The Plot Thickens...
Harry Potter Investigated by Fans for Fans

The Plot Thickens...
Harry Potter Investigated by Fans for Fans

Edited by

Galadriel Waters

Cover Art by

Melissa Rogers

Illustrations by

Michelle Heran
Christina Conley
Inkwolf
Nina Khosla

Wizarding World Press

B

Published in the United States by Wizarding World Press
8926 N. Greenwood Ave., Vault 133
Niles, IL 60714

Library of Congress Cataloging-in-Publication Data available at the Library of Congress

ISBN 0-9723936-3-3

Printed in the United States of America by TPS (Total Printing Systems), Newton, IL, and Pinnacle Press, St. Louis, MO
Distributed by SCB Distributors, Gardena, CA

Editor-in-Chief: Galadriel Waters

Editors: Cari Carlson, Nancy Davies, E.L. Fossa, Prof. Astre Mithrandir

Editorial Assistance: Madeyemuggle, Glenys and Andrea Reyes, S. P. Sipal

Communications: BeachBum, Christina Conley, E.L. Fossa

Layout and Cover Design: Dan Nolte – www.dannolte.com

Cover Art: Melissa Rogers – www.sandelwood.net

Illustrations: Michelle Heran – www.sherant.com
Inkwolf – www.inkwolf.net
Nina Khosla – www.kissedbyrain.com
Christina Conley

Web Design: Christina Conley – www.thedustyorb.com
Zach McCleary of harrypotterfanzone

Special Thanks to: Emerson, Webmaster of www.mugglenet.com
Matt, Webmaster of www.cosforums.com
Damon, MuggleNet Administrator for www.newclues.mugglenet.com
The many dedicated Admins and Mods of the New Clues and CoS Forums
All the HP Sleuths of the world
The wonderful staffs of: Borders, Mt. Prospect, IL and Barnes & Noble, Vernon Hills, IL

First Edition, October 31, 2004
First Trade Printing, November 5, 2004

The Authors dedicate this book to

Jo Rowling

and

Harry Potter Fans Everywhere

For the thinkers, the brains, the geniuses and the scholars.
The ones that don't deserve pennies for their thoughts—rather, a dollar.

For the editors, the artists, the proofers, the writers.
The ones that make that lightbulb illuminate just a bit brighter.

For the critics, the cynics, the skeptics, the flouters.
The ones who can convert the humblest fan into a shouter.

For the fanatics, the crazies, the sleepless, the buffs.
The ones who despite how much they get, it's never enough.

For the Harrys, the Hagrids, the Hermys, the Rons.
The ones from which some of our best characteristics are drawn.

For the wizards, the centaurs, the elves, the muggles.
The ones that inhabit this intriguing land that leave us befuddled.

For the revered, the reputed, the woman, the mother.
The one for whom it goes without saying...
Captures our minds, enflames our interest,
The one who writes, simply put, like no other.

-Christy Conley

✳ *Introduction* ✳

The title of this book required intense brain beating. That wasn't just because we wanted to be clever… it was because we wanted to be accurate.

What is this book about? Of course, it's about sleuthing Harry Potter. The discussions in this anthology delve deep into the riddles surrounding our favorite boy wizard, as the mysteries of JK Rowling's series become increasingly intricate. We are in the heart of the septology, and our heads are brewing with questions about the characters, the plot, and even the wizarding world. We could use a little magic to help boost our brain power and help sort through it all, and that is what Melissa has conjured for us with her cover art entitled "Pondering Potions".

This book is your recipe for a cauldronful of thought-provoking discussions. However, it's not just a slew of clues. You are about to be entertained with some of the most intriguing character profiles, brain teasers, and plot analyses you have ever read. And the best part of all, is that it is all in one place – right here in your hand.

Since this is a Wizarding World Press book, it has a very special perspective – a fan's perspective. These fan authors have taken some of the trickier subjects and pondered their meanings. There is a wide range of writing styles and subjects, so you may not love every one, but we are confident you will find many true gems to keep you busy sleuthing until the end of the series.

We now know a lot more about the mysteries that have bugged us through the first four books. Questions such as why Voldemort wants to kill Harry, why it seems as if Snape can read minds, or why Harry has to keep going back to the Dursleys each summer are now mostly resolved. Therefore, these fan-authors have looked ahead to who and what they feel will have significance for the ending as well as the entire septology, and provided fascinating studies into those subjects. We tried to cover as many popular topics as we could, but we can't possibly include them all. Nevertheless, we are sure you will have more than enough to fill your heads on this first such endeavor.

Consider this book to be a "snapshot" of what is going on with Harry Potter fandom at this moment in time. As JK Rowling is completing Book 6, fans are busy piecing together clues from interviews, chats, the previous books, and JK Rowling's own website. What are fans thinking? What theories do they have? What sparks their imagination? This book captures the essence of the fan's perspective. It documents the experience for us, and for any others who may wish to peer into our crystal balls.

Who are the authors? Now, don't let the word "fan" fool you. These authors aren't a bunch of "dunderheads". These are readers – just like you – who also have been inspired by the magic of Harry Potter. They are a bit more (hem-hem) addicted than the average fan, but as solving mysteries and puzzles is also what they love, they are a bit more clever than that fan image might imply.

First...these authors are definitely Harry Potter fans, and are lured by the mystery to spend time on the Internet forums inspecting and dissecting JK Rowling's works. What is especially intriguing is how each author brings an added dimension to understanding the series by drawing on their own areas of expertise. These authors are social scientists, lawyers, educators, physicists, literary scholars, musicians, mothers, grandmothers, students, etc; and include three who have a Ph.D., several with Masters Degrees, and at least one who has graduated kindergarten. ;) That eight-year-old has already written an article that was published by his 2nd-grade newspaper (okay, so he's a professional).

Second...these authors are members of discussion forums, and represent what JK Rowling calls the *"Mighty MuggleNet".** MuggleNet* is an elaborate fan site run by teenagers, and is (don't tell us you're surprised) the most popular fan-based Harry Potter site on the Web. They are host to two discussion forums: the "Chamber of Secrets Forum" (CoS), and the "New Clues Forum" (New Clues). CoS is known for both, its variety and quality of content, attracting kids and adults, alike. It is famous for the theories and debates that have drawn over 30,000 members. New Clues is a unique product of the digital age. It started with the book, *New Clues to Harry Potter: Book 5*, which contained *only hints* to what WWP saw as clues hiding in Book 5, and MuggleNet provided a forum on which over 10,000 HP Sleuths have congregated to solve these hints together (the most daring trying their hand in the "Brain Room"). The authors of *The Plot Thickens* book were solicited from those two forums. Many of the authors are eloquent and prolific online writers posting highly insightful (and witty) analyses, which are very popular among the other members.

In addition to their affiliation with those sites, the authors are a microcosm of our global community. Consider this book to be a Muggle-world equivalent for the Ministry of Magic's Department of International Magical Cooperation – crossing barriers of countries (and time zones) and working together on the challenges and themes that JK Rowling has presented. You might call this book a hardcopy rendering of the virtual community.

Finally, these authors are the ones who were brave enough to submit their words for the world to ponder. Most of them are first-time authors, and are using WWP as a first step toward their goals. We are providing this opportunity so that they may get closer to a dream that was dear to author JK Rowling:

> *"Firstly, you need to write something that a publisher would want to publish—it might take a while to find them—Wait. Pray. This is the way Harry Potter got published."*

> —www.jkrowling.com

There are some other contributors who need special recognition. As you gaze in wonder at the enchanting artwork, keep in mind that those are all the work of fans – they are not (yet) professional illustrators. This whole book has, indeed, been written, illustrated, and edited by fans (we meant it when we said it's "by fans for fans"). There is a lot of heart that has gone into this book, but even more exciting is that there is a lot of talent.

We are sure you will enjoy these works, as we at WWP have, but we are also sure that you will review their thoughts and opinions with the same scrutiny that you apply to their posts. So think of this before you get too critical – they are fans...just like you.

—*Galadriel Waters*

Some final thoughts from our house-elf:

I picked up a children's book once…it was called *Harry Potter and The Sorcerer's Stone*. When I finished reading, the book I put down was still called *Harry Potter and The Sorcerer's Stone*—but it wasn't a children's book. It was an adventure novel, a history lesson, a whole college English course, a morality play; it was an amazing demonstration of Stephen King's definition of writing as telepathy—the wholesale transfer of important ideas and images from an author's brain to a reader's.

The novels of JK Rowling have gifted us by expanding our definitions, by pushing out both literary boundaries (tell me if you can, now, what is a children's book?) and the mental boundaries of prejudice and convention. I hope that this book of discussions, in some small way, will pay tribute to Rowling's work by helping expand the definition of "analyses" and "essays". We tend to think of an essay as a vehicle for documentation—it can, indeed, be that. But it can, and should, also, be a vehicle for communication. There are brilliant writers from forums as varied as Playboy (we know you only read it for the articles) and The New Yorker that prove the point. In the end, it is the communication—the interaction— that lives, because it leaves the page and lives on in the brains and lives of those who invest the time to read and think.

The Internet has allowed Harry Potter fans all over the world the ability to contact each other at will, documenting their ideas in vibrant communities where age and education are not nearly as important as the excitement that comes from communication and cooperation. It is a fleeting medium, the Internet, so we have taken a screencapture for you of our lives— and perhaps of yours, as well. Here is what it is like to be a Harry Potter fan right now—at this very moment—in the breathless interim between Book 5 and 6 of what may be one of the best-loved literary epics of all time.

You have picked up a book of Harry Potter essays. What you put down—well, that's up to you.

—*E.L. Fossa*

Contents

Bloodlines and Blood Feuds

Wacky Weasleys

Love Potion #9^3/$_4$

Mischief Created: The Marauders

Travelling Picture Show

Shady People and Places

✳ *You Were There* ✳

Even if we don't have magic, the magical world that JKR created is rubbing off on all of us.

The Harry Potter phenomenon is apparently a "first". It is the first pop culture phenomenon to take place globally and bring this many fans together with a common interest through international forums on the Internet. This piece of literature has crossed all boundaries and touched people—no matter what their culture. It is not a UK event...it is not a Canadian event...it is not a Russian event. It is a global event that has brought together the children (and adults) of the world to experience it together as it is happening.

There may never be another experience like this, or there may be many more (hope, hope). Regardless, this will always be the first, and you will be able to say YOU WERE THERE! No other generation will have this adventure—no one else will have to wait for JKR to finish writing before they can grab the next book, to share their theories with their friends, to be able to push JKR for info, to be able to watch her website for clues, to give her feedback as she writes, or to tease her when she slips (no pressure, Jo!). You will talk about it, you will be asked about it by your children and your children's children.

Right now, you want the answer ASAP, but you will find out that is only a small part of the fun. All readers for the rest of time will miss the excitement and the challenge of having to solve the clues like us—without the answers already sitting on a shelf somewhere. Think about how great it would have been to have been there when Tolkien was writing his trilogy, when Michaelangelo was painting the Sistine Chapel, or when the Wright brothers were testing at Kitty Hawk? It's a privilege that you shouldn't take lightly, and you may want to reflect on the significance of that the next time you are so anxious to get the final answers. Savour this experience—make the most of it, don't feel frustrated if the ending isn't quite ready. The fact that it's not quite ready means you are experiencing something very unique. It also means you can have fun searching for clues, posting theories (even as wild as they may seem), and sleuthing the mysteries. We're really excited to share this experience with you.

See you in the queue for the next Warner Bros. movie and for the next Harry Potter book!

DEPARTMENT OF INTERNATIONAL FAN COOPERATION

Some of these authors shared what it's like to be a Harry Potter fan in their particular country. As always, it points out the truth of Dumbledore's wisdom—that even in the Muggle world, as different as we may appear, we are all the same...

AUSTRALIA

In a lot of chat rooms I've come across in my time on the internet I still find it surprising that some people say "oh, Australia gets HP?" This is understandable though, since Australia is a little hidden 'down under' and for such a big place we have got a rather small population, but it's true. Australians do indeed get Harry Potter! The movies, merchandise, JK Rowling updates—everything.

For those of you who are wondering if we get an Australian version of Harry Potter, this is not true. Since our spelling and grammar skills have derived from England we get Harry Potter books exactly as they are, including the cover. The only difference is that they are printed in Australia (although if anyone was lucky enough to snag a first edition Book 1 that was printed in Britain and worth a lot of money!).

There is only one Harry Potter item you can get in Australia that isn't available anywhere else and that is the stamps! Our stamp printing system is virtually the only one in the world that will print living people on stamps. So if you want HP stamps get a pen friend in Australia, pronto!

Well, other than the stamps I guess everything else is the same. Harry Potter hype gets bigger and bigger each year and people still dress up to see the movies (even if they are over 30 years old!). We even had a Harry Potter conference here earlier this year at a university. I went and found it really fantastic! We had people from America and Britain to tell us about Harry Potter, goodness!

—Angelwings

DENMARK

Fairy tales and fantastic literature for children has always been well esteemed in Denmark, even when it was not considered a proper subject of adult literature (that is fortunately changing). The Hans Christian Andersen's fairy tales have been an essential part of Danish culture (children's culture in particular) for almost 200 years (it will be his two hundredth birthday in 2005), and for the past 20 to 30 years the Danish book market has also been affected by her Majesty Queen Margrethe II, who is an avid fan of Tolkien.

When the first Harry Potter book was published in Denmark, sales were slow. In the last year of the '90s rumours began to surface about this Potter phenomenon—I heard about the books in 1999 from my daughter's godfather who was studying to be a librarian. Slowly the rumour spread: "these books are good", "these books are the latest craze in England and America". Even then, the Harry Potter books didn't really pick up until the release of Book 4 in the UK and US, when it got coverage in Danish news.

Today most kids know who Harry is—many have read some (or all) of the books, and the rest have seen the films or heard about him from their friends. They see the ads on the street, T.V., and they see the merchandise in stores. Even though the Harry Potter phenomenon is not as big in Denmark, as it is in the UK, we still get the same things, only on a smaller scale. The last couple of years have seen a decrease in children dressing up as Harry for the Shrovetide carnival (in February—that's when Danish children dress up).

Speaking with the friends of my own children (aged 5 to 13), many of the older kids have read at least one of the books, and it is not uncommon for 12 to 14-year-old children to struggle through the books in English. The adults are a bit harder to make out. I know several adults who read the *Harry Potter* books with great delight (though none with the dedicated obsession of myself), but the books are not normally discussed in adult company, and few people react when I start speaking about them. Most of the adult Danish Harry Potter fans that I know I have met on the Internet in parts of the English-speaking on-line fan community.

The Danish translations of the books are quite good, though they are a far cry from being brilliant. There are a number of errors, and a few last-second saves, but my pet grievances are the translations of Ron's owl, Pigwidgeon, into "Grisligiano" (shortened to "gris" which means 'pig') and the translation of the Firebolt to "Prestissimo". To be fair, though, these are exceptions—in general the British ambience in the books is maintained. I would still, to put it a bit rudely, say that the translations have a look of being works of craft, not of love.

As a curiosity, privet hedges are very common in Denmark—they separate the sides of small, detached houses all over the country. (I live in this type of house, complete with privet hedges—though mine are neither neat, nor well-tended). There are 7 exact matches for the Danish translation in the books of 'Privet Drive' in Denmark. Here, the Dursley-ish people who are sticklers for their property edges are often called 'privet-fascists'…

—Troels Forchhammer

GERMANY

As a general impression, Harry Potter is pretty popular. Mostly in the translated version though, because many children don't speak English yet or at least not well enough to dare attack a brick like Books 4 or 5. Besides, even for adults it's just more comfortable to read a book in your own language. (Good thing for those who prefer the originals, they're less often borrowed by others. ;))

It is hard to tell about "adults in general" and whether or not they are embarrassed to admit they read HP. There are those who discuss in the press about how beneficial or dangerous the HP phenomenon is for children (mainly teachers, parents, editors, and religious officials), there are those who think HP is just a childish fad which will soon die out (often without ever having read it), and there are those who like to publish quizzes or scientific research on it, write HP fanfiction, or discuss details and theories in the web.

People here are less directly hateful or terrified of magic than the Dursleys. However, disbelief in magic, magical beings or real effects of superstitions are fairly common. You do have to stand in line… especially when there's a new film, book, or book translation being presented! :D

Often it's OK (the translations of "Mirror of Erised" and "Tom Marvolo Riddle" were actually nicely done), but in some cases it's blatant. Colours, ways of speech or actions are at times rendered differently from the original with no obvious reason. The translations of OWLs and NEWTs are rather flat and un-funny (UTZ and ZAG? Huh?), and the worst translation mistake, in my opinion, was done with the card-game "Exploding Snap". I daresay no fan with a liking for the language and/or for the Potion Master enjoys having it mistranslated as "Snape explodes". Grumble. All in all, I prefer the original.

—Serpentine

GERMANY

A few weeks ago I witnessed a doctor and his collegue being told by a nurse the slightly unusual name of a patient they were going to see later that day. The two doctors didn't quite catch the name, which was something like "Vordenhort", and one of them said: "What? Voldemort?" and everybody around perfectly understood the gag. Harry is absolutely huge in Germany, throughout both genders and all ages.

When it comes to the neat little rows of houses, Jo's social satire perfectly applies to our society.

The translations, however, are rushed and full of mistakes. There is actually a website which lists and explains all the many mistakes.

—Stic

UK

Over here in Great Britain Harry Potter is pretty popular, as you can imagine. CBBC is frequently reporting Harry Potter news, and if kids didn't like it, then they wouldn't keep reporting it. I had to stand in line for the movie (it was packed) even in the sleepy county of Norfolk.

There are lots of adults that read Harry Potter books here (obviously), and I suppose a lot of them are embarrassed to admit they read it.

I'd like to say that it is a misconception that houses in England are in neat little rows. The only place you might find this on a large scale is Milton Kenes. We don't have blocks, and our villages and towns tend to be built higgledy-piggledy, with no real structure.

—Cookie

USA

It is truly amazing to me the response that the Harry Potter series has had throughout the world. I have lived in the US and Norway and, in both places, the series is incredibly popular with all ages…not just children. I personally believe there is something inherent in JK Rowling's series that stirs the imagination in a way that only literature can. Most importantly, it has encouraged children to read in an age where they are inundated with TV, movies, and video games. The incredible popularity can be seen in long lines at both movie releases and book releases. Often, there are just as many adults in those lines as children…and they're not just accompanying the kids! I think the adults are able to return to literature that they read in their childhood, such as The Lord of the Rings that stirred their imagination, but also had a moral to the story. Not to mention, both series consider the constant struggle between good and evil and how all characters are impacted by the leaders/heroes and their actions. This is a timeless topic and people in any culture can relate to it.

—fanofsirius

US - *Boston*

I live in a U.S. city, sustained by universities. Books are everywhere, merchandising is everywhere and Harry Potter is everywhere. In my opinion, the United States grabs onto new things a bit over-zealously and turns them into fads by over –merchandising, leaving the old as a "has been". I think Harry Potter has gotten trapped in the "fad system", too. I find this especially troubling because the merchandise focuses on a very small part of the Harry Potter audience: children.

People often ask me if I think Harry Potter will be as popular and relevant in literature 50 years from now. I don't know if Harry Potter will be as popular, certainly the jellybeans and the toys won't hold out, but I do think Rowling's septology will be just as relevant and take its place alongside other literary works we deem to be "classics". Most adults I know, from teachers and astrophysicists to "punk rockers" and activists, have read the Potter series. They are very comfortable talking about the books. It is the children I know who seem to be less interested in 'Harry'. While they find the movies captivating, they are a little lost when it comes to the 'Harry' text. They don't seem to have grown into him yet.

Although my peers do not find it strange that I read the books, they do find it strange that I am an "HP Sleuth". This is the first "popular" interest I have ever had and my friends are all a bit taken aback by my obsession. I am a "punk rocker", so my friends are simultaneously very tough and intellectual, and most of them cannot figure out why I would read *Harry Potter* over socio-political philosophy. The looks on their faces are priceless – dumbfounded awe! Many of them have read *Potter* and have enjoyed it … but spending so much time researching it is weird to them.

Researching Rowling is addictive. With each page there is something new to uncover…and researching "Harry Potter" is just as often about researching Rowling's influences as it is analyzing her own stories. Sleuthing is a global subculture that brings a diverse group of people together. I don't think that will change. Rowling's work is timeless and relevant to a wide range of people. Somehow we can all relate to a boy, who thought he was nobody, taking a stand against evil.

—ridgeback (RB)

US - *California*

One of the most positive effects of the Harry Potter phenomenon, for me, has been that this popularity crosses the age line. As a result of the Harry Potter books, I now have a subject of conversation that is as interesting to me as it is to my pre-teen daughter and her friends. They now think I'm really cool because I know so much about the Harry Potter world. They will even initiate conversations with me, asking me if I have any new theories about future books. Given that these girls would usually not have much to say to me, I consider this an added bonus to the Harry Potter phenomenon.

—siriusaddict

US - *New York (A Kid's Perspective)*

Kids find out about Harry Potter through parents & other kids who have the books & tell their friends, or they watch the movies. More kids watch the movies. You can tell because the kids who have seen the movie just play Harry Potter, but the kids who've read the book talk about it more. Plus, the kids who've seen the movie don't play the book parts. It's more fun to play with the kids who've read the books because they know more about the story.

The most interesting thing about the series is how JKR writes the books. For instance, you think someone is bad, but it turns out they're good. Plus there's always exciting things going on.

Harry is the most interesting character to kids because Harry does the most exciting stuff. A lot of kids want to be like Harry because he's a wizard and so powerful and cool. He can do neat stuff. That's why he's such a popular Halloween dress-up. Some kids are interested in the spells & like to make up their own. When we play, we like to do wizard duels. Lots of kids like to act-out scenes and some like to battle magical creatures (I don't like to, though). I think Hermione is cooler than Ron because she's so smart and she knows all these spells. My friends think Ron is cooler because Ron's a boy and he does lots of funny things.

I think the movies are scarier than the books. I think the evil spells in the books, like Imperio & Avada Kedavra, are the scariest. I think other kids find the Dementors scariest.

—The Crookshank

US - *Southeast Tennessee*

Even though the world of Harry Potter is well represented in all my neighborhood stores, with the books, toys, trading cards, and candy all easily available, that's not saying everyone buys them. I live in the Southeastern United States, in a very religiously conservative area. For various reasons, some parents in my part of the world steer their children to other books. Few adults, except college students and teachers, choose to read the Potter books. People here are much more likely to rent a movie than to read what they consider to be a "children's book" for fun.

Muggles here are quite conventional, live in spacious houses surrounded by large green lawns that must be fertilized, watered, and mowed on a rigid schedule. The Dursleys would enjoy that immensely! Of course, some of us grew up in older houses with crooked doors, rattling windows, and dark corners full of spiders. Petunia, though, would find plenty of "unnaturally clean" kitchens to enjoy in my neighborhood!

The number of people in Southeast Tennessee who are interested in the "wizarding world" is perhaps analogous to the number of people who celebrate Halloween. About half of the people in my town celebrate Halloween and half of them do not. Some buy bags of special candy, while others turn their porch lights off and don't answer the door. Some people encourage costumes and elaborate home decorations, while others forbid any mention of witches, vampires, or were-wolves. Similarly, some people here would be delighted to see their children reading a book—any book—and would find the Harry Potter books imaginative, well-written, exciting, and moral. Other parents would *not* be thrilled if their child checked a Harry Potter book out of the library, and would probably send it back the next day without letting them read it.

Even though many people here aren't super readers, some of the largest crowds I have ever seen in local bookstores were present for the "midnight" arrivals of the Harry Potter books. The bookstores were sold out within half-an-hour. When Book 5 debuted, I took my two teenagers, their friends, and my 8-year-old son on an odyssey through two nationally known bookstores and a discount store until we found copies for everyone. We were running through parking lots at midnight trying to beat other people to the front door! On opening day of the movie "The Prisoner of Azkaban" in my area, the first showing was at 10:00 a.m. on a weekday. There was a long line that stretched into the mall parking lot. Clearly, many people had taken the day off from work to bring their children to the movie. Many young people wore costumes with "house" insignia. I saw Hufflepuff capes and Slytherin robes. My daughter wore her "Quidditch" T-shirt. And that day, the crowd was obviously familiar with the books. They laughed in all the right places, and clapped and cheered. There was definitely a sense of camaraderie.

I really do not talk to a lot of other Harry Potter fans in my day to day existence. I am lucky that my children love the series and are always eager to discuss new aspects of the characters and the plot. My 14-year-old son, when he isn't playing football, likes to reread the entire series from time to time. My 8-year-old son hasn't read them yet, but enjoys it when I read passages to him and watch the movies with him. My 17-year-old daughter reads them with an eye for symbolism and foreshadowing, just as she reads books for English class. She is the person who introduced me to the online Harry Potter community, where I discovered that other adults, as well as young people all over the world love these books as I do. So even though I know very few adult fans in my community, I can find people with whom to discuss theories on the fan forums twenty-four hours a day.

—Silver Ink Pot

US – *Pacific Northwest*

The United States is a big place, and despite the homogenizing effects of television and popular culture, there are still regional differences. I'm coming from the perspective of someone living in the Pacific Northwest

Considering that in the U.S., "Harry Potter" has become practically synonymous with "children's books," I'd say the series is extremely popular. Sometimes I feel like I can't throw a rock without hitting something related to Harry Potter, at least when a new book or movie is coming out.

I think adults that I know are a bit shy of admitting that they like the books, but get two adult HP readers together and you can't shut them up.

There are strong fundamentalist Christian communities in my area, so I see a good deal of the same kind of nearly allergic reaction to words such as "magic" or "witch" that we see in the Dursleys. But there is also a good deal of quirkiness in the Northwest, and a great many people who would be perfectly at home in Hogsmeade.

—ArtemisMoonbow

US – *Wisconsin*

I work in a library in a small town in Wisconsin. We don't see a lot of Harry Potter merchandise or T-shirts come into the library (everyone's too busy wearing Green Bay Packers stuff), but kids are always happy to see the Hogwarts school and house crest banners hanging from our ceiling. We hang up Harry Potter news updates, and the plastic Harry Potter glasses were a very popular prize during this summer's reading program. On the night OOTP was released, the Barnes and Noble in Green Bay had a midnight release party, and it was so crowded that it was impossible to walk around, and very stuffy. Many people were dressed up! There were lots of Harrys and Hogwarts students, and even a few adult wizards and witches. We received six copies of OOTP for the library – but there were over four hundred people in the system who had reserved it! The next morning we had our own Harry Potter party at the library. My boss wore a turban! (Worrying...)

—Inkwolf

US

In America I don't run into many adults who read the series. Many of them buy it for their kids, but mainly I see teenagers showing the most interest. I find more adult fans of the movies.

The Internet community is different. They are mostly adults who have an unabashed interest in the many characters and layers present in the books. They realize it is not just a children's series and run the gamut from those with a passing interest, to hard-core fans who name themselves after characters, and dress up in HP costume. I'm in the middle and like the humor, the literature, the mythological parallels and the search for hints. I've always loved a detective story. Otherwise, I don't know if my own interest would have been sustained.

—Alexa

THE PLOT THICKENS: INGREDIENTS

Author Search

Once we came up with the idea to publish a fanbook, Wizarding World Press (WWP) posted a "Call for Proposals" on both MuggleNet forums. Additionally, we personally invited some of the authors, whose posts were especially intriguing, to submit proposals. A review committee with representatives from both, the Chamber of Secrets and New Clues forums, voted on which proposals would be selected for the fanbook. The start was a bit shaky. In spite of being communicators, we somehow had trouble getting communications started. However, thanks to Matt of CoS, we worked out our initial problems, and everything came together.

If you want to know more about these Fan-authors, please visit:

www.plotthickens.com

Contributing sites:
www.mugglenet.com
www.cosforums.com
www.newclues.mugglenet.com

Categories

The discussions in this book run the gamut of everything Harry Potter—from the Weasley twins to Egyptian mythology. After a lot of deliberation (and many attempts), we finally decided on 14 separate categories for the discussions. Like the characters in Harry Potter, many of the discussions could have been placed in multiple categories, but the final decision was based on the core theme of the discussion.

Editions and Translations

Because Harry Potter is a universal phenomenon, the published editions and translations vary greatly, in grammar, phraseology, and even character names and titles. In order to keep the discussions clear and concise, we have set a standard of referring to the name of the book by its sequential number in the series. For instance, in the US, the first book is known as Harry Potter and the Sorcerer's Stone, in the UK it is Harry Potter and the Philosopher's Stone, and in France, it is Harry Potter at Wizarding School, but we will simply refer to it as Book 1. For the same reason, we have referred to all chapters by the chapter number, instead of chapter title.

The edition of the series that the author used for citations is noted at the beginning of the discussion. Just because the author is from the US or UK does not necessarily mean that the books that they used as a reference guide were the respective editions for that country.

Abbreviations

We have kept most of the abbreviations that the authors may have used when referring to various Harry Potter elements. Here is a list of frequently encountered abbreviations and what they stand for:

Jo, JK, JKR – JK Rowling, author of the Harry Potter series

HP Sleuth – those who sleuth the clues in JKR's books

HBP – Half Blood Prince (title of Book 6)

WWP – Wizarding World Press

NC – New Clues Forum

CoS – Chamber of Secrets, both the Forum and the Chamber in Book 2

LV – Lord Voldemort

DE – Death Eater

DA – Dumbledore's Army

DADA – Defense Against the Dark Arts

DoM – Department of Mysteries

MoM – Ministry of Magic

Spelling and Grammar

Even though we at WWP live in the United States, many of our authors do not. We have not Americanized most foreign grammar or spelling. For example, in the United States, we have the word "favorite", but in the UK, it is spelled as "favourite". Likewise, the term Death Eater is separated into two words in the English language, but the German translation combines the two words into Deatheater. We tried to be consistent as possible with conventions while still maintaining the individual authors' styles. It was really tricky.

Author Information

Before jumping in and reading the discussion, please take note of the author's info at the top of the page. Our authors range in age from 8-years-old to adult and the age should be taken into account in regards to the complexity of the discussions. Also notice that our authors come from several different countries (see above) and many of them do not speak English as their first (or sometimes even second) language.

Also included in the author information is the forum in which the author most commonly posts, although some post in both. NC and CoS are the respective abbreviations for the MuggleNet New Clues and the Chamber of Secrets forums.

OWLs and NEWTs

The discussions in this book vary not only in subject, but also in complexity. In order to aid you, we have given each discussion a readability score. The scores used are: "Handful of OWLs", being the most basic (even Fred and George could handle that), "12 OWLs" and "NEWT" level. Remember that this is not a score of how insightful or well-written each essay is, but rather is based on overall writing level, content, and general HP knowledge needed by the reader to understand the discussion. There are discussions in here for all age levels, and no matter what the difficulty level is, we suggest reading them all!

HANDFUL   12   NEWT

Canon vs. Speculation

All of the authors have painstakingly researched their discussions and based them on the available (and ever-changing) Harry Potter canon. Some authors, following presentation of their findings, have speculated as to what may happen in Books 6 and 7. These speculations are clearly marked within the discussion and may go a bit beyond known facts.

References

All references to works by JK Rowling, including her personal website and any interviews are referenced within the text itself. The book, chapter, and page number (if provided by the author) are cited in {curly braces} following a quote or crucial piece of information from the story. All page numbers come from either the UK hardcover or the U.S. hardcover and trade paperback editions, but not the pocket versions. Any external references (websites and books) used by the author are cited at the end of the discussion, following Sleuthing Points.

Additional Sleuthing Notes

Following each discussion is a set of "Additional Sleuthing Notes" or extra possible clues to ponder that relate directly to the author's discussion. Unlike the discussions themselves, these are the thoughts of Galadriel Waters and WWP.

General Knowledge

All of these discussions have been written based on the assumption that the reader has a general knowledge of the events that take place in Books 1-5. Therefore, the authors do no spend a lot of time giving background information, unless the event is more obscure, or easily glossed over in the text. An example of this would be that everyone should know that Harry Potter lives with the Dursleys during the summer holidays without needing the background that he was left on their doorstep as a baby, after his parents were killed. However, WHY Harry needs to return to the Dursley's every summer may be addressed in the discussion in more detail

Disclaimer

The views expressed by the individual authors may not represent the views of Galadriel Waters and/or Wizarding World Press.

WWP firmly believes in presenting a forum for all perspectives and we have presented discussions with opposing and potentially controversial views. Therefore, if you don't like what one of our authors said—please don't send us a Howler!

MEGA SPOILER WARNING!

Don't even consider opening this book unless you've read all five of JK Rowling's Harry Potter series. All discussions in The Plot Thickens cover information leading up to and including the ending to Book 5. You have been warned! Untrained wizards proceed at your own risk...

How to Read
a Children's Story

ICEBERG AHOY!
WHY THE HARRY POTTER BOOKS SHOULD BE
RESTORED TO THE NEW YORK TIMES BEST-SELLER LIST

MARY AILES ✳ NC, "ZOEROSE"
USA (*US Edition*), AGE 43

Inspiration for this Discussion

I knew something was up after Order of the Phoenix *was released. Every day, I commute on mass transit to my office in Washington, D.C. For months, not a day would go by when I didn't see someone — and always an adult — reading* Harry Potter. *From college students in jeans to businessmen and women in suits, I'd find them, heads bent down poring over the prose of JK Rowling. "What's up with that?" I wondered. "Aren't these books for children?"*

Whether they are or not, that's what we have been conditioned to believe by the people who set these standards. Due to strong lobbying from other publishers, in 2000, The New York Times *"banished" Harry Potter from the Best-Seller List, and instead created a children's list where Rowling's books have resided ever since.*

Should The New York Times *have bowed to the pressure to change the list? What if these aren't just books for children after all? What if there's more to Harry Potter than meets the eye?*

 HANDFUL

"I always try to write on the principle of the iceberg. There is seven-eighths of it under water for every part that shows. Anything you know you can eliminate and it only strengthens your iceberg... It is the part that doesn't show."
—Ernest Hemingway, 1958[1]

The great twentieth-century American writer, Ernest Hemingway, described the writing process as being like an iceberg. The Harry Potter books are, indeed, a wonderful story for children. But their popularity as a children's story is only the tip of iceberg. What matters, as any sea captain will tell you, is what lies below.

The first time I heard about "Harry Potter" was from a child, my seven-year-old niece, Rebecca. Her mother and I were watching Rebecca playing in front of the house. She was skipping down the sidewalk, lost in a world of her own, when suddenly she stopped, stood perfectly straight, and then put her arms out at her side like a scarecrow. She stood there for a long time, a very long time, perfectly still.

"What is she doing?" I finally asked her mother.

"She's being fitted for her robes," her mother sighed. "Last night she changed her name to Hermione."

I thought it was amusing, but I am a busy, working woman and the thought of sitting down and reading a children's story didn't seem to fit into my schedule. But Rebecca wouldn't leave me alone, I started receiving copies of the books for birthdays and Christmas until finally I gave in, sat down and read them all.

If the tip of this iceberg was everything and there was nothing more, then yes, *Harry Potter* more than deserves its place on the Children's Best Seller List. But as Hemingway said, "it is the part that doesn't show" that matters.

And the part "that doesn't show" in *Harry Potter* makes all the difference.

On the surface, the part that is easily seen, even by the most casual or young reader, is the story of Harry Potter, a young wizard, and his friends, Ron Weasley and Hermione Granger. Over the course of a seven-part series (five of which are currently published) we are seeing Harry develop from an eleven-year-old boy to a seventeen-year -old young man. The books tell a classic adventure story that leaves both children and adults spellbound by the imaginative plots, memorable characters, and exciting twists and bends that take us through one rollercoaster ride after another.

The moment of illumination came for me when I read the third book, *Prisoner of Azkaban*. Until this particular moment, I saw the books as wonderful and imaginative adventure stories. But all that changed with the "Shrieking Shack" scene.

In that scene, I realized that there was far more than meets the eye to the entire series. I suddenly stopped, just like Ron, dumbfounded, and began to reflect in a deeper way on the pages I had already perused. I continued reading the next two books with the same careful reflection, and I expect this exciting reading experience will be with me until the last page of the septology.

Like Hemingway's iceberg, the publishing industry has only looked at the top one-eighth of this book and deemed it a children's book. But I challenge everyone – including those few adults who have not yet read these books – to recognize that there is another world below the surface…a world as large, as multifaceted, as significant, as intriguing, as meaningful as anything we might find on today's *New York Times* Best Seller List.

Look with me below the iceberg's tip now, and see what amazing secrets lie just under the surface. With each book, JK Rowling dives deeper and deeper into the iceberg of her story. Just as with any piece of classic literature, when you finish the fifth book, you can start all over again—rereading the entire series, and finding jewels, hints, clues, allusions and themes that are completely missed on the first read.

One example—and there are so many—comes in the first chapter of Book 1. In what appears to be a throwaway line, or one tiny bit of information, turns out, in reflection, to be a significant event. Fifteen-month-old Harry is being transported by Hagrid from the horrific murder scene where Harry's parents were killed. Hagrid is delivering Harry (bearing a nasty scar on his forehead) to Dumbledore, a wizard, who will leave the orphaned baby on the doorstep of Harry's aunt and uncle. With great drama, Hagrid arrives from the skies on a strange flying motorcycle:

> *"Hagrid," said Dumbledore… "Where did you get the motorcycle?"*
> *"Borrowed it…Young Sirius Black lent it to me."* {Book 1, Ch1, p13 US}

We do not hear mention of Sirius Black again until the third book, and in fact, by then most of us had forgotten this brief mention from Book 1, but it was a key element of this mystery. Black is a significant character of tremendous importance to the entire series. The next time Harry encounters Black he is thirteen years old and Sirius is an escaped "murderer" from the wizard prison of Azkaban. The character of Sirius Black, his triumphs and his tragedies, his conflicts and his ultimate fate in Book 5 is the stuff of legend. His character, by the end of Book 5, has become mythic. He is not unlike Boromir in Tolkien's *The Lord of the Rings*: rich young men from noble bloodlines with great passion for truth, who falter by their own blindness to evil, paying a dear price for that error, and ultimately redeemed through self-sacrifice. This is, indeed, the stuff of legends. And that is only one of many subtle twists in Rowling's books.

As we go deeper into the text, we find ourselves exploring many of the great themes of British literature. Issues such as class struggle, government corruption, social satire, and tragic heroes can be found along with classical mythology.

Rowling's wizarding world is not one of princesses and Prince Charmings. The characters in the Harry Potter novels are multi-faceted. Those who seem perpetually wrapped in darkness can be suddenly revealed to possess increased psychological and emotional depth. A prime example of this is the unexpected traps into which we readily fall. Those who appear to be friends may be enemies. And those who appear to be enemies are friends. A teacher, Remus Lupin, carries a horrible secret in Book 3. When that is revealed, we are sympathetic to his plight. Another teacher in Book 4 also carries a secret, but when his secret is revealed, we shudder.

As we continue below the surface, we find that Rowling is deeply influenced by some of the great social satirists of British literature. Jane Austen wrote of the highly structured social hierarchy of early 19th century England. Her characterizations were sometimes brutal as she lampooned the class and wealth divisions of her period, and her humor is buried in those character sketches and the situations in which they find themselves. Rowling follows in this tradition in each Harry Potter book. The more she reveals the details of the wizarding world – be it Hogwarts (the wizarding school for the youth), the Ministry of Magic (the center of Wizard government), Diagon Alley (the center of Wizard Commerce), or St Mungo's (the center of Wizard Health Care…or lack thereof)—the more we see a remarkable world parallel to our own. By creating a society of Wizards and Muggles, Rowling places herself in a unique position to comment on the real world in which we live.

Rowling presents a world where social class and bloodlines can be examined, turning her literary magnifying glass on it. The reader provides the judgment. It is world where some want society ordered by bloodlines or by wealth or by influential connections, with pockets deep enough and magically pure enough to rule the rest of the world. But it is also a world of sheep and goats, where friend and foe are side by side and it is not yet clear who is friend and who is foe. This is much like our own world and it is certainly not the safe and comfortable world created by Hans Christian Anderson.

Rowling's wizarding world is one of strict classes, financial status, and inherited birthrights. Those at the bottom of the social classes are often enslaved by those at the top. Despite the serious subject, rather than getting into some kind of socialistic propaganda, Rowling will even poke fun at any attempts to take herself too seriously. Her pen leaves no one untouched.

It is in Book 2 that Harry meets Dobby, the house-elf servant slave of the autocratic Malfoy family. In the chapter, "The House-Elf Liberation Front" in Book 4, Hermione Granger attempts to enlist Harry Potter and his best friend, Ron Weasley, into an activist group she is organizing to free house-elf servants from their lives of enslavement in the wizarding world. Harry later provides one of his own articles of clothing, which results in Dobby's freedom—an act that infuriates the pureblood, upper-class Lucius Malfoy, who is a strong sympathizer of the Dark Wizard, Voldemort. Hermione witnesses what she sees as unfair and inhumane treatment of the house-elves, and is determined to do something about it.

Hermione's ongoing crusade to free house-elves is sometimes humorous and sometimes poignant, especially since she appears to be having little success in gaining the support of the house-elves, themselves. Rowling's satirist view of do-gooders who launch into moralistic crusades without first finding out from the subjects what they want is familiar to anyone who has had any kind of a political activist background. I am not sure how many children will find Hermione's attempts at crusading for justice humorous or familiar—but those of us who have histories of marching in the streets may find Hermione's struggles hit just a little too close to home.

It is a reflection of the world in which we live. And in the tradition of morality plays, it prepares us, alongside Harry, for dealing with the real world. The deeper the reader goes into that submerged part of the iceberg and reflects on the world that Rowling is creating, the more assuredly we find it is not a place that is fairy-tale safe, sound, and forever free. It is, in fact, a world that is filled with corruption, both from the inside and the outside.

At the center of this world is Cornelius Fudge, the Minister of Magic. He could have walked right out of a Charles Dickens novel. He is blustering and swaying with the winds of power. He is more interested in keeping his own head then protecting the rights of others. By the fifth book, it is clear that he is corrupt and weak and will cover up the truth no matter what the cost.

The themes Rowling is working with here are as grim as any political novel or crime thriller. Evil is on the march—and, no different than in our own world, it can corrupt through action, as in practicing a form of terrorism called the *Dark Arts*, or through inaction as in the conscious dereliction of government power and authority. Both forms of corruption are very present in all of the Harry Potter books. It is not hard to hear the whisper of Macbeth or the ghost of Hamlet's father within these pages. The darkness that Rowling reveals is not the darkness of simple fairy tales—where a kind wave of the fairy godmother's wand or a kiss from a prince is simply enough to stave off evil. No, Rowling creates a world that is very much like our own and just as terrifying. In a world that knows firsthand what terrorism is like, we see the characters struggling with the issues that we struggle with ourselves in the dawn of this new century.

For me, the themes and the characters are the strongest elements of these books. They convince me to look beyond the mere tip of the iceberg and contemplate what lies below. The themes that Rowling wrestles with through her imaginative prose are those of classic literature. One hears in her writings the echoes of Homer, Joyce, Milton, Shakespeare, Orwell, the Brontes, Tennyson, Tolkien, Lewis, Dickens, and H.G. Wells. We also hear the earliest mythology of western culture—of Greek and Roman, and even Norse myths reflected with sometimes a slightly eastern twist. What we see in the Harry Potter series is a continuation of these elements and Rowling captures our imagination as she takes the old themes and molds them into a new mythology for the 21st century. She reaches back to the past, using as her foundation the great themes of the western literature, and then weaving into them rich characters, theology, philosophy, humor, and mystery. In many ways, like a good teacher, she points us back to the literary roots of England, but in the process she never forgets to tell a really good story.

The characters in Rowling's novels are rich and complex. The prose of each of the books is written from the point of view of Harry's chronological age in that book. Book 1 (*Sorcerer's Stone*) is from the perspective of an eleven-year-old, Book 2 (*Chamber of Secrets*) being from a twelve-year-old, Book 3 (*Prisoner of Azkaban*) from a thirteen-year-old, Book 4 (*Goblet of Fire*) from a fourteen-year- old; and the latest Book 5 (*Order of the Phoenix*) from a fifteen-year-old. But this doesn't mean that what Harry, the character, chooses to see reflects the entire world that Rowling has created. As Hemingway said about the iceberg theory, "*a writer knows enough about what he is writing about, he may omit things that he knows. The dignity of movement of an iceberg is due to only one ninth of it being above water.*"[1] This is exactly what Rowling does in her prose. As we explore the text, we discover that while Harry is limited to see what he can for his age, we—the adult readers—can see more, if we look. Rowling gives subtle and sometimes rather witty hints and clues throughout the entire series—if we are willing to do the work to uncover them. Readers are invited to become a Sherlock Holmes, themselves, uncovering the mysteries of the text and developing theories of what may be revealed in the future.

The biggest mystery in the Harry Potter septology continues to be: Who is Harry Potter (really) and what is he going to do with his life? Given that famous scar on his forehead, he is a "marked man." While much of his destiny seems to be planned for him, it is also very apparent that Harry has choices—that he does have the freedom to choose. *"It is our choices, Harry, that show what we truly are, far more than our abilities,"* Dumbledore tells Harry at the end of *Book 2.*

The New York Times also has a choice, a choice that will reveal the character of those who decide what truly belongs on the Best Seller List. If it is true, that *Harry Potter* is merely the tip of the iceberg, if it is true that JK Rowling's works may be appreciated in many other ways—as a children's book, a mystery, mythology, a political thriller, a morality play, or the heir of great British literature—then the time has come to fight the pressure and restore this series to the main Best Seller List where it belongs.

When it comes time for our cultural leaders to look back and assess the impact that this series has had on literature and the book trade, will we see *The New York Times* literature section suffer the consequences of inaction—by following in the wake of the rather infamous ocean liner that didn't take the tip of an iceberg seriously?

EDITOR'S NOTES

✳ Mary Anne Grossmann, in "Magical Facts about Harry Potter", stated that, *"Harry's intergenerational appeal shows in the Book Industry Study Group report that of the nearly 8 million Potter book sold in the US in 1999, 57% were bought for readers 14 and younger; the rest were purchased by those over 14, most of whom were 35-49."*

> Grossman, Mary Anne
> "Magical Facts about Harry Potter". 1 Sept 2004.
> http://www.contracostatimes.com/mld/cctimes/6114784.htm

✳ In a *Time* magazine article, they thought it particularly interesting that the Harry Potter books don't specify a reading level, which would be expected for a children's book.

That same article also addressed the controversy over the Best-Seller List. Although there are those who blame *The New York Times*, it wasn't an arbitrary decision – it was the result of extreme pressure that was put on them by the whole publishing industry, *"The Times' decision was a response to complaints from many publishers...that Harry Potter was hogging and clogging the top of the best-seller list, depriving the public of access to other popular fiction."*

> Corliss, Richard
> "Why 'Harry Potter' did a Harry Houdini" 1 Sept 2004.
> http://www.time.com/time/nation/article/0,8599,50554,00.html

1 Hemingway, Ernest. "The Art of Fiction". Interview with George Plimpton. *Paris Review.* #18, Spring, 1958

✴ TWO DEGREES OF SEPARATION ✴

BEACHBUM ✴ NEW CLUES FORUM
USA (*US Edition*), AGE "OLD ENOUGH TO BE A MEMBER OF AARP"

Inspiration for this Discussion

Most of the folks I had talked to told me that reading the *WWP Ultimate Unofficial Guides* was like "WOW! Somebody turned on the light in a dark room. I saw the Harry Potter books in a whole new way!" That enthusiasm prompted me to jump into a discussion forum with both feet. It was great! All these folks talking about the Harry Potter books and guessing what various points might really mean. But also I noticed something in that forum: the temptation to engage in an ever-growing series of "what ifs". What if this, and then based on that idea, what if THIS, and then based on that what if …YOWZA! Suddenly, you've gone from figuring out that Aunt Petunia just might know way more about the wizarding world than she lets on to theorizing that Delores Umbridge is actually Aunt Petunia on Polyjuice potion.

Only two degrees of separation keeps imaginations from running rampant. This essay grew out of a post of mine on my favorite web site (where I was moderating) that was intended to help some lost souls find their way back toward reality (away from fan-fic) with their theories.

 HANDFUL

Sleuthing *Harry Potter* is one of my favorite activities. Instead of just reading a good book, I can search for clues about future events, hints on things to watch for in various characters, correlated images and symbols and several underlying themes and plot lines (based on JK Rowling's *intentional* hints). But just recognizing those hints and clues can be tricky, and the subsequent analysis can generate any number of theories – all of which are potentially valid.

So, how do we determine a valid theory? One of the principles of being an HP Sleuth is to support *all* theories with evidence. Therefore, if you feel you have spotted a possible clue and you can support it with evidence, you can "invent" as much as you can *justify* so long as you have canon to back it up (see discussion in "Loose Canons").

Those of you who are familiar with the game "Six Degrees of Separation," can apply that same concept. When used for sleuthing, Galadriel Waters calls it "Two Degrees of Separation". The idea is: if the only way a theory works is by using unsupported assumptions (as opposed to canon evidence), it doesn't qualify for our purpose as a valid theory. A speculation is one degree separated from canon, and then any theory based on that would be two degrees separated. For those of you who relate more closely with visual cues (or those currently enrolled in an algebra class), it looks like this:

One Degree of Separation ➔ theory based on fact (canon)

Two Degrees of Separation ➔ theory based on a theory ➔ that was based on fact

Although the original assumption may have been based on canon, the new theory (now 2 degrees off)

is not. *A valid theory must be separated from canon by only 1 Degree.* Another way to look at it is whether you can find any canon to *disprove* your theory (again, see "Loose Canons" for more details).

You can use this Two Degrees of Separation to help evaluate whether a theory is a wild-yet-totally-valid analysis, or just fan-fic. That is how WWP distinguishes the difference between analysis and fan-fic.

Let me give you some valid examples of One Degree of Separation using everybody's favorite dweeb, Neville Longbottom, and some of his family history:

> Canon: We know that Neville has a terrible memory {B1, Ch9, p145}. We also know that a bad memory is one of the symptoms of having had a powerful memory charm performed on you. {B4, Ch35, p685}
>
> One Degree: A valid hypothesis (within 1 degree of separation) would be that Neville's memory is bad because a Memory Charm was placed on him.

> Canon: We know that some Death Eaters (Bella and the Lestrange boys) attacked the Longbottoms and tortured them into insanity after the attack on the Potters at Godric's Hollow. {B4, Ch30, p595}
>
> One Degree: A valid hypothesis (again, within 1 degree of separation) would be that Neville was present at the attack of his parents.

> Canon: According to canon (Headmaster Dumbledore, to be exact), Professor Snape used to be a Death Eater. {B4, Ch30, p590}
>
> One Degree: A valid hypothesis would be that Snape was present at the torture of Neville's parents.

The problem arises when I, or someone else, take a *theory* and then use it as the basis for *another* theory. For instance, we know that Neville is terrified of Professor Snape {B3, p125, 135}, and since it was the Death Eaters who attacked the Longbottoms it becomes tempting to extrapolate:

> One Degree: Neville, who has a memory problem, could have been present at the torture of his parents.
>
> Two Degrees: Since Neville, who has the symptoms of a Memory Charm, was present at the torture of his parents it could mean the Death Eaters placed a Memory Charm on the infant so he would not remember the attackers.
>
> (Although this seems quite plausible, it requires that Neville be present – which is only a theory.)

> One Degree: Neville could have been present at the torture of his parents and Snape could have been one of the Death Eaters there.
>
> Two Degrees: Since both Snape and Neville were present, Neville (consciously or subconsciously) recognized Professor Snape as one of his attackers – so he is now terrified of Prof. Snape.
>
> (But this is now 2 degrees away because we are assuming that the theories about Snape and Neville are true.)

It is easy to jump to conclusions that seem perfectly plausible (and could even turn out to be true); however, if they are based on too many assumptions, they are only guesses (and therefore fan-fic) – and not based on the clues JKR has planted:

Canon: Snape was working undercover for the Order of the Phoenix.

One Degree: Neville could have been present at the torture of his parents.

Two Degrees: Neville recognized Snape as one of the Death Eaters who attacked his parents.

Three Degrees: I speculate that Dumbledore ordered the Memory Charm performed on Neville to protect Snape's espionage and the Order.

(Intriguing or likely as this seems, it is actually only fan fiction.)

We try really hard to keep our theories at just one degree of separation from canon because we are trying to stick to the clues that JKR purposely gave us. This isn't always easy because some of the fan-fic guesses are REALLY nifty. I mean if Snape WAS there, and *Dumbledore* ordered the Memory Charm performed on Neville, then that means…See what I mean? Wandering into the realms of fan-fic can really let your imagination run wild. Unfortunately, it doesn't do much for sorting out the intentional clues in JKR's works.

There are a lot of big clues to uncover, so even if a theory may seem a bit outlandish, as long as there is nothing in canon to *disprove* it, it could certainly be valid. Think of it this way: in the first Harry Potter book, Scabbers was a rat, Mrs. Figg was a crazy old Muggle, and the Weasleys didn't come from a family of Dark Wizards!

Loose Canons:
On the Use and Misuse
of Canon Evidence in Theories

K.E. Bledsoe ✳ NC, "ArtemisMoonbow"
USA (*US Edition*), Age 42

Inspiration for this Discussion

"Do you have canon evidence to support that?"

You don't have to be on the MuggleNet *New Clues* or *Chamber of Secrets* web forums very long before you hear that refrain. Just offer a guess or a hunch with no supporting evidence on any of the threads and you can count on a mod or an experienced HP Sleuth trilling, *"Where's your canon evidence?"* What is canon evidence, and how do we find it, use it, and not have our theory smell like a dungbomb?

 HANDFUL

In this case, "canon" (meaning "a list of recognized genuine works of a particular author, composer, etc."[1]) primarily refers to the Harry Potter books themselves, and secondarily, to information provided directly by Ms. Rowling via interviews, online chats, or her personal website. These are HP Sleuths' sacred sources of evidence in supporting story-line theories.

Yet, while canon can and should be used as evidence to support theory, there are many examples of misuse of canon all over the online discussion boards. It's not enough to say, "Look, I found a clue for this in the book, so it must be true!" It's how you use and support suspected clues that counts.

BACKWARD-CHAIN OR HYPOTHETICO-DEDUCTIVE REASONING

How do you do that?

The best way I have to explain is by example. Let's start with a theory, and then turn to the canon for supporting evidence. This, in cognitive science circles, is known as *backward-chain reasoning* — that is to say, reasoning which begins with theory and moves toward data (you postulate a theory and look backward for data to support it). It's also called *hypothetico-deductive reasoning*, the kind of reasoning associated with scientific methodology. Properly applied, it can lead to new discoveries. Improperly applied, it drives you directly into a theoretical rut (i.e., ridiculous theories), as I will now demonstrate.

First, you must start with a theory. My model and (ridiculous) theory, then:

> ### Dudley Dursley is a Death Eater who has been placed at Privet Drive to keep
> ### tabs on Harry.

Do I have canon evidence to support my Dudley Dursley is a Death Eater? Why, yes! Sure, I do! I have a whole pocketful of evidence to support my theory. ☺

First of all, how do we identify Death Eaters? By the Dark Mark on the forearm which became visible as Voldemort returned to power, and burns when he called his faithful followers. We also know the Dark Mark can be cast into the sky as a sign or a beacon. Several "clues" tie Dudley to the Dark Mark. In Chapter 2 of Book 1{p26, 27 US}, we have the reptile house scene. The book clearly states, "*Dudley and Piers wanted to see huge, poisonous cobras and thick, man-crushing pythons. Dudley quickly found the largest snake in the place.*" Snakes are the symbol of Slytherin and form a significant part of the Dark Mark. Interesting that Dudley is so interested in large, dangerous snakes.

Does Dudley wear a Dark Mark? While we've never had the chance to observe his forearm closely, we do know that he was "marked" significantly in Book 1 when Hagrid gave him the pig's tail. Think of the shape of a pig's tail: curly, twisty, worm-like. "Curly" and "worm" are running bits throughout the book, and a worm-like tail brings us to Wormtail, a known Death Eater {Ch4, p59}

But the most telling connection between Dudley and the Dark Mark is in Book 4, when Fred and George drop the Ton Tongue Toffees on the floor. Dudley's tongue lolled "*like a great, slimy python*". {Ch2, p50} A snake coming out of a mouth — remind you of anything?

Next, let's look at some Death Eater Behavior clues. Dudley has a penchant for violence, from explosive video games to real-life acts of bullying. We're told many times that he beats up on Harry, and focuses specifically on breaking his glasses. We've been told that eyes are the most vulnerable feature, and "eyes" are a running bit. Why does Dudley keep focusing on Harry's vulnerable eyes? Dudley is also the first to notice that Harry has a letter from Hogwarts, and he alerts Vernon. {Ch3, p35} Interesting that Dudley is the first to interfere with Harry's going to Hogwarts.

On page 31 of Book 1, Dudley knocks down Mrs. Figg on his new racing bike, *even though he doesn't like exercise.* This has to mean he goes out of his way to attack her. We know from Book 5 that Mrs. Figg is watching over Harry. Is it a coincidence that Dudley runs over Harry's only guardian in the neighborhood?

In the opening chapter of Book 5, Dudley really gives away his Death Eater behavior. On page 10, Dudley appears on the scene thus: "*A soft ticking noise came from several expensive racing bikes that they were wheeling along.*" Clocks (ticking) and wheels are both running bits, so this must be important. We're told that Dudley and his gang cruise the neighborhood to beat people up, *just like the Death Eaters at the Quidditch World Cup*!

Then comes the Dementor attack. We know that in Book 4, the Dementor Fudge brought with him swooped down on Barty Crouch immediately. Of course, in the Dementor scene in Book 5 both Harry *and Dudley* are attacked by the Dementors. We find out later that they were ordered to attack Harry, but they also went for Dudley *just as they went for another Death Eater!*

There are a few other oddities that I can point to that may help support this theory. In Chapter 1 of Book 2 {p1}, Harry asks to be allowed to let Hedwig out, but Vernon refuses. Harry tries to argue, but Dudley *drowns him out* with a long belch. An interrupted clue! Why is Dudley trying to keep Hedwig caged? Later {Ch2, p23}, Harry dreams that he's in a cage and Dudley is on the outside, rattling the bars to taunt him. This ties with Hedwig's cage, but it also ties with the "cage" of light in the graveyard scene with all the Death Eaters in Book 4.

Also extremely interesting is Dudley's school uniform of maroon and orange. Those two colors are associated with Ron, who wears maroon sweaters, pajamas, and dress robes, and whose bedroom is done in Chudley Cannons orange. Is it a coincidence that in Book 1, Dudley is going to a school whose colors are associated with Harry's *future* best friend? I think we have some foreshadowing.

But how, you ask, can Dudley be a Death Eater when he's Harry's age? The answer to that lies in the Department of Mysteries. Recall the Death Eater from Book 5 who got his head stuck in the bell jar? His head turned into a baby's head.{Ch35, p790} This is a clue pointing back to the numerous "baby" clues throughout the book, and to the opening chapters of Book 1: Dudley's baby pictures, the ones that looked like a beach ball in a bonnet. How hard would it be to take a volunteer Death Eater, put him in the bell jar, and place him in the Dursleys' home? Either the Dursleys were in on the scheme, or someone exchanged the Death Eater "Dudley" for the real Dudley and used a memory charm on the Dursleys to make them think that this "boy" was their own son. Simple!

There it is, then, a theory completely supported by canon and only canon (except for a bit of hypothesizing at the end). A bit scary, isn't it?

The theory, as ridiculous as it sounded at the start, is highly convincing (or at the least seemingly plausible) with all that canon evidence behind it.

But what's missing?

The crucial piece that is missing is an active search for refuting evidence. This is an essential part of critical thinking.

REFUTING EVIDENCE

Any good scientist knows that the way to test a hypothesis is not to seek out only the supporting evidence, but to actively look for refuting evidence. If, after an exhaustive search, no refuting evidence can be found, or what little can be found is unconvincing, then the hypothesis is accepted — for the moment.

And refuting evidence for this theory is abundant. As being a Death Eater usually implies also being a wizard, that alone would negate most of my "evidence". We've never seen Dudley use any kind of magic, not even the spontaneous magic that Harry emits when he's threatened. All of Dudley's bullying techniques are conventional: punches, kicks, and verbal abuse. Dudley is, in fact, *absolutely petrified* of magic. His parents are also terrified of magic, and Dudley picks up on their refrains as he taunts Harry about his "freak" school. He has no idea where Harry's letters are coming from until Hagrid reads one out, and is genuinely puzzled as to why anyone would write to Harry. As for the "mark" Hagrid left on Dudley's backside, Hagrid himself explains that: *"Meant ter turn him into a pig, but I suppose he was so much like a pig anyway there wasn't much left ter do."* {B1, Ch4, p59} Definitely just a pigtail.

Backward-chain, or hypothetico-deductive reasoning, without an active search for refuting evidence, leads to theoretical dead ends. We've seen numerous theories sprout up on the Harry Potter fan boards and many HP Sleuths offer evidence in their favor: metamorphmagus theories, animagus theories, relationship theories, polyjuice theories. We've all seen HP Sleuths cling to pet theories so tightly that they not only refuse to accept refuting evidence, they twist it to fit their ideas. It can get so bad that when Ms. Rowling tells us straight up in an interview, "No, he/she is not a Death Eater," there is always someone who will cry out, "Oh, but look at how she said it. I'm sure she was being sarcastic, so she meant the opposite." No matter how hard one clings, the theory is dead, and should be buried quickly before it smells. HP Sleuths, all of us, would do well to examine our own pet theories with complete open-mindedness to see how their vital signs are holding up, and, as your HP Sleuth membership card states, refrain from attacking people who offer differing ideas.

FORWARD-CHAIN OR DEDUCTIVE REASONING

Well then, if backward-chain (hypothetico-deductive) reasoning has pitfalls, what about forward-chain (also called inductive) reasoning—moving from data to theory? In this type of reasoning, we begin with canon facts. By sifting through the facts, we search for patterns, which become hypotheses and theories. The whole "running bits" business is an example of forward-chain reasoning at work: as we notice many instances of mirrors, eyes, and similar recurring features throughout the books, we watch for emerging patterns. Where do we see mirrors? In what circumstances? What do they look like? How are they being used? Are all mirrors significant, or only certain ones?

But forward-chain inductive reasoning can have as many pitfalls as backward-chain reasoning. One problem that even the most experienced researchers have is that humans are natural-born pattern detectors. We tend to "discover" patterns even when none really exists. Seeing animal shapes in the clouds is an example: we all know there aren't really elephants in the sky, but we recognize certain forms as being elephant-like. We also have a natural tendency to notice only outstanding clues and ignore contradictory clues when we think we're on to something. An example is the belief that the phone always rings when we're in the shower. We know very well it rings when we're not in the shower, and we've all had plenty of showers where the phone didn't ring at all. But let it ring once when we're in the shower, and we notice the outstanding exception, reinforcing our perception that the phone always rings when you're in the shower. Casinos take full advantage of this human trait when they ring the bells and flash the lights for big winners, but quietly ignore big losers, leading other gamers to believe, "Hey, it'll happen for me, too!" Once again, the problem is the failure to recognize refuting evidence as important.

So, what do we do then? How do we avoid these pitfalls?

CYCLING THE BEST METHOD

First and foremost, HP Sleuths have to recognize that all theories are tentative. Even scientific theories (which are not guesses, but explanations of natural phenomenon) are tentative, and change as new data are uncovered. Part of this recognition involves the acceptance that one's pet theories might be incorrect, with a willingness to let go of ideas that fail to hold up under scrutiny. Another part is an openness to recognizing refuting evidence when it is presented by fellow sleuths.

Second, using inductive-deductive cycling is an excellent way to develop theories. In plain English, this means cycling between using facts to spin hypotheses, and testing those hypotheses by looking for new facts that support or contradict the hypotheses. Sifting through data creates questions; out of the questions come hypotheses. We test the hypotheses against more canon data, always keeping in mind that refuting evidence is as important as — indeed, more important than — supporting data. Hypotheses that hold up against all evidence cluster together into larger story-line theories that inspire more questions and more searches for data. Best done as a group process, inductive/deductive cycling is an efficient way to process large amounts of data. And (as we have come to appreciate) Ms. Rowling's books certainly qualify as *large* amounts of data!

By cycling between backward-chain and forward-chain reasoning, and by always remembering the value of refuting evidence and of openness to letting pet theories go, we can build good theory about the future stories without falling into hypothetical pitfalls.

---

[1] Shorter Oxford English Dictionary. 5th Ed. Oxford University Press. Oxford, 2002.

Magic
and the
Mind

PONDERINGS... DOES THE WAND CHOOSE THE WIZARD?

—"CECI" ✳ NEW CLUES FORUM
ARGENTINA (*UK Edition*), AGE 30

Inspiration for this Discussion

Ever since I started reading the Harry Potter books, I've had some questions that are still unanswered. One of those questions was related to the wands—why some people would use wands that were not meant for them. Were they aware that a wand makes its selection to help the wizard? Most importantly, why did Harry end up with a brother wand to Voldemort's? I had been re-reading all the information we have about wands and I came up with some answers. Of course, those also raised more questions. But now I'm seeing the situation with a new perspective that I feel is worth discussing.

 HANDFUL

THE CHOICE

"*The **wand** chooses the wizard*"...

That is the phrase Mr. Ollivander, purveyor of fine wands, imprinted in our memory. {B1, Ch5, p63 *UK*} Who doesn't remember Harry's first day at Diagon Alley when he had just found out that he was not only a wizard, but a very famous one as well? "...*only place fer wands, Ollivanders, and yeh, gotta have the best wand*" {p81}. The best wand? If the wand is the one making the decision then it's not necessarily the best wand, is it? Rather it's the wand that *likes* him best – which definitely isn't the same thing.

In spite of how often we see wands, they are still truly mysterious objects. I will ponder the apparent inconsistencies by presenting a series of questions that have bugged me about wands in JK Rowling's world.

Having just met the pureblood Slytherin, Harry learns that Draco's mother was looking at wands for him. {p77} That's where the first of many questions arises: why would someone from an old family think that it's okay to choose someone else's wand? Could it be: the information about the wand choosing the wizard (or that you can't do as well with another wand) is well-hidden, and only a few wizards ever knew this seemingly important fact, or maybe they didn't believe or care about Ollivander's statement?

Picture Harry at Ollivanders wand shop. Ollivander asks which hand he uses more often. Then he starts to measure Harry. {B1, Ch5, p64} Presumably using that information, he starts to search for some wands to try. Are there some specific kinds of wands that prefer left-handed wizards and witches and other kinds that prefer right-handed? If not, then why would Ollivander need that info? Or, is he the one who makes the choice, and all that information helps him to make the best choice? Hagrid, a giant, has a long wand, while Umbridge is short and "stubby" with an "unusually short" wand. {B5, Ch12, p216} Is there a correlation? Does the wand give more power to the wizard? All this leads the reader to three very important questions: why does Ollivander need measurements? Why does he need to know which one is his best hand? Does the size of the wizard/witch make a difference in the fit of the wand?

If the answer is yes to any of these, is it really the wand that is making the choice? There are many more such questions to ponder...

Harry had waved what felt like every wand, until at last he had found the one that suited him. {B4, Ch18, p272} How do you know if it's a good fit? "...*excellent for transfiguration...I say your father favored it.*" James *favored* his wand? And Harry found the one that *suits* him? Not the other way around? Does everyone "try out" wands? "*Well, it's really the wand that chooses the wizard, of course.*" {B1, Ch5, p63} Ollivander also says that there are some wands better for charms, and others for transfiguration. {p63} How does it know?

After several tries, Ollivander and Harry come across the correct wand—a wand, which has some particular similarities to Voldemort's wand. It has the same core as the wand that chose Lord Voldemort— a tail feather from Fawkes the phoenix. {B4, Ch30, p605} Ollivander links Harry's scar to Voldemort's wand and in turn to Harry's new wand, creating several bonds between both wands. {B1, Ch5, p64} This clearly relates to Book 4, when Harry's wand was bound to its brother (Voldemort's wand) producing the sound of a phoenix song that he "connected with Dumbledore". {Ch34, p576} Is Harry associated with Fawkes in some way? But then again, how does the wand make the choice? Can the wand predict what the wizard will do in the future? Could Ollivander have done anything to change the selection? "*...and in the wrong hands... well, if I'd known what that wand was going out into the world to do....*" {p64} Can it read wizards the same way the Sorting Hat can? We never saw any evidence that the wand can do that, so how can it choose? If the wand really chose Harry, I want to know why. Does it have anything to do with his scar being made by Voldemort's wand? One more thing to ponder—in the Priori Incantatem scene, we never saw the echo of the spell hitting Harry. Why?

The Best Wand

On the Hogwarts Express we find out that Ron has Charlie's old wand. "*...a very battered-looking wand. It was chipped in places*"..."*Unicorn hair's nearly poking out*". {B1, Ch6, p78,79} This brings up all sorts of questions about second-hand wands. Why would Charlie want a new wand? If that wand chose him in the first place, I think it's reasonable to presume that he would want to keep the wand that fit him best. Then there's the situation when someone gets expelled from wizarding school or sentenced by the Ministry of Magic – they get their wands destroyed. {B5, Ch8, p136} Why do they get destroyed? Why not confiscated? Is it because the rest of the wizards would not want it?

As the years pass, we discover that there are several wand-makers and some wands can have a "personality". At the wand-weighing ceremony in Book 4, before examining Krum's wand minutely, Mr. Ollivander identifies it as a "Gregorovitch" wand. {Ch18, p271} How did Harry's perfect wand know to show up in Ollivander's shop? How do we know his perfect wand isn't sitting in Gregorovitch's bargain bin?

As we know from Ron's mishaps throughout Book 2, wands can malfunction if they are broken and cannot be fixed, so a replacement is required. Apparently, wand performance, *even with the same person,* can vary. Bagman explains to Harry why they have to "weigh" the champions' wands, "*We have to check that your wands are fully functional...*"{B4, Ch18, p265} Wands can also be less effective if not taken care of in the proper way, as Ollivander discusses with Cedric. "'*It's in fine condition...You treat it regularly?' 'Polished it last night,' said Cedric.*" {p271} Was Harry ever informed of the proper care for his wand? Who knows more about that than Ollivander? Did he ever mention it to Harry? How do we know if it is true? Sounds like a great excuse to check the others' wands—especially Krum's (student of a "former" Death Eater). They all know that someone submitted Harry's name for the tournament. Since some extra safety precautions may have been added, having the wand inspected was another means for Dumbledore to protect

Harry. Mr. Ollivander notices that Fleur's wand core is a Veela hair, and then he states, *"I find it makes for rather temperamental wands...however, to each his own, and if this suits you..."* {p270} The wand suits Fleur and not the other way around?

At the most critical moment in Book 4, we see that the wands do not always perform the way the wizards want. {Ch36, p575} Two wands with the same core don't work as they should if they have to duel each other. *"Every Ollivander wand has a core of a powerful magical substance...No two Ollivander wands are the same, just as no two unicorns, dragons, or phoenixes are quite the same. And of course, you will never get such good results with another wizard's wand."* {B1, Ch5, p64} If there actually is a difference in the performance of a wand, it's more likely to be related to the material of the wand.

At the Ministry of Magic, we discover that Neville has been using his dad's wand all these years. He comes from a pureblood family {B3, Ch11, p201} and his parents had been Aurors. It is logical to expect some knowledge about wands and their limitations. Why would Grandma Longbottom give him his dad's wand—especially when they thought that Neville wasn't magical enough to make it to Hogwarts? You would think she should want to give him the most appropriate wand, as a way to help him improve his magic.

If the wand chooses the wizard and it's the best match, does this mean it cannot be "matched" to another wizard and have the same performance? What happens when someone dies? Is their wand destroyed? We are told that you can't do as well with someone else's wand, but Sirius didn't have trouble using Snape's or Ron's wand. {B3, Ch19, p377} In the graveyard, we witnessed how Peter Pettigrew, not a very talented wizard, was capable of performing the difficult Killing Curse on Cedric with someone else's (Voldemort's) wand. *"...swishing noise and a second voice, which screeched the words...'Avada Kedavra!'"*. {B4, Ch32, p553}

So we keep returning to Book 1 and our introduction to Ollivander at his shop. Harry gives us an eerie description of Ollivander's eyes and the way he gazes:

> *"Mr. Ollivander fixed Harry with his pale stare"..."Harry wished he would blink.*
> *Those silvery eyes were a bit creepy."* {B1, Ch5, p63,65}

See if that reminds you of something:

> *"Remembering what Snape had said about eye contact being crucial to*
> *Legilimency, Harry blinked and looked away."* {B5, Ch26, p520}

Could Mr. Ollivander be a Legilimens? Or is Mr. Ollivander just good at reading people, especially after having years of experience? Does he judge his wand-making skills by the success his customers have into their adult years?

DUMBLEDORE'S PLAN

When Harry entered the shop, looking so much like his dad, {B1, Ch5, p82} Ollivander knew right away who he was. Harry had just met Draco, and was feeling more out of place and worried than before. Mr. Ollivander knew how important Harry was (who didn't) so, maybe Ollivander thought if Harry had a special wand, it would give him some confidence. After all, there were plenty who refused to believe that Lord Voldemort (LV) was gone for good. Presumably, Ollivander would have known about the Priori Incantatem spell; perhaps he helped the choice — allowing Harry something else against LV, something that could be useful for Harry, if they were confronted again.

Dumbledore told us in Book 4, {Ch36, p605} that right after Harry left the shop, Ollivander sent him a note saying that Harry bought the other wand with a Fawkes feather as a core. This fact raises a few questions in itself. Why tell Dumbledore? Had Dumbledore contacted Ollivander to find out what wand

Harry got? There was probably an agreement to inform Dumbledore who it was that bought each of the Fawkes' feather wands when the wands were first made – but was that just idle curiosity? Dumbledore tells us that he made his *"...decision...with regard to the years ahead,"* convinced Voldemart would survive and come back to kill Harry. {B5, Ch37, p736} Did Dumbledore think, in his perfectly outlined plan, that he could help the outcome by giving Harry the brother to Voldemort's wand and asking Ollivander to do so (but without letting Harry know)?

Dumbledore took several measures to make his plan work. With the wand having such an important role in the wizarding world, it would be reckless of him not to have thought about it and taken action. *"The wand chooses the wizard, remember...I think we must expect great things from you, Mr. Potter..."* {B1, Ch5, p65} But did Dumbledore, Ollivander, Harry or the wand actually do the choosing? What do *you* think?

ADDITIONAL SLEUTHING NOTES

* How does the mind of the wizard interact with the wand?
* Did Voldemort himself somehow subconsciously yet directly influence Harry's wand choice via their scar link?
* Was Charlie's "old wand" new when he got it? Ron is casting tricky spells on Quidditch Quaffles and doing well at DA lessons – doesn't he seem to have improved with his new wand?
* How many wand-makers are there? Are there cheaper wand-makers, and if so, do their wands choose as well?
* Does Ollivander have a "best-fit" wand sitting in his shop for everyone, or is there an "almost fit" or a "one-size-fits-all"? Does the wand take the owner's financial situation into account?
* What makes a wand-maker "the best"? How does Mr. Ollivander choose his materials or "victims" when looking for feathers, hairs, or heartstrings?
* Why did they do a wand weighing before the Triwizard Tournament? They claimed it was to make sure they were in proper working order {B4, Ch18, p270}—but what would they have done about it if one of the Champions' wands malfunctioned? (A handicap?) If the "weighing" was to look for improprieties then what could be done to "enhance" a wand that would disqualify it?
* What happened to James' and Lily's wands?

✳ Unity Inside: The Sorting of Harry Potter ✳

—Diane Heath ✳ NC, "9Moons"
USA (*US Edition*), Age 49

Inspiration for this Discussion

My husband joined a book club a few years ago and the "welcome to our club" gift was a set of Harry Potter books, which numbered 3 at that time. My first attempt to read them was interrupted as I had just finished Chapter 1 of Book 1. It was at least 6 months before I picked up the first book again, but once I started reading it, I promptly read all of the others and have continued to do so since. While waiting for Book 5 to be released, I came across the Ultimate Unofficial Guide by Galadriel Waters. My essay, entitled "Unity Inside: The Sorting of Harry Potter", was written because I got to thinking about the need for unity as stated by the Sorting Hat in Book 5. In my opinion, Harry Potter represents the unity, and need for unity at Hogwarts because he could have been sorted into any of the four Houses. He is not the Heir of Slytherin and may not be a true Heir by blood of Godric Gryffindor, but Harry is the hope of the wizarding world.

 HANDFUL

Second in importance only to the receipt of the Hogwarts letter of acceptance into the school, the Sorting Ceremony is the one event with the most profound impact on the education and future of wizard students. Professor McGonagall tells the first-years, "*your house will be something like your family within Hogwarts.*" {B1, Ch7}

Like all families, the Houses can be identified by the pride, expectations and history of the members that belong to it. Although Professor McGonagall assures the students that every House has a noble history full of outstanding witches and wizards, the individual student brings his or her own personality, ideas, and family background into the process. Harry noticed this when he saw that Draco Malfoy felt sure that he would be sorted into Slytherin because, "*all our family have been.*" {B1, Ch5} Ron Weasley, on the other hand, has the family expectations of being in Gryffindor. "*I don't know what they'll say if I'm not.*" {Bk 1, Ch 6} He later tells Harry "*if the Sorting Hat had tried to put me in Slytherin, I'd've got the train straight back home...*" {Bk 1, Ch 9}

In the sorting of Harry Potter, the readers get an inside look into the Sorting Hat's method of selection. As we see from its process of contemplating where to place Harry, the Sorting Hat pointed out four characteristics: courage—*plenty of courage*, intelligence—*not a bad mind*, talent—*there's talent*, and ambition—*nice thirst to prove yourself.* {Ch 7} You probably recognized that The Sorting Hat's profile of Harry represents the core characteristics of each of the 4 houses. What can we learn from these descriptions? What does that parallel tell us about the Houses? About Harry? Just as the Hat warns that Hogwarts needs to "*be united from inside or [it'll] crumble from within*", so too must Harry.

"Plenty of courage..."

is quickly identified as the trademark of Gryffindor House. The House's founder is Godric Gryffindor.

There are three Sorting Songs found in the Harry Potter books published so far, and in all three, bravery is the identifying mark of a Gryffindor.

The Gryffindor ghost is Sir Nicholas de Mimsey-Porpington (whose nearly-successful decapitation earned him the nickname, Nearly Headless Nick). One can safely say that facing a beheading, especially one as botched as Nick's *"...getting hit forty-five times in the neck with a blunt axe..."*, requires a degree of bravery. {Bk 2, Ch 26} Professor Minerva McGonagall is the Head of Gryffindor House. She exhibits bravery, both in her work with the Order in the ongoing fight to defeat Lord Voldemort, and in her fight, on behalf of Hagrid, when she is struck down by four stunning charms to the chest {Bk 5, Ch 31}—brave deeds indeed. Yet, it is from the adventures of Harry accompanied by his friends, that we learn of the bravery, chivalry and deeds prized by the Gryffindor heart.

"Not a bad mind..."

in spite of Harry's lackluster academic performance. He *could have been* sorted into Ravenclaw *"where those of wit and learning, will always find their kind."*{Bk 1, Ch 7} The Sorting Hat lets us know that the founder of the house, Rowena Ravenclaw, prized the intelligent, clever and witty. We know little about their House ghost, the Grey Lady, but we have met some of the Ravenclaw students. Penelope Clearwater (Percy's girlfriend) is introduced in Book 2. She met Hermione Granger in the library and bravely faced the possibility of a Basilisk with a small mirror. Evidently, Gryffindor would have been a comfortable fit for Penelope, just as the Sorting Hat considered placing Hermione in Ravenclaw (surprise, surprise). Professor Lupin referred to Hermione as the cleverest witch of her age while Terry Boot seemed astonished that she had not been sorted into Ravenclaw from the very beginning. {Bk 5, Ch 19}

In Book 5, we are introduced to Luna Lovegood. Upon examining the uniqueness of Luna Lovegood, one realizes that Ravenclaw is home to more than the academically brilliant. Luna looks at the world with faith—both mature beyond her years, and yet, still child-like in its steadfastness. She acknowledges the truth in Harry's story before any other students, while still maintaining belief in her (supposedly non-existent) Crumple Horned Snorkack and the Blibbering Humdinger. Her acknowledgement of those creatures could be a sign of "second sight", or merely faith in her father, the editor of the magical tabloid *The Quibble*r. She accepts the truth of her mother's death, yet has faith that she will meet her again. It is this faith that comforts Harry in dealing with the loss of Sirius Black.

Although the Eagle is the mascot of Ravenclaw house, one cannot help but consider a Ravenclaw namesake, the ravens of Odin. Odin was a one-eyed god in classical Norse mythology, which JK Rowling draws some of her themes. His ravens are referred to as *Thought* and *Memory*[1]. Odin's wisdom is reflected in those two birds. Perhaps they represent aspects of character that cause one to be sorted into Ravenclaw as well: the ability to think for oneself, to remember what history teaches, coupled with the desire to not only search out the truth but to apply it to one's life so that it is a way of living.

Harry must get over his anger towards the fate that has placed him in the role of icon for the wizarding world and use both Thought and Memory to accept his title of "The Boy Who Lived", and the one on whose shoulders rests the fate of the wizarding world. The Memory of what Voldemort has done must be accompanied by the Thought of the consequences that result not from inaction, but from hasty, ill-considered action. As a Gryffindor, Harry is brave enough to face any consequence—but he needs to put his mind to work, and like a good Ravenclaw, come up with the appropriate strategy. At the end of Book 5, Harry has lost his source of guidance with the death of Sirius Black. He has lost faith in Dumbledore—both in his infallibility and perhaps even in his love. Harry needs to learn how to deal with his ravens of *Thought* and *Memory* through the tools of Occlumency and Legilimency, in order to begin to work on his inner unity.

"There's talent ..."

a quality for placement in Hufflepuff. Professor Sprout teaches Herbology and is the Head of Hufflepuff House. The linking of these two functions is not a coincidence. We learn from the various songs that Helga Hufflepuff chose the hard workers, the patient, the loyal, the just and the true. In spite of the reputation as "duffers"{Bk 1, Ch 5}, Hufflepuff is home to more than all "the rest". {Bk 4, Ch 11} Of the 4 qualities that the Sorting Hat used to describe Harry, courage, intelligence and ambition are quickly and easily matched up with Gryffindor, Ravenclaw, and Slytherin. This leaves the characteristic of talent in the hands of Professor Sprout. Talent is a trait not readily discerned. It requires hard work, patience and determination in order to be cultivated and then come to full fruition. What better hands to guide these students than the Herbology professor? She is trained to plant, water, tend and prune where necessary in order to get the most growth and greatest fruit from whatever plants come into her greenhouse. As the Head of Hufflepuff, she would help each student identify and acknowledge particular strengths and talents, and insures that they get the proper attention and training, regardless of the student's background or personality. While we know that Hannah Abbot, Ernie MacMillan, and Susan Bones all belong in Hufflepuff, the student most often associated with Hufflepuff-like characteristics is Neville Longbottom. Perhaps this is because the Hat took considerable time debating Neville's fate—or it could be because hidden within Neville's memory is a great talent.

In Book 1, Neville tells his new friends that his *"family thought I was all-Muggle for ages...You should have seen their faces when I got in here—They thought I might not be magic enough to come..."*{Bk 1, Ch 7} The Sorting Hat could have seen talent hidden inside of Neville and considered the possibility that Professor Sprout's guidance would be the key to unlocking it. Neville is known to excel in Herbology. Although he ultimately landed in Gryffindor, perhaps Professor Sprout is helping that talent along after all.

Harry is known to have a great talent (in Quidditch and Defense Against the Dark Arts). So, on that basis, he would have qualified. Yet, just as his academic performance leaves his intelligence in doubt, his lack of patience and determination to work hard in order to succeed negated any chance of his being placed in Hufflepuff House.

"A nice thirst to prove yourself..."

in the House of Salazar Slytherin and Lord Voldemort. The reputation of Slytherin as the home of Dark wizards caused Harry to plead against his placement there.

Did the Sorting Hat recognize the connection Harry has with Lord Voldemort? Was it because in attacking Harry, Voldemort made Harry a Parselmouth—the "mark" of Salazar Slytherin? Were these the aspects of Harry's character that the Hat marked as interesting? Ambition, in and of itself, is neutral—it is neither good, bad or interesting.

The reputation of Slytherin House was formed by the division within Hogwarts from Salazar Slytherin leaving the school due to his pureblood mania, and was deepened by the rise of Lord Voldemort. That reputation continues in the current student body through the actions of Draco Malfoy and his followers. But just as Hufflepuff is more than a house of last resort, Slytherin House is more than the home of the Dark Arts. The Sorting Hat sings of cunning folk who use *"any means to achieve their ends"*. {Ch 7} Just as Salazar himself was described as shrewd, one has only to look at the current Head of House, Professor Severus Snape, to see a cunning, shrewd individual whose own ambitions and goals are hidden while he plays the dangerous game of spy. The only other known Slytherin Headmaster is Phineas Nigellus, who epitomizes the cunning nature found among the Slytherins. Dressed in silver bloodstains, the Bloody Baron, the Slytherin House ghost is a menacing and brooding presence. Slytherin House must be accepted and acknowledged before it can be integrated and united with the other Houses. Dumbledore once told Harry that he shared, along with the students of Slytherin House, a disregard for rules. In Book 5, Harry's anger revealed his darker side, while the growing influence of Voldemort on the mind and actions of Harry revealed the dangers.

In conclusion...

Harry has proven himself brave, but in order to unite Hogwarts and the wizarding world so that Voldemort is defeated, Harry needs to be united **inside of himself**. He has to use his *intelligence* effectively and rely on the knowledge and support of those around him. He has shown loyalty and compassion but he will have to develop the *patience and tenacity* of hard work in order to bring his talents to full fruition. I believe that Harry will have to deal with his own Slytherin-like traits, and acknowledge the dark side of his soul while at the same time, guarding against it. It will require every bit of cunning and shrewdness in Harry's possession to see that Voldemort is vanquished, never to return.

— ADDITIONAL SLEUTHING NOTES —

* If there is some of each House in all of us, does Voldemort have other Houses in him?
* Since it is "choices" that are at the core of JKR's message, it is likely that Harry will face a lot more decisions—not only Slytherin ones. For instance, will he be willing to work hard enough on his Occlumency?
* In what way does Harry's mind sync with the external world?
* How does this mesh with the yin and yang themes we keep seeing in the septology?
* Anybody want to wager what house Ludo was in?
* Wonder if Gildroy remembers his school house?

---

[1] Lindow, John. *Norse Mythology: A Guide to the Gods, Heroes, Rituals, and Beliefs.* Oxford University Press. New York: 2001.

The Timing of Voldemort's Plans

Alexander Benesch ✳ CoS Forum
Germany (*UK Edition*), Age 20

Inspiration for this Discussion

This discussion along with "Voldemort's Pawns" was originally part of a larger paper submitted by this author. We, at WWP, felt it was significant enough to stand alone as an extremely fascinating discussion.

12

The same Monday evening of Harry's first Occlumency lesson, Lord Voldemort (LV for short) successfully freed his ten Deatheaters from Azkaban prison. However, In Book 5, LV had two other plans that ultimately failed. We know when the first one ended in a fiasco: shortly before the day of Harry's first Occlumency lesson (and the Azkaban-breakout of ten Deatheaters (DEs), LV had to accept the realisation that months of preparation didn't pay off because Broderick Bode, a Department of Mysteries (DoM for short) employee who they had under the Imperius Curse, failed to steal the prophecy and instead landed himself in St Mungo's where he was later assassinated.

It is more of a secret, and maybe more important to know, when LV's second plan to get the orb was really made.

One would assume that LV's servants would feel their Dark Marks burn and join their master the minute they were outside Azkaban and had their wands back. I would think LV would question Rookwood instantaneously about the Department of Mysteries. However...strangely, almost TWO CHAPTERS' WORTH OF TIME passed after the Azkaban breakout until Harry had the dream of LV questioning Rookwood. The Dark Lord asks: "*You are sure of your facts, Rookwood?*"{B5, Ch26, p515 UK} It would appear the servant had told LV that only he himself or Harry could lift the prophecy off the shelf in the DoM. I refuse to believe that the Dark Lord had set Rookwood free and sent him on a few weeks' vacation before asking him a few simple questions about the security measures in the DoM. No sir, that just does not sound like the Dark Lord I know. The Voldemort *I* know has already been forced to wait *15 years* to get his hands on the complete prophecy and would not allow his servants time to take a single breath.

The answer to this is a set of proposed questions:

1. Who says the interrogation of Rookwood happened exactly *when* Harry saw it in his sleep?
2. Could it not be that Harry had just caught LV's "thought", the *memory* of it?
3. Couldn't the thing have actually happened shortly after the Azkaban breakout, just when you'd have logically expected it?

When Harry saw the attack on Arthur Weasley in his sleep, shortly before Christmas, he *really* saw what was going on at the same moment, but from another location. The big difference is, prior to that, LV was unaware Harry could enter his mind. Harry seemed to "*have visited the snake's mind because that's where the Dark Lord was at the particular moment*", and when his mind is "*most relaxed and vulnerable*" he is "*sharing the Dark Lord's thoughts and emotions*" and "*this process is likely to work in reverse*". {Ch24, p470} Now, during the attack on Arthur Weasley, LV's mind was not in his own head; he was possessing the snake, so his mind could therefore have been more vulnerable and easier to invade. Harry witnessed the attack on Arthur from the snake's point of view; saw him close-up getting bitten even *felt* splintering ribs and gushing blood. We can be quite sure that Harry abruptly "pulled out" just because of the sheer terror he felt from it, and that forceful act of "pulling out" was what LV recognized. Having his enemy invade his mind, moreover at such an important point, of course infuriated LV, and poor Harry felt the usual consequences: blinding pain.

After the attack on Arthur Weasley, Dumbledore ordered Harry to be taught Occlumency to defend himself against LV's mind-intrusion. One can surely assume that LV had upped *his own* defence against *Harry's* intrusion and it would mean that *since then,* all later visions (like the Rookwood questioning) were most likely not viewed by Harry in *real* time (the same time they were happening). The last vision Harry had, about Sirius getting tortured, was even a complete fabrication of Voldemort's mind, and Harry was still convinced that "*Sirius is being tortured NOW!*" {Ch32, p648}

It is my firm belief that, since the attack on Arthur Weasley, Harry has caught only a few *truly real* impressions from LV: some pangs of emotion and one thought/memory of the Rookwood questioning, when LV was letting his guard down for a moment. Obviously, Harry received *intentionally-transmitted,* manipulated images of the Sirius-torturing and those of the DoM.

So, how would that affect Harry? Lord Voldemort may well have made up his second plan on the same Monday when his DEs were freed and Snape gave the first Occlumency lesson. The lesson started on a Monday evening at six o'clock and the Tuesday edition of the *Daily Prophet* reported that "*ten high security prisoners escaped in the early hours of yesterday evening*" from Azkaban prison {Ch25, p481}. Sounds like the two events happened at about the same time (Monday).

Now, consider this: It's not really what you'd call a typical breakout if the prison guards are *all on your side and let you go,* is it? The Dementors obeyed Voldemort and I imagine they would have conducted the whole operation very silently, to not draw attention to it so it would be more safe and to give the Deatheaters more time to disappear. The Dementors could have very well smuggled them out around four or five o'clock without creating any fuss (what method would they have used?) and *given them their wands back* – as they had them later at the DoM! By the time the DEs were outside the prison walls, they probably would have already been feeling their Dark Marks burn, kissed the island goodbye, and Disapparated to Dark Lord Headquarters, pronto! Hours could have passed until the authorities recognized the breakout. That would give LV more than enough time to ask Rookwood a few quick questions about the DoM before the first Occlumency lesson had even started at six o'clock. I mean, how long does it take to explain that "**only the one to whom the prophecy belongs can take it from the shelves and all others go crazy if they try it**"? Heck, I just explained it to you and it only took me 5 seconds and 23 words!!

I find it highly possible that LV didn't take very long coming up with the idea of making Harry go get the thing so he could steal it from him afterwards. And LV just might have come up with the idea the same Monday evening before six o'clock before Harry's Occlumency lesson even began. The timing of the idea's conception and Harry's first Occlumency lesson have been a favourite coincidence for LV, however, it gave the Dark Lord prime opportunity to deceive Harry.

ADDITIONAL SLEUTHING NOTES

* If we don't know for sure what was realtime and what wasn't, how will we know the difference in the future?
* During the first Occlumency lesson, Snape rubs his arm – had he felt the Dark Lord calling through his Dark Mark? Did Harry's use of Voldemort's name have anything to do with it?
* Can Voldemort place thoughts in anyone else's mind, and does he control other creatures?

✷ Occlumency and Legilimency ✷

E. Lingo ✷ NC, GinnyWeasley31
USA (*US Edition*), Age 32

Inspiration for this Discussion

Occlumency and Legilimency are just two of the great new mysteries in Book 5. I wanted to explore how Voldemort was able to tap into Harry's mind and plant images that were not his own. I wondered how this new skill would be used in the final two books, for both sides, good and bad.

🦉 12

There have been suspicions for quite some time that certain characters could 'read minds'. Professor Dumbledore always seems to know what is going on and his gaze has been described as "x-raying". {B2, Ch9 p144 US} Harry also has felt that "*Dumbledore looked at him as though he knew what Harry was thinking.*" {B3, Ch22, p427}

When we are first introduced to Lord Voldemort we see that he somehow knows things that he shouldn't. During Harry's first encounter with him in Book 1, Voldemort says, "*He lies…He Lies…*" {B1, Ch17, p364} when Harry says he saw himself winning the House Cup in the Mirror of Erised. Even more surprising is when Lord Voldemort soon thereafter tells Harry, "*Now, why don't you give me that Stone in your pocket?*" {p365}. Lord Voldemort appears to do this several more times when we are reintroduced to him in Book 4. He accuses Wormtail and later Frank Bryce of lying several times during the first chapter. These are just a few examples throughout the books showing Lord Voldemort's and Professor Dumbledore's mind skills. From these inferences, we can guess that they could be examples of Legilimency.

Professor Severus Snape also accuses others of lying. There are several instances in the previous four novels in which Harry worries that Professor Snape was reading his mind: During Chapter 13 of Book 1, Harry felt as if Snape knows that they've figured out about the Sorcerer's Stone and "*he sometimes had the horrible feeling that Snape could read minds.*" Later in Book 2 {Ch5, p79}, Harry thinks, "*This wasn't the first time Snape had given Harry the impression of being able to read minds.*" Furthermore, there are instances in both Book 3 and Book 4 where Harry wonders if Professor Snape is able to read his mind. Thus, when Professor Snape explains the skill of Legilimency to Harry, Harry's "*worst fears are confirmed*". {B5, Ch24, p530}

Legilimency

Legilimency can be dissected into "legi", meaning *to read* and "mens", meaning *the mind*. (www.dictionary.com) Thus, Legilimency would be *to read the mind*. Professor Snape tells Harry that this skill is not as simple as just "mind reading". That would make the mind too one-dimensional. Snape describes the brain as being "*complex and many layered,*" but that "*the skilled Legilimens can interpret the findings*". {p530, 531} Legilimency is easier to perform if the wizard who is casting the spell is in close proximity to the person on whom it is being cast. Snape informs us that, "*eye contact is often essential to Legilimency.*" {p531} We also learn during Occlumency lessons that it is easier to perform Legilimency on a person who is relaxed, emotional, and/or caught off-guard.

Legilimency seems like it has the potential to be highly useful, although not always reliable. In Legilimency, it seems that you must interpret the results, which can leave a lot of slop. That is possibly the main reason this skill is most often used as a "lie detector". Do they rely on magic alone, or do they take the images that they witness along with physical attributes associated with lying such as sweating, nervous twitching, elevated heart rate, not wanting to look someone in the eye, etc.? The Legilimens is most likely really good at taking whatever information is available to determine if a person is being truthful. I also see the word "Legilimency" as being similar to the word *legitimacy*. Lord Voldemort is said to use this skill to tell if he is being lied to. {B5, Ch24, p531} The word "legitimate" can mean several things; however, in this context the definitions that fit best are: *authorized, real, genuine*. (www.dictionary.com) Trying to determine what is really, or genuinely, on someone's mind is precisely how we are told Lord Voldemort uses Legilimency.

We can also look at the way Harry's mind is manipulated later on in the Book 5 to see that there are other possible uses for Legilimency. Lord Voldemort is able to *plant* into Harry's head images of Sirius being tortured to lure Harry to the Department of Mysteries. But we are not sure exactly how Voldemort does this. In Book 2 (as Tom Riddle), he tells Harry, "*I've always been able to charm the people I needed to.*" {Ch17, p310} This also sounds like Legilimency. However, this sounds like so much more than just reading minds; it's almost on the verge of "mind control".

When Professor Snape performs Legilimency on Harry, he utters the spell "*Legilimens!*" However, it is highly unlikely that these words are needed to actually perform the spell. For example, in Book 2, Voldemort knows that Harry is lying when he says that he saw himself win the House Cup in the Mirror of Erised, instead of actually seeing the stone being placed in his pocket – without casting a spell. In Book 5, Chapter 35, Hermione silences a Death Eater, yet he is still able to zap Hermione by making a "*sudden slashing movement with his wand*". The Death Eater was able to successfully cast a spell without saying a word. As with many spells, it can be inferred that saying the spell aloud makes the spell more powerful, but this is an example where concentration may work best. {B5, Ch38, p847} Besides, would you want someone to know that you were delving into his or her mind to see if he or she were telling you the truth? That would be a cue to put them on-guard and be ready to practice Occlumency.

OCCLUMENCY

Occlumency can be broken down several ways: "Occlude", meaning *to block passage through* and "mens", being Latin for *the mind*. Thus, we have *to block passage to the mind*. Essentially, this is what Professor Snape appears to be trying to teach Harry. The goal is for Harry to block his mind to the entry of Lord Voldemort. Unfortunately, we are not exactly sure how this is done. Professor Snape tells Harry that he will need many of the same powers that he used to repel the Imperius Curse. Professor Snape consistently tells Harry to block his emotions and that "*fools who wear their hearts proudly on their sleeves*", namely Harry, will become easy prey for Lord Voldemort.{Ch24, p536} Snape also tells Harry that he may use his wand to attempt to disarm Snape or defend himself in some other way. The trouble is (as we know too well), Snape never exactly tells Harry how to block his mind – just that he try to do it. Harry seems to effectively block Snape when he subconsciously uses a Stinging Hex, and also when he uses a Shield Charm. {Ch26, p592} The Shield Charm takes the spell and alternatively repels the Legilimens spell back on Snape, thus resulting in the *reverse* flow of memories from Professor Snape that Harry then views. This appears to be the most effective for Harry, as it makes the Legilimens spell backfire into Snape. So, are we to make from this that a really great use of Occlumency is to produce a spell that either repels or hurts the person performing the Legilimens?

Professor Snape seems to be trying to teach Harry to hide his emotions. What I gather, from the information that Professor Snape gives us, is that when people are emotional, their defenses go down and it is much easier to delve into their minds and extract information – or in some cases, deposit information. Professor Snape also tells us that a person skilled in Occlumency can very effectively lie to an accomplished Legilimens. {Ch24, p531} Again, this reiterates that a person's emotional control is important in Occlumency.

Snape's *motives* or *methods* of teaching Occlumency to Harry are not understood. There are many hints from Harry, Ron, and Hermione that Harry's defenses are down following his Occlumency lessons with Snape, thus making Harry easier prey than he was even before the lesson. However, Harry also admits that he didn't work very hard at perfecting his Occlumens skills.

SUMMARY

Okay, according to Snape, it's not mind-reading. However, in my opinion, it's close enough to make me nervous. I am sure this will be a key skill for both sides. It will definitely be interesting to see how both Occlumency and Legilimency will be used and portrayed in the final two books of the *Harry Potter* septology. It surely gives a whole new meaning to "mind games".

ADDITIONAL SLEUTHING NOTES

* Will Voldemort continue trying to "pick" Harry's brain or to plant more false information? Can Harry think "love" thoughts to ward off Voldemort – like he thinks "happy" thoughts to ward off Dementors or "silly" thoughts to ward off Boggarts?

* Hagrid conjured a pigtail onto Dudley without our hearing him voice a spell – is that an example of highly-focused magic? {B1, Ch4, p48} Does this relate to wandless magic?

* Is Lupin a Legilimens? Could Hermione be a Legilimens?

Birds
of a
Feather

How is Harry Potter Like a Phoenix?
(And Why Should We Care?)

K. E. Bledsoe ✳ NC, "Artemis Moonbow"
USA (*US Edition*), Age 42

Inspiration for this Discussion

Great strength, healing powers, deep loyalty, and the ability to rise again from death—these are the characteristics of the Phoenix. But Fawkes, the phoenix, isn't the only character who shows these qualities. Harry Potter has shown some interesting phoenix-like characteristics himself (and I don't mean his unusual hairstyle with its perpetual ruffled hair—as crest-like as it might be). I'm talking about Harry's unique relationship with death. The themes of death and rebirth greatly intrigue me and I was wondering how Harry's role as a phoenix will play out in future books.

 HANDFUL

"Phoenixes burst into flame when it is time for them to die and are reborn from the ashes... They can carry immensely heavy loads, their tears have healing powers, and they make highly faithful pets." {Dumbledore, B2, Ch12, p207}

Of all the characters in the book, Voldemort included, Harry has the strangest and most interesting interactions with death. How phoenix-like is Harry? Let's consider those qualities of the phoenix as Dumbledore describes them.

"They can carry immensely heavy loads..."

When we think of Harry, we don't usually think of great physical strength. Harry is small, skinny, and practically helpless without his glasses. We could, perhaps, attribute considerable *mental* strength for enduring heavy *emotional* loads. Living ten years with the Dursleys without becoming a psychopath, by itself, shows enormous mental strength. His firm sense of self, of what is right and what is wrong, shows plainly in Book 1 when Harry turns away from Draco's offered alliance, choosing Ron as a friend, and insisting "not Slytherin" to the Sorting Hat. But even Harry's mental strength shows cracks, in Books 4 and 5, as his strange mental connection with Voldemort grows more and more obvious, just as Voldemort becomes aware of the connection and the use he can make of it.

Great *magical* strength, yes! In his third year Harry masters the *Patronus* Charm, though it's highly advanced magic and even many adult wizards never learn it. When given a powerful incentive to learn the Summoning *("Accio!")* Charm in Book 4, Harry masters it practically overnight. Despite his lukewarm academic performance, Harry's magical abilities are so advanced that in Book 5, fellow students insist that he become the underground Defense Against the Dark Arts teacher. And, of course, there are the dramatic displays of power when Harry battles Voldemort—from his first encounter in Book 1, to the Department of Mysteries battle in Book 5. Several of the battles have other phoenix connections: phoenix song, Fawkes' appearance, and, in Book 5, the members of the Order of the Phoenix pop in.

Harry also shows a remarkable physical resilience. He falls from his broom from great heights in Books 2 and 3, yet survives. He isn't affected by Acromantula poison, even when one of the giant spiders bites him in the maze in Book 4 (though Newt Scamander assures us in *Fabulous Beasts and Where to Find Them* that the Acromantula bite is poisonous). Though he is nearly overcome by Basilisk poison, he resists the effects long enough for Fawkes to reach him and drip healing tears on the wound. Perhaps this resilience relates to the next phoenix-like trait.

"Their tears have healing powers..."

This attribute is much harder to find in Harry. He's shown no inclination toward being a healer, and his only connection to the healing trade seems to be his ability to end up in the hospital wing of one kind or another in every book, either as a visitor or a patient.

There are two events, though, that are subtly suggestive. The first is when Harry finds Ginny in the Chamber of Secrets. She is still, cold, and nearly dead. Harry, nearly in tears, says, *"Don't be dead!"*—and she survives. The second is in the battle in the Department of Mysteries in Book 5. Hermione is hit with a spell that appears as a strange bolt of purple light that whips across her chest. Harry, again filled with emotion, says, *"Don't let her be dead!"*—and she does survive.

Now, there's no real indication that Harry's spoken words caused either Ginny or Hermione to live through their ordeals. Still, one wonders... when Sirius fell through the veil, Harry shouted, *"HE'S NOT DEAD!"*

"They make highly faithful pets..."

Harry is nobody's pet, to be sure, but *highly faithful* describes Harry's relationship with those he cares most about. It is Harry's loyalty to Dumbledore that draws Fawkes to his aid in Book 2. His friendship with Ron endures a stressful bout of Ron's jealousy in Book 4. Even when Sirius' worst traits are revealed to Harry in Book 5, his first impulse when he believes Sirius to be in mortal danger, is to rush to his aid. Harry staunchly stands up for Hagrid during the Care of Magical Creatures classes, even when he secretly believes Hagrid's teaching style could use a great deal of polish. HP Sleuths can easily recall numerous other examples of Harry's fidelity to his friends, that endures in spite of numerous trials.

"[They] are reborn from the ashes..."

It is in this third quality of a phoenix that Harry shows his most obvious and most interesting phoenix-like characteristics. Harry's survival on the fateful Halloween night at Godric's Hollow is an almost literal embodiment of the phoenix rebirth. Voldemort attacked Harry with the fatal Killing Curse (*"Avada Kedavra!"*) – but, while Voldemort was nearly destroyed and the house blown to pieces, Harry is "The Boy who Lived".[1] Hagrid removed Harry from the ruins, and while no one knows yet what happened between that night and the next (when Dumbledore deposited the infant on the Dursley's doorstep), Harry survived to promise the Dursleys in Book 1 that he wouldn't "blow up the house." Interesting promise, Harry.

Harry has cheated death on other occasions, too. In recovering from the Basilisk poison in Book 2, Harry also cheated death. Voldemort, in the form of his youthful Tom Riddle-self, tells Harry that the Basilisk poison is invariably fatal, and stands back to watch Harry die. Yet by the healing powers of Fawkes' tears, Harry lives, and turns the same poison back on Riddle when he stabs the diary. In Book 3, Harry saves himself and Sirius from the Dementors—the only creatures he's come across so far, to which he's vulnerable. Of course, Dementors don't just kill. They steal the soul completely, suggesting that they may be the only creatures that can destroy an immortal. No wonder Voldemort wants them on his side.

In his other conflicts with Voldemort, too, Harry turns Voldemort's own weapons against him. In the graveyard battle in Book 4, the wands join when Harry and Voldemort attempt to duel, and Harry forces Voldemort's Killing Curse back into its originating wand—to the tune of a phoenix song, interestingly enough. Again, themes of time and death come into play in the Department of Mysteries. Later, in the Ministry of Magic in Book 5, Harry battles Voldemort, and endures a psychic attack when Voldemort possesses him and tries to force Dumbledore to kill him. Harry escapes death by embracing it, hoping that Dumbledore will kill him—releasing him from his pain and allowing him to see Sirius once more. His great love for Sirius (and acceptance of death), forced Voldemort to flee—after all, "*vol de mort*" means "fly from death."

Even more interesting and subtle than Harry's dramatic, death-defying encounters are his *symbolic* interactions with death. For example, in Book 1, Harry and his friends had to get past Fluffy, the three-headed dog in order to get down the trap door to rescue the Philosopher's (Sorcerer's) Stone. Exciting enough by itself, but it is even more interesting when one considers who Fluffy is. Recall that Hagrid bought him, significantly, from "a Greek chappie" Fluffy would seem to be of the same lineage as Cerberus, the three-headed dog who, in Greek mythology, guarded the gates of Hades. By getting past Fluffy and down the trap door, Harry symbolically had entered the underworld.

Another symbolic passage into death—this time literally "beyond the veil"—occurred in Book 2. Harry and his friends were invited to Nearly Headless Nick's Deathday Party. To reach the chamber where the party was held, Harry, Ron, and Hermione had to journey down a long passageway lit by black candles that burned with blue flames. Nick was there to greet them, and held aside a thick black curtain, through which they passed to reach the strange party – literally a land of the dead.

The graveyard duel in Book 4 can also be seen as a symbolic descent into death. Harry maneuvered his way through the maze, battled dangerous monsters, and was magically transported to a terrifying underworld of Death Eaters among graves, where an almost dead man was resurrected using Harry's life blood. Harry returned after a hard battle, bearing the dead body of his companion, Cedric Diggory.

An echoing passage into a world of death, rebirth, and twisted time occurs in Book 5. When Harry and his friends were in the Department of Mysteries, they again faced the mysterious black candles burning with the blue flames. Again, they encountered a black drapery in the form of the strange veil with mysterious whispers behind it, but this time there was no friendly ghost to bow them through. Only Sirius passed through, and he did not return.

Finally, in a metaphorical sense, Death *is* Harry's guardian. Sirius takes the form of a giant black dog, which Professor Trelawney identifies as a Grim, a herald of death. Furthermore, the rising of Sirius, the Dog Star, is tied to mythic accounts of disease, death, and the cycles of life.[2] Sirius is also Harry's godfather. Although he has so little time with Harry and so few opportunities to truly help him, Sirius – a character associated in multiple ways with death – is Harry's legal guardian.

Why we should care…

By Book 5, the signs are growing stronger. Clues about death, rebirth, time, and resurrection abound. According to the Prophecy, Harry has been marked by Voldemort as an equal, and is the only person who has the means to vanquish the Dark Lord. How he will do that, no one can know until the final book is in our hands. But the clues pointing in the direction of another descent into death are strong. Some HP Sleuths speculate that Harry will have to die in order to vanquish Voldemort. Others believe he will have to follow Sirius beyond the veil, possibly emerging elsewhere (or even else *when)*. The outcome, it seems clear, won't be as simple as a wand-slinging, Western movie type of shoot-out between Harry and Voldemort, with Harry then riding his broom victoriously off into the sunset. Death, birth, and time are complex forces, and it appears that Harry will have to tangle with them all before this adventure is ended…until he rises like a phoenix, from the ashes, to victory.

——————————— ADDITIONAL SLEUTHING NOTES ———————————

✴ In *Fantastic Beasts and Where to Find Them,* Newt Scamander notes that few wizards have ever been successful in domesticating a phoenix – should that attribute be applied to Harry as well?

✴ In Book 5, phoenix "loyalty" even extended to self-sacrifice when Fawkes took the hit for Dumbledore – is that parallel a possibility too?

✴ Does this point to Harry needing to take on part or all of Dumbledore's role?

---

[1] *"The killing curse rebounded, so he should have died. Why didn't he?"*, JK Rowling appearance, the Edinburgh Book Festival, August, 2004.

[2] Allen, Richard Hinckley, Star Names: Their Lore and Meaning, Dover Publications, Inc., New York, 1963, p 126.

HARRY POTTER AND ALBUS DUMBLEDORE:
AN INTERPERSONAL CHEMISTRY

SARAH DEBORAH WARD ✳ NC, "ANGELWINGS"
AUSTRALIA (*UK Edition*), AGE 17

Inspiration for this Discussion

I have always been interested in the character of Dumbledore and his relationship with Harry. Dumbledore is always the voice of reason, and the color of his eyes always has a calming affect that helps bring into focus issues of communication and self-expression, both in what we say and how we present ourselves to the world. I was especially intrigued how Dumbledore may have influenced Harry so that he has stayed rather normal with good morals.

 HANDFUL

"What did I care if numbers of nameless and faceless people and creatures were slaughtered in the vague future, if in the here and now you were alive, and well, and happy? I never dreamed that I would have such a person on my hands." (Albus Dumbledore, talking to Harry in Chapter 37 of *Harry Potter and the Order of the Phoenix* {p739 UK})

So what's so special about this friendship? Normally, for teenagers, the company of an 'older person' would certainly be considered boring. But to Harry, the bond he holds with the 150-year-old-Headmaster is a source of strength and admiration. In fact, if it weren't for Dumbledore, Harry may very well be considered dead today.

At the start of the series, Harry had never met the person who left him at the Dursleys' front door step that night eleven years ago. That notwithstanding, before Harry had even spoken to Dumbledore for the first time, some sort of invisible friendship was already taking place. Having grown up with his horrible relatives, the Dursleys, Harry never once felt remotely related to them. Conversely, he'd barely met Dumbledore three times through the whole first book, yet already Harry had created a much closer bond with Dumbledore than all three Dursleys combined.

Harry's first impressions of Dumbledore began in Book 1 on that fateful night at the island shack where the Dursleys had retreated to avoid receiving any more letters. {Ch 4} Hagrid was telling Harry about his past. When the conversation moved onto whether Harry should go to Hogwarts or not, he quickly learnt his aunt and uncle weren't particularly fond of Albus Dumbledore, especially when Uncle Vernon called him a 'crackpot old fool'. Since they are both greatly hated by the Dursleys, Harry was able to immediately relate to this 'crackpot.' As Hagrid revealed more, Dumbledore became an intriguingly mysterious character and Harry wanted to know all about him.

The number of things Harry and Dumbledore have in common is almost scary. Both these brave Gryffindors own pet birds, have glasses, and rather unusual scars (Harry with his famous lightning bolt slash and Dumbledore with the '*perfect map of the London underground*' above his left knee.{Ch 1}) They've both survived Voldemort's attacks and protected people more than once in their lives. They're both particularly famous in the wizarding world for defeating Dark Wizards, both were falsely accused by the *Daily Prophet,* and both deemed crazy by the rest of the wizarding community throughout Book 5. All these things, and possibly each character's past, are adding to why Harry and Dumbledore understand each other so well.

Rowling is very crafty with the way she presents this professor-pupil friendship. She uses many colorful adjectives to describe what Harry perceives Dumbledore could be thinking. She specifically exaggerates the twinkle in Dumbledore's blue eyes. This wonderful technique sets the mood for us readers. If we see a twinkle, we know Dumbledore may be amused, happy, or even proud. If the elusive twinkle is gone, his mood is often tired, wary, and almost negative.

We are also rewarded at the end of every book when Rowling presents a deep conversation between the two characters, during which Dumbledore is always giving counsel to Harry. It's as if JK Rowling turns Dumbledore into an outside narrator who can explain and summarize the whole novel for us. I especially love (as I'm sure everyone else does) these parts of the book, as we finally get some well-needed answers!

As the series progresses, Harry's illusion that Dumbledore can solve anything slowly begins to fade. *'He had grown used to the idea that Dumbledore can solve anything. He had expected Dumbledore to pull some amazing solution out of the air. But no…their last hope was gone.'* {B3, Ch2, p288} Deep down, it seems Harry has been looking for guidance that few people can give him.

Through all his years at Hogwarts, Harry has shown nothing but respect for Dumbledore, and looked to him for guidance and answers. It has only been in his fifth year that we begin to see all that change. Harry is going through his teen years and learning more about himself. Dumbledore must've watched Harry very closely as he was growing up, and is probably seeing part of himself inside the boy. Unfortunately, for his own good, Harry was ignored by the headmaster for the whole Book 5 school year. All the anger this caused in Harry towards Dumbledore, along with all the other frustrations that had happened during the year, created a very exciting event in Harry Potter history. We have never seen someone get that emotional with Dumbledore nor have we ever seen Dumbledore, himself, cry (although, he did sniff once in Book 1{Ch 1}).

Unfortunately, we don't get to see that rift completely resolved. Sure, we find out what information Dumbledore was hiding from Harry for fifteen years, but what will Harry's feelings towards him be like in Book 6? We were not told enough to know for sure. Will Harry still look to Dumbledore for guidance, or tell him to stop interfering with his life? Harry is aware from past experience that although Dumbledore can't solve everything, he often takes the right course of action in a situation (even if it means something like sending Harry back in time to save his own life!). {B3, Ch21}

After a whole year of making Harry's load a little heavier, Dumbledore surely needs to make up for it in the next book. JK Rowling said in her website (www.jkrowling.co.uk) that Harry has his shortest stay at the Dursley's ever for the coming summer holidays. Maybe this means Dumbledore could take Harry away from his relations' care early so he can teach Harry Occlumency or just get him away from people who pretend he doesn't exist. After all, Dumbledore did say, *'You need return there only once a year…'*{B5 p737}, when he referred to Harry's imprisonment with the Dursleys.

Ever wonder what Dumbledore may have seen in the mirror of Erised? He told Harry that he saw himself holding a pair of socks, but Harry didn't think this statement was truthful. We now know there was one humongous thing Dumbledore wanted to keep hidden from Harry, and that was *the Prophecy.* So, is what he sees in the mirror a happy Harry with his family in a Voldemort-free world? That could be possible – it would explain why he fibbed to Harry about it (as we don't think he was hiding an evil desire to take over the world!).

Whatever significance this friendship holds, wherever it could lead, we can be sure that it will only become more and more important. The creativity that JK Rowling has used to demonstrate this bond between two people with such a wide age difference can teach many things. In a way, this friendship may be telling us that those who care for us most will stay hidden in the shadows, always making sure we're safe – and that seeing someone else happy can be the greatest gift you can receive.

────────────── ADDITIONAL SLEUTHING NOTES ──────────────

* Will Harry's shortest stay at the Dursleys be a result of trouble, or of Dumbledore personally teaching Harry Occlumancy? Could Harry become a true apprentice of Dumbledore's?

* Is there any chance there is a link between Dumbledore's and Harry's scars? What role will Dumbledore's scar play?

* Isn't it interesting how JK Rowling's Harry Potter series creates the same interpersonal chemistry between young and old readers that exists between Harry and Dumbledore?

Fowl Play with Owl Post

"Hedwig at Heart" * New Clues Forum
USA (*US Edition*), Age Adult

Inspiration for this Discussion

Ever since Hagrid bought the beautiful owl, Hedwig, for Harry in Book 1, I have been fascinated with these amber-eyed creatures and the messages they carry. An ordinary day becomes extraordinary when using one of the most magical and mysterious forms of wizard communication. I began to look for techniques that unsavory wizards might use to take advantage of Harry's desire to keep in contact with his companions.

 12

Remember how upset Harry was in the beginning of Book 2 when Dobby the house-elf prevented him from receiving his letters? It's most likely the same way we feel when our e-mail goes down. Wizards probably regard owls and Owl Post with the same nonchalance we often reserve for Muggle post. Harry relies on Owl Post for important everyday services such as letters, news and message deliveries to his friends. When Harry's mail was intercepted by Dobby as blackmail to keep him from Hogwarts, and again when Hedwig was injured in Book 5, the risks associated with using owls became clear. Have you ever considered how Lord Voldemort and his followers might exploit owls and owl communication to further their plans? Although Dobby obtained letters sent to Harry by Hermione, Ron and Hagrid, we are not told how the powerful house-elf was able to accomplish this. However, in both Book 4 and Book 5, JK Rowling gave us a few pointers to the ways in which an enemy might use owls.

Lord Voldemort's covert operations at the beginning of Book 4 clued us in that the level of intrigue was growing. Voldemort had made a plan that included murder and he had someone willing to execute it. Harry, a witness to this plan via a dream, awakened with scar pain, and fearful, sent Hedwig with a message to his godfather, Sirius Black. This opening chapter not only set the stage for Voldemort's eventual rebirth, but also the undercurrent of espionage. When Harry and Sirius corresponded throughout Book 4, we observed how spies might use owls and Owl Post to their advantage.

Because of the necessity for Sirius to stay undercover when hiding out in Book 4, and especially upon returning to the Hogwarts area, he wrote that Harry should "*keep changing owls.*" {Ch15, p240} As Hermione reminded Harry, owls outside the range of their usual habitat, such as snowy owls like Hedwig, can "*attract too much attention.*" {p240} We already know that there are many types of owls available for use. In Book 3, we learned all about them when Hermione and Ron described the Hogsmeade Post Office: "*...two hundred owls...color-coded depending on how fast you want your letter to get there!*" Harry saw them for himself when he went to Hogsmeade: "*From Great Grays...to...little Scops owls (Local Deliveries Only).*" {B3, Ch14, p278} Draco Malfoy received his packages from home via an eagle owl. {B1, Ch9, p144}

In Book 4, while following Sirius' advice, Harry also used Ron Weasley's owl, Pigwidgeon. Tiny "Pig" could barely manage one of Harry's more lengthy letters to Sirius. {Ch21, p364} In the case of Pig, excitable owls may be a bit too noticeable, due to the twittering distraction they make. Ron reinforced this when Pig delivered a message and garnered the attention of nearby students. Ron scolded Pig: "*You don't hang around showing off!*" {Ch23, p405} Pig is small, and yet quite noticeable. Pig seems likable enough, but was he described in this way to remind us that flamboyancy in a delivery owl can be dangerous? If the Hogsmeade Post office uses the small owls for shorter deliveries, how was Pig able to fly so far? Is he, as GW dubbed him, "the little owl that could"?

Sometimes the number of owls or their behavior can be conspicuous too. Many owls flying around a particular area may tip off alert observers that wizards are nearby. Professor Dumbledore warned of the dangers of letting the owls pursue their nighttime hunting around the square at number twelve Grimmauld Place in Book 5. {Ch6, p99} In Book 1, even Muggles stood "open-mouthed" at the number of owls flying around at odd hours of the day after Lord Voldemort was temporarily vanquished by baby Harry. {Ch1, p6}

Sirius first alerted Harry in Book 4 that owls can be "intercepted". {Ch18, p312} After the Second Task of the Triwizard Tournament, the March weather became cold and windy, and the mail was late "*because the owls kept getting blown off course.*" Harry had sent an owl in reply to Sirius and it "*turned up...with half its feathers sticking up the wrong way...it took flight...afraid it was going to be sent outside again.*" {Ch27, p510} Harry was desperate to talk to Sirius, and these events foreshadowed similar circumstances that occurred later in Book 5. Harry was sitting in Professor Binn's History of Magic class when Hermione called his attention to Hedwig sitting on the windowsill outside. Questioning why Hedwig would be arriving at an odd time and place, Harry surreptitiously grabbed Hedwig. He then noticed her injury. Hedwig's "*feathers were oddly ruffled...bent the wrong way, and she was holding one of her wings at an odd angle.*" {B5, Ch17, p356-361}

Notice how JK Rowling used similar language when describing both the injured Hedwig in Book 5 and the ruffled feathers of the barn owl from Sirius in Book 4. Harry assumed the barn owl was afraid because the weather was so windy, but was it possible that owl was intercepted in a similar way to Hedwig? The barn owl was delivering a message telling Harry to meet Sirius outside Hogsmeade, while Hedwig's note was letting Harry know when Sirius would be appearing in the fire. Both times, Harry was concerned that Sirius was exposing himself to danger – could his fears have been real?

With the appointment of Dolores Umbridge as Defense Against the Dark Arts Professor, we discovered the Ministry of Magic was keeping tabs on the professors, students, staff, and curriculum at Hogwarts. Professor Umbridge used her powerful Ministry connections with the Minister of Magic, Cornelius Fudge, to allow Argus Filch, the caretaker, to inspect Harry's Owl Post. Remember Hermione's and Harry's conversation after Hedwig was injured in Book 5? Harry questioned Hermione about how secure a sealed letter could be. Hermione responded: "*I don't know...it wouldn't be...difficult to re-seal the scroll by magic...*"{Ch17, p360} Would they? Could they?

When Harry took the wounded Hedwig for treatment, Professor McGonagall cautioned him that the "*channels of communication... may be being watched.*" Afterwards, as Harry, Ron and Hermione discussed Hedwig's injury, Hermione was not surprised, and asked the question we all wished to know: "*she's never been hurt on a flight before, has she?*" But Ron interrupted. {p359, 360} (Grrr.)

The circumstances concerning Hedwig's injured wing raised more questions than just Hermione's. If it was Filch that intercepted Hedwig, what does it say about his character that he was willing to inflict such an injury on an animal? Considering how upset Filch was when Mrs. Norris, his cat, was "petrified" by the Basilisk in Book 2, should we be concerned that Umbridge perhaps was able to persuade him to do so?

When and where could Filch have injured Hedwig?

Hermione later remarks that Umbridge is "*frisking all the owls.*" We know she was monitoring Harry closely, so was there any way she could have had his owls followed? {Ch29, p657} In Book 5, we became aware not only of ways in which the political climate can influence communication, but also of the vulnerability of even Hedwig, herself. Odd, isn't it, that we've never seen a human able to intercept owls …are we sure we saw one this time?

If owls can be intercepted, can the knowledge they possess about their delivery be intercepted as well? Is JK Rowling illustrating both a weakness in the communication link and secrecy charms? Should we be wary of all wizarding communication devices?

We now know owls can locate persons who are residing in locations that are "Unplottable" and/or under the Fidelius Charm – even before the sender of the owl has been told the secret by the Secret-Keeper. In Book 5, Harry sent three letters with Hedwig to Sirius, Ron and Hermione, without knowing where they were, after he and Dudley were attacked by the Dementors in Little Whinging. {Ch3, p42} Hedwig was able to deliver them at number twelve Grimmauld Place. {Ch4, p63} When Harry finally arrived at number twelve Grimmauld Place, *then* we learned that Secret-Keeper Dumbledore has placed the house under the Fidelius Charm and that Sirius Black's father made the house Unplottable. {Ch6, p115} Just as Sirius said, owls can obviously find even the most well-hidden people. {B4, Ch22, p433}

If Hedwig can deliver to number twelve, what does this mean in reference to the charms and restrictions on Grimmauld Place? How would this kind of magic work? What about owls that deliver newspapers such as the *Daily Prophet* or the *Quibbler?* Would it apply to Transfigured objects as well?

By hampering and harassing the information network at Hogwarts, Dolores Umbridge demonstrated some of the weaknesses of Owl Post. Sirius Black had warned Harry to heed his advice (even though Sirius, himself, ignored his own words at his own peril).

Book 5 concluded with the beginning of the Second War. What role will owls play in this battle? Now that we are aware of the risks involved in using owls and Owl Post, shouldn't we be wary of other ways in which Voldemort might use them to further his objectives? Owls have an understated yet vital role in the wizarding world, and seem to hold as many secrets as they reveal. What will JK Rowling tell us about them next? I can't wait to learn more!

ADDITIONAL SLEUTHING NOTES

* How are owls able to interact with humans? How does Hedwig understand Harry when he talks to her? Will Pig's enthusiasm get him into trouble?

* What exactly is the magic behind owl deliveries? How can you send a letter that is addressed to a pseudonym [Snuffles] and why did Harry think he had to "whisper" to Hedwig in the Owlery? {B5, Ch14, p279 *US*}

* How does anyone intercept an owl? If they do it themselves, do they use magic or another owl? How can Dobby intercept Harry's mail – do house-elves have special powers/skills to communicate with owls?

* Is tampering with a delivery owls the same as "tampering with the U.S. Mail (a federal law) and protected by wizard law?

The Prophecy
and the Legend
of Godric's Hollow

HARRY'S SCAR

Lily Goldman ✳ NC, "Lily G"
USA (*US Edition*), Age 23

Inspiration for this Discussion

My inspiration for this essay has two parts. First, is my obsession with all things Harry Potter. I think it must have something to do with bunking for a year with my roommate's Harry Potter quilt. Second, the reason I chose to write about Harry's scar is simple—I see it as central to the story that I love to dissect. The inspiration for the words and ideas in my analysis come from JKR's incredible works, plus hours of discussion with my family, patient friends, and obliging fellow booksellers at work.

🦉 12

Without the jagged scar on his forehead, Harry Potter just would not be...well...Harry. Not only is it crucial to Harry's own identity, but that lightning bolt mark may be a link to what is perhaps the crucial septology question: what is the significance of Harry's scar, and how will it factor into his struggle against Voldemort? At the end of the fifth book, Harry learns a lot about his infamous scar. He knows something of how and why he got it, the reasons it sometimes hurts, and how to utilize the knowledge the pain gives him. Yet, even as of Book 5, Harry's most identifying feature has only *some* of its mystery explained.

SEPTOLOGY SCARS (WHY HARRY'S SCAR STANDS OUT)

In Rowling's wizard world, Harry Potter is not the only character with a telling mark. Most "scars" in her invented universe are signs of a connection to Dark Wizards. The Death Eaters have a snake tongue or "snake-swallowing" skull on their forearms, called the "Dark Mark", which serves as a summons to Voldemort, and Mad-Eye Moody's pockmarked face is a reminder of his career as an Auror. We can only imagine what events could have put a scar the shape of the London Underground on Dumbledore's knee. While physical characteristics are typically little more than signs of a past adventure, Harry Potter's scar is central to his development and the story's plot. Plus, it continues to link him to one of the most evil wizards, Voldemort. Most wizards find the scar fascinating, since it is the relic of Voldemort's downfall caused by little baby Harry. In the magical universe, Harry's name is famous because he has that scar.

NOT AN ORDINARY CUT (HOW HARRY GOT THE SCAR)

One of the first things we learn about Harry, before he ever meets the Dursleys, is that he has "*a curiously shaped cut, like a bolt of lightning*" on his forehead. {B1, Ch1 p15 US} This bit of information is frequently repeated. Even the title of the second chapter of Book 4—the book in which Voldemort returns to power—is "The Scar". The Dursleys pretend it is a reminder of the car crash in which Harry's parents supposedly died – until Hagrid shows up and forces them to acknowledge the truth. Hagrid informs Harry, the scar is not "ordinary"; it is the sign of an encounter with "*a powerful, evil curse,*" one that killed his parents and destroyed his house. {Ch4, p55, 56} But, even by the time he is almost sixteen, Harry still doesn't know a whole lot about how he got his famous scar.

Harry remembers very little about the attack and only recalls a "blinding flash of green light". {Ch2, p29} He can't connect that green light with the Unforgivable Killing Curse—"*Avada Kedavra!*"—until Mad-Eye Moody's class during his fourth year. Imposter Moody claims that is the spell that hit him and Harry is the only known survivor of it. Yet, the deadly curse does not normally leave a mark on its victims. When Wormtail kills Cedric with the curse in the graveyard, Harry sees the same flash of light; however, we do not yet know the color of many curses or spells. Since Harry does not have a clear memory of the attack when he was a baby, we don't know exactly what happened. During her appearance at the Edinburgh Book Festival in August of 2004, JKR confirmed that it was, indeed, a Killing Curse that rebounded on Voldemort, "*The killing curse rebounded, so he should have died,*" but we still don't know what protected Voldemort or what the process was that gave Harry this strange scar.

MARKED AS EQUAL (WHY HARRY GOT THE SCAR)

Harry does know a great deal about *why* he has been marked. Harry matures from his scar being his favorite feature in the first book to resenting it, at the end of the fifth book, as the symbol of his misery and destiny. After Harry successfully battles with Lord Voldemort four times Dumbledore finally reveals to him the reason why he carries the lightning bolt scar. As Rowling explained to the *Houston Chronicle* (March 20, 2001), Harry is "*physically marked by what he has been through.*" More than that, the scar is, Dumbledore finally admits, "*a sign of a connection between [Harry] and Voldemort,*" {Book 5, Ch 37 p827}. Of course, Voldemort is not aware that he would only be able to "mark" Harry as an infant; Voldemort, not aware of the full account of the prophecy, thinks he can just murder Harry. Voldemort thought Harry is the one to whom the prophecy was referring because of his own similarity to Harry, but we don't know if he had any reasons to specifically reject Neville Longbottom. Yet, as Dumbledore reminds Harry, Voldemort *did* mark him, and Harry *has* proven himself (even as a child) a match for Voldemort.

ACTING LIKE AN AERIAL (PAIN IN HARRY'S SCAR)

The paralyzing pain Harry still experiences in his scar gives him warnings about Voldemort's intentions and Harry has learned to utilize this information. The intensity of his pain allows Harry to determine the evilness of Voldemort's activity at the time, but it is not until Book 5 that Harry understands this connection. Prior to Voldemort using Harry's blood to regenerate his body, Harry's scar only pangs occasionally, which results in Harry's understanding of his scar's usefulness to develop slowly.

Before rejoining the wizarding world, the only "pain" Harry had experienced was a triggered memory associated with his parents' "car crash."{B1, Ch2, p29} Even after meeting Voldemort in the Forbidden Forest during his first year and collapsing to his knees from the ache in his scar, Harry is confused as to what caused his pain. After that incident, he comes to recognize pain in his forehead as "a warning" and a sign that "danger's coming," {B1, Ch16, p264} but it is not until he faces Voldemort/Quirrell the first time that he associates the threat directly with Voldemort.

Surely, it is Voldemort, alone, who makes Harry's scar hurt. Coming in contact with Death Eaters, and even those who wish to kill him, does not affect Harry's health. Harry's forehead is fine after meeting Lucius Malfoy in Flourish & Blotts in Book 2, encountering Peter Pettigrew in the Shrieking Shack in Book 3, and spending a year with Barty Crouch Jr. masquerading as Mad-Eye Moody in Book 4. The Death Eaters' parade at the World Quidditch match in Book 4 does not hurt Harry's head, nor does the uttering of the spell casting the Dark Mark in the sky. His scar does not even hurt when he battles the diary-preserved version of Voldemort, personified in Tom Riddle.

Only the post-attack, adult Voldemort can hurt Harry, and that hurt is only severe when Voldemort uses an Unforgivable Curse on another wizard. *"Agony such as he had never felt in his life,"* {Book 4, Ch 32, p637} occurs after Harry's vision of Voldemort and Wormtail at the Riddle House in Book 4. {Ch 2, p16} Harry does not remember the Muggle dying, but he does remember the plotting of his own death. Harry is able to calm himself by rubbing a finger over his forehead, so it is real, physical pain. By the end of year four, though, Harry clutches his scar, his eyes water from the pain and he becomes alarmed enough to alert Dumbledore when Voldemort uses the Cruciatus Curse on Wormtail. When Voldemort orders Cedric killed, Harry collapses, feels as though his head is "about to split open," {Book 4, Ch 32 p637}, and retches.

After Voldemort regains his own body, Harry's scar often prickles uncomfortably and he increasingly experiences more violent scar attacks. I believe this may be happening for either of two (yet unclear) reasons: (a) it could be hurting more because Voldemort forged a further connection by using Harry's blood in his regeneration, or (b) the scar hurts simply because Voldemort has returned to his full power.

There are different levels of pain in Harry's scar. His scar sears or burns when Voldemort feels a strong emotion; such as the great joy Voldemort's feels when Harry's scar hurts (for example, during Harry's detention with Umbridge), or when Harry experiences Voldemort's fury (such as, when he was in the lockers with Ron in Chapter 18 of Book 5 {p380}). Harry's scar also hurts and makes him violently sick when Voldemort intends to injure or kill a wizard, as shown during the snake attack on Mr. Weasley or the Death Eater's punishment. Harry wishes for it all to end when his scar explodes as Voldemort uses an Unforgivable Curse on him—which is similar to when Voldemort uses the Cruciatus Curse in the graveyard, or possesses Harry in the Ministry of Magic.

The pain does have its benefits. Harry begins to realize that he can understand Voldemort's emotions. Apparently, he unsettles Bellatrix in the Ministry when his scar sears, by letting her know that Voldemort is aware the prophecy is smashed and that he is furious. Just as significantly, Harry becomes conscious that his scar pain is a sign of Voldemort invading his mind.

THE FOGGY FUTURE (WHAT WILL HAPPEN TO HARRY AND HIS SCAR)

Will Harry's scar aid him in finally defeating Voldemort? How exactly did Harry get his scar? Mythology may lend some clues to these questions, but any answers at this point are still speculation. Intriguing evidence backs two particular theories. One is that Harry's scar is actually a Norse eihwaz rune, and another is that it is his literal Hindu "third eye." Hermione mentions the eihwaz when discussing their O.W.L.s in Book 5; perhaps Rowling is clueing readers into its importance. If it does represent the thirteenth rune (eihwaz) it could be relating to the combination of Voldemort's evil curse and Lily's protection—as the rune symbolizes the deadly yew tree (the wood of Voldemort's wand) and has the divinatory meanings of psychic protection and endurance[1]. Maybe Harry's scar is, literally, a symbol of his being the embodiment of good versus evil.

Alternatively, perhaps Harry has a visible third eye in the form of his lightning bolt. In Hindu mythology, third eyes may burn white-hot, to the point of gods using their fire in battle. By often juxtaposing Harry's scar with his eyes in her writing, Rowling may be hinting at this possibility. When Harry's scar hurts, it often does so by "burning," "searing," or feeling as though he has a "white-hot poker" applied to his forehead and such pain temporarily blinds him. As his eyesight fades with the onset of pain, he is forced to look inward where he should discover Voldemort's presence in his mind.

The legend of the development of the third eye also has correlations with Harry's story. Shiva, one of the great Hindu gods, was the first to attain an inner eye, when his wife Parvati (the name of a Gryffindor in Rowling's world and Harry's Yule Ball date) temporarily covered his eyes. If Rowling plans to incorporate this myth into her books, Voldemort would most resemble Shiva, who was the god of destruction, but also of regeneration. Shiva, pale white, is associated with serpents and demons wearing skull necklaces. Harry often sees Voldemort's red eyes gleaming out of his chillingly white skull-like head. And of course, Voldemort's serpent, Nagini, and his demon-like Death-Eaters, who bear snake-"eating" skulls on their arms, accompany him.

If Voldemort is to parallel Shiva, then Harry would likely fulfill the role of Jalamdhara, a creature created out of Shiva's anger.[2] Jalamdhara was created in Shiva's image, an attribute reminiscent of how closely Harry resembles his father. Jalamdhara was a good flier (as Harry is), and had the power to tame lions (the Gryffindor mascot). Jalamdhara had the power to raise the dead. If the Hindu myth of the third eye is to be entirely fulfilled in Rowling's world, though, Harry seems doomed to fall at Voldemort's hands, as Jalamdhara eventually does at Shiva's.

With more knowledge about his scar as an inner eye, perhaps Harry will be able to use the information to his advantage and successfully vanquish Voldemort. Whatever the case may be, Harry's scar is certainly central to the development of Rowling's remaining books. It is both key to understanding his past and "unfogging his future."

✳ Additional Sleuthing Notes ✳

✳ Why are scars so unique in the wizarding world – is it because wizards are typically healed completely (think re-growing of bones)?

✳ From what we know of Lee Jordan in Chapter 25 of Book 5 {p551}, Umbridge's quill probably left scars on more students than just Harry.

✳ What is the mechanism of Harry's scar functioning as an "aerial"?

✳ Is Dumbledore's scar a map of the Tube or of other Underground landmarks (such as the concept of an underground community similar to the TV series *Beauty and the Beast*)?

---

[1] Melville, Francis. The Book of Runes. Quarto Publishing plc. London: 2003
[2] Cotterell, Arthur and Rachel Storm. The Ultimate Encyclopedia of Mythology. Hermes House. London: 2004.

The Charming Lily Evans Potter

"SASKIA" ✳ NEW CLUES FORUM
THE NETHERLANDS (*UK Edition*), AGE 24

Inspiration for this Discussion

*My interest in this particular 'subject' has become greatly augmented after reading Book 5. The Department of Mysteries has an alluring name to start off with. The key to the story is, at the very least, **investigated** in one of these rooms. The first thought that came into my head after reading the chapter "The Lost Prophecy" is that Lily is my favorite character above all others because she is so mysterious. Even though she was murdered so many years ago, she is one of the most important characters in the book. And yet, she is also one of the people we know the least. Since I am drawn to a good mystery (as Doxies are to a good curtain), I can't help but be intrigued by Lily. Still, from the little we do know about her, she seemed to be not only a very fair character, but quite powerful as well. I am sure we will see more of her in the last two books.*

So, take a seat, fetch a drink, grab your Sleuthoscope and let me share my thoughts (and at times ramblings, tee-hee) with you. Our "subject": Lily Evans Potter. I have but one request for you: keep an open mind. At the end, you can decide if you agree with me—or if you think that a good course of Shock Spells at St Mungo's would be the best treatment for yours truly. J

Everybody ready? Let's go!

 HANDFUL

We'll recap what we have on Lily Evans:

- ✳ Muggle-born witch
- ✳ Wife to James/mother to Harry/sister to Petunia
- ✳ Placed in the house of Gryffindor at Hogwarts
- ✳ Head Girl
- ✳ Green eyes (same as Harry's in case you haven't heard yet) and dark red hair
- ✳ Excellent at Charms, most likely augmented by her 10¼ -inch-long swishy wand, which was made of Willow (core of the wand remains unknown)
- ✳ Died trying to protect her son on October 31, (Halloween) by the wand of Lord Voldemort
- ✳ While in school, she stood up for Snape (sorta)
- ✳ While in school, she verbally sparred with James
- ✳ Was doing some kind of work that is so revealing JK won't tell us about it

Unfortunately, the list of what we *don't* know is much longer than what we do know. However, I'll try to show you what job Lily could possibly have had. (Yes, I am quite aware that JK said on several occasions that Harry's parents had inherited a lot of money and they didn't *need* a job.)

Q: *What did James and Lily Potter do when they were alive?*
JK: *"James inherited plenty of money, so he didn't need a well-paid profession..."*
{AOL Online Chat, October, 2000}

(We all know that when JK neither answers, nor refutes a question, this means that we have some red herring on the menu.)

Q: *What did the Potter parents do for a living before Voldemort killed them?*
JK: *"I'm sorry to keep saying this, but I can't tell you because it's important to a later plot..."*
{Scholastic Online Chat, February, 2000}

(Anyone up for another portion of red herring?)

Can you imagine the Potters as a stay-at-home, do nothing couple? I cannot. For some reason, I can't think of these vivid people without a job. So what would an intelligent woman who excels in Charms do for a living?

Based on the scraps of evidence we have from JK, this is what I believe Lily did for a living.

In Chapter 37 of Book 5, Dumbledore described an always-locked room in the Department of Mysteries in which "the most mysterious" of all the department's subjects is studied. He said that room holds "*a force that is at once more wonderful and terrible than death, than human intelligence, than the forces of nature.*" {p743 *UK*} This is a description of what the "Locked Room" in the Department of Mysteries is all about. A Logical conclusion suggests that "Love" is the subject of study.

Love also happens to be the force that saves Harry at the end of Book 5—because it flows through his body, and Voldemort can't stand it. *Love* was what Lily spilled for Harry when she died to protect him. {B1, p216} But Voldemort even told us that Lily didn't have to die—he gave Lily the chance to save herself. {p213}

Lily sacrificed her young life to protect her baby son, and in doing so, cast a charm to protect him. We have word from Dumbledore (who, according to JK Rowling, is the only one whom we can always trust), {p216} as well as Riddle, that the spell Lily cast was a powerful charm. {B2, Ch17, p233}

So how does one learn these charms? Surely it was not at Hogwarts because it's probably too old. Haven't we been told that this ancient magic which protects Harry is a magic which Voldemort neglects? *"...an ancient magic of which he knows, which he despises, and which he has always therefore, underestimated."* {B5, p736} I have a theory. Remember the room, where the force contained is both wonderful and terrible? The most mysterious of all studies in the Department of Mysteries? What if Lily Potter worked in there? Could she have been seeking the mysteries of Love, and, perhaps, developing charms, which involve all forms of Love?

Ponder the Dark Lord Voldemort again. He is assumed to be the most powerful wizard alive (except perhaps Albus Dumbledore) and still he underestimates the ancient magic that protects Harry. Not only is he very powerful, but he also has spies everywhere in the Ministry of Magic. Therefore, he may not have thought he needed a spy guarding the "Locked Room". Without a spy, Voldemort would have very little detail of the goings on in the room or about those who worked there. People working at the Department of Mysteries are called "Unspeakables" because of the fact that no one (not even they) can speak about what they do. So, if she worked there, Lily Potter would not even tell her husband what she keeps busy doing all day.

The murder of his parents is imprinted in Harry's memory. He relives it thanks to the presence of the Dementors in Book 3:

> *"Lily, take Harry and go! It's him! Go! Run! I'll hold him off."* {B3, Ch12, p240}

> *"Stand aside. Stand aside, girl!"* {p239}

But, as we know, Lily did not move. She stayed. She shielded her son until her very death. It is quite clear that Lily Potter knew what she was doing. She knew what the effect of her Charm would be on her son or she would never have risked leaving him alone at the mercy of the Dark Lord. Why else would she ignore what her husband had shouted at her to do...what her husband died for?

I believe the Potters went into hiding because of the prophecy made about their young son. They knew the Dark Lord would quickly figure out which boys fitted into the prophecy (the part he heard). If Lily had been told the whole prophecy, it must have been clear to Lily what she had to do. She seemed to have had options other than death—she could have Apparated to the former Headquarters of the Order of the Phoenix or to any other location where Albus Dumbledore was present—seeing as Dumbledore is the only one who the Dark Lord has always feared. Instead, *she chose to stay.*

Lily Potter was on a mission. She knew what had to be done and she did it. She made choices based on what she felt she had to do and somehow fulfilled the terms of the prophecy – with her powerful and loving legacy.

——— ADDITIONAL SLEUTHING NOTES ———

✳ When Lily said to Voldemort *"I'll do anything"* {B3, Ch12, p239}, what exactly was it that she thought Voldemort wanted her to "do"? If Lily was an Unspeakable in the Department of Mysteries, why didn't he spare her and use her to get to the prophecy?

✳ If Riddle only respects power and he complimented Lily's spell, what does that say about Lily's power? {B3, Ch17, p317}

How We Know What Happened During the Attack at Godric's Hollow and Baby Harry's Arrival at Privet Drive

NISHA E. THAMBI ✳ CHAMBER OF SECRETS
INDIA (*UK Edition*), AGE 19

Inspiration for this Discussion

There's been a whole lot of speculation about what's going to happen in Harry Potter's future. Considering that past and future are becoming very tangled in this septology, I just thought it would be helpful to try to understand certain events in the past, even though our questions about them may never be clearly answered in the books. The particular chunk of Harry's past that I chose to deal with is also the one that marks the beginning of his time as "The Boy Who Lived"; I refer, of course, to the day that elapsed between Voldemort's attack at Godric's Hollow and the time that Harry was left on the doorstep of Number 4, Privet Drive.

 12

Just to review the facts, this is the chronology of what happened that night in Godric's Hollow. Voldemort arrives at Godric's Hollow on the night of October 31. He first kills James Potter with a Killing Curse (*"Avada Kedavra!"*), then kills Lily Potter with another Killing Curse after she refuses to stand aside as he tries to kill Harry.

How do we know all of this? How do the characters know all this? In Chapter 17 of Book 1, Voldemort says to Harry, "*I killed your father first… but your mother needn't have died…she was trying to protect you…*" {p213 UK} Following that, he aims another Killing Curse at Harry – the third to hit its target that night. The curse, however, is unsuccessful – it not only fails to kill Harry, but rebounds onto its originator, Voldemort, as a result of what Lily did — sacrificing herself in place of Harry. (Note: we don't know if the protection she left Harry was the result of her death alone, as no one has said whether the "ancient magic" mentioned was done consciously or not, and whether it consisted only of Lily's death, or if other spells and charms were involved.) Whether Lily knew what would happen if she died is also debatable. {B4, Ch33, p566} Also while we know what happens to Voldemort; we just don't know why. In Book 4, he explains that he was experimenting with immortality. Voldemort says, in reference to the curse, "*And now, I was tested, and it appeared that one or more of my experiments had worked…for I had not been killed.*" {p566} What the curse did was to separate him from his powers, leaving him "*less than the meanest ghost*". {p566}

But the Killing Curse is supposed to destroy whatever it comes in contact with – if it's people, it wipes out their life force and sends their souls to a different plane, but leaves their bodies unmarked; if it's an object, it blows it up.{B5, Ch36, p717-719} So the Killing Curse most likely destroyed the Potters' house. Following the events at Godric's Hollow, Voldemort, lacking corporeality, flees, while Harry (thanks to the innate protection that all magic-capable children have against *relatively* ordinary disasters like a house falling on them), survives (as best he could with the Dursleys).

I have a theory on why the house fell after a single rebounded Killing Curse: I think it was because of the negative energy resulting from the separation of Voldemort's powers from his body – if he was one of the most evil Dark Wizards of all time, then it stands to reason that the destruction of his powers would generate a *lot* of bad energy – definitely enough to bring the house down.

Following the attack on the Potters, there are a few possibilities as to how Dumbledore was alerted to what had happened. The first is that a member of the Order of the Phoenix may have been posted at Godric's Hollow and witnessed the destruction of the house. Another theory is that Dumbledore was alerted through the "clock" that he held on Privet Drive. According to Book 1, "*the clock had twelve hands, but no numbers...it must have made sense to Dumbledore, though.*" {Ch1, p15} The clock may have been a monitoring device for the Potters and the rest of the members of the Order of the Phoenix—something similar to the Weasley family clock. It seems logical that Dumbledore would have a way to keep track of the Order's whereabouts for the very purpose of knowing when they were in danger.

When Dumbledore dispatches Hagrid to Godric's Hollow to fetch baby Harry, Hagrid does as told—he reaches Godric's Hollow and picks Harry out of the ruins of the house. Dumbledore, most likely, chose Hagrid for the job not only because he trusted him, but also probably because he is one of a few wizards who could have quickly shifted the rubble aside without using magic. Not only would this allow easy retrieval of the baby without alerting any Muggles, it would also not alert the remaining Death Eaters to Harry's survival.

Sirius, alerted to what has happened by Peter Pettigrew's disappearance, arrives at Godric's Hollow and finds Hagrid with baby Harry. In Book 3, "The Marauder's Map", Sirius says to Hagrid, "*Give Harry ter me, Hagrid. I'm his godfather; I'll look after him.*" Hagrid, recounting the story to Harry says, "*I told Black no, Dumbledore said Harry was ter go ter his aunt an' uncle's.*" Here we get one important piece of information: **Dumbledore knew where he had to send Harry almost as soon, if not as soon as, he heard of the attack.** Did Dumbledore know Harry was alive or was he sending Hagid only to check? Also, it's almost as if he knew the protection of blood would be necessary, and he had kept this in mind as a contingency plan in case Lily and James died at the hands of Voldemort.

When Dumbledore saw the scar on Harry's head, he must have realized what it meant – that Harry was the child the prophecy spoke of, and that he would be safest under the protection of blood– his mother's blood in the form of the much-reviled Aunt Petunia – till he was old enough to attend Hogwarts.

By the morning of November 1, word of Voldemort's disappearance spreads through the wizarding world. Among those who have heard of Harry's survival is Minerva McGonagall. She spends 24 hours hanging around Privet Drive in her Animagus form waiting for Harry and Dumbledore. Meanwhile, the "Boy Who Lived" spends the day in protective custody and/or in hiding—most likely with Hagrid—while Dumbledore and maybe other wizards (probably members of the Order of the Phoenix) cast protective spells and charms around Number four, Privet Drive in preparation for Harry's arrival.

Shortly after midnight, when Albus Dumbledore arrives in Privet Drive, Professor McGonagall, who has gotten wind of Dumbledore's plan, wants to verify the rumors she has heard. When Hagrid arrives, the three wizards leave Harry at the Dursleys' doorstep with Dumbledore's letter of explanation. Mrs. Dursley then finds Harry on her doorstep on the morning of November 2.

That's all we can deduce, at least for now, of the events of that day. I hope this essay helped at least a few people make sense of some of the little nagging questions they may have had about the events following the attack at Godric's Hollow.

ADDITIONAL SLEUTHING NOTES

* ✷ JKR said this is the key piece of information: Why didn't Voldemort die?
* ✷ Why was Professor McGonagall not informed directly by Dumbledore following the death of the Potters? Was she even a member of the Order last time?
* ✷ How did Dumbledore know that Harry had survived in order to send Hagrid to retrieve him?
* ✷ Was the Potters' house normally hidden from Muggles like the Black mansion, and if so, did the destruction of it cause it to become visible?

THE ATTACK ON FRANK AND ALICE LONGBOTTOM

LAUREN COFFMAN ✳ NEW CLUES FORUM
USA (*US Edition*), AGE 24

Inspiration for this Discussion

I can remember the exact moment when I fell in love with Harry Potter. Before that, I was just another skeptic of the entire series and had dismissed it as a "kiddy book" – something that wouldn't interest a college student. Sometime around Christmas Day in 2002, I picked up Book 1, on a complete whim at a local bookstore. I realized I was in trouble when I was back at the bookstore later that afternoon, quickly using my Christmas money to buy Books 2 and 3.

However, the exact moment when I knew it was love occurred during the scene in the Shrieking Shack in Book 3, when the truth was revealed about Scabbers, Sirius Black and Remus Lupin. It was the most incredible plot twist I had read. From that moment on, I was hooked...waiting in line for the release of Book 5...waiting in line for hours for the midnight showing of Harry Potter and the Prisoner of Azkaban movie.

For this essay to be here in print for you, the eager Harry Potter reader, I must thank: My parents— for continuing to buy books for me (even though they would be finished by the next day); Jason— for being his creative, wonderful self and loving Harry Potter as much as I do; Joia—for being my Harry Potter idea springboard and writing editor; World Wizarding Press—for allowing my writing to grace this book; and finally, JK Rowling—for allowing everyone to experience Harry's world (if only for seven years).

🦉 12

"The one with the power to vanquish the Dark Lord approaches... Born to those who have thrice defied him, born as the seventh month dies..." {B5, Ch 37, p841 US}

One of the many mysteries in the Harry Potter novels is the attack on Frank and Alice Longbottom and the aftereffects on their son, Neville. Throughout the unfolding tale of Harry Potter, readers have been given small, tantalizing bits and pieces of information about Neville's past. In fact, the information about Neville's past has been given in the same vague manner as it has for Harry's past and his face off with Voldemort in Godric's Hollow. Now that JK Rowling has revealed both Harry and Neville were originally considered "the prophecy child", it has become important to examine what happened to Frank and Alice Longbottom.

JUST THE FACTS, MA'AM

So, what do we know about Frank and Alice Longbottom? What do we know about the attack on them in comparison to the attack on the Potters? What has JK Rowling hinted in passing that could be very significant later? Don't worry, these questions made my head spin, too. Let's look at the facts that we have been given.

On the surface, Frank and Alice Longbottom seem to be just another set of background characters in JK Rowling's mystically complex world of Harry Potter.

...Or are they?

Frank and Alice Longbottom were both members of the Order of the Phoenix and Aurors under the Ministry of Magic. In addition, according to the Prophecy, they thrice defied Voldemort, but details about these escapes from the Dark Lord are not known. Their son, Neville, born on July 30, (according to JK Rowling's website) was thought at first to be the child of the Prophecy! Dumbledore states in Book 4 that the Longbottoms were "very popular" {Ch30, p603}, and they were clearly very important wizards at the time. Finally, we know that they reside in St Mungo's Hospital in the permanent spell damage ward after being tortured into insanity by a group of Death Eaters. Those Death Eaters were Bellatrix Lestrange, Rastaban Lestrange, Rodolphus Lestrange, along with Barty Crouch Jr.—all of whom were sent to Azkaban for this deed.

The Longbottoms also had a very important son, who may still have a link to Voldemort. Dumbledore tells Harry, *"The attacks on them came after Voldemort's fall from power, just when everyone thought they were safe."* {p603} If the Potters were attacked on October 31, the year of Harry's first birthday, and the attack on the Longbottoms occurred "sometime" after that, it is possible to discover exactly when this attack occurred and, most importantly, whether Neville was present. Voldemort had been terrorizing the wizarding world for almost ten years, so it would take some time for wizards to return to a "safe" state. Also, considering that Frank and Alice were Aurors and on their guard for over a year, it seems unlikely that they would have felt very safe immediately after Voldemort's fall. So, months pass in the wizarding world and things seem to finally settle down. The Longbottoms begin to let their guard down after having dealt with such a long period of terror and battle. It seems most logical to assume that the Longbottoms were attacked the year following the attack on the Potters and three to six months after Voldemort's fall from power.

Since the Potters chose to keep Harry close with them, we can only assume the Longbottoms did the same with their child, and that they always watched over Neville. This would indicate that Neville, like Harry, was present during the attack on his parents. However, Neville would have been anywhere from one-and-a-half years old to one-and-three-quarters years old during the attack—older than Harry's one and one quarter years. Neville's memories of the event would be even more detailed than Harry's detailed recollection of his parent's attack. Before we discuss Neville's memory, another crucial question must be asked...

WHY THE LONGBOTTOMS?

Is it possible the Longbottoms knew more than the Death Eaters suspected? Is there more to their torture than meets the eye?

Now, I was never one for logical reasoning in philosophy classes. Just think of those logical paradigm problems, they always reminded me of those ridiculously annoying "two trains that never seemed to meet" word problems. However, based on the information given by Dumbledore in Book 5, we can formulate a basic logical statement:

* We know from the various books that James and Lily Potter were extraordinary wizards, Aurors and members of the Order of the Phoenix. Their son, Harry, follows in their footsteps. James and Lily Potter defied Voldemort three times.

* We know from Dumbledore in Book 5 that Frank and Alice Longbottom were extraordinary wizards, Aurors and members of the Order of the Phoenix. Frank and Alice Longbottom also defied Voldemort three times.

* Therefore, Frank and Alice Longbottom were *equal* to James and Lily Potter in wizarding abilities.

According to Dumbledore, the Longbottoms *"...were tortured for information about Voldemort's where-abouts after he lost his powers."* {p602} Since the Potters died, the Longbottoms are now the closest thing the Death Eaters had to the parents of the real prophecy child. Obviously, Dumbledore would be the most knowledgeable; however, it's highly unlikely that Bellatrix would go stomping up the Hogwarts grand staircase in an attempt to speak to Dumbledore. So, the Death Eaters chose their next best option – the Longbottoms. Because the Longbottoms were highly respected and very popular in the wizarding community, the Death Eaters knew their attack would serve two purposes: (1) possibly find information on how Voldemort was defeated, what form he would be in, his location and most importantly, how Harry or Neville could have the power to defeat their "master" (2) deal another blow of terror to the wizarding community, which was finally starting to return to normalcy after Voldemort's fall from power.

The Death Eaters had known the Longbottoms were hiding crucial information, and in their fury, Crucio'ed them into insanity. It was assumed that Frank and Alice knew of Voldemort's whereabouts, yet was that the reason? They must have been well-versed about the prophecy because it involved their son, Neville. Could it have been that the Longbottoms were protecting prophecy secrets?

If Neville had been in another room of the Longbottom household, Frank and Alice would have fought the Death Eaters and refused to answer their questions, knowing that if they told the Death Eaters about the additional prophecy information—they would kill Neville. To complete the parallel, Frank and Alice (like James and Lily) may have sacrificed themselves for the welfare of their child.

NEVILLE—JUST FORGETFUL?

Since the beginning of the series, Neville has been displayed as a clumsy, forgetful, yet well-natured boy. Neville tells Harry, *"...my family thought I was all-Muggle for all ages."* {B1, Ch 7, p125} In fact, until the conclusion of Book 5, no one put much stock in Neville Longbottom.

Why is Neville so seemingly inept at wizardry when his parents were powerful Aurors? He obviously isn't a squib after all. Could something have happened to him during the attack on his parents or as a direct result of this attack?

I hold the widely shared belief that at sometime in his life, and maybe repeatedly, Neville has been the recipient of a Memory Charm. Throughout the Harry Potter series, his memory seems lacking—from forgetting whatever his Remembrall was supposed to help him remember to having his Hogsmeade permission slip owled directly to Professor McGonagall because she knew he'd forget to bring it. {B2, Ch8, p149} However, if that is the case, the question is: what is Neville being charmed into forgetting?

Here is a list of possible explanations, as well as my own theories, as to why and how Neville could be Memory Charmed (in the true Gryffindor spirit, I needed extra amounts of bravery to present these educated guesses about Neville's memory and possible plot twists):

A. <u>One of the Longbottoms' attackers cast a Memory Charm on Neville.</u>

> ✳ In a moment of weakness following the attacks on Frank and Alice, one of their attackers only Memory Charmed Neville instead of using the Killing Curse on him.

> ✳ Years later, during Barty Crouch Jr.'s stint as Mad-Eye Moody, he "visits" with Neville to see if he remembers anything from that night. *"Come on, Longbottom, I've got some books that might interest you."* {B4, Ch 14, p219} If Barty was present at the attack on Neville's parents (or even performed the Memory Charm himself), then what did he say or do when he was alone with Neville?

B. Neville is being Memory Charmed by Gran Longbottom

✻ *Gran Longbottom is trying to protect Neville—ensuring he is inept at wizardry, turning him into an "Anti-Harry Potter".*

⋯ ⋯hildren from evils in the world, parents have been known to do extreme ⋯⋯ ⋯ottom could be purposely Memory ⋯ediocre wizard. Gran watched her son ⋯ the Cruciatus Curse; now she wants to ⋯5, Ch 35, p794} (knowing that it will not ⋯ Charm on him, so he will not easily

⋯ !ping him forget the event and maybe some

⋯rture and Gran could be trying to protect ⋯Memory Charms Neville in order to help ⋯leville because she is hiding information ⋯lim to ask any questions about his parents.

⋯e's questioning.

⋯)ecause she does not want him to question ⋯ecause she had something to do with them ⋯)m Book 3 that Neville does not want the ⋯Maybe Neville is dimly aware that his Gran ⋯aptured and attacked by Death Eaters.

⋯s ready to know about the prophecy.

⋯et by his parents before they were attacked. ⋯)e Memory Charming Neville to protect him ⋯ have learned about the prophecy. Neville ⋯iran is hiding the prophecy until it becomes ⋯n Neville.

⋯While some ⋯⋯ ⋯ ⋯an others, I felt it was necessary to include all aspects of this theory so that other Harry Potter fans could ⋯⋯/be draw their own conclusions or expand on these.

So What? Wrapping it All Together

I love plot twists, especially JK Rowling's, because they are so intricate and mind-blowing. These twists are what cemented my never-ending love for the Harry Potter series. The most appealing factor is that JK Rowling has always laid the necessary foundation for these twists in the previous books. That being the case, we have undoubtedly been given the necessary information for a twist regarding the Longbottoms and their role in the Harry Potter universe. I am sure that Book 6 will answer many of my questions and lead me to ask a lot more, but I would expect nothing less.

See you in line for Book 6!

—————————— Additional Sleuthing Notes ——————————

✻ Did Neville receive a memory charm, or is he an example of a "late bloomer"?

✻ Could someone be using a Memory Charm to protect Neville from the Death Eaters? If he had seen something but they think he doesn't remember, would they leave him alone?

✻ If Neville is also being protected from knowing about the prophecy Dumbledore-style, now that everything has been revealed to Harry, is anyone going to tell Neville? Should he/does he know about his past in all this as well as his near-miss with destiny?

NEVILLE AND HARRY: CHILDREN OF THE PROPHECY

"SIRIUSADDICT" ✳ NEW CLUES FORUM
USA (*US Edition*), AGE 44

Inspiration for this Discussion

"Appearances are deceiving" is a major theme of the Harry Potter books, and nowhere is this more evident than in the character of Neville Longbottom. From the beginning, Neville is portrayed as a clumsy inept child, yet, when we carefully review what JK Rowling writes about him, we find there is more to see than what a superficial reading of the books would lead us to believe. In Book 5, we discover that Neville could have been the one chosen to destroy Lord Voldemort, and even as early as Book 1, we are made aware by Dumbledore that Neville is more than he appears, for it is because Dumbledore awards Neville ten points for bravery that Gryffindor wins the House Cup. So, what is JK Rowling concealing by portraying Neville as incompetent? Could Neville be a key to unraveling the Harry Potter mysteries? These questions have fascinated me and motivated me to find all the Neville references and examine these passages for clues regarding his connection to Harry in the search for the true Neville.

 HANDFUL

The parallels between Neville and Harry begin with the similarities in their background. In Book 5, Dumbledore tells us that, like Harry, Neville was born at the end of July (July 30) to parents who had thrice defied Voldemort. Both sets of parents endured tremendous adversity in the battle against Voldemort. In the first four books, we find out that Neville, like Harry, grows up in an environment where his self-esteem is beaten down. While Harry is treated like a pariah by his aunt and uncle because of his magical traits, Neville is nearly drowned by his Uncle Algie and dropped from a window to test him for magical aptitude. {B1, Ch7} The fact that Neville and Harry both have particularly cruel uncles is probably more than just a twist of fate.

It is much too coincidental how often Neville plays a significant role in the pivotal events of Harry's life. The first example occurs in Book 1. McGonagall notices Harry's flying talent, and places him on the Gryffindor Quidditch team when he performs a spectacular dive to save Neville's Remembrall {Ch9}. Quidditch turns out to be one of the most satisfying parts of Harry's life at Hogwarts and Neville is inadvertently responsible for bringing it to him. A further illustration of this takes place later when Neville is responsible for Harry's remembering the identity of Nicolas Flamel. After Draco bullies Neville, Harry gives Neville a chocolate frog as a kind gesture, and in return, Neville gives back to him the Dumbledore wizard card that came with it. That's how Harry discovers the key information in Book 1 for on the back of the card, it names Nicolas Flamel as Dumbledore's partner in alchemy. In Book 2, Neville is the one who discovers that the contents of Harry's trunk have been scattered throughout their dorm room when Tom Riddle's diary is taken from Harry. In Book 5, the dream in which Harry first sees the locked door ajar begins with Neville waltzing with Professor Sprout. Ironically, Neville is responsible for breaking the prophecy during the battle in the Department of Mysteries. Although we are told that Harry could not hear the prophecy over the noise of the battle around him, it is left as a question whether Neville did hear it, which suggests to me that he probably did.

In addition to his crucial role in many of the significant events of Harry's life, Neville is also linked to him by some of the significant people in Harry's life. Harry and Neville have similar relationships with Severus Snape. Snape appears to be cruel to all students, except to those in Slytherin. However, JK Rowling makes it a point to remind us that he is particularly evil to both Harry and Neville. In fact, Severus Snape is the one thing that Neville fears the most.{B3, Ch7} We have some knowledge from Book 3 as to why this is true for Harry, but we are not told why Snape mistreats Neville.

There are several references that may tie Neville to Sirius Black. In Book 1, Neville tells the story of how his Uncle Algie pushed him off Blackpool Pier to force some magic out of him. As we know, it was common to name a landmark after the resident family or vice versa, so could there be a Black family connection? (Of course, Blackpool Pier is a real place.) In Book 2 and 5, Neville is described as "snuffling" when he sleeps (readers may recall that Sirius' nickname is Snuffles), and in Book 5, Neville is responsible for Sirius getting the password that lets him into Gryffindor Tower.

Neville seems to have a sixth sense when Harry is in trouble. In Book 1, while Quirrell is attempting to jinx Harry off his broom in his first Quidditch match, Neville is sobbing into Hagrid's jacket before anyone notices there is anything wrong with Harry. In Book 5, when Harry experiences the attack on Arthur Weasley, Neville seems to be the most alert to the scale of the distress that Harry is experiencing and reacts very quickly seeking help from McGonagall. Later, in the Department of Mysteries, Neville is the only one to notice that Harry is dying when he is being choked by a Death Eater. Neville rescues Harry by jabbing Hermione's wand in the eyehole of the Death Eater's mask.

Neville has similar sensitivities to Harry's. On the train in Book 3, when the Dementors show up, Neville is almost as disturbed by the Dementors as Harry. In Book 5, we discover that, like Harry, Neville can see the Thestrals and has been able to see them all along. Later, we find out that Neville, like Harry, is affected (mesmerized) by the veil in the Department of Mysteries.

Harry seems to be aware of his connection with Neville at a subconscious level. In Book 1, when Harry runs away from Privet Drive and gets picked up by the Knight Bus, the name he gives the driver is that of Neville Longbottom. Later, Harry dreams that he has overslept and missed the Quidditch game with Slytherin. In his dream, Neville replaces Harry in the game.

JK Rowling often uses Neville's character to foreshadow events. In Book 1, Neville receives a Remembrall from his Granny. The description of the Remembrall has an uncanny resemblance to the prophecy orb in Book 5. Later, when Hermione uses the full Body-Bind spell on Neville, it foreshadows the petrifaction caused in Book 2 by the Basilisk. In Book 4, Neville is the one who forgets to jump the trick step found halfway up the staircase and ends up stuck. Harry gets stuck in this same trick step when he is returning to his dorm from the Prefect's bathroom. Interestingly, when Neville tries to use the "Stupefy" curse he says, "Stubefy", which using the Philological stone can be read as "Stubby Fly". Does Neville's sixth sense regarding Harry expand to make him sense that Sirius (known as Stubby Boardman in the *Quibbler*) is in trouble?

With the recent release of the title for the sixth book "The Half-Blood Prince" and the information that the "Half-blood" is neither Harry nor Voldemort, there has been much speculation regarding Neville as the potential prince. Those who argue against Neville point out that there are many references to Neville's pureblood status. However, we still don't know very much about Neville, especially his mother's side. Is it possible that like Harry, Neville is actually a half-blood?

In closing, I would like to share some speculations I have with regard to Neville's role in future books.

Why is Neville so forgetful? One possible explanation is that like Bertha Jorkins and Gilderoy Lockhart, his memory problems are due to a Memory Charm gone awry. I believe there could be another explanation. What if Neville's memory problems are due to the connection between him and Harry? We know that Voldemort and Harry can at times know what the other is feeling and thinking. Could the curse that connected Harry and Voldemort's minds somehow be responsible for the problems with Neville's mind?

Lastly, I'd like to throw this out for consideration: Given all the references to time travel in Books 3 and 5, could Neville have gone back in time at some point and been at Godric's Hollow on the night that Voldemort attacked the Potters? In Book 3, when Harry gets near the Dementors he recalls events from the night his parents died. In one such recollection there is a mention of someone stumbling from a room. JK Rowling makes a huge point of the fact that Neville is clumsy – could this be the reason? Could this be a clue to how truly important Neville is in Harry's life?

JK Rowling weaves a web of intrigue when she writes her books. She deliberately leaves clues for readers to determine future events but she also cleverly misleads. She has trained us in the first four books to overlook Neville by making him forgetful and weak while other characters are competent and strong. The growth we observe in the character of Neville in Book 5 could be just the beginning to JK Rowling's revelation of the real Neville Longbottom.

ADDITIONAL SLEUTHING NOTES

* In Chapter 15 of Book 3, Harry had a dream that Neville had replaced him for the Quidditch match – was that an allusion to the prophecy, or is there more to it?{p302}

* Was it just a story line clue or a more significant septology clue that in Chapter 21 of Book 5, we are told Harry gets partnered with Neville "as usual"?{p454}

Bloodlines
and Blood Feuds

PETUNIA: THE WOMAN WHO KNOWS TOO MUCH

"FANOFSIRIUS" ✳ NEW CLUES FORUM
USA (*US Edition*), AGE 30

Inspiration for this Discussion

When we first met Petunia Dursley, none of us liked how she treated our hero, Harry. As the series progressed, however, it became clear there was more to this character than met the eye. In Book 5, we finally learned that Harry's aunt has a tremendous amount of knowledge about the magical world. It is this revelation that intrigued me and led me to the idea of looking at Books 1-4 on the assumption that Petunia knows much more about Harry's magical world than we could possibly imagine. What possible clues to her knowledge are hidden in the first four books?

 HANDFUL

From the start, we were sure to dislike Petunia. After all, none of us liked how she (and the rest of the Dursleys for that matter) treated Harry. Then we discover in Book 5 that Petunia has been holding out on us. She *does* know about magic. What is Petunia so afraid of? Better yet, has JK Rowling left us clues all along?

In Chapter 2 of Book 5, the Dursleys seem rather overwhelmed by the magical events in Little Whinging. Dementors…owls…it's all too much! But, it is during Harry's explanation of the night's strange events when we are shown a side of Petunia that we have not seen before. Vernon asks about Dementors and Petunia immediately responds, *"They guard the wizard prison, Azkaban."* Thankfully, Harry asks the burning question for us: How does she know this? She heard *"that awful boy—telling **her** about them—years ago."*{p31,32 US} Why doesn't she just use Lily's and James' names? And, as Harry wonders, why does she remember this bit of information from supposedly so long ago when she tries so hard to pretend the magical world doesn't exist?

As a result, we can conclude she knows, and has known for quite some time, much more than we could imagine. Does Petunia possess magical abilities? Or, is she simply still jealous of her talented sister? How can she understand all this and be a simple Muggle like Vernon? Even more significant is her reaction to the Howler. Petunia has been in contact with a wizard! (Dumbledore, no less.) And he's on a first-name basis with Petunia. Her magical agreement is so important that she refuses to let Vernon throw Harry out of the house. But, are there any clues in the first four books that could help us to answer some of these questions?

In Book 1, Petunia describes her sister as a "freak".{Ch4, p53} She also shows a certain disdain towards Lily because of their parents' joy in having a witch in the family. One possible clue is that not everything is as it seems with Petunia. She is, in fact, just like her name. Petunia is a flower that is a part of the night-shade family.[1] The name is even defined as a bittersweet nightshade that contains a poisonous juice. Sounds like our Auntie, doesn't it? It would seem this is sibling rivalry in the extreme— a jealousy that continues throughout the series.

Continuing to Book 2, we may have our first clue that something is not as it appears with Petunia. Harry has a moment of fun with Diddykins, pretending to jinx him. When Dudley runs to tell his mum, *"Petunia knew he hadn't really done magic."* {Ch1, p10} If she is really no more familiar with wizards than Dudley or Vernon, how does she *know* that Harry was only torturing Dudley psychologically and not actually using magic? Had she seen Lily doing her magic? If so, would this also explain why she knows something about the wizarding world? In Books 3 and 4, Petunia takes a back seat to Aunt Marge and Vernon. So often in this series, we get a glimpse or hint of something then it disappears—possibly even forgotten by us—before JKR springs it back on us in a rather sneaky manner.

In Book 5, our glimpse of Petunia takes an unusual turn. It is quite odd that she is juxtaposed to Mrs. Figg when Harry asks her about her knowledge of the Dementors.{Ch2, p31} Now, this could simply be because those are two characters who share the common aspect of knowing things they should not; however, I believe that this juxtaposition is indicative of much more—a hint that Petunia is not what she seems to be. Mrs. Figg turned out to be a Squib. Can Petunia logically be a Muggle with latent magical abilities? Can this help us to explain her? Well, we know that Lily is described as a "Mudblood". This, of course, means "dirty blood" because she is not descended from a pure-blood wizarding family. We have been told that Lily's and Petunia's parents were Muggles. However, it is still plausible that they had a wizarding ancestor. Due to our lack of information regarding their family, these aspects are sure to prove important.

As everyone knows, Lord Voldemort's pure-blood followers consider *anyone* with *even one drop* of Muggle blood to be a Mudblood. Also, Squibs are seen as equal to Muggles. So, logically, the parents could be any of these combinations and still be Mudbloods. This would explain the utter elation of Lily's and Petunia's parents at having a witch in the family, especially if Petunia was not fortunate enough to have magical abilities like her talented sister. Then it's not surprising she would be jealous of how much attention her parents gave to Lily. We can see that Petunia would want to know as much about the magical world as she could, yet show a complete contempt for Lily and her world. Therefore, we have a classic case of sibling rivalry. This explains Petunia's complete disdain for anything magical. It hurts too much for her to admit that her parents possibly appreciated Lily more because of her magical abilities. So, what more of a human thing to do than to hate the aspect that draws her parents' attention away from her and to her sister?

The crux of the Petunia paradox is that she hates magic and anything abnormal, but at the same time obviously knows an awful lot about the wizarding world. Petunia is not just a magic-hating Muggle, but also one who obviously understands the power of The Dark Lord and those who follow him. She exhibits great fear at the news of Voldemort's return. Harry is even a bit awestruck by her reaction. For the first time, he relates to her as his mother's sister. Harry goes as far as to state that it seems as if all of the antagonism over magic that he had felt from his Aunt Petunia had dissipated in a moment.{B5, Ch2, p38} Furthermore, her reaction to the Howler reinforces the idea that she has had some sort of continuing contact with the wizarding world. We know from JKR's Edinburgh chat that Petunia is not a Squib, but there is something peculiar about her and her relationship with the wizarding world.[2] We must not forget that she did take Harry in after all that had happened. And now, JKR has also informed us on her website[3] that Petunia has exchanged letters with Dumbledore *prior* to the one left on her doorstep with the orphaned baby Harry. Clearly, Petunia is no ordinary Muggle.

So, will she have an appreciation and understanding of what or, more precisely, *WHO* Harry is facing? Does she understand what this could hold for herself, her family and the rest of the world? I believe she does!

——————— ADDITIONAL SLEUTHING NOTES ———————

✳ Is Petunia's "unnaturally" clean kitchen {B5, Ch3, p51}the result of incredible diligence, or could a little extra magic be seeping out to help? What kind of magical protection is there around Privet Drive? How did Dobby get in?

✳ Vernon gets upset and wants to beat the wizard out of Harry, while Petunia is always trying to cover up the magic – could that be a crucial distinction?

✳ Who did Petunia overhear talking about Azkaban? She didn't use names, so do we know for sure who "her" and "that boy" are? Are we sure she meant James? Are we sure she meant Lily?

✳ Can a Muggle "sign" a wizard agreement? Does Petunia's sealing of a wizard contract, by taking in Harry, imply that she has magical ties? What would be the consequences (as a Muggle or wizard) if she were to break the contract?

1 "Nightshade". Online dictionary www.dictionary.com 20 August 2004
2 JK Rowling chat, World Book Day, March, 2004.
3 www.jkrowling.co.uk – FAQ Poll

SOMETHING DURSLEY THIS WAY COMES

ELYSE SCHULER ✳ CoS "THETHIRDMAN"
USA (*US Edition*), AGE 21

Inspiration for this Discussion

In the beginning, Petunia and Vernon seemed united in their loathing of Harry. However, as the books progressed, I have watched Petunia stand up to Vernon and allow Harry to remain at Privet Drive. That raised questions in my mind. Is a rift growing between Petunia and Vernon? Is Petunia's connection to Harry interfering with Vernon's perfect, magic-free world? Will Petunia have to choose between living her perfect life with Vernon and honoring her bloodline? This is how I see it.

HANDFUL

They're despised and loathed…

They're the self-righteous, social-climbing scourges of suburbia…

They are *the Dursleys*.

But they can't be dismissed as nothing more than stock elitists. As *Book 5* has shown us, the Dursleys are key to an important part of the story, Petunia especially. Now that she's revealed more knowledge of the wizarding world than we first thought, what lies in her future? Will her relationship with Harry grow at the expense of her marriage?

Skimming back more carefully through the books, it becomes apparent that Vernon's and Petunia's understanding of magic is completely different. Let's look at an example in *Book 2*, "*As neither Dudley nor the hedge was in any way hurt, Aunt Petunia knew that he hadn't really done magic…*" {Ch 1} How can a Muggle like Petunia know that no magic has been done? Even if there is no visible damage, wouldn't someone without knowledge of magic suspect that a spell was cast to cause latent or non-visible damage? Isn't that what Vernon would think? I'd say it's safe to assume that Vernon wouldn't have checked for damage; he would have torn right into Harry. It certainly seems, therefore, that Petunia has a much better grasp on magic than Vernon. And, after Book 5, it now appears to be true.

In the second chapter of Book 5, Petunia explains the Dementors to Vernon. She says she heard "*…that awful boy [presumably James] – telling her [presumably Lily] about them…*" But even more importantly, *she knows who Voldemort is.* Upon hearing of his return, Petunia's "*large, pale eyes…were wide and fearful.*" Why was she so terrified? Obviously, she must have some idea of Voldemort's power, and how many people (both magical and Muggle) he's killed.

So where did she get all this knowledge of the wizard world? From Lily? It's logical, but Petunia seems to have wanted nothing to do with her sister, dead or alive. Perhaps the parents had family/friends who were wizards? The only mention of Petunia and Lily's parents is that they were very proud when Lily got accepted to Hogwarts. What Muggle parents would have found such pride in having an owl drop a strange piece of parchment through their mail slot? For example, wouldn't Dean Thomas' parents have been scratching their heads when the first owl from Hogwarts arrived? According to JKR, they were definitely Muggles. So, what was different about Lily's and Petunia's parents?

Petunia has (so far) shown no magical ability, just tidbits of knowledge about important figures in the wizard world. She may be incapable of doing magic and therefore wants nothing to do with the magical community. Why else would she marry such a painfully normal man like Vernon? It was a sure way of severing herself from magic. The only affectionate gesture we see between Petunia and Vernon is the peck on the cheek in the first page of *Book 1*. Their lives revolve around showing how much better they are than their neighbors, spying on the block, pampering Dudley and yelling at Harry: not exactly a functional marriage. Can it be that the Dursleys' marriage is a sham? Perhaps a separation is in their near future....

There are hints about how a separation may occur. It can be the result of what a good number of people are already proposing: Petunia will take Harry's side for once. That would do it. Just think of the row that would cause at Number 4! It would tear the household apart. Let's face it—Vernon wouldn't want anything more to do with Petunia. He's not exactly what you'd call tolerant. Remember how Moody declared that what Vernon didn't know could fill several books? {B5, Ch38} He obviously has no clue that his wife may be in communication with wizards. How would someone so prejudiced about anything magical deal with that? Probably like he always does— squash it. He forbids even the mention of the "M" word. Even if there is nothing magical about Petunia, there is the great possibility that she is holding major secrets about Harry, the Evans family, and the Howler that arrived in her kitchen.

Building off what is already known, I propose that Petunia will reveal a broad understanding of the wizarding world. Based on her reaction to Voldemort's name, she is likely to recognize (if she already hasn't) the immense threat that Voldemort's return poses and that Harry is important in stopping him. This could cause her to overcome her jealousy of Lily and begin to show Harry more sympathy (and maybe even some respect?). Petunia may be the one who will show some magic ability, causing Vernon to resent her or simply end their marriage. In that case, it is likely that Harry will end up with Petunia. JKR has specifically said that Dudley is just Muggle Dudley {JKR chat – Edinburgh Book Festival, August, 2004}, so Vernon may take "Big D" away in order to protect him from the wizarding community.

If my hypothesis is correct, then Petunia could be placing herself in more danger than she's been in so far. As Lily's sister, she carries the blood protection. If Voldemort discovers this (if he doesn't already know), then killing Petunia would be an easy way to reduce Harry's safe havens to none. Voldemort and his followers have infiltrated Hogwarts multiple times, Kreacher was able to leave Grimmauld Place and leak information to the Malfoys, and Umbridge was able to cause danger right near Privet Drive. However, her Dementor attack proved futile. So, the Dursleys' is the safest place for Harry, unless Petunia is removed from the equation. By now, Voldemort has had fifteen years to realize that his demise was brought about by Lily's love for Harry and that Harry is only safe at Privet Drive because of Petunia. I expect Voldemort to come after the Dursleys at some point.

As I reread the books, it seems logical that events will play out this way. The Dursleys are not just going to fade into the background. Something big is coming — and it's coming their way.

ADDITIONAL SLEUTHING NOTES

* Why would Petunia fear Voldemort? Was he in any way responsible for Petunia deciding to reject the wizarding world?

* JKR said that someone might use magic "late in life" {BarnesandNoble.com chat, 1999} – would that be Petunia? If so, what terrible emergency would cause her magic to pop out?

* JKR revealed that her most disliked character is Uncle Vernon {World Book Day Char, March, 2004} – why would she say that? Will Vernon be sucked in by Voldemort through his prejudices? Is Book 6 going to be Harry's shortest stay at the Dursleys so far because Uncle Vernon kicks him out? Could he kick Petunia out?

WHAT HAS BECOME OF THE HOUSE OF BLACK?
THE DISAPPEARING FAMILIES IN JK ROWLING'S BOOKS

SUZANNE FOSTER, CRAIG L. FOSTER ✳ CHAMBER OF SECRETS FORUM
USA (*US Edition*), AGES 35, 42

Inspiration for this Discussion

A genealogist, whether by profession or hobby, sees the world slightly differently than the average person. He sees the world as a series of interlocking family connections: who is related to whom, and how they are related, becomes a topic of conversation with almost anyone. Ever since we read Book 2, the sparseness of such family relationships in the Harry Potter universe has not passed without our notice. Book 5, however, drove the issue home for us. We realized Rowling was not just using the "last heir" theme as a dramatic device, but was actually trying to make a point. In discussions with other Harry Potter fans, we developed our feelings on this and cited examples until we felt that we had an actual insight into Rowling's thought process. So, when presented with the possibility of writing a discussion about anything from the septology that interested us, we jumped at the chance to commit to paper the ideas that had been floating in our minds for almost a year. Here, then, are the first scant summaries of a topic that is so deeply entrenched in the Rowling texts that there is reference to it on almost every page: the love of family, the heritage of blood, and (ironically) the need to rise above it and become your best self. We hope this article inspires its readers to look at the Rowling texts in a new light.

 12

As fans, we read the *Harry Potter* books with an absolute love for the characters and the story, but as genealogists, we find one element of the septology story line to be particularly interesting. That is the virtual extinction of so many of the wizarding families. The theme of a certain person being the last of his ancestral line is repeated so many times that we are sure JK Rowling is trying to make a social statement through it, rather than it just being a coincidence. Now, you may be saying to yourself that we just have a little bit too much time on our hands if we can read something into that, but let's consider the way genealogies work for a few minutes and then discuss why Rowling is so obviously contradicting this in her wizarding universe.

As we all know, ideally two people marry and have children. These children grow and have children of their own, and through a slow, but steady multiplication, the family grows. Mathematically, it does not take very many years for the total number of descendants of one person to be very large. Making some assumptions about family size of three living children per family, who then marry and have three living children each, it only take four generations, or about 100 years, for the number of living descendants of one individual to reach 108. If a typical "Muggle" lived in the year 1500, which is slightly over 500 years ago, and these conditions held true up to the time of the *Harry Potter* stories, he could be estimated to have 172,186,884 descendants.[1] Knowing this, when we read that Tom Riddle is "the last remaining descendant [ancestor]"[2]{B2, Ch18, p332 US} of Salazar Slytherin, we took notice. After all, Slytherin lived 1,000 years ago and the number of his descendants should be huge. But Riddle is certainly not the only one in the predicament of being the last of his line. Draco Malfoy, Barty Crouch, Jr., Sirius Black, (Neville Longbottom?), and even Harry Potter are all specifically named as the last living heirs of their respective families.

We don't believe you have to think very hard to realize that if too many wizarding families find themselves in a situation where they only have one descendant, the outlook on the survival of wizarding society is not optimistic. In fact, we would be so bold as to state that in the septology, wizarding society is hovering on the edge—of not only war, but of complete extinction.

So, why is this the case? Why has Rowling set up this situation? We know she frequently incorporates certain themes into her plot points in order to make important social statements, and she is apparently doing that here as well. Now, we realize there are two more books forthcoming, so it is possible that she may change course completely; however, we doubt it. The blood feuds and potential demise of the race of wizards is such an ingrained part of the stories so far, we are positive that by the end of Book 7, this same problem will emerge as being crucial to the entire septology. Deplorably, for both themselves and others, the hate and distrust among the members of pure-blood wizarding families have led to their elimination. To help illustrate her point, Rowling uses the Black family as an example of everything that is wrong in wizarding society, dooming it to destruction.

Sirius Black told Harry in Book 5 that he was the last Black left {B5, Ch5, p79}, thus, when he was killed, the Black line died with him. Even more telling in our opinion is that it was a family member – his own cousin Bellatrix – who killed him, and sealed the fate of the entire Black family. There are numerous examples in the books of family members killing their own relatives – such as: Tom Riddle's murder of his father and grandparents {B4, Ch1, p2}, and Barty Crouch killing of his father.{Ch35, p690} Now, killing a parent obviously does not do anything toward eliminating a bloodline, as their chance to procreate has typically come and gone, but the fact that there is no love lost between family members in these pureblood families is extremely clear in these passages. The Black family is certainly a prime example of this. Mrs. Black hates her son, the *"blood traitor, abomination, shame of [her] flesh"* {B5, Ch4, p78}, with a vehemence that shatters the air and makes Grimmauld Place…well…grim. This is interesting, because typically as people get older (or in this case, deader), their thoughts turn toward their posterity and the continuation of the family bloodlines. But Mrs. Black doesn't seem to care a whit that Sirius is her last chance for descendants. She just hates him and everything to do with him. This anomaly is reinforced, in our opinion, when we are told that the one book Harry mentions as being found at Grimmauld Place, is a large volume called *Nature's Nobility: A Wizarding Genealogy.* {Ch6, p116}

While we may feel certain sympathy toward Sirius for hating *his* parents (and dead brother), his embittered emotions seem to go even deeper than that. He has no love or respect for the entire *Black family line* and he has no sentimental attachment to any of it. *"The china, which bore the Black crest and motto, was all thrown unceremoniously into a sack by Sirius…"* {p117} Indeed, Kreacher, the house-elf, has more reverence for the Black family treasures than Sirius does. Sirius hates his family's blood intensely; he never had children, thus ensuring that the line ended with him. Now, we can see you thinking, *"Yeah, but he was in Azkaban for 12 years and he wasn't exactly available when he was hiding out in caves as Snuffles, living off rats."* And that is true. However, his friend James Potter—exactly the same age—had managed to marry and have a child in the time before Sirius went to Azkaban. In fact, it is worth pointing out that from the five friends (Peter, Remus, Sirius, James and Lily) one child was produced. Exactly one. With statistics like that, it's not hard to see why wizard society is in extreme trouble.

We find it sadly ironic that the motto of the Black family is "Toujours Pur" or "Always Pure". Why? Because Harry is told on several occasions that it is the pure unselfish love of his mother—his family— that preserved his life that fateful Halloween night. *"… to have been loved so deeply, even though the person who loved us is gone, will give us some protection forever."*{B1, Ch17 p299} Indeed, pure love is hinted to be the thing that Voldemort cannot understand or tolerate. *"It was your heart that saved you."* Dumbledore tells Harry concerning the night in the Department of Mysteries. {B5, Ch37, p844} But despite the Black family motto, their love for each other is anything but pure; it is filthy and (to put it bluntly) black. That is what has doomed them to extinction.

We are quite certain Rowling is trying to make an important statement, rather than just demonstrating an appalling ignorance of genealogy. What convinces us most is that, while showing us these pure-blood families extinguishing themselves through their own self-hatred, Rowling also presents us with a complete contrast. The difference is so stark that it startles us to read about it. This is the Weasley family—the one non-dysfunctional wizarding family we meet in the septology. Arthur and Molly love each other and they love their children very much. The scene from the first five books that best illustrates this is in Book 2 where Ron, Fred and George rescue Harry from the Dursleys and bring him home in the flying Ford Anglia. Molly is mad at them, very mad, but after yelling at them for the danger that they put themselves in, *"You could have died!"* {B2, Ch3, p33}, she welcomes them home, feeds them breakfast, and places the blame where it probably rightly belongs in this case—on Arthur's shoulders. Her children love her and Arthur with no underlying fear. And they love each other. That love is manifest in their large number of children and in the love that the children have for their siblings (even if they do get on each-other's nerves).

This love, present *within* the Weasley family, is also extended to those in their circle of friends who are *outside* of the blooded family. They seem to like almost everyone, and to always look for the good qualities in people, reaching out to those the other pure-bloods despise—including Muggles, Muggle-born wizards, half-breeds such as Hagrid, and even the outcast, Remus Lupin. Indeed, everyone who hates Arthur lists his Muggle-loving tendencies as one of his least desirable qualities. *"Arthur Weasley loves Muggles so much he should snap his wand in half and go and join them,"*{Ch 12, p222} Draco Malfoy mocks with an opinion that is undoubtedly picked up from hearing his father voice similar sentiments. It is our belief that one of Rowling's main goals is to demonstrate that the hatred most pureblood families have toward those outside of their own bloodline, tends to turn inward and destroy these same families. This hatred is a slow-acting poison, spreading and killing anything it touches.

But the Weasleys have avoided this poison because of their intense love for their family members. Yes, this love has been tested by Percy's betrayal of the family. *"[Percy] was going to make sure everyone knew he didn't belong to our family anymore,"*{B5, Ch 4, p72} Whether or not Percy comes around in the next two years or not, that love for him and despair at this (hopefully temporary) absence from the family circle can be overcome by Weasley family.

Conversely, Rowling uses the Black family and what happens to Sirius as a symbol of the self-destructive mentality that is tearing apart the pure-blood wizarding families. She illustrates their lack of love for each other, feeling no compunction in killing other family members. Sirius avoids passing on his hated blood to another generation, and his other family members do not care. The Black family hates "blood traitors" so intensely that they are ready to poison their own family relationships rather than intermarry, leading directly to their own extinction. But at this point is it too late? Is there anything that can save them? Is the entire wizarding world doomed?

Rowling answers these questions by presenting her readers with an obvious solution: a family that could serve as an example to everyone else, the Weasleys. Their love for each other and their quiet acceptance of other magical and non-magical persons are the reasons they thrive. Rowling has brought us full circle. As the love of Harry's mother saved his life and conquered one threat to wizarding society, the love of other mothers for their children could save them all from an even greater threat. What will be the legacy of the House of Black?

ADDITIONAL SLEUTHING NOTES
---

* Could the Black Family house, itself, be "evil"—similar to the "Turn of the Screw"?

* We saw Lucius berate Draco for being only second best {B2, Ch4, p52} – is it possible for Lucius to praise and show love to his son? Does Lucius treat Draco with the same contempt that he showed to Dobby? Could that be what is wrong with Draco? Didn't Crouch Sr. also treat his son the same way?

* Would that book, *Nature's Nobility*, be propaganda, or could it be a play on words and be implying ties to "Nature" (as in princely lions)?

* What other evidence do we have that the wizarding race could be dying out? Is it a coincidence that in Harry's class there are 5 males in Gryffindor, but only 3 females? JKR said in her Edinburgh Book Festival chat that *"Ginny…is the first girl to be born into the Weasley clan for several generations"* – is that typical for all wizarding families? If so, then wouldn't they be facing an emergency right now?

---

1 http://freepages.genealogy.rootsweb.com/~pamonval/howbig.html, June 2004, p 3.

2 The text in the book said "ancestor," which would normally be a mistake; however, in an interview, JK Rowling said it was an "intentional error." It was changed in some editions to "descendant," but the "error" is still showing up.

**PHINEAS NIGELLUS:
PORTRAIT OF A SLYTHERIN**

LELA JANE PAGE ✳ CHAMBER OF SECRETS
USA (*US Edition*), AGE 26

Inspiration for this Discussion

I welcomed the addition of scene-stealing Phineas Nigellus to the world of Harry Potter with great delight and relief. Not only did this self-absorbed painting add a new level of magic to Hogwarts, but he also brought a much-needed sense of balance. I had been growing troubled by the continued portrayal of Slytherin as a house of villains; the idea that eleven-year-old children were destined to a life of certain evil unsettled me deeply. Then came Book 5, and in strolled Phineas Nigellus to show just how a Slytherin, working for the light, behaves. Proving JK Rowling's ability to sketch a character in just a few words, Phineas' brief appearances helped to show the futility of stereotypes.

 HANDFUL

"*There's not a witch or wizard who went bad who wasn't in Slytherin*," Hagrid proclaims in Book 1.{Ch5, p80 US} Further descriptions add little to dispel the notion of this particular House as a genuine nest of vipers. Established by the wizard who broke the unity of the founders of Hogwarts, Slytherin House boasts two famous alumni including the main villain, Lord Voldemort, and house-elf kicker, Lucius Malfoy. The more Slytherins we see introduced to the story, the more tempting it becomes to twist Hagrid's remarks into "*there's not a witch or wizard in Slytherin who* didn't *go bad*," which was not what he meant. Just because a few bad guys were from Slytherin, it doesn't mean that *all* the Slytherins will become bad.

It falls to the talkative portrait of a long-dead headmaster to correct this misconception. Phineas Nigellus embodies many of the characteristics for which Slytherin House is known, while at the same time assisting the heroes in Book 5. By using Phineas as a model for the way a Slytherin behaves if he is "on the side of good", readers can begin to see hints of which characters will be aligned with the Dark Lord in the Second War, and which ones will not.

Phineas does not make the best first impression, but where does he stand? His true nature soon begins to emerge. He is initially mentioned by Sirius, who declares his great-great-grandfather to be the "least popular" headmaster in Hogwarts' history. {B5, Ch6, p113} However, the offense of "unpopularity" is put in perspective by the fact that the other family members were known for attempting "to make Muggle hunting legal" and chopping the heads off house-elves.{p113} Later, Phineas is seen being threatened by a fellow portrait for his seeming unwillingness to follow the orders of the current headmaster.{Ch 22, p475} Phineas may not be happy about his role as errand boy for Dumbledore, but his displeasure takes the form of grumbling and non-deadly subversion. If a house-elf can find a way to get around orders and get his master killed, one would expect a former headmaster to be able to twist messages and reports if it suits his wishes. True, Phineas delights in winding people up like bits of clockwork for his own amusement;

nonetheless, he is never seen being deliberately misleading. His feigning of sleep and announcement that he is "too tired" to deliver a message are not laziness or disloyalty, but rather an attempt to amuse himself by sparring with people. {p472} It is hinted that the paintings in the Headmaster's office get bored, when one says to Harry, "*I hope this means…that Dumbledore will soon be back with us…It has been very dull without him*" {Ch37, p821} To move from the powerful position of headmaster to being confined to only observing a few rooms and trading messages, must be hard for the portraits' personalities. Phineas obviously enjoys the spotlight and his complaints allow him to feel that he is still needed.

What Phineas says about Dumbledore while out of his presence emphasizes his loyalty and respect for the current headmaster. When Harry gets angry because Dumbledore sends Phineas with just some vague instructions (instead of visiting in person), the portrait jumps to the headmaster's defense. He points out to Harry that Dumbledore may have "*an excellent reason*" for "*not confiding every tiny detail of his plans to you.*"{Ch23, p496} Phineas seems frustrated at Harry's lack of trust and confidence in Dumbledore, and reminds him pointedly, "*following Dumbledore's orders has never yet led you into harm.*"{p496} If Phineas wished to plot against the Headmaster, Harry's anger at not receiving more information would have given him the perfect opportunity to feed this discord. Even if prevented by spells from speaking against the Headmaster, it seems hard to believe that Phineas would be required to speak up for him quite so forcefully. It doesn't feel as if he would be a "bad guy".

Perhaps the clearest sign that Phineas should *not* be counted as a villain comes with his reaction to Sirius' death. His shock over this loss allows Phineas to be emotionally aligned with the heroes, and with readers. His refusal to accept that his great great grandson is gone shows not only that the portrait is capable of a very human response to death, but also echoes what Harry is experiencing. When informed that Sirius was killed, Phineas (who usually loves to hear himself talk), can only manage a short, "*I don't believe it,*" before going off to his portrait at Grimmauld Place.{Ch37, p826} Harry's belief, that he left to walk through the frames in the empty house, looking for the last of his family, is a haunting image of his inner unity with the heroes.

Readers of this series are not invited to ignore the fact that Phineas is a member of Slytherin House; rather it is pointed out several times. When properly introduced to the character, he is described as "*painted wearing the Slytherin colors of green and silver*" and later reappears "*in front of his Slytherin banner.*"{Ch22, p472 & 474} His next appearance makes his House loyalty even more apparent. Phineas does not try to distance himself from Slytherin, rather, he takes it upon himself to speak on behalf of the House: "*We Slytherins are brave, yes, but not stupid…given the choice, we will always choose to save our own necks.*"{Ch23, p495} Phineas also reminds readers that the Sorting Hat nearly placed Harry in Slytherin saying, "*you would have been better off in my own house.*"{p495} Portraying Phineas not as an anomaly but as a *proud* Slytherin who works for the Order, reflects well for his entire House.

Phineas must balance out the evil natures of the others in his house because Professor Severus Snape, one of the most visible Slytherins in the series, is unable to take on this ballast role. The possibility that Snape simply pretends to be a loyal member of the Order, or that he could turn his back on those fighting to defeat Voldemort, hovers over the story. Much suspense hinges on his ability to retain a sense of ambiguity. This mystery and uncertainty means he cannot come out for the side of good in the same way that a minor character like Phineas can. Despite Snape's sense of humor and his disdain for students, (much like Phineas'), his loyalty to Dumbledore probably is not an act.

Another notable Slytherin, Draco Malfoy, does not come across as favorably when compared with Phineas. He backs up his taunts with deeds that hinder the heroes. Draco puts the Trip Jinx on Harry that allows Umbridge to capture him running from the raided DA meeting. Draco's reaction to Dumbledore's removal as headmaster differs greatly from Phineas' response. His reaction immediately acknowledges Umbridge's authority; he works with the Inquisitorial Squad showing his desire to curry favor with the Ministry and Professor Umbridge — the same people who oppose Dumbledore.

After Dumbledore's dramatic escape from Minister Fudge upon being removed as Head of Hogwarts, Phineas does not say anything that could be useful in capturing the former headmaster. Instead, he simply remarks, "...I disagree with Dumbledore on many counts...but you cannot deny that he's got style."{Ch27, p623} Coming from the attention-loving portrait, this is certainly a remark of great admiration.

Phineas Nigellus adds much-needed humor to the gathering darkness in Book 5. He is an easy character for readers to become attached to—we laugh at his snide remarks, cheer his attempt to berate some much needed sense into Harry, and mourn with him the loss of Sirius. This Slytherin proves that allies for the "good" can be found in surprising places, if one only takes the time to study the techniques not of the painter, but of the painted.

ADDITIONAL SLEUTHING NOTES

* In what ways are portraits bound to serve?
* If the Slytherin mentality is to save his own skin, can a Slytherin be trusted when the going gets tough (think Snape)?
* Is it right to have fun at the expense of others – even if it is just being difficult? Can we truly trust that kind of person?
* Why was Phineas the "least favorite" headmaster? Could that be a red herring and have nothing to do with his personality or affiliation?

Barty Crouch Jr: A Good Son Gone Bad

Erin Knutson * NC, "momthatsafan"
USA (*US Edition*), Age 31

Inspiration for this Discussion

My infatuation with Barty Crouch Jr. started in Book 4. His character seemed intriguingly multi-faceted. I found myself constantly rereading the section where he revealed himself to Harry. How did a kid from a strong-minded, wizard family become such a bad apple? What happened in his childhood that would cause him to become a Dark Wizard? What were the influences outside of his family that led him to become a Death Eater and, eventually, a faithful servant of Lord Voldemort?

12

Our introduction to Barty Crouch Jr. {henceforth Crouch Jr.} in Book 4 is a complex and devious one. We first meet Crouch Jr. (as himself) in Dumbledore's third memory in the pensieve. He is described as "...*a boy in his late teens, who looked nothing short of petrified...shivering, his straw-colored hair all over his face, his freckled skin milk-white.*" {B4, Ch30, p594} Nothing in this description leads us to believe that Crouch Jr. is anything other than a normal teenage boy just out of school. He seems out of place with the other people on trial for the same atrocity. Is he just a mistreated, un-loved youth? Are there other dark secrets we don't know about? What childhood influences could have turned him bad? Was there a family or a school influence that turned a well-to-do young wizard toward the Dark Arts?

During the trial, we see a side of Barty Crouch Sr. {henceforth Crouch Sr.} that is noticeably different than the calm, cool, and collected one we met at the Quidditch World Cup. He almost seems to take on a maniacal personality. "'*You are no son of mine!' bellowed Mr. Crouch, his eyes bulging suddenly. 'I have no son!'*"{p596} We have sympathy for Crouch Jr. as a mistreated, misjudged, and misguided youth sentenced by his father to life in prison. Yet, he wasn't alone in suffering the consequences of this action. Crouch Sr.'s sentencing of his son begins the downfall of his own aspiration – that of becoming the next Minister of Magic. We have to ask: who paid more for the deception, father or son? In this case, Crouch Sr. did, by losing a promising career in the Ministry of Magic and ultimately losing his life to his only offspring. What inspired Crouch Jr. to dabble in the Dark Arts? Would his home life have led him down the path of the Dark Order?

Crouch Sr.'s love of power and position caused him to ignore his family, including his own son. By doing so, he pushed Crouch Jr. away from a more positive lifestyle, and directly into one ruled by prejudice and destruction. Upon the completion of Book 4, we learn that there may be valid motivation for disowning his son. We see the dark and sinister side of Crouch Jr. (who borders on crazy at times) when he interrogates Harry after Voldemort's rebirthing. We hear about Crouch Jr.'s lengthy infatuation with Voldemort's evil past and how much Crouch Jr. relates to that past by seeing parallels in their backgrounds, "*Both of us suffered the indignity, of being named after those fathers. And both of us had the pleas-*

ure...of killing our fathers to ensure the continued rise of the Dark Order!" {p596} He describes how Voldemort wants absolute devotion; his loyalty to the Dark Lord is unquestionable. In fact, Crouch Jr. says he wants nothing more than to risk all for Voldemort's cause, *"to serve him, to prove myself to him."* Voldemort, himself, spoke of his *"... faithful servant at Hogwarts."*{Ch28, p555}

Crouch Jr. was obviously a very talented wizard. In Chapter 28 of Book 4, his father mentioned he had received 12 O.W.L.s. He was smart enough to know what he was doing. In my opinion, I am convinced from the evidence that he has proven to the readers that he was indeed a Death Eater upon entering Azkaban. Otherwise, he would not have been able to *re-enter* his Master's service {B4, Ch33}. The big question is where, when, or how does the love of the Dark Arts blossom in Crouch Jr.'s young life? Crouch Jr. had to be influenced by someone to become a loyal Death Eater. To whom did Crouch Jr. confide his interest in the Dark Arts? It seems safe to say that his father was not his mentor. Crouch Sr. had an intense dislike of Dark Magic, which bordered on hatred for those who practiced it. Harry tells Sirius about Moody's comment, *"Crouch is obsessed with catching Dark Wizards,"* to which Sirius responds, *"I've heard it's become a bit of a mania with him..."* {Ch27}

If Crouch Jr. was influenced by anyone, a close family friend seems to be a likely candidate. While rambling incoherently to Harry and Viktor Krum, Crouch Sr. discloses, *"My wife and son will be arriving shortly, we are attending a concert tonight with Mr. and Mrs. Fudge."*{Ch28, p555} The fact that he had social as well as working relations with the Fudges could be the link to a family friend's influence.

Fudge's "influence" may have extended to Crouch Sr.. Could Fudge have affected Crouch Sr.'s career? This leads us to consider the many "coincidences" that surround Crouch's downfall and displacement from assuming the Minister of Magic position:

1) Crouch Jr. was caught with other Death Eaters while torturing Alice and Frank Longbottom for information.

2) Crouch Sr. sentenced his own son to Azkaban.

3) Crouch Sr. was shuttled sideways into another Ministry position while Fudge took over as the new Minister of Magic.

4) Fudge was in the Magical Catastrophes Department and first at the scene of Peter Pettigrew's "murder".

Was there something going on to ensure the failure of the Crouches and the success of the Dark Order? All these coincidences seem to point a finger towards Cornelius Fudge, so you have to wonder if he could be a Death Eater, or at least highly sympathetic to their cause (see discussion on Judge Fudge).

Fudge's close relationship with the Crouch family allows Crouch Jr. to see the power, position, and money that can be gained by aligning oneself with Voldemort's inner circle. The close relationship between Fudge and Crouch Sr. is one possibility for the beginning of Crouch Jr.'s fall into the Dark Order. A second possibility occurs during Crouch Jr.'s school years. Crouch Jr. may have attended Hogwarts at the same time as Severus Snape, and the gang of students that later became known as Death Eaters. *"Snape ... was part of a gang of Slytherins who nearly all turned out to be Death Eaters."* {Book 4, Ch. 27, p531} Since we know that most of the Dark wizards and witches were in Slytherin, we may be able to place Crouch Jr. in Slytherin House during the same time as Snape and company. Could Crouch have been in Slytherin? If so, Crouch Jr.'s placement into Slytherin would surely have disappointed his father and may have been the catalyst for their estrangement. No matter what, it would seem they are approximately the same age, so they could have attended Hogwarts simultaneously.

All of these negative influences on Crouch Jr.'s life could have led him to the Dark Arts and ultimately to the Dark Order. Crouch Jr.'s dysfunctional relationship with his father would not have created a positive home life in which to grow up. Instead, it created not only a hatred for his father but the desperate desire to be the antithesis of him.

Lord Voldemort's quest to rid the wizard community of Mudbloods is leading to the demise of pure-blood families. The Dark Order's members are consumed by evil and hatred for those unlike themselves. Do they not realize that Voldemort is destroying the very bloodlines they claim to preserve? The incapacitating evil and hatred that Voldemort inspires is also destroying their community. It affects everyone, and we see how it even caused a talented son from a prominent wizard family to go bad.

ADDITIONAL SLEUTHING NOTES

* Can we be sure Crouch Jr. is the "faithful servant" that Voldemort mentions at the gravesite in Book 4? Can we be sure Crouch Jr. was a Dark Wizard before he went to Azkaban?

* Is there a "Dark Order" as Crouch Jr. states in Chapter 35 of Book 4? {p678}

* Did Crouch Sr. hate Dark Wizards with a passion, or could he have been over-reacting to cover for his true nature? Was Crouch Jr.'s father his mentor? If Crouch Sr. was not a Dark Wizard, and we know Hogwarts only teaches defenses-it doesn't train kids how to do the spells, then how did he learn the Imperius Curse in order to use it on his son? {B4, Ch 35, p685}

* Was Crouch's pure-blood family also an elitist family? If so, could Crouch Jr.'s mother have been a Death Eater?

✳ KNIGHTS OF WALPURGIS ✳

CINDY ERIC ✳ NEW CLUES FORUM ✳ WWW.DESIGNERPOTIONS.COM
AUSTRALIA (*UK Edition*), AGE 25

Inspiration for this Discussion

Ever since I found out that the Death Eaters used to be known as the Knights of Walpurgis, I have been extremely interested in their past. This essay attempts to shine a light on what they were, and why they have become what they are today.

🦉 12

> **"...in here is the history of the Death Eaters ... which were once called something different - they were called the Knights of Walpurgis..."**

—JK Rowling,
BBC Newsnight, 19 June 2003

ETYMOLOGY OF THE KNIGHTS

Knights of Walpurgis is a play on the words W*alpurgis (K)night*:

> "Walpurgis Night *(in German folklore) the night of April 30 (May Day's eve), when witches meet on the Brocken Mountain and hold revels with the Devil...*"
>
> (Oxford Dictionary of Phrase & Fable)

Brocken Mountain is also known for a natural phenomenon called the "Brocken Spectre", in which a rainbow-like shadow is cast onto the clouds by a person standing on the mountain.

Dumbledore defeated the Dark Wizard Grindelwald in 1945, which coincides with the end of World War II in Muggle history. That makes the German connection to the Knights of Walpurgis interesting – because we *know* JK Rowling has referenced Nazis through the Grindelwald defeat. She has also stated in an interview that Lord Voldemort is "like Hitler". [1] Another "coincidence", connecting pure-blood wizards to Nazis and World War II, is the SS (the Nazi special police force). Those are, of course, the initials of both Salazar Slytherin, founder of Slytherin house, and Severus Snape, Slytherin's current head of house.

What does Walpurgis Night tell us about the Knights of Walpurgis? It reinforces what we already know about the Death Eaters—that they are a closed, secret society. But when were the Knights of Walpurgis founded? Why were they created? And by whom? What made them join Lord Voldemort and take on a new name? To even begin to formulate a plausible theory it is necessary to go right to the very beginning (at least, the beginning of what we know…).

THE SALAZAR SLYTHERIN CONNECTION

In Book 2, Professor Binns (who is only interested in the honest facts, thank you very much) gives us quite a bit of information about Salazar Slytherin. Here are my thoughts on what he covered:

1. Salazar was one of the greatest wizards of the age.
   Is there a parallel to Voldemort and Dumbledore?

2. Salazar helped build a school castle, far removed from Muggles, symbolising what the four founders were feeling at the time—defensive. It was built to educate wizard children as well as shield its occupants from the persecution that witches and wizards were suffering at the hands of Muggles.

Castles were also built for war, so will we perhaps get to see Hogwarts in use as a fortress in future books?

3. Salazar did not trust Muggle-borns.

His fears were not unfounded, considering that the magical world was being persecuted by Muggles during his time; he most likely believed that Muggle-borns would stay true to their ancestry, and end up working as spies inside Hogwarts, crumbling the foundations of the castle school from within.

4. Salazar realised that he was fighting a losing battle, as none of the other three founders agreed with him, so he left.

Where did he go? What became of one of the greatest wizards of the age after that?

Is it possible that, after leaving Hogwarts, Salazar Slytherin rounded up the Knights (if they already existed), or else other witches and wizards who shared his ideals, banding them together to form the Knights of Walpurgis? But why the title of Knight?

Let's look for hints in the meaning of the word, Knight:

Etymology: Middle English, from Old English cniht *man-at-arms, boy, servant; akin to Old High German* kneht *youth, military follower*

Date: before 12th century

1 a (1): a mounted man-at-arms serving a feudal superior; especially: a man ceremonially inducted into special military rank usually after completing service as page and squire." (Merriam-Webster Dictionary, 11th Ed.)

From this meaning, it is possible to theorise that the Knights of Walpurgis may have followed Slytherin (as youthful military inductees). They probably also followed Grindelwald, and they are now following Lord Voldemort. This is important because, no matter what name they may take, they will always exist and they will always find a powerful leader to serve, who shares their pure-blood ideology. The Knights of Walpurgis/Death Eaters will live on, even if Lord Voldemort does not.

It is like the opposite side of a coin – the antithesis to the Order of the Phoenix, another society of dedicated members. Professor Dumbledore founded the Order only to fight against Lord Voldemort and the Death Eaters, while the Death Eaters are much older with apparently deeper roots than the Order of the Phoenix.

THEORY

So here is my little theory, based on mere crumbs of evidence:

The Knights of Walpurgis could have been founded around one thousand years ago to protect witches and wizards from Muggle persecution. However, once wizarding society managed to convince Muggles that magic didn't exist, the services of the Knights would have been no longer required. The Knights maybe did not share that belief, thinking Muggle-borns might still betray them, and decided to continue their work by cleansing the wizarding world of Muggle-borns. In continuing their war with Muggles, who no longer believed in magic, these Knights could have been the cause of much suffering for witches and wizards.

The Knights of Walpurgis were most likely very active during the time of Grindelwald. So, when Professor Dumbledore defeated Grindelwald, the Knights would have needed to go into hiding, just as they did when Lord Voldemort disappeared. Meanwhile, Lord Voldemort was undergoing Dark transformations {B2, Ch18 *UK*} and most likely knew about the Knights of Walpurgis, waiting for another powerful leader to lead them to victory. Lord Voldemort probably recruited those modern-day Knights to work for him. It is very likely that it was Voldemort who changed their title to Death Eaters (much more fitting for someone who wants to escape death, wants to terrorise, and is openly Dark). Then he branded them all with his own personal insignia—the Dark Mark. I am also willing to bet 1000 Galleons that down through history, the Malfoys' ancestors were all Knights of Walpurgis, and that is how Lucius Malfoy became such a prominent Death Eater (remember - he led the battle at the Department of Mysteries in Book 5).

Why Did They Fail Their Mission?

So, if the Death Eaters are the descendents of this knightly Order, then why did they perform so atrociously at the Department of Mysteries?

1. They were not allowed to let the prophecy break.
2. They were supremely overconfident (probably not believing that a group of children was capable of causing them any harm).
3. Dumbledore and the Order arrived.
4. Lucius told them to kill if necessary, not to go on a murderous rampage.

To summarise, I believe they failed because they were fighting children. Some of them have children of their own, and know that it is wrong to kill a child; others just did not take the children seriously enough.

We know from what Moody told Harry when showing him his old photo of the members of the Order of the Phoenix, that Death Eaters are ruthless fighters. We also saw this first-hand when they were fighting against the Order at the Department of Mysteries prior to Dumbledore's arrival. Moody was defeated, Kingsley Shacklebolt was defeated, Tonks was defeated, and Sirius Black was killed.

In spite of their failure on this mission, they are clearly still a strong force and a threat – and we really don't know how many more of them are secretly out there....

──────────────── ADDITIONAL SLEUTHING NOTES ────────────────

* St. Walpurga, where the Walpurgis name originated, is a Halloween-like Christian celebration that involved making a lot of noise (including bangs) – could JKR's reference go back to that as well?

* Evil memberships are often old because they need to keep recruiting and fighting to exist, while those who fight evil don't need to keep active unless there is a present danger – so, how well-prepared is Dumbledore's Order compared to the "Knights"?

* Yes – why did the Death Eaters fail their mission? Is it possible that Snape could somehow have been responsible for the Death Eaters' downfall?

[1] JRK Interview on the BBC, Fall 2000

Wacky Weasleys

✳ Is Percy a Stupid Git? ✳

RYAN McHUGH ✳ NC, "IRISHWIZARD"
USA (*US Edition*), AGE 17

Inspiration for this Discussion

*The magical world of Harry Potter is fascinating, not to mention inspirational. Who wouldn't want to live in a world filled with magic, mind-boggling creatures, and butterbeer to the brim? I began reading the **Harry Potter** series about three years ago, and within no time, I had read all the books and wanted more. When I finally began to get involved with Harry Potter sleuthing, I joined the MuggleNet New Clues forum and soon became a moderator. With help from other sleuths, I began the research to find out what truly was wrong with ever-perfect Percy Weasley in Book 5. Had JK Rowling prepared us for why Percy was acting strangely? I intended to find out.*

HANDFUL

"I am a Prefect!" *"Yes Minister, coming!!!"* *"Ministry business."* Yes, you guessed it: these are some of the most well-known phrases uttered by none other than Percy Weasley.

It was a shock when we read that Percy yelled at his parents and moved out of the house. This certainly was not the pompous, yet caring son and brother we all knew, was it? He had always been so strict and rule-abiding, addressing his parents very formally (and respectfully) as "Father" and "Mother." How could "perfect Percy" change so much in such a short span of time?

What I seek to explain is why Percy has changed—or *has* he? Doesn't it seem a bit odd for a role-model son, who has never (that we know of) gotten so much as one point taken from his school House, to all of a sudden lash out at his loving parents? Have there been any hints as to how it could have happened? In analyzing Percy's motives, it's important to remember that JKR assured us Percy is working on his "own accord" {World Book Day Chat: March , 2004}, so we'll have to consider that Percy's just a big power-hungry git. We'll also consider the clues leading up to this.

Let's give the time turner a few clicks and go back to Book 2, when Harry saw Percy "*deeply immersed in a small and deeply boring book called **Prefects Who Gained Power**.*" According to Ron, "'*Course, he's very ambitious, Percy, he's got it all planned out….He wants to be Minister of Magic.*"{B2, Ch4, p58}

There had already been several occasions where Percy has felt that his position or rank put him above others. When Harry and Ron (Polyjuiced as Goyle and Crabbe) are in the dungeons on their way to find the Slytherin common room, they run into Percy: "*What're you doing down here?*" said Ron in surprise. *Percy looked affronted. "That," he said stiffly, "is none of your business."* {B2, Ch12, p219}

Then in response to Ron's query about Percy wandering around the corridors as well: "*I,*" said Percy, *drawing himself up, "am a prefect. Nothing's about to attack me."*

When Percy gets his Ministry job, he is clearly caught up in the "importance" of his position right from the start. "*Just don't get him onto the subject of his boss. Mr. Crouch…*" and then, there is no stopping him. According to Ron, "He's obsessed…"{B4, Ch5} Harry says Percy "idolized" Crouch.{B4, Ch7}

Fudge or Voldemort's henchmen positioned in the Ministry would have no trouble brainwashing the git.

We know Percy is embarrassed by his family's lowly situation. But would he turn on everyone he loves and respects—including Dumbledore? Think back to another young man, hungry for power, whom we met in Book 1. We were told that Quirrell was "gullible" and that's how Lord Voldemort got to him. *"A wizard—young, foolish, and gullible—wandered across my path in the forest I had made my home....he was easy to bend to my will... I took possession of his body, to supervise him closely as he carried out my orders."* {B4, Ch33, p654}

I challenge anyone to convince me Percy's not gullible. In Book 4, he believed anything Mr. Crouch told him without questioning, as if it were gospel, even though Crouch was barely aware of who Weatherby (uhh...Percy) was. Percy switched this loyalty to Fudge in Book 5, denouncing his own family in the process. It is interesting that Percy is originally promoted in Book 4. The Ministry was in a bind, yet, why would a junior member of the Ministry continually be given so much responsibility and an even greater promotion as Fudge's "right-hand man?" Keep in mind that Quirrell willingly let Voldemort in, and was working of his own accord.

Think back to the summer between Harry's fourth and fifth years; Lord Voldemort is back again on the loose, and his followers are slowly returning to him. We know that he has spies inside and outside the Ministry. During the summer, I am sure that Percy must have been busy working at the Ministry, working long hours into the night, due to Crouch's death, and rumors of He-Who-Must-Not-Be-Named's return from the "dead." He would have been an easy target for recruitment by the people Voldemort has working within the Ministry. Why would Voldemort use Percy? Percy is a follower—not a leader—no matter how badly he tries to be one; he just can't do it. But that makes him a good candidate for Voldemort. The Ministry has identified Percy as a hard worker...who will do *anything* for a higher-ranking person (and fall all over himself getting it done). The question is... is he aware that he is being sucked in? Is he being stupid, or is he conscious of what he has become?

Now that Percy is the assistant for the Minister of Magic, I'm sure there are tons of spies for Lord Voldemort trying to get their claws on a person in a position like that. Voldemort wants to get as deep into the Ministry as he can, and who better to choose than Percy Weasley—Assistant to Cornelius Fudge, and someone who rubs shoulders with Harry Potter?

The question keeps getting asked regarding who will be the next Minister of Magic, and JKR said on her website that Arthur Weasley won't be it. Could you see Percy as Minister? I bet Voldemort would like to.

In the end, the only person who truly knows what is wrong with Percy is JK Rowling. But do keep this in mind.... There are so many things we do not clearly know that could affect Percy's development, but I don't expect him to just come back home, his tail between his legs. What is going to happen to Percy? One way or the other, I feel it will not be good.

————————————— ADDITIONAL SLEUTHING NOTES —————————————

✴ How do we know Percy is gullible – would a certain rat ring a bell? Is Percy even aware of what happened with his former pet, Scabbers, including who Wormtail is?

✴ In Book 2, were Percy and Penelope in the dungeons only for a lover's rendezvous?{Ch18, p340} Was his hanging out by Slytherin a hint at his "ambitious" side? Where is Penelope now? Where are her loyalties?

✴ Could Percy really be as gullible as Quirrell? Could Percy have even been on his way to becoming Death Eater? Voldemort is probably not inhabiting Percy when we've seen him (Harry's scar never hurt around Percy), but it raises the question that if you let Lord Voldemort in willingly (like Quirrell), does it hurt like it did with Harry?

✴ What are the chances that the return of Voldemort will knock some sense back into Percy? The Sorting Hat put Percy in Gryffindor – should we assume the Sorting Hat is always right?*

*World Book Day chat March, 2004
  Arianna: "Can we believe everything the sorting hat says?"
  JKR: "The Sorting Hat is certainly sincere."

✦ Dragons and Dungeons: Charlie and Bill Weasley ✦

New Clues Forum, "Alexa"
USA (*US Edition*), Age 40(ish)

Inspiration for this Discussion

I believe the *Harry Potter* books come with instructions. You will find many instances of wordplay, which is surely designed to clue us into JKR's tricky style. For example, when Sirius Black says "OUT," he means, "Get out of the kitchen," but to Kreacher it meant, "Get out of the house." In Book 4, Dumbledore shows us his trick for interpreting ambiguous information as he attempts to sort through his own clues. He stirs his thoughts in a special stone basin explaining, *"It becomes easier to spot patterns and links, you see, when they are in this form."* {B4, Ch30, p597} The MuggleNet board gives me my own Pensieve. I get the chance to sort through my findings with people who possess a formidable knowledge of the books. Since theorizing can be hazardous to one's credibility, I just highlight links to see what is going on, which is the best way to get a sense of where the series is going. I decided to look at the links between Bill and Charlie Weasley and see how they connect to the septology as a whole.

 HANDFUL

In the beginning, it is easy to brush over Bill and Charlie Weasley as support players whom we'll never see. We find out that Bill works at Gringotts Wizarding Bank and Charlie works with dragons. Interestingly, those are two tantalizing plot lines that have been sustained throughout all five books and yet, haven't really been played out—a sign that Bill and Charlie will be back in a big way. How? Looking at their connections to other characters and events will show what has been going on with them since early on in Book 1. They may not be directly involved, but these characters form a template that touches on most of the major subplots.

Just as Bill, Ron and Percy resemble each other, so do Charlie and the twins. From that, we can draw parallels and make some assumptions.

Appearance

Their descriptions tell a tail…um… I mean tale.[1] Bill resembles Ron and Percy, except he is very cool. He is tall, and has long red hair that he ties in a ponytail. He wears an earring with a fang dangling from it and boots made of dragon hide. The most powerful wizard, Dumbledore, has long (formerly auburn) hair and a beard, and the statue of Salazar Slytherin has a beard that actually reaches his feet. Ginny remarks that her mum is old fashioned for thinking Bill should cut his hair, since it is not nearly as long as Dumbledore's.{B4, Ch5, p62 US}

Could long hair, as with Samson, relate to strength or power in wizards? Samson and Delilah's parable is one of blindness (literally and figuratively) and treachery. Due to his amazing strength, Samson is unbeatable. The "scarlet woman", Delilah, repeatedly asks him how he can be defeated. He eventually confides in her that his strength is in his hair and she then betrays him to people who cut it. The hair is symbolic of his consecration to God and after it is cut, he is shorn of his strength. He is taken prisoner and his eyes are put out, but he later regains his strength when his hair grows back, and defeats those who bound him.

I am wondering if it could somehow affect Bill's power if Molly ever cut his hair? Of course, in Bill's case it's his mother, not his girlfriend, who wants his hair cut. Harry notices Fleur eyeing Bill over her mother's shoulder and we get the impression long hair and earrings with fangs don't offend her. In fact, Fleur and Bill are now working together, and we can see the goblins plot line will be important during the war.

Molly's boggart, or deepest fear, includes an image of Bill spread-eagled on his back with wide-opened, empty eyes—much like Cedric after Wormtail killed him off in Book 4. She may be mistaken in thinking old-fashioned conformity will keep Bill from harm. The already-short-haired Percy seems to be the one blinded and bound by mistakes, seeking power through Fudge rather than obeying his father. (I think if we ever see Percy with longer hair, it'll be a sign he is coming around.)

While Bill appears to be more image-conscious, Charlie is definitely an outdoors kind of guy. He is described as "shorter and stockier", and has a "broad, good-natured face" resembling Molly's side of the family. We can see how the twins take after him. Charlie has callused hands and by looking at his face, Harry can tell that he spends all of his time outside. Charlie's freckled arms are muscular, marred by a shining burn that is implied was received from one of the Dragons he had encountered.{Ch5, p52} So far, we know nothing about the females in Charlie's life.

Based on appearance, the two oldest Weasley boys seem to be complete opposites but both are brave in what they do for a career and both are greatly admired by the rest of their family.

PERCEPTIONS

The other characters' attitudes towards Bill and Charlie say a lot.

Ron (who doesn't respect Percy) looks up to both of them and feels as if he has to fill their shoes. Bill was Head Boy and Charlie was a Quidditch captain. These are two of Ron's deepest desires as is reflected in the Mirror of Erised.

Professor McGonagall compares Harry's Seeker talent to Charlie Weasley. She was obviously impressed with Charlie.

Percy, in Book 2, talks about Charlie when helping Harry choose subjects for the next year. He points out that Charlie picked Care of Magical Creatures over Divination. We also know that Hagrid considers Charlie to be "great with animals" {B1, Ch8, p141}

Ginny, the youngest Weasley, absolutely adores her brother Bill. When Harry rescues Ginny in the Chamber of Secrets, her main concern is being expelled because she had wanted to come to Hogwarts ever since Bill did. {B2, Ch17, p323} Because Ginny is smart, practical and is turning out to have the same wizarding potential as the rest of her family, her opinion carries a lot of weight.

Even the twins don't pick on Bill and Charlie – which translates into respect.

THE CAREERS OF BILL AND CHARLIE WEASLEY

We don't know much about Charlie's job in Romania except that he is working with dragons. During the Triwizard competition at Hogwarts, it is Charlie who brings in the dragons that the Champions are meant to fight. What we do know is, every time the subject of Dragons comes up, Charlie's somehow involved. It is Charlie, of course, who takes Baby Norbert from Hagrid in Book 1, since it is illegal for Hagrid to keep the little tyke. The whole Weasley family is becoming more central to the plot (if that is possible), and Voldemort does use beasts for his cause. One way or the other, I see Charlie having an important role.

When Ron says in Book 2 that the Chamber of Secrets "rings a sort of bell" he claims that it "might've been Bill" who told him. {Ch9, p145} What would Bill know about the Chamber of Secrets? His most obvious connection is to Gringotts, gold and pyramids. Bill is a curse-breaker in Egypt for Gringotts Wizarding Bank and pyramids have chambers that are cursed by old Egyptian wizards. He also is working for the goblins, who everyone seems to think are pivotal in the upcoming war. {B5, Ch5, p85} He is currently holding down a desk job, which keeps him closer to the Order (and Fleur). In Book 4, after the Triwizard competition ends, Mrs. Weasley and Bill wait in a side chamber, off the Great Hall. I think this is meant to point out symbolic parallels—I wonder what curses still need to be broken in the Chamber of Secrets?

THE FUTURE

Not only do the two brothers have successful careers abroad, but they also do their part for the Order of the Phoenix. Charlie tries to contact foreign wizards in Romania and Bill attempts to win over the Goblins. I can't think of Bill and Charlie as anything but "good guys". Both of their areas of expertise will most likely come in handy during the Second War and most likely during an event connected with the Chamber of Secrets (I really think we'll see inside it again).

We all wonder how crucial the Weasleys will turn out to be. Bill and Charlie must be powerful wizards to handle fire-breathing dragons and to break ancient curses in the pyramids of Egypt. Even repairing the tables that they smashed for fun at the Burrow in Book 4 barely took any effort. One thing seems clear from these two Weasley brothers—Weasleys are leaders, with or without long red hair.

⁎ ADDITIONAL SLEUTHING NOTES ⁎

* ✳ Does Charlie have scars from dragons because no wizard medics were nearby when he was injured, or was there something about the dragon injury, itself, that prevented full healing?

* ✳ We know that Ginny has secretly picked things up from Fred and George who didn't even want her around – could she be have gotten any help from Bill, her role model?

* ✳ Is it possible that Bill has "friends" among the goblins? Does he speak Gobbledegook? If the goblins side with Voldemort, what will happen to Bill and his job (not to mention the entire wizarding economy)?

---

1 Galadriel Waters. *New Clues to Harry Potter: Book 5*. Niles, IL: 2003

FRED AND GEORGE: THE ORDER'S SECRET WEAPON?

MARIA RICO ∗ NC, "MARIA"
USA (*US Edition*), AGE 17

Inspiration for this Discussion

I decided to write about twins Fred and George Weasley because they've always kept me laughing and I think they deserve a chance in the spotlight. To be honest, they aren't my favorite characters, but I still feel attached to them, maybe because deep down I'd like to be as carefree as they are and love life as much as they do. We've all wanted to toss out the rulebook at some point in our lives, and they do it every day. I really wanted to reflect their personalities in my essay, so I've added some humor, of course. ;) Thanks to my friends on the New Clues Forum; they were really the ones who inspired me to write this. I've taken my time making sure this essay is all I want it to be, so happy reading and enjoy!

 HANDFUL

Fred and George – our favorite twins, masters of mischief, kings of laughter…secret weapons for the Order of the Phoenix? OK, maybe not, but they could be very useful. They have the one thing that no one else in the Order possesses in quantities enough to weaken You-Know-Who: *laughter.*

It's becoming increasingly obvious that Harry's strength comes from love and that is the one thing Voldemort cannot stand. Laughter isn't exactly love, but it is happiness. The twins are capable of making anyone laugh (not that I expect them to tickle Voldything to death). But soon enough, a lot of people are going to need laughter, as Harry wisely stated when he handed over the Triwizard winnings to the twins.

Fred and George might be more useful than they seem, for not only are they a source of laughter, but they are extremely clever. They have invented things that require considerable talent as wizards. And those inventing skills could come in handy. They have experimented with a lot of magic—some of it very powerful. Invisibility cloaks, for example, are very rare, yet the twins have created Headless Hats, which make your head invisible. Who's to say they can't invent Bodyless Clothes? (Maybe Moody can use them as a replacement for his lost invisibility cloak :p)

The twins are known for their obsession with jokes and mischief, rather than seemingly more important things, like helping out in the Order. (It's not for their lack of trying, though.) However, they have been very busy over the last two years. They've been making, perfecting, and recently testing their merchandise. Given what we've been introduced to so far, the twins have created quite a few items:

Fake Wands *(Laughter is only one spell away!)*…change into a rubber chicken or mouse whenever a witch/wizard attempts to do magic with them.

Canary Creams *(They make you chirp with every bite!)*…temporarily turn the eater into a large canary.

Ton-Tongue Toffees *(Tons of fun for your tongue!)*…make your tongue grow and grow and grow…

Extendable Ears *(Overhearing just got better!)*…can extend into other rooms and allow you to overhear conversations.

Weasley's Wildfire Whiz-Bangs *(The Bigger the Better!)*… large and very noisy fireworks that are very difficult to extinguish.

Headless Hats (*Laugh your head off!*)…make your head invisible when you put them on.

Portable Swamps (*A Bog-full of fun!*)…are exact replicas of a swamp that can be placed anywhere including indoors…ideal for pet toads.

Skiving Snackboxes (*Have a snack attack – skive off a class!*)…include Nosebleed Nougats, Fever Fudge, Blood Blisterpods, Puking Pastilles and Fainting Fancies (not advised to be tried all at once). Skive off classes with the illness of your choice! Take one end of the candy and it makes you sick. When you leave to go to the hospital wing, take the other piece and voila! You skive off the class of your choice.

The twins have proven to be capable wizards. Even Hermione is impressed by their achievements (at times). They want to help with the Order and protect their family (*especially* if it means they get to eavesdrop). And, they'll find their way around *anyone* who stands in their way. For example, in Book 5, the twins have been making guinea pigs out of Gryffindors—by testing experimental charms on them. Hermione threatens the twins by promising to tell Molly what they are "up to".{Ch13, p253} Knowing that Hermione would be a problem, I think they took matters into their own hands.

Our trio had been assigned to look up the properties of moonstone, an ingredient for the Draught of Peace. This is a potion that calms anxiety and soothes agitation, but too much of the ingredients can put the drinker into a heavy sleep.{Ch13, p252} When Hermione became upset with the twins, she decided to go to bed, but first left some hats out and covered them with "rubbish" (part of her S.P.E.W. campaign, of course). The rubbish *could have* been notes on the potion, which could've easily been picked up by Fred and George and given them the idea to use the potion on Hermione (spiked her butterbeer) so they could test their products on first-years without any problems.

The day of the Quidditch tryouts, when Harry comes back into the common room, Hermione is asleep in a corner, holding a bottle of butterbeer. {Ch13, p276} Coincidentally, there are first-years who have been trying Nosebleed Nougats in the room, but in her condition, Hermione can't object. Now, we know from Book 3 that the twins sneak out to Hogsmeade through a secret passage and come back with butterbeer whenever Gryffindors have a celebration in the common room, so we can be fairly sure that they were the butterbeer providers in this occasion. They also entertain the crowd by juggling butterbeer bottles (usually, the repetition of something means that it is a clue).{Ch13, p277} It is very likely that the twins would have done this, especially if their plans were threatened. If they will do that to Hermione, think of what they could do to their enemies!

There's also been some speculation about the twins being capable of time travel. In Book 4, during the Quidditch World Cup, the twins bet with Bagman that Viktor Krum would catch the snitch, but Ireland would win anyway. Normally, this is a very risky wager. What a *coincidence* that the bet happened to come true! It's easy to think that the twins went forward in time and saw who won the Cup, I mean they're not exactly afraid of breaking the rules, especially if it is for profit. If they really have managed to get a glimpse at the future, that could be useful for the Order, since they'll be able to see Voldemort's attack before he even does it—the trouble is that they wouldn't be allowed to because they'd break a million wizard laws doing it! Book 5 doesn't provide any overt clues as to the twins actually going back or forward in time, but we do get a glimpse of something very important in the Department of Mysteries: the Time Room. The room showed that there are other ways to turn back time besides using a Time-Turner, so it's very possible that the twins have managed it.

Either way, the twins have shown that they are willing to do anything to achieve their goals. Ginny says in Book 5, *"The thing about growing up with Fred and George is that you sort of start thinking anything's possible if you've got enough nerve,"* {Ch29, p655} which does show how bold and daring they really are. They also, however, are driven partly by money and I'm not sure this could lead to good things. They're really ambitious, very much like Percy, though I doubt they're willing to betray their family like he did.

Nevertheless, the twins have proven to be very capable and talented wizards.

The twins' talent could be useful in the fight against Voldy. The Headless Hats might be of use for stealth, since they work like an invisibility cloak, especially if they can also create clothes that make your body invisible so you don't have to worry about your cloak slipping off (like what happened to Harry's infamous head at Hogsmeade). Their fireworks could be used as a distraction and the Portable Swamp is an easy way to put distance between two people—just imagine being chased by a Death Eater who all of a sudden finds himself in the middle of a swamp! Extendable Ears can also be helpful, obviously to overhear conversations. Bear in mind that the twins are out of school, and in the next book they will be 18 – which means they could now join the Order. They could be very useful as the Order's own creators of weapons or other items. Inventing is the twins' area of expertise (plus, they probably wouldn't be useful to the Order in any other way). They aren't interested in boring hexing and jinxing, and I doubt Molly would allow them to fight anyway.

While the twins' products provide wonderful jokes and entertainment, there are two things that their inventions have that are more important: (1) the talent behind actually making the products, and (2) their uses in the fight against Voldy. The twins use all sorts of ingredients and spells to make their products— some are even dangerous or illegal, such as venomous Tentacula seeds, wart cap powder, doxy eggs and doxy venom. Not only have the twins managed to actually get hold of these items, they've also managed to overcome the poison in some of the products and use it to their advantage. Most impressively, the twins have never been hurt (as far as we know) during the testing of their products. The worst they've encountered has been boils in…unlikely places. This makes me wonder whether they have become immune to certain poisons, or if they've found cures for illnesses without even realizing it. I guess testing products without knowing what will happen can be considered brave, which would explain why they're Gryffindors (or it could just be that they're really stupid ☺).

If the twins really do join in the fight against Voldy, it will be very interesting. Voldemort and his Death Eaters only know how to fight through deceit, blackmail and evil. The twins could provide an interesting turn of events because they are fighting him with things that are silly, happy, and joyful. It's almost like fighting a boggart. When you laugh at a boggart, you take the fear away and the thing you are afraid of becomes funny, giving a person the security and motivation to fight the thing they fear—in this case, Voldemort and the Death Eaters.

It is my opinion we can all expect great things from the twins. Their love for life and happiness are very powerful. We've learned that the twins are capable of finding their way around any obstacle, that they will especially fight back if something they love is threatened, and that they are clever and capable of doing just about anything they put their minds and hearts to do. So, we'd better keep an eye open for Fred and George— their part in the books isn't over. Whether it's time traveling, creating weapons, opening more joke shops or joining the Order, I'm sure that they will continue to be just as much fun. You didn't expect *them* to Apparate quietly into the background, now did you? Of course, we're not sure they can do anything quietly.

─────────────── ADDITIONAL SLEUTHING NOTES ───────────────

* Fred and George are always just skirting the law when acquiring and using their inventions – will they be able to keep out of legal problems?

* Is Ginny right – that with the twins, "anything's possible"? If so, do they have this effect on everyone? …And what does she mean by "anything"?

* What new project are the twins working on (a secret weapon?) The twins are working on potentially dangerous products – should we be worried that something could happen to one or both of them while doing their experiments – similar to what happened to Luna's mum?

THE TWINS: A BALANCING ACT

NINA KHOSLA * CHAMBER OF SECRETS FORUM
USA (*US Edition*), AGE 16

Inspiration for this Discussion

As I was leafing through and skimming my Harry Potter books one early Sunday morning (not an unusual occurrence), I began to notice Fred and George Weasley's reactions to the people around them. I noticed that as funny and silly as they are, they also are very serious. They care deeply for the people they love, which creates an interesting dynamic between their "silly" characters and "serious" values. Here, I wanted to look at that more closely. I started by searching for every reference to the Weasley twins in all the books. From there, I was able to examine their interactions and then draw conclusions about them. Those conclusions are presented in this discussion.

 HANDFUL

The Weasley twins, Fred and George, are the most hilarious characters in the Harry Potter series. They entertain us with portable swamps and rubber chicken wands, and they are the life of the Gryffindor common room. On the other hand, they also have a serious side.

The twins are extremely protective of the people they love. When Voldemort's snake bites their dad in Book 5, they are very incensed about not being allowed to go to him immediately. When Lucius Malfoy insults Mr. Weasley, one of the twins eggs his father on, "*Get him, Dad!*" {B2, Ch4, p62 *US*} The family insult hits particularly hard, and is not something the twins are going to take lying down. It's not just their direct relations who they defend. At the end of Book 4, the twins know Draco is up to no good; the Dark Lord had just risen after all, and they are particularly watchful over Harry. On the train ride home, Malfoy and his goons approach Harry, Ron and Hermione in order to harass them. The trio hits the bullies with curses, but they find out they aren't the only ones doing the zapping—Fred and George are also attacking them with curses. "*Thought we'd see what those three were up to,*" Fred says, as George "*… was careful to tread on Malfoy as he followed Fred inside.*" {Ch37, p730} In Book 5, when Zacharias Smith doubts Harry's abilities, Fred and George threaten to clean out his ears for him—or any part of his body—with "*a long and lethal-looking metal instrument*"{Ch16, p343} from Zonko's. The twins won't stand for anyone hurting members of their family, their close friends, or even talking smack* about Harry!

In a reflection of the Weasleys as a whole, family is very important to the twins. They participate in family events, such as watching Bill and Charlie smashing tables together, or finishing off a twilight dinner with Filibuster fireworks for the family's enjoyment. The two are also very social outside of their family. At Hogwarts, the duo spends time with Harry, Hermione, and Ron in the Gryffindor common room, along with their sibling, Ginny. They play their favorite game, Exploding Snap, challenging Harry and Ron to a few games of it in Book 2, and on the train ride home in Book 4. They also have several snowball

---

* "Talking Smack" (v) is American slang for putting down or insulting someone, usually behind his or her back.

fights around Christmas during Harry and Ron's first and fourth years at Hogwarts.

At the same time, the twins like to work diligently by themselves on their projects. They're very ambitious people; actually succeeding in their greatest dream at the end of Book 5—their own joke shop. We can see their determination in moments when they are quietly conversing between themselves in the common room or during their ongoing experiments at the Burrow (in spite of the various explosions that would deter anyone else).

The twins know when to be loyal to their family, and when it's okay to differ. This comes in handy—especially when they face differences in opinions from loved ones (Mrs. Weasley and Hermione, in particular). They are respectful of others' feelings and try to accommodate them, but still follow their beliefs on what's best for them. They decide to stay in school their seventh year because they "...*didn't think Mum could take us leaving school early, not on top of Percy turning out to be the world's biggest prat.*" {Ch12, p227}

But what about Percy? In Harry's fifth year, we are well aware that no one in the Weasley family is very happy with Percy. The twins have picked on Percy for years—ever since he became a prefect. They steal his badge at Christmas in Harry's first year, and in Book 3 at the Leaky Cauldron, they enchant it to say, "Bighead Boy". They also make fun of him and play practical jokes on him, such as sending dragon dung to his inbox at the Ministry in Chapter 5 of Book 4. Actually, their picking on him really begins when he starts taking his success and ambition too seriously—when Percy seems to value his career more than his family. Through Book 1, they try to keep Percy in balance, but eventually they realize it isn't helping—George has to remind Percy "*Christmas is a time for family*". {Ch12, p203}

I am sure that part of the reason Fred and George give Ron a really hard time about his becoming a prefect is because they fear that Ron's successes might go to his head, as well, and further upset the Weasley family. They fear having another Percy in the family. This is why their initial reaction to Ron's becoming a prefect is to roll their eyes and ridicule him. {B5, Ch9, p161-165} They try their absolute best to keep Ron's ego at bay.

Fred and George also like to poke fun at Ron and give him a hard time simply because older brothers will do that. Teasing Ron while de-gnoming the Weasleys' garden in Book 2 and teasing him about his Quidditch playing skills in Chapter 4 of Book 5 are all part of the job description of being older brothers. But don't let it fool you—they're really supportive and caring about Ron. When Crookshanks chases Scabbers across the common room, in Chapter 8 of Book 3, George is the only one who leaps for him. You see, they just want Ron to become independent and deal with his own problems. They don't jump to his defense every time he is in trouble—like in Book 5, when Malfoy begins choruses of "Weasley is our king". They want him to be able to defend himself, but they do try to help him out when things get serious. They even try their very best (the best you can expect from the twins) to comfort him in Chapter 13 of Book 3 when he believes Scabbers is dead.

We see that there is a serious side to Fred and George. We also see that they won't tolerate *anyone* being mean, arrogant, or rude toward those they love. This leads me to speculate about what they will do about Percy. Because of their history with Percy, I believe the twins may actually be the most upset and reluctant to let Percy back in to the family now. They were so upset with Percy that they told Mrs. Weasley that "...*Percy's nothing more than a humongous pile of rat droppings.*" {Ch23, p502}

The twins are, all in all, talented, fun-loving, practical, and highly loyal people. They are ambitious, but they absolutely adore their family and keep an amazing balance between family and career. This balance is the key to their personalities. They are goofy, but very loving at the same time. They are ambitious, but loyal. They both want to make sure nothing bad happens to those they care about, that they are happy, and finally that nothing comes between them and splits them up.

And now you have the serious side of Fred and George, which is just as crucial to understanding their characters as their goofiness and ambitions.

Overall, the twins' attitudes towards their loved ones and life are summed up at the end of Chapter 17 in Book 1:

> After Harry's escapade with Voldemort, the twins were really worried about Harry and wanted to send him something to make him feel better, so they came up with the best Gred and Forge treat they could think of... they attempted to send him a toilet seat!

───────────────── ADDITIONAL SLEUTHING NOTES ─────────────────

✴ The Second War is coming and we know that at least one more character is going to die in the next book – how would one of the twins react if something were to happen to the other one?

✴ Is it Love that is behind the locked door in the Department of Mysteries, or could it be Happiness or Emotion? Do the twins have this power?

✴ If Fred and George are so driven by galleons and goals, along with all this love for others, what are the chances that Voldemort can use any of those as a weakness to get to the twins? How vulnerable are they?

Love Potion #9$^3/_4$

✳ WHAT KRUM SAW ✳

MARK PHILLIPS ✳ CoS, "HAWK92"
USA (*US Edition*), AGE 30

Inspiration for this Discussion

Having heard that the Harry and Hermione shippers can't see a forest for the trees and that those of us who are H-H "Pumpkin Pies" base our theories on wishful thinking and over-reading of text, I think that this is long overdue. Now I can almost hear everyone who has been on the Internet forums debating the love aspect groan with pain as we are about to study Hermione's relationship with Fleur, with Krum, and (we'll get there soon enough) with Harry. How about now?

 HANDFUL

In an attempt to take all evidence into consideration, we will begin our analysis with a simple time-line of events that culminates in Hermione's realization of her feelings for Harry.

1. Hermione is disgusted by Fleur's disrespect towards Dumbledore during his welcoming speech. {Book 4, Ch 6, p250 US}

2. The first Rita Skeeter article appears, proclaiming Harry and Hermione to be a couple. {Ch 19, p315 US}

3. Krum visits the library and attempts to work up the courage to talk to Hermione. {Ch 20, p339}

4. Hermione and Krum are introduced as a couple at the Yule Ball. {Ch 23, p413}

5. Hermione is taken as what Krum "will sorely miss". {Ch 25, p463}

6. Krum directly admits his feelings to Hermione. {Ch 26, p504}

7. Hermione seems to ignore Krum when he tries to remind her of his admission and focuses her attention on Harry. {p504}

8. Fleur gives Ron and Harry a kiss on the cheeks. Hermione is furious. {p506}

9. Rita Skeeter's second article proclaims Hermione to be simultaneously toying with both Krum and Harry. {Ch 27, p512}

10. Krum confronts Harry about his relationship with Hermione. {Ch 28, p552}

11. Krum and Hermione have a conversation before Krum leaves Hogwarts. Hermione returns with an unreadable look on her face {Ch 37, p725}

12. Hermione gives Harry a kiss on the cheek.

Let's start at the beginning of the time-line and look at these events in closer detail.

While Dumbledore gives a welcoming speech to the students of Beauxbaton and Durmstrang, extending hospitality and being a gracious host, *"One of the Beauxbatons girls still clutching a muffler around her head gave what was unmistakably a derisive laugh."*{B4, Ch16 p250, 251}

Now, a derisive laugh is a contemptuous laugh. Therefore, this particular student is making sure that people know exactly what she thinks of Hogwarts and its hospitality right from the start. We should also take a close look at the way it is phrased—it says *unmistakably* derisive. JKR is making sure everyone knows that this student is being scornful of Hogwarts and its headmaster—there is no mistaking it. Another point of interest is the description of Fleur clutching a muffler around her head. This girl is literally bundled from head to foot. Our first Hermione/Fleur interaction takes place before we receive any physical description of Fleur. I feel this is a deliberate ploy by JKR to clearly establish that Hermione's reaction to this girl is based on observation of her actions and her actions alone. *"'No one's making you stay!'" Hermione whispered, bristling at her."* {p250, 251} JKR leaves her bundled with a muffler clutched around her face so that we don't get a look at her beauty. Plus, JKR does not confirm that Fleur is part veela or possesses any veela charms or traits at this point. When she finally removes her muffler, there is no doubt that Fleur and the girl who laughed are one and the same. {p252}

We know that the first Rita Skeeter article appears in Chapter 19 of Book 4 and states that Hermione and Harry are a couple. Shortly after the article comes out, we know that Krum has *"...been coming up to the library every day to try and talk to [Hermione]..."*{Ch23, p42} If Rita's articles had influenced Krum, he would have had to eliminate the possibility that Hermione was dating Harry before he asked her out. This leads us to two conclusions: 1 – Krum is not reading Rita's articles or 2 – Krum is not basing his decisions on Rita's articles. Krum is not likely basing his decision to ask out a girl, whom he hardly knows, on an article that is claiming her to be the girlfriend of another student. This is important to establish for Krum's future responses when it comes to Harry and Hermione.

Hermione and Krum are first recognized as a couple at the Yule Ball, even though there is clearly a relationship before then. At the ball, we know that Hermione *"...didn't seem to be thinking about S.P.E.W. She was deep in talk with Viktor Krum..."* {p416, 417}. Later, Hermione says about Krum, *"He's really nice, you know,"* {Ch24, p444} and Krum says about Hermione that, *"he'd never felt the same way about anyone else."* {Ch27, p514} At this point, it would seem that Hermione and Krum equally care about each other and the progression of their relationship is quite normal.

Before embarking on our analysis of the second task, I feel that it is important that we look a little at Hermione and Krum and their relationship. The Hermione/Krum relationship is important to our analysis of potential future relationships and is all too often overlooked or merely dismissed. By Hermione's relationship with Krum, JKR gives us several clues to the development of Hermione's feelings. One of the most important and interesting aspects of this relationship is the simple fact that Krum asks Hermione out after the first Rita Skeeter article comes out. The article proclaims that Harry has found love at Hogwarts—love in the form of Hermione Granger.

The Krum/Hermione relationship drastically changes during the second task, however, when Hermione is taken, as Krum's *"something that he will sorely miss".* {Ch25, p463} This is a very important point because the thing that is taken away from the Champions is established as someone who is extremely important to them. The hostages and their respective champions are as follows:

> Harry—Ron
> Krum—Hermione
> Cedric—Cho
> Fleur—Gabrielle

We know that Harry and Ron are the best of friends that Cedric and Cho are dating exclusively, and Fleur and Gabrielle are extremely close. It only takes two months, from the Yule ball in December, to the second task, where Hermione is rescued in February, for Krum to become infatuated with Hermione. Hermione says that, in a conversation by the lake, he told her *"he'd never felt the same way about anyone else."* {Ch27, p514} This is a big leap from visiting the library everyday, trying to work up the courage to talk to her.

Just after the second task, Krum notifies Hermione that she has a water beetle in her hair. {Ch26, p504} Now, if we combine it with this piece of our puzzle, where Hermione says: *"Viktor pulled a beetle out of my hair after we'd had our conversation by the lake,"* {Ch37, p728} we have not only verified Hermione and Krum's conversation where he tells her how feels in relation to our timeline, but we start to see Hermione's interest in Krum…well, crumble.

What if the story had run along these lines:

1. Harry walks up to Hermione and Krum
2. Krum has just finished telling Hermione how he feels and possibly asks her to visit him
3. Hermione turns away from Krum and begins to cheer and focus on Harry.

What conclusion would you come away with? This did happen, and precisely in this manner; however JKR did not write it openly.

Harry gets a clear impression that *"Krum was drawing her attention back onto himself; perhaps to remind her that he had just rescued her from the lake…"* {Ch26, p504} I believe Krum is not just trying to draw Hermione's attention back to the fact that he had just saved her from the lake, but that he is trying to draw her attention back to their conversation—the very conversation in which Krum may have invited Hermione to visit him and definitely admitted his feelings for her—the very same conversation in which Krum made that powerful statement. We know that when Krum attempts to direct Hermione's attention back to his admission of his feelings for her, Hermione does not seem to be focused on Krum, but rather on Harry. *"… Hermione brushed away the beetle impatiently and said, 'You're well outside the time limit, though Harry…'"* {p504} Hermione seems to ignore Krum and has a possible change of heart in her feelings towards him. *"[Krum] attempted to engage Hermione in conversation again, but she was too busy cheering for Harry to listen."* {p507} Krum is able to take Hermione's attention away from the house-elves, S.P.E.W., and the extra work for the house-elves, but Krum is not able to take away her attention from Harry. At this point, Hermione is focused on Harry and Harry alone. By failing to make this connection, we do not see all the other pieces of evidence that surround the second task.

It is interesting to note that when Fleur gives Harry a kiss on the cheek following the second task, Hermione is furious. {Ch26, p506} As seen from the initial meeting between Fleur and Hermione, we know that Hermione already has a reason to dislike Fleur. Initially, Hermione was upset that Fleur laughed at Dumbledore during his speech, but now Fleur has gone a step further and is displaying signs of affection towards Harry. Is Hermione simply finding any reason to be "furious" at Fleur or is she jealous of the attention Fleur is giving Harry? It seems odd timing, since Krum has just admitted his strong feelings for Hermione.

It is no wonder that, when the second Rita Skeeter article comes out, (claiming that Hermione is toying with both Harry and Krum) that Krum's suspicions are based on Hermione's actions following the second task and not on the article itself. Afterall, he didn't base asking her out in the first place on the articles; therefore, it is unlikely that he would base the decision to confront Harry about their relationship because of Rita's claims.

"'Hermy-own-ninny talks about you very often,' said Krum, looking suspiciously at Harry." {Ch28 p552, 553} Krum obviously sees Harry as a rival for Hermione's affection. Harry, of course, stops just short of mak-

ing this connection. *"We're just friends. She's not my girlfriend and she never has been. It's just that Skeeter woman making things up."*{Ch28 p552, 553} But the Rita answer is not enough to satisfy Krum. This is further proof that Krum is not basing his suspicion on either of Rita's articles, but on what he has seen between Harry and Hermione. Had the articles been the primary factor, we would have seen Krum become less jealous right here. But Krum is still suspicious. I don't think Krum is one hundred percent satisfied at this point.

Before he leaves Hogwarts, Krum asks Hermione if he can have a word with her. Even though prior to this point, they seem to have a close relationship, Hermione agrees, but is "slightly flustered" {Ch37, p725} It is almost as if Hermione is nervous to be alone with Krum.

What takes place during this conversation is open largely to speculation. This is the last piece of the puzzle that JKR has kept for herself until she is ready to reveal it to us. We might not know details, but we know the conversation took place. Here I've assembled enough of the puzzle to deduce four possible conversations that could have occurred.

1) Hermione and Krum discussed Ron: I'm not sure why anyone would think that Hermione and Krum are talking about Ron. There is no indication anywhere that Krum has been jealous of Ron or even knows that much about him.

2) Hermione and Krum spoke about her having feelings for someone else but didn't use a name and talked in rather general terms: Krum could have confronted Hermione about her feelings for another person and simply left the name out. Something along the lines of

> Krum: *Hermy-own-ninny you are in love with (or like) someone else.*
> Hermione: *Who?*
> Krum: *A boy here at Hogwarts.*

And it would go on. I don't think that Krum would be able to make much of a case for the change in his feelings, after his admission at the Lake in the second task, so he probably would have had to speak in general terms. One would also think that Hermione would not take this well at all and not remain in contact with him after the conversation. To speak in general terms would appear that Krum was simply through with Hermione after this year, and was moving on. Note, they returned very shortly and this type of conversation, in which Krum would have had to convince Hermione that she was in love with someone else, would take a bit of time.

3) Hermione and Krum spoke about Harry: Krum could have talked about what he has observed between Hermione and Harry. Remember the second task and how Krum tried twice to draw Hermione's attention back to himself. He failed. We also have the confrontation between Harry and Krum in which we are given another clue: that Hermione talks about Harry often. Given the progression through Book 4 of the Krum/Hermione/Harry interaction, this is the most likely conclusion. Krum brings Hermione's feelings to the surface and she confronts feelings that she has never felt before, but which readers have witnessed forming, quite without her realizing it. And yet Krum saw it.

4) Hermione and Krum may have spoken about Hermione visiting Krum over the summer and that they are still dating. However, Hermione's references to Krum as a pen pal in Book 5 put some kinks in this conversation, as do the events that follow this. While we can't rule it out completely there is little to support it at this point.

What we do know is that Hermione returns with an "unreadable" look on her face. {Ch37, p725} If we go back and look carefully at the second task and follow our chain of events, we see that is the seal of Hermione's caring for Harry. Having feelings for Harry that she has never had before, or realized before, she does something she has never done. When she said goodbye to Harry, she "kissed him on the cheek". {p725}

JKR is an excellent writer who loves a good mystery and a terrific plot twist. She writes the *Harry Potter* series in the "third-person limited". This style of narration (along with the first-person narrative) is often favored by mystery and suspense writers, as it allows them to focus their audience on the clues while giving misleading conclusions and steering their captive readers away from the final conclusion. By doing this, the writer misleads without conning the reader. We have seen how JKR can be showing that Hermione has feelings for Harry, while effectively steering us away from realizing this.

My purpose in this essay was to show you the pieces of the puzzle that JKR has scattered throughout Book 4 and to assemble these pieces to the best of my ability in order to reveal the completed picture. I am aware that one piece of the puzzle remains safely in the hands of JKR—the conversation with Krum—but hopefully I have assembled enough pieces of the puzzle around the conversation to at least present you with a general outline of what may have transpired between the two. Also, we have been told that we will see Krum again, though not soon, and he could shed the light we need on this very mystery.

ADDITIONAL SLEUTHING NOTES

* What is the exact sequence of the Fleur kissing Harry scene?

* How will their personal relationships enhance or interfere with their efforts during the upcoming war?

* WWP has been accused of not giving enough credence or support to a possible H<->H relationship. While we personally don't feel there is anything between Harry and Hermione besides close friendship, we find this perspective fascinating. Have you been swayed at all by the evidence?

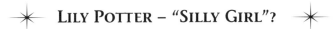

✴ Lily Potter – "Silly Girl"? ✴

Jill Atkinson ✴ Chamber of Secrets
Northern Ireland (*UK Edition*), Age 18

Inspiration for this Discussion

Lily has always been one of my favourite characters. We learn a lot more about her in Book 5, yet her character is still shrouded in mystery. So many questions… who were her parents? What did she do? Why did her husband not avail himself of the wizarding equivalent of hair gel?

LILY – SYMBOL OF PURITY

What do we know about Harry Potter's mother? Lily Evans Potter seems a paragon of virtue by all accounts. Although Professor Snape, the Potions Master, constantly derides James, Harry's father, Lily is never mentioned. *Everyone* loves Lily (perfect in every way: how very Mary Poppins-like), with the exception of her sister Petunia Dursley.

Petunia says rather condescendingly that her parents were 'so proud' of Lily. Prim-and-proper Petunia thought Lily was a 'freak', abnormal – she thinks of her as someone who 'turned teacups into rats'. {B1, Ch 4} This suggests to me (Petunia's ability to exaggerate aside) that Lily was a rather powerful child.

Petunia resented her sister: quite apt, considering petunias are the flowers of anger and resentment.

Lily flowers, however, are symbolic of purity, chastity, death and rebirth. Purity and chastity…well, I can't really vouch for her there…but death and rebirth are integral to the plot of *Harry Potter* and to Lily's life. Her sacrifice invoked an ancient magic, one that is to be greatly revered: the power of love, the heart, the bond of parent and child. Lily's final spell protected Harry from certain death.

Lily's purity is also shown through the fact that Quirrell was not able to touch Harry. The strength of Lily's love and the absolute purity and selflessness of her sacrifice meant Quirrell, possessed by Voldemort, could not bear to touch him. {Ch 37} She stood over her son and defied Voldemort without ever trying to cast a spell against him. To stand defenceless in front of the most evil wizard alive and try to plead with him—shows real courage. No wonder she was a Gryffindor. Of course, Lily's protection of Harry plays a part in Voldemort's return:

'*His mother left upon him the traces of her sacrifice…old magic…no matter. **I can touch him now.**'*{B4, Ch 33} This is important to the prophecy. Up until Book 5, Harry had never faced Voldemort without his mother's protection. The 'old magic' to which Lord Voldemort refers may well have an impact on future books—after all, Voldemort has been reborn with Harry's blood. Voldemort may now be carrying a power within him that he does not understand and, therefore, 'underestimates'.

LILY AND JAMES

There are relatively few Muggle-borns that we know of, so I find the similarities between Hermione and Lily to be worthy of note. First of all, Hermione and Lily both tell their schoolmates exactly what they think of them through sarcastic wit. For instance, Hermione tells Ron that, '*just because you have the emo-*

tional range of a teaspoon…doesn't mean we all do.' {B5, Ch 21} Similarly, Lily calls James Potter an *'arrogant, bullying toerag.'* {Ch 28} We can imagine that a toerag probably also has the emotional range of a teaspoon. Other than their witty nature, both Hermione and Lily are considered very pretty (see the Yule Ball in Book 4 if you don't believe me). When provoked, Lily and Hermione will both passionately defend the underdog, no matter how ungrateful the underdog may be about it. For instance, Lily stands up for Snape when James is bullying him at Hogwarts, and Hermione stands up for the house-elves and their slave-like conditions. Finally, Hermione and Lily are both occasionally infuriated by the person who fancies them, namely, Ron and James, respectively.

Because of the many similarities, we can get a glimpse of the relationship between Lily and James through Ron and Hermione. For instance, we know that Ron is infatuated with Hermione through several different instances in the series. In Book 5, during the Quidditch match, Hermione gives Ron a kiss on the cheek. Ron, in turn, *'touched the spot on his face where Hermione had kissed him'* {Ch19}, apparently at a loss for words. There is also the ill-fated attempt at impressing Hermione by buying her perfume for Christmas. *'That perfume's really interesting, Ron.'* {Ch23} 'Interesting', of course, being the universally accepted word for, *'How on earth do I avoid having to say I like the putrid thing?'* James, on the other hand, tries the unconventional way of getting Lily's attention; however, like Ron, he ends up looking like an idiot. When Lily says to James, *'I'm surprised your broomstick can get off the ground with your fat head on it'"*(Can you feel the love in the room?) and then tells him that his actions make her 'sick', {Ch28} It would have been a good time for Sirius to give his mate a few pointers—Really, Prongs, there are more reliable ways of impressing a girl: flowers, chocolates, keeping your mouth shut... Clearly, both Lily and Hermione are not easy to impress.

We have seen people react to Hermione and Lily in the same way, and both witches can deliver zingers if they want. In Book 4, Rita called Hermione a "silly girl", and we know how Hermione dealt with that (boy, was Rita sorry!). {B3, Ch24} Lily was also called a "silly girl" by Voldemort, and you might say he was sorry too…. {B3, Ch9}

The relationships between Ron and Hermione and James and Lily are alike in a lot of other ways. While Hermione and Lily are Muggle-born, Ron and James come from pure-blooded, wizarding families. Both pairs constantly fight with one another; however Ron sticks up for Hermione, even when she takes the opposite side, just as James jumps to Lily's defence when Snape calls her a "filthy little Mudblood." {Ch28} Note that these are precisely the same words that Draco used in Book 2 when he describes Hermione and Ron jumps to her defense. Ron and James are also both very arrogant at times. Ron messes up his hair to look like he just came from a Quidditch match, and Lily also claims that James is always messing up his hair {Ch31, Ch 28} (most likely for the very same reason as Ron). Now that we have an idea of Lily's younger personality and relationship with James by comparing it to Hermione's and Ron's relationship, let's take a look at Lily's magical capabilities.

LILY'S MAGICAL CAPABILITIES

The impression of Lily is that of an excellent student—also like Hermione, but Ron is not yet like James in this respect, though that may be partially due to his confidence problem.

Lily's first wand was ten and a quarter inches, willow, swishy and apparently good for Charm work. {B1, Ch5, p82} Now what other charms could Lily have performed? The Fidelius Charm is an 'immensely complex spell, involving the magical concealment of a secret inside a single, living, soul.' {B3, Ch10} It is entirely possible that Lily was the one to perform it, given that James' wand was, 'excellent for Transfiguration'. {Ch5} We infer Dumbledore could not have performed it because he didn't know that

Sirius wasn't the Secret-Keeper. {Ch21}

I do wonder what other Charms she may have been placed on Harry that he will discover in the future. Is her spell of love such a powerful charm that no wand was required? We will, I gather, also be hearing more about Mrs Potter's career in Book 6. Did Lily perhaps experiment in the field of Charms? As for the future in general—well, we know we will not see Lily alive again: 'No spell can reawaken the dead.' {B4, Ch36} However, in the Harry Potter universe, a character's death is not really necessarily a problem. After all, we've seen Harry's parents in their pictures and the Mirror of Erised, we've heard the voice of Lily in Harry's memory, and we've seen their younger selves in the memory of another.

Lily and the Power of Love

We know that Ms Rowling has a big surprise about Lily waiting in the wings for us. What could it be? She was secretly in love with Snape? She had an affair with Lupin? No, I really didn't think those were very likely either. But you never know. I think there will be a lot more attention paid to Lily and James in the last two books. The first power that 'the Dark Lord knows not' is Lily's sacrificial love for her son. I doubt this is the last thing she left him, and I doubt this will be the last we hear from her…

Additional Sleuthing Notes

* Is there a correlation between Harry hearing his mother's voice in his head {B3, Ch9}and his often hearing Hermione's voice in his head?{B5, Ch30}

* What changed after the Pensieve scene {"Snape's Worst Memory"} in Book 5 that brought Lily and James together? Could it have been Voldemort or yet another parallel to the Troll that brought the trio together?

* …and we still keep asking: What's so special about those green eyes?

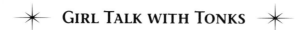

GIRL TALK WITH TONKS

ELYSE SCHULER ✳ CoS "THETHIRDMAN"
USA (*US Edition*), AGE 21

Inspiration for this Discussion

I know that JK Rowling never does anything without a reason, and she introduced Tonks very late in the series. Therefore, Tonks must have a special role. I find the character of Tonks to be very unique. She is the only adult female that we've met, thus far, without a several-decade age gap between her and the main young characters. As Hermione and Ginny grow up, I feel that Tonks will play an important role in guiding the girls through future decisions regarding love.

HANDFUL

How can someone who only appears as a minor character and falls down a lot be considered important to the plot? It's not too hard to be important when you're the only non-student, young female role model in the series. Nymphadora Tonks is an Auror in her early twenties working with the Order of the Phoenix and, through her involvement, has developed an important relationship with Hermione and Ginny.

In the fourth chapter of Book 5, the first time we see Ginny, she's been following a bit of information she got from Tonks. Ginny now knows how to detect if a door's been Imperturbed. Even though Tonks is one of the members of the Order involved in the meeting on which Ginny and the twins are trying to eavesdrop, she gives Ginny tips on how to eavesdrop more successfully. In the next chapter, Tonks is entertaining the girls by changing her nose. And after Ron and Hermione receive their prefect badges, Tonks once again, entertains the girls with a joke about why she'd never been a prefect. In that scene, Tonks is described as looking like "Ginny's older sister." Upon returning from the Christmas holidays, Tonks rides the Knight Bus with the twins, Ginny and the trio. However, when the group has to split up, Tonks stays with Ginny and Hermione.

This sets her up as the perfect adult female friend and confidante for Hermione and Ginny. After all, Harry has Sirius and Lupin to look up to, but until Book 5, Hermione and Ginny don't have that kind of influence. Sure, there are strong females in the books, but would Hermione or Ginny actually feel comfortable talking to Molly about those tangled, complicated emotions of puberty? Or how about sitting down for a discussion of boys, love, and all that mushy stuff with McGonagall? No way, right? That's the sort of stuff a girl feels most comfortable talking about to an older friend—not a mother figure or a teacher. And, having been there, I can say that the girls are happy to talk with someone closer to their own age.

During the party for Ron and Hermione, we see Tonks listening to Ron go on about his new broom. There's no hint of her being bored with the conversation or looking for an escape, even when Ron is going into detail about the kind of wood used in the handle. So Tonks must be a listener and easy to relate to.

That's why the girls like her. She is fun, entertaining, and she listens well. So, whom would the girls rather take their teenage woes to? Someone who would interject advice and when-I-was-young stories at every turn? Or someone who will listen to their problems, give a bit of advice, and leave the decision to the girls? The former is probably what Molly would do. She pressures her children to do what she thinks is right or what she would do. But Tonks seems to be different. It's safe to say that she's the most easy-going person in the Order.

This is what makes Tonks the perfect counselor for Ginny and Hermione. She is also an ideal role model as they reach their career years. She listens to the girls, laughs with them, and most importantly, treats them like friends.

I see Tonks becoming a big sister figure in the future.

ADDITIONAL SLEUTHING NOTES

* What kind of interesting potions would an Auror know?
* Who is going to help the girls with fashion, cooking, and cleaning – as Tonks admits she isn't too good with those kind of feminine traits?
* What are the chances that her career might influence Ginny to become an Auror? How would Molly react to that news?

Mischief Created:
The Marauders

MARAUDERS—SO, WHAT'S IN A NAME?

MISSY RUZICKA ✳ NC, "KATIELBELL"
USA (*US Edition*), AGE 32

Inspiration for this Discussion

Missy was kind enough to help research and write up the background on this fan nickname. We found it interesting enough to turn it into its own discussion.

 HANDFUL

It is common for Harry Potter fans to refer to Moony, Wormtail, Padfoot and Prongs as the "Marauders". However, until very recently, we have never heard JK Rowling use the name when referring to the fearless foursome. We knew the map had that title, but not necessarily the mapmakers…

Marauder is the noun derivation of the verb "maraud", which means to roam about and raid in search of plunder; to pillage (www.Dictionary.com)—so, it's another term for "pirate". This description fits James and company to a tee. Whether they are searching for food in the school's kitchens (a tasty plunder) or roaming Hogwarts looking for new secret passageways, these young men were constantly seeking some form of adventure. There is no question that they qualified as "marauders".

Now, even though fans have dubbed them "The Marauders", there is nothing in the books that verifies the use of the term. In the books, the only place we see that word is in the title of their map. In fact, they referred to themselves, there, as "Purveyors of Aids to Magical Mischief-Makers".{B3, Ch10, p192 US} The Marauder's Map, was intended for any single user who would like to be considered a pirate-like mischief-maker (i.e. marauder). We know of several pirate-like mischief-makers who have used the map, but we hadn't known if they ever referred to themselves, singly or together, as a Marauder or "the Marauders". For example: you can create or use a pirate's map without actually being (or calling yourself) a "pirate"—but the map is most useful, of course, for pirates.

So, did they use the name, Marauders? It seems that they could have. In May of 2004, JK Rowling posted her fan website award to Immeritus. In describing why she likes their site so much, she referred to James' gang of mischief-makers as the "four marauders" (lower case). While they may not have used it as a proper name, it definitely appears that they considered themselves to be marauders.

Most importantly, who are these marauding friends and what are their connections to each other? Hopefully, Rowling will map out more of that for us.

ADDITIONAL SLEUTHING NOTES
✳ What other "pirate-like" activities would these Marauders have gotten involved in?

SCHOOL YEARS OF THE MARAUDERS

TAMMY MUN. ✳ CoS, "LIL_KATS13"
USA (*US Edition*), AGE 13

Inspiration for this Discussion

Since the third Harry Potter book came out, the Marauders have been my main point of interest. I have always been curious about them and have always wanted to share my insights into the kids that were the Marauders. Now I can. I put a lot of work into this discussion. I hope it is a great experience for you.

 HANDFUL

When we hear the name "Marauders", the first thing that comes to mind is a bunch of mischievous boys. The Marauders were a group of extraordinary students with many talents. Getting into trouble, making people laugh, trying to impress others, and having fun is what they were all about, just like any kids. Despite their actions, they were very clever and creative (making their pranks so much more exciting, of course!). If you think about your own school days—now, or a few years from now—I bet you recall who the class clowns were, right? They always manage to leave their mark and that is exactly what the Marauders did.

James Potter and Sirius Black, the ringleaders of the group, were the best of friends, almost brothers. {B3, Ch10, p204} Their backgrounds are similar in some ways—both boys come from Pure-blood (and seemingly rich) families. Yet, while James' home life was apparently great, Sirius' childhood was a bummer. Now many of you probably have a little brother or sister who is always bothering you and somehow is the apple of your mother's eye, yes? Sirius' younger brother, Regulus, was just that, while Sirius was the black sheep. Sirius had a rebellious "bad boy" image—he was a tough guy. The Black family supported Voldemort, and those that remain still do. Sirius was against his family's belief 110%, which caused him to be an outcast from them. Thankfully, James' parents seemed to be very supportive of Sirius and were probably very good people because they let him hang out at their place. The boys have an "I'll be there to catch you before you fall" friendship going on.

Remus John Lupin, another member of the Marauders, was the frailest in physical stature. He apparently came from a good home of two loving parents, one Muggle and one magical {World Book Day Chat}. When he was a young boy, a werewolf bit him. So, every full moon he becomes a monster. Therefore, Lupin probably had no friends as a kid. The other parents most likely kept their children away from him, due to his illness. Hypothetically speaking, during his early childhood, anything good that happened to him he most likely would not have taken for granted because of all the isolation and pain… But then, he met James and the gang at Hogwarts. I mean, imagine being alone…friendless…for a great part of your childhood and suddenly getting three wonderful friends. Would you take them for granted, or would you be thankful?

Even though Lupin was weak, physically, he was very strong, personality-wise. For example, in Book

3, he gives "*the merest half-glance at Harry, warning him not to interrupt.*" {Ch 14, p288} and who can forget when he blasts Peeves with the chewing gum using "*Waddiwasi!*" Lupin not only has a commanding presence, but he deals with the huge burden of being a werewolf. There are people who will hate you or reject you because of something you can't control. It takes a really strong person to deal with all that—especially as a kid.

Peter Pettigrew is a very easy character to figure out (at least in hindsight). He was the "odd one out". He was not as talented or handsome as the other guys were. He was always having trouble functioning. If it weren't for the other Marauders, we wouldn't know he existed. Think of the class outcast—the one who was always in a corner being ignored by anything that breathed….that is who Peter might have become if it hadn't been for the other boys. He was a very insecure and self-conscious person. Peter always allied himself with the stronger group. He was easily influenced by those around him, and that probably caused him succumb to peer pressure later on in life.

Even though the boys spent some of their time—no, most of their time—pulling pranks on people, they were very smart. We know that Lupin became a prefect and James a Head Boy. Things just don't come so easily that you can accomplish them without any study (trust me I've tried). They must have spent a lot of time studying and doing homework in the library (or in detention). Against popular belief, they didn't sit around all day planning pranks, talking, or playing Quidditch, but it sure sounds as if James liked being a jock. We know he was a talented Quidditch player, however, we aren't sure what position he played. Was it Seeker as the movie suggests? Or was it Chaser, as JKR said in her chat on Scholastic.com {October 16, 2000}? Whichever it was, he obviously liked showing off to the females (we watched him ruffle his hair around Lily).

The four boys had to have scouted out every corner of Hogwarts in order to produce the Marauder's Map. They also had to be very skilled to have enchanted the parchment, and studied very hard to learn Transfigurations.

We've established that the Marauders had one of the strongest bonds, like the ones you can only have with those special people who have been with you since you were knee-high to a dragon's eye. When James, Peter and Sirius found out about Lupin's illness they researched becoming Animagi, and by their fifth year, all accomplished it.

This is where we find out most about what drove those Marauders. JK Rowling stated that you can't pick your Animagus form. It sort of picks you. It reflects your personality. Imagine that, after all the hard work and dedication, you discover you are a toad or a slug—now wouldn't that be disappointing? The Marauders' Animagi forms really do reflect their personalities. This is also where we get the Marauder nicknames. Moony is obviously Lupin's nickname because he turns into a werewolf during the full moon. Sirius becomes a dog (Padfoot); dogs stand for friendship and loyalty. Sirius would die before he betrayed his friends. Peter's Animagus form is a rat (Wormtail). Rats represent betrayal. His form certainly foreshadows his future. James becomes a stag (Prongs—like the antlers of a stag). Stags stand for power and are the enemy of serpents and Satan. Again, it foreshadows what he is destined to do.

During their time at Hogwarts, the Marauders were most likely popular. Based on what we've heard and seen of their reputation, everyone loved their pranks and jokes. Their "audience's" laughter probably added to the Marauders' egos. That looks like what Harry saw, and it most likely led them to think that they were the best all around and could do anything they wanted. The ego boosts could have affected James and Sirius the most, and that led them to pick on Severus Snape.

Snape, a Slytherin in their year, was a total and complete outcast, like what Peter might have been if he hadn't been tagging along with James. In everyone's eyes Snape was a dork, a freak. It did not help his self-esteem that James and Sirius picked on him a lot.

Most Lily and James fans would like to believe that they got together because he saved her life or because her parents died. Is that realistic? If she hated James why would she go running to *him*? She surely had friends, people she could trust.

I have a speculation that Lily witnessed or found out about James saving Snape's life from werewolf Lupin in their sixth year. And what if Lily had discovered that, and it changed her feelings? (Not that Snape's feeling was changed any by it).

Knowing about Muggle kids helps us understand the Marauders better. Knowing about the school years of the Marauders helps us understand better why characters, such as Lupin and Snape, are who they are today. The Marauders' era makes up a great part of the Harry Potter series. It is when Voldemort started to gain power, when best friends met and formed life-long relationships that will help Harry; it is when it all started.

ADDITIONAL SLEUTHING NOTES

* Four Marauders plus Lily…Harry, Ron, Hermione, Neville plus Luna. Coincidence? Should we be looking at how choices are the difference?

* How did James become Head Boy if he was not a prefect? Did he do some great deed (similar to Riddle "capturing" the monster from the Chamber)? Did it, again, have anything to do with Snape?

THE MARAUDERS – WHAT WENT WRONG

MISSY RUZICKA * NC, "KATIELBELL"
USA (*US Edition*), AGE 32

Inspiration for this Discussion

Three years ago I went down to our local Blockbuster and rented a movie called Harry Potter and the Sorcerer's Stone. I just wanted to see what all the fuss was about. As I watched, the scene with the Mirror of Erised really moved me, and I wanted to know everything about this couple whose son looked like his father (but with his mother's eyes). I ran out that next day and bought Books 1 - 4. I was absolutely in love with this story and all its characters. When I reached the chapter in Book 3 where Harry received the Marauder's Map from Fred and George, I was already intrigued with the Marauders. When the Map talked back to Professor Snape, I had to know all about its creators, and by the time I reached the chapter of Cat, Rat and Dog, I was completely hooked on these four friends. It might be because I'm a parent, myself, and am closer to the Marauders' ages rather than Harry's, but I love this generation of characters JK Rowling has included in her stories and I can't wait to find out all the mysteries of the Marauders.

HANDFUL

To hear Remus Lupin speak, you would never find a group of friends as close as the Marauders. This prank-pulling clan consisted of James Potter, Sirius Black, Remus Lupin and Peter Pettigrew. All four boys started at Hoggy Warty Hogwarts together and were all sorted into the brave and noble house of Gryffindor (I am assuming, from JKR's World Book Day chat, she intended to include Pettigrew). Their friendship was like that of legends. Yet, the betrayal by one shattered the lives of those around. No one was left unaffected by the coward, Peter Pettigrew. How could they be so close, and yet not see that someone amongst them was a traitor?

The ringleaders of this band of troublemakers were none other than James Potter, father of Harry, and his best friend Sirius Black. Professor Flitwick says, *"You'd have thought the two were brothers".* {B3, Ch10, p204 US}

James and Sirius were "inseparable". When Black was fed up with his Pure-blood-fanatical family at the age of 16, he ran away from home, and where did he run? He ran to James' house.{Ch6, p111} In treacherous times like those, it would really have meant something to have friends that would risk anything and everything for you, and they believed in that.. *"DIED RATHER THAN BETRAY YOUR FRIENDS…"* {B3, Ch19, p375}

Another of the Marauders, Remus John Lupin, was a kind and gentle person with a very dark secret…so dark that he hid it from his very closest of friends. Eventually, they did find out, and even his being a werewolf couldn't get between them. Not only did his Marauder friends not abandon him *"…they did something for me that would make my transformations not only bearable, but the best times of my life.*

They became Animagi." This was needed since a werewolf is not a danger to other animals, only to humans. {Ch18, p354}

Last (and definitely least) of all is Peter Pettigrew. Not much is known about the background of the fourth member of the Marauders. What we do know is that he was a far less talented wizard than the others were. "*Hero-worshipped Black and Potter,*" said Professor McGonagall. "*Never quite in their league, talent-wise.*"{Ch10, p207} He needed help becoming an Animagus and when he did transform, it was in the form of a 'rat'. Little did they suspect how rat-like he could be.

Individually, they were known as Prongs, Padfoot, Moony, and Wormtail. Together, fans have dubbed them the "Marauders". There is no evidence that this friendship was anything but solid and unwavering at the time they left Hogwarts.

After they mapped out Hogwarts, the Marauders put their talents to nobler things, such as fighting the Dark Wizards of the age. Instead of the four Marauders, they became the four Marauders *plus Lily.* They all joined Albus Dumbledore's secret society called the Order of the Phoenix, where they fought together for what they believed. We have "seen" their photographs of that era. From the descriptions of the images, you would never know they were facing such dark times. In the wedding picture: "*There was his father waving up at him, beaming,*" … "*There was his mother, alight with happiness.*" {B3, Ch11, p212} In the Order picture: "*His mother and father were beaming up at him*" … "*all waving happily out of the photograph forever more, not knowing that they were doomed*". {B5, Ch9, p174,175} Was it because of their trust for one another that they could put the darkness aside for these brief moments?

As we all know, when you grow up you tend to drift away from the friends you once had. Is it possible that the Marauders became so involved with the events in those dark times that they drifted apart? We have been told many things about the Marauders and some of the events that lead to Lily and James's deaths, but there are also a lot more questions. Do you remember that picture Mad-Eye showed us of the original order members…do you recall who was sitting in the middle of Lily and James? Yes, the rat-fink, known as Wormtail. {p174} What made them so blind to the evil that was literally sitting right between them?

The Potters decided to go into hiding with Harry and place a Fidelius Charm on their home in Godric's Hollow. Now for those of you who don't recall how a Fidelius Charm works, it involves concealing your secret inside your most trusted comrade. {B3, Ch10, p205} Therefore, James and Lily put their faith in this person to keep them safe—their 'Secret-Keeper'.

Albus Dumbledore had a network of spies that told him there was someone close to the Potters that was passing information to Lord Voldemort. Dumbledore, himself, volunteered to be their 'Secret-Keeper', but "*Potter trusted Black beyond all his other friends. Nothing changed when they left school.*"{p205} James insisted that **Sirius would rather die than give them up.** So what convinced him it was safe to switch the 'Secret-Keeper' over to Peter Pettigrew—how did he make the wrong choice? Something is really odd. James decided on the change. WHY?

Why did they put so much trust into Peter and not Remus? Did the other Marauders shun Remus because he was a Dark Creature and figured him untrustworthy? And after Peter betrayed Lily and James by telling their secret to Voldemort, why did Remus believe that it was Black who betrayed them? He should have known that Sirius would never have put Lily, James and Harry in harm's way. What happened between these four friends to cast so much doubt upon one another? Could it be that they let Voldemort splinter their friendship and love?

I truly hope that in the next 2 books JK Rowling helps answer some of the questions we have about the Marauders. But one thing is certain; friendship is one of the most fragile yet greatest things one can acquire. I believe that if Harry puts his faith in his friendships and believes in his love for his friends, he will have the "*power the Dark Lord knows not.*" {B5, Ch37, p841} As Albus Dumbledore said about fighting evil, "*We can fight it only by showing an equally strong bond of friendship and trust.*" {B4, Ch37, p723}

ADDITIONAL SLEUTHING NOTES

* If the Marauders started to go their own ways, is that what happened to Wormtail? Did he feel alone and deserted again? Was he resentful?

* It is interestingly symbolic that Peter had wormed his way in *between* James and Lily in the picture Moody showed to Harry.{B5, Ch9, p174} Could the Wormtail have been jealous of James and Lily?

* Because of the scene with Lupin and Harry on the bridge in the Warner Bros. movie, *Harry Potter and the Prisoner of Azkaban*, we can't help but speculate about "Lupin and Lily" – could there have been a personal relationship or some kind of secret between them?

Travelling
Picture Show

PORTRAITS AND PHOTOS: CAPTURING AN AURA

JEANNIE PLOEGMAN ✳ NC, "MADEYEMUGGLE"
USA (*US Edition*), AGE "SAME AS SNAPE"

Inspiration for this Discussion

"Farewell!" cried the knight, popping his head into a painting of sinister looking monks.
"Farewell, my comrades-in-arms!" {B3, Ch 6}

I fell in love with the idea of painted subjects that can move and talk when I first visited Harry Potter's world. There are many questions to ask concerning both, the portraits and the photographs – the first of which is "how"? It is easy, at first glance, to think of the two as the same. However, it seems that portraits and pictures each have a different set of rules, although it looks as if they may break a few.

In my research, I visited all five books to examine the differences and similarities in the artwork. Sadly, there was no way that I could include them all. The examples that I did use continue to be some of the most memorable and puzzling. I realize that only one person knows all of the secrets... So, I am not saying that I have found the answers; I have tried to distinguish some of the many forms involved and shed some insight as to how they might have been produced. I would like you to join me on a tour of the wizarding world's most dazzling dust catchers and the other fantastic findings in the artwork, that grace the hallowed halls of Hogwarts and the wizarding community.

 HANDFUL

Some of my favorite things in JK Rowling's magical world would have to be the portraits and pictures. I find the fact that they move, and in some instances speak, fascinating…if only I were a fly on the wall of JKR's study (*Animagi, of course!*). The fact that JKR rarely puts things into her books "just for show" has me wondering: just what is the real purpose of these "moving memories"?

As you are aware, the portraits are paintings of "real" individuals who were at one time alive. They tend to show the personality traits of the subjects that they resemble. There are portraits that have fairly significant roles—such as The Fat Lady, Sir Cadogan, Phineas Nigellus, and those former fellow headmasters in Dumbledore's office. They interact with the living characters as if they were alive. Taking into consideration that we have never been introduced to a portrait of someone from the present whom Harry has met in person, we had suspected that portraits are of the deceased. JKR verified, during the 2004 *Edinburgh Book Festival*, that the subjects of portraits are indeed dead. I find it interesting that Harry has never encountered any paintings of the Hogwarts ghosts, such as Nearly Headless Nick or the Bloody Baron, nor has there been any evidence of a portrait of Lily and James. That answer came up as well during the Edinburgh chat. JKR said that it is not the same as being a ghost (*and that is the key here, isn't it?*) Portraits only speak in the "catchphrases" that their subjects used when they were alive.

This has me questioning now if there are options that one might have in the event of one's demise. Evidence has brought me to the possibility that one could *choose* to become a portrait the way that wizards choose to become ghosts.

Nearly Headless Nick mentioned that one could choose to stay behind as he did (being that he was afraid of death). Moaning Myrtle also chose to become a ghost so that she could haunt Olive Hornby. The Potters, however, did not make that choice, and they have only appeared in photographs (and the Mirror of Erised). We have now learned that the former headmasters left behind a faint imprint of themselves or as JKR said, it was their "*Aura **almost, in the office** and they can give some counsel to the current occupant.*" {Edinburgh Book Festival} The definition of "aura" is *a distinctive but intangible quality surrounding a person or thing.*[1]

There is the question of how the portraits were fashioned. I feel that someone would have had to personally paint them. Whether they would use a paintbrush or a wand is still open for discussion. So, how does the actual aura arrive into the painting? That is a tricky one indeed. I have some ideas how this aura is preserved. Another definition of "aura" uses the word *air*, such as *an air of mystery* or *the house had a neglected air.*[2] Would this tie into the room where the portraits had once used such catchphrases when they were alive? We know that many subjects have more than one frame in different buildings. Would all of the canvases have to be present at the time of a person's death in order to absorb some of that aura? On the other hand, is it the room in which they are hung that resonates with that certain vibe that they had left behind? These questions are crucial because of what JKR said about the former headmasters having had left their aura; she used one phrase that shouted out at me—the "in the office" part. That makes me think the imprint or aura was specific to the office and not necessarily in the portrait itself.

I would love to hear the details of portrait creation…which leads me to the question of how many times has there been a hint about Dean Thomas' artistic flair? I wonder if he has what it takes to create a portrait? I want to know how his artistic talent can help Harry (other than forging permission slips and making banners). There has to be more…I hope that JKR will indulge us with that information soon.

Since I am mentioning artists, I should also bring up Dobby's painting of Harry: the Christmas gift with the uncanny resemblance to a gibbon. Harry did not mention that it moved or spoke. Since it said on the back that it was Harry, was that enough to capture his essence, or does it require highly complex magic? Does it mean when Harry dies his aura will bring the gibbon to life? Could Dobby have been able to do anything special to it without Harry's participation?

Portraits have very unique and intriguing capabilities. In the case of The Fat Lady and her friend, Violet, *they consume considerable amounts of Chocolate liqueurs!* {B4, Ch23} They can also leave their frames to visit other canvases in the same building or if they are lucky enough to have more than one portrait of themselves, they can go to other dwellings where they have a frame, as long as they are not currently "in" that portrait.

We do know that portraits are not just there to make the walls look pretty. Human portraits can communicate with the living and with each other. As the portrait of Dumbledore's predecessor Armando Dippet, explained, "*We are honor-bound to give service to the present Headmaster!*" {B5, Ch22} The Fat Lady has the duty of guardian to the Gryffindor common room entrance. (Though she wasn't able to keep out a knife-wielding prison escapee). Then there is everyone's favorite: Mrs. Black. I find it hard to believe that her only job is to hurl insults at passers-by, and why the permanent sticking charms? Could Mrs. Black have a duty we had not seen from the Hogwarts portraits? Is she always behind her black curtain when not in hysterics? Could she possibly have another frame somewhere other than "The Noble And Most Ancient House of Black?" When Harry first encountered her he "*thought he was looking through a window*". {Ch4} That idea still has me a little wary. I am reminded of the ties to glass/mirrors/windows as a form of spying and communication.

One portrait has me completely befuddled, though. It is the bowl of "still-life" fruit at the kitchen's entrance. I wonder if that ticklish pear ever "lived". (If so, was it ticklish, then?)

Photo-type pictures, on the other hand, seem to have a different set of rules. Again, like portraits, the question is how they came to be. Book 2 gives us many hints as to what makes these moving-mementos tick. We have obtained key information about how the moving photos are created, first by Colin Creevy, who owns an ordinary Muggle camera. Colin tells Harry that if the film is developed in a "special potion" {B2, Ch6} the pictures will move. We also learned, in Flourish and Blotts, that a picture could also be taken with *"a large black camera that emitted puffs of purple smoke with each blinding flash."* {Ch4}

Photos seem suspended in time and just happily wave from their frames or shuffle along when prodded, typically showing their subject's personality. Most importantly, since pictures can be of living people, we see that they mirror how they act in life: such as Harry trying to break free of Gilderoy Lockhart's grasp {Ch6} and Percy walking out of the family photo {B5, Ch7}.

We also learned that there are times when a picture seems to communicate with the living. For instance, in Lockhart's office, the walls were covered in pictures of him (some were even signed). When the teachers and Dumbledore meet there after the first attack, we see the photos *"nodding in agreement."*{B2, Ch9} That was something I found especially odd. Then there is the case of the Black family photos. While Sirius is cleaning house, he tosses out the old photographs in tarnished frames and they squeal shrilly when their glass is shattered. Now, I have seen no evidence that photo subjects can leave their pictures for another frame of their own image nor do they seem to visit photos of their friends.

Another thing that I have really wondered about is the Chocolate Frog cards. Where do they fit in? In the Muggle world, trading cards are photos, but in Book 1, Dumbledore leaves his card and Ron is unconcerned—there are also cards of historical witches and wizards such as Agrippa. There is no evidence they contained the aura of those people from the past. In fact, one thing that makes me scratch my head is that Dumbledore is alive. So that must be a significant difference between a picture and a photo. *Also, who would want to paint the thousands of cards that exist anyway?* Dumbledore joked that he would not want his image removed from the Chocolate Frog cards—some suspect they could be a way for him to see what is going on anywhere his card exists. Unless his card is a portrait, how is that achieved?

Though we have never heard a Chocolate Frog card speak, *(let alone croak)* it seems they must rest somewhere between the two media forms of portraiture and photography. I also understand that while creating this wonderful world, JK Rowling could have taken a few artistic liberties. It seems that we have only brushed the surface in the intricate secrets behind the frame.

Additional Sleuthing Notes

* What kind of processes do they have to print all the images on cards, newspapers, and all the other mass-production items?
* Can you permanently change the location of a frame? The Fat Lady's portrait was switched with Sir Cadogan's in Book 3 after the attack by Sirius Black, but if the room is important, what happens with the Headmasters in Dumbledore's office? When Filch moved the Fat Lady's portrait to repair it, was she still able to roam the other portraits or was she temporarily disabled?
* Why does JKR describe the portrait of Sirius' mother as a "window", "life-size", and as the "most realistic" Harry had ever seen? Could she be guarding a doorway like the Fat Lady or the pears?

1 www.hyperdictionary.com
2 Ibid.

✳ Phineas Nigellus: Wicked Wit on the Wall ✳

Jeanne Perry Kimsey ✳ CoS, "Silver Ink Pot"
USA (*US Edition*), Age 44

Inspiration for this Discussion

I minored in art history in college, and love the idea of a painting coming to life… let alone speaking. I wish there were more details in the Harry Potter books about magical painting and the process involved. In the meantime, I just enjoy Phineas Nigellus—he's a hoot! I've noticed that on many Harry Potter websites and forums, his quotes are some of people's favorites. One night on the Chamber of Secrets Forum, we were talking about his distinctive name and I started researching how many meanings for Phineas I could discover – as it turned out there were quite a few. He is a bossy, irritating, yet strangely elegant character, and I look forward to seeing him again in future books.

 12

One of the most memorable characters in Book 5 isn't a living character at all; he isn't a ghost, either. Sometimes he is just a voice "sniggering" in a blank frame. {Ch9, p166 US}. That's because he is the subject of a painting on the wall. He is the sly and witty Phineas Nigellus, the *"least popular Headmaster Hogwarts ever had,"* according to his great-great grandson Sirius Black.{Ch6, p113}

We know he has two magical portraits—one in Dumbledore's office, and one in the Headquarters of the Order of the Phoenix, number twelve Grimmauld Place in London. The second portrait just happens to hang in the bedroom where Harry Potter was staying, and that is probably no accident. Phineas plays the role of a guardian to Harry, watching over him at times while he sleeps.{Ch23, p497} At other times, he delivers messages to Harry from Dumbledore, though often Phineas seems more like a childish tattletale than a concerned adult (well, you know these Slytherin types!).

For that is what Phineas Nigellus really is—the ultimate Slytherin, next to old Salazar himself! He is portrayed as a *"clever-looking wizard with a pointed beard,"* wearing the green and silver of Slytherin House. {Ch22, p472}

Phineas is scathing in his appraisals of Harry, and seems to take delight in vexing the boy. In one incident, when Harry is hurting from the scar on his forehead, Phineas just makes a snide remark. {p178} Also, when Ron and Hermione receive their Prefect Badges in the mail, Harry is a bit jealous that he was not chosen. Phineas hides out of sight, and Harry hears the blank picture frame begin to "snigger" at him. {Ch9, p166} How irritating!

While portraits in the Headmaster's office are "honor bound" to serve Dumbledore {p473}, Phineas seems quite reluctant. He pretends to be asleep even though Dumbledore calls to him five times. {Ch22, p472, 473} Then he gives a "theatrical jerk" and a "fake yawn" and tries to beg off following orders. The other portraits are scandalized. In the course of the story, we learn that Phineas "loathed being a teacher" {Ch23, p495, 496} and detests Harry's "adolescent agonizing". (A child psychologist he definitely is not!) No wonder he was so unpopular as Headmaster!

What else can we discover about this character? How about his unusual and old-fashioned name? Can it tell us something about Phineas Nigellus?

THE NAME "PHINEAS"

The first name, "Phineas" (pronounced FIN-ee-as) is an ancient name.

It may be derived from the Egyptian name "Panhsj" meaning *Nubian* or *dark-skinned*. [1]

In Hebrew, the name means *serpent's mouth*.[2] Does that remind you of anyone? Was Phineas, perhaps, a Parselmouth like Voldemort or Harry? Or does being a "serpent mouth" refer to Phineas being a spokesperson for the Slytherin point of view? In Hebrew, the name can also mean *oracle*, as in someone who foretells the future.[3] Perhaps we should listen to any warnings Phineas Nigellus gives to Harry?

The ancient Etruscans spelled the name differently: "Phinius." Surprisingly, in that language the name means *Phoenix*.[4] So even though Phineas Nigellus often seems at odds with Dumbledore and Harry, his name may imply a strong connection to the Order of the Phoenix.

There are at least two stories from Greek mythology that include a person named "Phineas."

In the first, Phineas was a prophet who could accurately predict the future. However, he did it so often that he gave away too many secrets, angering Zeus, the king of the gods. To punish Phineas, Zeus blinded him and sent him to live on an island with a bunch of harpies—evil, flying creatures that would swoop down at the slightest sign of food and prevent the blind man from eating. Eventually, Phineas was saved by the hero Jason, and his Argonauts, who captured the harpies and freed Phineas from his torture.[9] This story is a little disturbing, since our Phineas is keeping Dumbledore's secrets. Will Phineas cause problems for the Headmaster in the future? Could the fact that the mythological Phineas was blinded be a hint that this painting will be destroyed someday? I sincerely hope not. How dreadfully we would all miss his wicked wit! Of course, there is a "harpy" who resides at Grimmauld Place—the portrait of Sirius Black's mum, who shrieks horribly at the slightest sound. {Ch4, p78}

The other Grecian "Phineas" appears in the myth of Perseus and Andromeda. Perseus was a great young hero with winged sandals and a shield given to him by the gods. He was the son of Zeus. After he killed the horrible Medusa (a woman with a head covered in snakes that turned onlookers to stone), he then rescued the beautiful princess Andromeda from a sea monster sent by some angry sea nymphs. He immediately asked Andromeda for her hand in marriage.[10] One problem, though—she was already betrothed to a man named "Phineus", who interrupted the wedding party with his men in order to kill Perseus. Phineus hurled a spear at the young hero, but it missed the mark. He then turned coward by running to hide. Perseus picked up the head of Medusa, which he luckily still had in a bag. Telling all his real friends to hide and look away, Perseus raised the head of Medusa and turned his enemies into stone. Phineus, trying to be clever, crawled toward Perseus and asked for mercy. But Perseus showed him the head anyway and Phineas became a statue of a man crawling on his knees.[11]

The Phineas in the myth of Perseus really is a coward. Phineus never attempted to save Andromeda in the first place, and was going to let the monster have her. Then, he let Perseus risk his life to save the girl. When Phineas decided to steal the girl for himself, he let his men do the fighting while he hid. Perhaps this is why Phineas Nigellus is often "out of sight" in his blank frame—in effect, hiding. He tells Harry his Slytherin Philosophy which is: "*given a choice, we will always choose to save our own necks.*" To his credit, however, Phineas Nigellus does stop Harry from running away at one point in the story, making him realize that it is not "noble" to flee. {Ch 23, p494, 495} Of course it helps that Dumbledore *ordered him* to stop

Harry – would he have done it on his own?

Other characters in Book 5 also share the same names as people in the Perseus and Andromeda myth. Minerva, the goddess of wisdom, could be Minerva McGonagall. There is "Andromeda" Black Tonks, also a great-great-grandchild of Phineas and cousin to Sirius Black. (Andromeda's name had been blasted off of the family tapestry because she married a Muggle-born named Ted Tonks. {Ch5, p113}) Her grown daughter is named Nymphadora (but don't call her that).{Ch3, p49} It is certainly reminiscent of the sea nymphs in the myth. Many people in Internet forum discussions, however, believe that "Perseus Evans", an anagram for *Severus Snape* has relevance. "Evans" is the maiden name of Harry's mother. {Ch28, p647} If this anagram has any validity, as the myth suggests, Snape could have an interesting past with the Black family.

THE NAME "NIGELLUS"

The name "Nigellus" also has quite a history. It is originally from the Viking *Niul*, which then traveled to England as *Njal*, then changed in Ireland to *Niul* or *Neil*. The name "Neil" means *Champion*.[5] Eventually, when the main written language of the British Isles became Latin, many names were changed to their Latin forms. "Neil" was written down in documents or records as *Nigellus*.[6] The modern form of Nigellus is, of course, Nigel.

"PHINEAS + NIGELLUS"

What is humorous about Phineas Nigellus' name is that "Nigellus" in Latin also means *black*. So if Phineas means *black* and Nigellus means *black*, then his name could be translated as *Black Black*.

Phineas Nigellus was also the name of a knight of old who founded the town of Blackley in Great Britain. That knight reminds me of the Knight Bus, which is also a pun on the term "Night Bus". If you think about knight Phineas Nigellus's name, you could technically call him the "*Black Black Knight*"! How fitting for a Slytherin (known to fall into the category of Dark wizards) to have a name like that! *Snigger*.

Around 1066, that Blackley knight was given land by William the Conqueror. The land included a five-acre Roman fort near the beautiful forest of Arden, known as "The Great Wood". The descriptions of this land resemble Hogwarts and the Forbidden Forest. In the same area was a township that came to be known as "Blackley" and a manor house known as "Blackley Hall".[7] Over the centuries many families lived there, not all named Black. But there are certainly some uncanny stories that resemble the House of Black in Book 5. For instance, around 1760, a schoolmaster who lived in the Blakely manor reported seeing what he called a "boggart" in the hall. At that time, "boggart" was another name for *ghost*, and this was supposedly the ghost of a woman who walked about at night, accompanied by a large and unearthly black dog. Can anyone say "Grim"?[8]

THE CHARACTER OF PHINEAS NIGELLUS

Phineas Nigellus has some of the same mannerisms as Severus Snape, and perhaps might share a common ancestor. He strokes his beard as he talks to Harry, just as Snape is seen repeatedly "*tracing his mouth with his finger.*" {Ch24, p531} Phineas speaks to Harry "lazily" {Ch23, p495}, as does Snape. {Ch28, p638} At one point, Snape "raises one eyebrow."{Ch24, p519} Phineas Nigellus is seen "*raising a thin black eyebrow as though he found Harry impertinent.*"{p495} They are both sarcastic, often to the point of rudeness, yet they still follow the orders of Albus Dumbledore and respect him. As Phineas says, "*I disagree with Dumbledore on many counts, but you cannot deny he's got style.*" {Ch27, p623}

All through the book, Phineas displays a rather jaded view of his great-great-grandson, Sirius Black, calling him "worthless", {Ch37, p821} disdaining him for his "odd taste in houseguests,"{Ch22, p473,474} and complaining to Dumbledore that Sirius might destroy his portrait. Yet when Sirius dies, Phineas cannot hide his emotions. He listens from the wall as Dumbledore and Harry talk about who is to blame for the death of Sirius Black, and finally asks, *"Am I to understand . . . that . . . the last of the Blacks—is dead?"* Disbelieving what he has heard, Phineas marches out of his painting and goes to Grimmauld Place. In a poignant thought, Harry imagines Phineas walking *"from portrait to portrait, calling for Sirius through the house."*{Ch27, p826} Harry obviously thinks Phineas cares.

Though Phineas is merely a portrait on the wall, he is not a two-dimensional character. He displays a depth of thought and emotion that rivals the living people in the Order of the Phoenix. Since he is tied to Grimmauld Place, the fate of that house is also his fate. The owner of the house now is dead, but the work of the Order of the Phoenix goes on. Will Phineas remain true to Dumbledore and to the Order? Will Harry return to Grimmauld Place and Phineas' canvas? Will Phineas continue to tell Harry what's on his mind—even when the lad doesn't want to listen? I expect that Phineas may be a little ticked-off about the death of Sirius. Will he give Harry a tongue-lashing about the Department of Mysteries?

And finally, will we ever learn how magical portraits are painted and meet some of the artists? Let's all hope so; although Phineas would probably say this is none of our business! ...or just snigger.

ADDITIONAL SLEUTHING NOTES

✳ Why did the family name change from Nigellus to Black? There is also the connection to the phoenix, the legendary Egyptian bird – is Sirius' family tied to Africa and Egypt?

✳ During what era in history did Phineas live?

✳ Is there a "Perseus" in the Harry Potter series? Is Percy just plain "Percy", or could his name be a modern version of the name *Percy-us*?

✳ How does Rabastan (a Rowlinguistic for Rastaban, which means *serpent's head*), fit in with all the snake and dragon-like references for that family? (www.astro.uiuc.edu/~kaler/sow/rastaban.html)

---

[1] "Phinehas." http://www.behindthename.com/nmcleng12.html

[2] Ibid.

[3] "Phineas." http://www.babynamenetwork.com/deta

[4] "Phinius." http://etruscans1.tripod.com/Language/EtruscanPH.html

[5] "Nigel." http://www.geocities.com/edgarbook/names/n/nigel.html

[6] Ibid.

[7] Blakely, Allen. "A Short History of Blackley." http://www.fdjohnson.co.uk/shorthistory.html

[8] Ibid.

[9] Hamilton, Edith. Mythology. Penguin Books (New York, 1969), pg. 120.

[10] Ibid, pgs. 146-148.

[11] Bullfinch, Thomas. The Age of Fable or Stories of Gods and Heroes. Heritage Press (New York, 1958) pg. 76.

✦ ARRESTING MOTION ✦

Dana Bielicki-Maffei ✳ NC, "DBMaff"
USA (*US Edition*), Age 33

Inspiration for this Discussion

Throughout the passage of time, man has been consumed with the need to preserve an image of his being through visual representation. I have been fascinated, while studying art history, by how human beings seem to have a deep-seated, almost instinctive desire to capture lasting images of our person and character for future generations to view. To this need, we can attribute much of the development of portraiture and photography as fine arts and as communication devices. They appear in all facets of our cultural imagination and manage to weave their way into the fabric of popular literature. Portraits serve as key elements in story plotlines, such as Oscar Wilde's *The Picture of Dorian Gray*, Daniel Webster's *The White Devil*, and popular fiction like David Seltzer's *The Omen*. And now I have seen that they are encountered frequently in all five of JK Rowling's *Harry Potter* books. I have a theory as to how these art forms "come alive."

🦉 12

"The aim of every artist is to arrest motion, which is life, by artificial means and hold it fixed so that a hundred years later, when a stranger looks at it, it moves again since it is life."

—William Faulkner[1]

I will investigate the strong ties between Rowling's magical images and those found in our Muggle world. In addition, I will offer suggestions as to how these magical devices function, the magical principles that may govern their use and the workings of each. What is behind portraits and photos in the wizarding world?

MUGGLE PORTRAITS

"A man paints with his brains and not with his hands."

—Michelangelo

Throughout time, man has been fixated with a need to preserve images of his likeness. To this need, we can attribute the development of portraiture as both an art and a mode of communication. How has the portrait evolved? In the strictest sense, a portrait is an "artistic representation of a person, especially one depicting only the face or head and shoulders."[2] Before the camera's invention, portraiture was the prominent method of capturing a lasting image of a person. Since rendering a portrait could take long hours of work by a skilled artist, it tended to be a form of expression limited to the wealthy. Examples of portraits depicting and glorifying the life and times of individuals can be found in tombs of the rich and powerful, dating as far back as ancient Egypt, Mesopotamia and Asia.

While artistic techniques used to render an image certainly progressed with the passage of time, even in the Middle Ages, the primary function of the portrait was to preserve a likeness of a person after death. During the Renaissance, the number of portraits began to slowly increase, but they were still seen as a luxury and often interpreted as a celebration of one's wealth.[3] In the early 1500s artists moved away from side-view profiles and what is known as a "three-quarter pose" became popular. This position offers more of a face-on look at the person and invites us to study the face, and most importantly, the eyes, which were previously obscured from view in the profile pose.[4] Clearly, the artist's goal was to create more of a connection between the viewer and the subject—to open a dialogue of sorts. The portrait offers the viewer a chance to see not just a physical representation, but a glimpse of the character and personality of the subject. The portrait is moving toward telling a story about the person it depicts in addition to preserving a likeness.

With the spread of industrialism throughout Europe (c. 1750), more money filtered down into the hands of common folk, making art accessible to them. Artists began to work for whomever they pleased, named their prices and incorporated distinct styles.[5]

The idea of portraits as interactive art (that tells the viewer a story about the subject) was further developed through objects and backgrounds. Colors became more vibrant (and form less restrictive). The push for realism lessened and images began to be more about the person and his distinct characteristics than the artist's interpretation of these qualities.[6]

While the underlying goal of portraiture is to preserve the physical likeness of a person, portraits create an active dialogue with the character and tell about his or her behavior, as well as the popular attitudes and trends at the time the image was rendered. It is on this note of interaction, between subject and viewer that we turn to the portraits we find in Harry Potter.

WIZARD PORTRAITS

"...painting is...an offensive and defensive weapon against the enemy."
—Pablo Picasso

What are portraits in the wizarding world? There is no formal definition to which we can refer nor do we have a window into Rowling's mind. Or do we? Based on canon, we know that:

1. Subjects can move from portrait to portrait, so long as there is another portrait (a "destination") canvas available at the next location, and that the other portrait can be of someone else or a blank canvas.
2. Portraits can interact with viewers in very complex ways—engaging in meaningful conversations, fulfilling requests, responding to orders and exhibiting emotion.
3. Portraits may be bound to serve their "owner" in some fashion.
4. Portraits can, to some extent, think and act of their own accord.
5. The characteristics of the person represented in the portrait are *in some way* captured; however these characteristics, according to JK Rowling, are typical but parrot-like qualities (or "catchphrases" that the person exhibited during his life). {Edinburgh Chat}

Hogwarts houses a vast collection of portraits—and what a collection it is![7] All of them have unique positions within the castle's culture.

One of the most frequently encountered portraits, the Fat Lady's, hangs over the (hidden) entryway to the Gryffindor Common Room. {B1, Ch7, p129 US} This portrait depicts a large, regal woman wearing a fussy, pink silk dress. As we find out early in Book 1, her primary job is to guard the entryway, allowing access only to those who are able to provide her with the current password. While dedicated to her job, she has been known to get a bit testy with people who wake her up and even to wander out of her frame to go visiting. In Book 4, at the Yule Ball, the Fat Lady and her best friend, Violet, an aged, pallid witch whose painting hangs in the antechamber off the Great Hall, did get a bit tipsy on chocolate liqueurs.{B4, Ch33, p411}

The Fat Lady only truly abandons her post after a vicious attack by Sirius Black in Book 3. Her flight is an example of a thinking reaction to a perceived, and in the end real, danger. It shows her ability to assess a situation and act appropriately. Likewise, her visits to Violet show that she has an emotional desire for companionship and is affected by food. The portrait of the ornery Sir Cadogan, hanging in a corridor near the South Tower, is another of the more widely seen portraits in the books. This little knight is a Don Quixote-style clown who frequently offers the reader a bit of comic relief with his tendency to be led astray by his overwhelming sense of gallantry and bravado. {B3, Ch12, p236} His bravery, combined with his predisposal to fight (made clear through his various dialogues and encounters with students like Harry and Ron), goes a long way to show us Cadogan's character.

The portraits of former Hogwarts Headmasters hanging in Dumbledore's office are also worthy of note. {B5, Ch22, p467-474} Often described as snoozing and ignorant to the activity in the room, the subjects of these portraits are obviously listening to everything that goes on within the walls of the office, and are merely faking their slumber. These portraits appear duty-bound to assist the current Headmaster upon request. Often this means visiting other portrait canvases that hang in separate locations for spying purposes. In Chapter 22 of Book 5, upon Dumbledore's command, Dilys Derwent, Headmistress from 1741-1768, visits St Mungo's, where she had been a healer from 1722-1741. Everard, reportedly among the most popular of former headmasters, first visits his own portrait at the Ministry of Magic, where he sounds the alert about the attack upon Arthur Weasley. He then travels to a portrait of Elfrida Cragg to get a better look at the injured Weasley being carried from the Ministry building. {p469-471} Here again, we have Dilys and Everard, two clear examples of portraits that are both interacting with the viewers and providing information—thinking on their own parts. Everard goes beyond what is requested of him, rationalizes a plan, remembers a picture in a place that suits his needs, and takes action—all to provide a more accurate account of the situation to Dumbledore. All this points to the portrait subjects clearly having minds of their own.

On two separate occasions, we have seen Dumbledore dispatch Phineas Nigellus to his familial home, number twelve Grimmauld Place, to deliver messages. These examples are of particular interest with regard to the historical concepts of portraiture. {p472, Ch 23, p495} On one occasion, Phineas tries to disobey his orders, feigning fatigue:

> *"Visit my other portrait?" said Phineas . . . giving a long, fake yawn . . .*
>
> *"Oh no, Dumbledore, I am too tired tonight…"*

This attempted resistance to a command supports the assumption that the portraits have some degree of self-determination. The implication here is Phineas, a former Slytherin, may resist providing assistance to Dumbledore if at all possible. Small clues such as this lead us to realize that elements of character and views held by the portrait subjects in their lifetimes are transferable to the representational "being" in the portrait.

While it is important to remember that portraits are not the actual persons they depict, it is apparent that, as is the case with Muggle portraits, wizard portraits are instilled with certain character qualities attributed to the subjects during their lives. JK Rowling described it as a faint imprint or aura. {Edinburgh Chat} Could they be similar to the "echoes" we saw produced by Priori Incantatem in Book 4? {Ch 24, p466-468} The portraits' actions provide us insight into what the real persons may have been like and, at the same time, support the assertion that portraits can think creatively and react independently.

One final point regarding wizard portraits is that, like Muggle portraits, they can be restored or fixed. Following the attack by Sirius, the Fat Lady stays with Violet in another canvas while her own painting is restored and repaired by Filch.

MUGGLE PHOTOGRAPHY

"It takes a lot of … looking before you learn to see the ordinary."

—David Bailey (English Photographer)

By the end of the 18th century, members of the working ranks of society were accumulating disposable wealth at an increasing rate. This trend resulted in the ability to obtain products and services (such as portraits) that were once limited to the upper class. The advent of the camera, in the mid-nineteenth century filled this demand and placed a mechanism that captured and preserved images quickly and inexpensively within reach of the lower classes.

A photo (in Muggle terms), as defined by *The Concise Oxford Dictionary,* is "a picture made with a camera, in which an image is focused onto film and then made visible and permanent by chemical treatment."[8] At present, it is almost impossible for us to move throughout the day without encountering a photograph.

While photography is a recognized artistic medium, for the purposes of this discussion, we should recognize that photographs serve more of a utilitarian purpose. Photography and cameras fill a need in our society. They are used to tell of news and world events, they help us preserve our life and times, they decorate interior and exterior spaces, they help promote and advertise products and services, and, finally, allow us to recall and preserve past events.

WIZARD PHOTOGRAPHS

"Make visible what, without you, might perhaps never have been seen."

—Robert Bresson

Having described photography in our Muggle world, we should define what we known about photography in Harry's world:

1. Photos in the wizarding world can be, but are not always, enchanted, animated objects.
2. Wizard photos represent "captured" moments in time.
3. Subjects of wizard photos react to commands.
4. Magical cameras apparently exist and produce animated photos.
5. Muggle film, processed with magic, photographic developing potion, produces animated photographs.
6. Wizard photos serve purposes similar to photos in the Muggle world.

Most frequently we see wizards use photos to preserve, recall and support the communication of news and events in publications like *The Daily Prophet* and *The Quibbler*. For example, Harry learns of the Weasley's financial windfall and their subsequent family trip to Egypt when he receives from Ron an article clipping from *The Daily Prophet* that is accompanied by an animated photo of the family. {B3, Ch1, p8} Who can forget Gilderoy Lockhart snagging the opportunity to pose with Harry in Flourish & Blots to gain some coverage in *The Daily Prophet*, unabashedly flashing his five-time, award-winning smile in the opening chapters of Book 2? {Ch4, p58-61} Finally, the various articles penned by Rita Skeeter throughout Book 4 are accompanied by the images snapped by her trusty sidekick, Bozo.

Wizards also use photos to preserve and recover their personal history. One of the most treasured gifts Harry receives is a photo album, assembled for him by Hagrid, containing pictures of his family and friends. Among the photos is a wedding picture of James and Lily in which a young, happy Sirius Black appears standing as James's best man. {B3, Ch11, p212} The photos are of the animated wizard variety—waving and smiling at the viewer—but the album itself is much more than simply a collection of images. For both Harry and Hagrid {B4, Ch24, p455} photos preserve the lives of loved ones who have passed, just like they do for Muggles. The images of Harry's parents prove the existence of a past to which Harry can claim ownership—they make his life and all the events leading to his present real and undeniable. The power of these images is incredible in a symbolic as well as tangible manner. By having those photos, Harry has proof that he, too, is part of the wizarding world.

Magic photos appear as illustrations in many of the books Harry encounters while attending Hogwarts. In Book 4, Ron and Harry peruse the pages of *Flying With The Cannons* {Ch 1, p18}; in Book 4, Harry reluctantly views the image of the grim on *Death Omens: What to Do When You Know the Worst Is Coming* {Ch4, p53, 54}; and in Book 5 Harry receives *Practical Defensive Magic and Its Use Against the Dark Arts* as a gift from Sirius and Lupin {Ch23, p501}. All these books contain animated images to help depict objects and other ideas explored in writing. Photos in wizard books, therefore, serve as communication aids or enhancements, similar to photos in Muggle books.

Just as interesting as the actual images is the magic used to create wizard photographs. At this point, it appears there are three ways to generate animated images: 1) magic cameras, 2) photograph developing potion, and 3) enchanted Muggle cameras. A reporter on the scene during Lockhart's book signing in Book 2 snaps some shots for *The Daily Prophet*. With each photo, the camera emits a small cloud of purple smoke with the flash indicating that there is likely some form of magic during the picture taking. {B2, Ch4, p59} Bozo's camera in Book 4 acts in very much the same fashion as he snaps off shots during the Triwizard Tournament and at other times in the book. {Ch18, p311, Ch24, p437} It is important to note that not all cameras are magical objects. Colin's camera appears to function like a normal Muggle camera and the pictures he takes with it move only because he develops them in a special potion. {B2, Ch6, p96} The correlation between the uses of photography in the Muggle and wizarding worlds is apparent.

Photography serves similar purposes and is used on a large scale in each population. There is, of course, one major difference – if you're a Muggle you don't have to worry about getting annoyed looks from your mom's photo as you slump around all day on the couch watching TV when you know you have chores to finish!

PORTRAIT OR PHOTOGRAPH: HOW'S A WIZARD TO CHOOSE?

It's apparent that portraits and photos share certain similarities, but we begin to see some glaring differences. The first, notable difference in Harry's world concerns their abilities to move, act and react to the world around them. While it is obvious that photos can move, there is yet no single instance wherein a photo does anything other than move within the context of its frame in response to a viewer's command (as subjects in the photo of the original Order of the Phoenix do in response to Mad-eye Moody's command). {B5, Ch9, p173, 174} But photos lack the ability to interact on a personal level with the viewer—as we have seen portraits do in earlier examples—by carrying out conversations, fulfilling orders, and making decisions or taking action on their own.

Rowling apparently uses photos in the wizarding world to preserve memories, capture images of people and places, communicate news, support ideas and concepts found in books—exactly as we do in the Muggle world. And while photos move, unlike portraits, the subjects in photos appear to be limited to that particular space. Additionally, we have yet to see the subject in a photo have a direct conversation with a viewer. All of these combined elements lead us to conclude that Rowling's photos capture a moment in time, and are intended to "preserve" and "depict", rather than interact.

Portraits, as we have shown, have purposes that extend beyond preserving and depicting a moment or likeness of a witch or wizard. Portraits seem to be an "echo" of the person, imbued with certain qualities and behaviors exhibited by the person depicted while he/she was alive. For example, the exchange between portrait-Phineas and Harry in Chapter 24 of Book 5 provides a glimpse of the views held by the living Phineas concerning young people, as well as a feeling of why he might have been unpopular with Hogwarts students during his tenure. This idea can also be applied to the "echo" being in the portrait of Sirius' mother. As she roams from canvas to canvas, hurling insults and curses at visitors to the Black family home, we are shown possible reasons for her son's disdain as well as the Black family reputation.

Finally, there is a major distinction by which photos and portraits are created, the key being the presence of an external machine or process to produce the animation seen in a photograph. In using a camera or a special developing potion, the wizard is introducing a third element into the magical equation. The camera or potion appears to be a conduit, of sorts, through which the magic presumable is imparted onto the image to animate it. The use of a third agent suggests a less personal brand wherein there is no direct contact between the wizard and object. The camera or the potion, while created by a wizard is the sole instrument of the magic used to produce a photo. This may explain why photos don't carry the personal qualities exhibited by portraits.

At this point, we have never witnessed the creation of a portrait in any of the books, nor has Rowling explained the process. Yet, we can theorize that there is a more direct relationship between the portrait and the wizard. We know magical media exists— magic ink like that used for the Marauder's Map and the magical paper seen in Tom Riddle's diary. So, it is likely that an enchanted agent is used to create a portrait—perhaps the paint, canvas and brushes (or all of them) are at work in magical portraits. What is important is that the media (brushes, paint, canvas, etc.) are in direct contact with the wizard's hand. Like a wand, this allows an element to work as a conduit for the magic used to produce a portrait that is missing in photos—that element is intent. We know wandless magic (magic that needs only the intent and focus of the caster's mind and no external aids like a wand) exists and that this form of magic can be very powerful—Occlumency, Legilimency, Transfiguration and Apparation, for example. Further, we know that when using wand-assisted magic it is critical that the intent of the use be clear and focused. Even Unforgivable Curses don't work without intent.

This being said, I believe the artist's intent, in combination with direct contact with the actual portrait, imparts the kind of magic needed to generate an interactive, thinking "echo" of a person—and assign to that wizard (and their heir?) the role of "task master" establishing who the portrait will serve. Must the wizard who rendered the image also have the ability to control its actions and elicit its service?

In conclusion, it is important to keep in mind that while photos require the presence of someone to "take" the picture, they remain a product of a mechanized process. The photographer can control the technicalities that contribute to the rendering of the image, but the camera is still the actual device of image production. With portraiture, the artist-wizard is the direct source of image production because no machine separates the subject and the artist. Even the language of photography is mechanical and scientific—(lens, aperture, film, speed, shutter)—when compared to the language of portraiture (strokes, rendering, hands, style). It is this concept of indirect creation (photography) versus direct creation (portraiture) that I believe is the key to understanding the magic used to produce these images as well as the abilities of one to simply react, while the other can interact.

Of course, this is all speculation, since magic doesn't really exist... right?

———————— ADDITIONAL SLEUTHING NOTES ————————

✳ Would non-electric/mechanical cameras (Argus, Brownie, etc.) work at Hogwarts?

✳ Are there famous wizard artists? Can a portrait be done in a different style (eg. cubism)?

✳ When and how is the aura captured for the portrait, and how is it "activated" upon death? Is there a portrait of Sirius somewhere?

1 "Simpson's Contemporary Quotations". www.bartleby.com/63/45/6845.html

2 portrait. *The Concise Oxford Dictionary*. Ed. Judy Pearsall. Oxford University Press, 2001. *Oxford Reference Online*. Oxford University Press. University of Pennsylvania. [19 March 2004],
http://www.oxfordreference.com/views/ENTRY.html?subview=Main&entry=t23.e43729

3 Campbell, Lorne. 'Portraiture', *The Grove Dictionary of Art Online*, (Oxford University Press, [March 19, 2004]),
http://www.groveart.com

4 Cranston, Jodi, *The Poetics of Portraiture in the Italian Renaissance*. (Cambridge, UK, 2000), 1-15.

5 Hayes, John. "Some Unknown Early Gainsborough Portraits," *The Burlington Magazine*, 107, (February 1965): 62-74.

6 Hayes, John. "Some Unknown Early Gainsborough Portraits," *The Burlington Magazine*, 107, (February 1965):

7While there are certainly numerous examples that work well within the context of this essay, there is simply not enough space to explore each. The following is a list of other prominent and not-so-prominent portraits along with the title and chapter of the book in which each can be found:
    Little girl who curtsies to the first years on their way up to their common room after the welcoming feast (*Sorcerer's Stone*).
    Woman who walks into a room and sits by a bed, in the Hospital Wing (*Sorcerer's Stone*)
    Anne Boleyn, second wife of Henry VIII, mother of Elizabeth I, popularly believed to be a witch located on the shifting staircase (*Sorcerer's Stone*).
    Wizard with walrus mustache; next to Violet in the antechamber off the Great Hall.
    Painting of a group of women in crinolines (*Prisoner of Azkaban*, Chapter 6).
    Map of Argyllshire on second floor; Fat Lady hid here once (*Prisoner of Azkaban*, Chapter 6).
    Mermaid painting hanging in the Prefects' Bathroom; apparently watches people take baths (*Goblet of Fire*).

8 "photograph" *The Concise Oxford Dictionary*. Ed. Judy Pearsall. Oxford University Press, 2001. *Oxford Reference Online*. Oxford University Press. University of Pennsylvania. 28 May 2004
http://www.oxfordreference.com/views/ENTRY.html?subview=Main&entry=t23.e42271

Shady People
and Places

BUBBLES AND BRIBES (GOINGS ON AT ST MUNGO'S)

K. ECSEDY ✳ CoS, "FURRYFREAKFERRET"
USA (*US Edition*), AGE 15

Inspiration for this Discussion

Here it is, Harry Potter fans: my lovely little discussion all on the wonders of bubblegum. I've been working on some anagrams and I think I have something for you to chew on. Time to pop a stick of chewing gum in your mouths and turn on your thinking caps. Wait! Don't throw out that wrapper just yet… stick it in your pocket, you'll want it later…

 HANDFUL

We know Alice Longbottom, Neville's mum, has been giving empty gum wrappers to her son for a while. Neville's Gran remarks that his mother must have given him "*enough to paper [his] room by now*". {B5, Ch23, p515} If your Sneakoscope *isn't* whistling away like a boiling teapot just yet, you might want to bring it over to Dervish and Banges for a check-up. Where would Alice, who isn't even allowed to leave her shared room, get so much gum? And why does she keep giving all of her empty wrappers to Neville?

ANAGRAM CLUES

Take out that gum wrapper again. It says 'Drooble's Best Blowing Gum' on it, right? Well, hand it over to your Philological Stone* and see what anagrams** you can get out of it. A few of them ought to come up, which relate to Harry Potter themes: *Gold Bribe Below St Mungo's*, *Goblins Were Sold Tomb Bug*, and *Mr. Tibbles Eats Owl Dung*. Now, what significance could any of these have?

Looking at them in reverse order, the third one is sounds like something Peeves would say and I'll leave you all to ponder possible significance for it.

The second anagram conjures a theory shared by me and "Dedalus Diggle" (also of the Chamber of Secrets' Forums). It is based on the knowledge that the goblins have wizards like Bill Weasley poking around for valuable artifacts, plus Egyptians were very big into the "afterlife" and immortality (note – Phoenixes come from Egypt). The goblins could be looking for, or already have obtained, an ancient magical scarab beetle, or "tomb bug," that might hold the key to unlocking the secret to immortality – which, of course, has been Voldything's aim from the beginning.

Think it's far-fetched? Try counting the number of times goblins and Egypt (or things connected with it, like scarabs) are mentioned throughout the series. While that is a fun theory, there isn't enough support to back it, and so it is to the first I turn my attention.

*Philological Stone – see *New Clues to Harry Potter: Book 5*, {p xv}
**anagram is a word or phrase made by scrambling the letters of another word of phrase

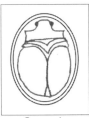

Scarab

What does "Gold Bribe Below St Mungo's" mean? Is there something going on at the hospital? Let's investigate this.

Please flip back to the Quidditch World Cup in Book 4. Remember what Minister Fudge so conveniently let slip? Lucius Malfoy, who was there as Fudge's guest, had just given a "*very* generous" donation to St Mungo's Hospital for Magical Maladies and Injuries. {Ch8, p101} I assume you all need no reminder that Lucius is a person with more nastiness in his forefinger than the Big Bad Wolf has in his whole body. But do we really, honestly, and truly believe that this bad man, who is loaded with money***, was actually trying to better the world by giving to "excellent causes"?{B4, Ch36, p706} As if. No, I assure you, Lucius has his own nauseating motives for giving gold to the Wizarding hospital.

Later, in Book 4, we get a second mention of St Mungo's Hospital – this time by Dumbledore, soon after he pulls Harry from his "thoughts". Dumbledore says Neville's parents were tortured to insanity by Death Eaters, and they now reside in St Mungo's, where Neville often visits them with his grandmother. Coincidence?

Fast-forward a bit. Voldemort has risen again, Fudge is an idiot, and Harry, himself, is an angry teenager only too willing to vent a bit of anger upon any innocent passers-by. Arthur Weasley has been bitten by Har - I mean, a *snake* and Harry, Hermione, Moody, Lupin, and the Weasley family are going to bring Mr. W a bit of Christmas cheer as he lies recovering in a bed in St Mungo's. Ducking for cover as the nuclear explosion that is Molly goes off, Harry, Ron, Hermione, and Ginny pelt up the stairs and onto the fourth floor - Spell Damage - where they are apprehended by none other than wanna-be defense genius Gilderoy Lockhart. Before they can slip away by a side passage, a "motherly looking Healer" {Ch23, p510} bustles up to them and persuades them to stay a while. The Healer (Miriam Strout?) tells the trio and Ginny that the door to Gilderoy's ward is usually kept locked and that he must have slipped out. (Sneakoscope still working? Is it still jumping up and down before your eyes, trying to grab your attention and alert you the presence of suspicious persons?) All right, then....

Obviously, the occupants of the ward aren't watched as carefully as they ought to be, if Gilderoy can slip out. And it seems he has done it repeatedly, because Miriam appeared to know exactly where she should look for the escaped patient, didn't she? Hmmm. Also, did you notice her word choice? "*with intensive remedial potions and charms ... we can produce some improvement*".{B5, Ch23, p511} Not even ten pages later, Snape's telling Harry that to cover up that he is getting Occlumency lessons, they're to tell others that he's taking "*Remedial Potions.*" Tapping your Philological Stone with your wand and saying the word 'remedial', should give you back two definitions: 1) 'providing, or intending to provide, a remedy'; 2) 'designating or of any special course for helping students overcome deficiencies'[1]. So, of course, Miriam wants us to believe her to be using the first definition, to remedy an illness. But what if she really means the second, and the potions and charms they use to combat the illnesses of people, like Gilderoy, are second-rate (made by someone who could have used a course of Remedial Potions)? Or is it something even more dubious?

J K Rowling also provides us, in that short stretch of a few pages, with the name of the ward: the Janus Thickey ward. For those who don't know the tale of Janus Thickey, I will now relate it to you. Janus Thickey feigned death by a Lethifold, a magical creature that devours its victim, leaving no trace of themselves or the victim behind. Janus' family was convinced by his spotless bed and a hastily scribbled note

*** "loaded" = English idiom for having lots and lots of money.

that this fate had indeed befallen poor Janus. Their mourning was brought to an abrupt halt when he was discovered five miles away, living with another woman.[2] If this man was ever hospitalized at all, he would have most likely been brought to St Mungo's to recover from injuries dealt him by his enraged wife. So, why would he have a ward named for him? Curious.

Leaving a helpless Harry, Hermione, Ron, and Ginny to be tortured by Gilderoy's sickening personality, Miriam Strout flitters around the ward, finishing her delivery of presents. Before his little accident, Broderick Bode was an Unspeakable (someone who works in the Department of Mysteries – the place where the weapon was kept that Lord... *Thingy* wanted so badly). He was placed in St Mungo's when Lucius Malfoy put the Imperius Curse upon him in an attempt to force him to retrieve the afore-mentioned weapon. If you recall, he was given a potted plant for Christmas, which turned out to be a cutting of Devil's Snare that killed him. Why was he murdered? Presumably, it was a Death Eater trying to silence him. Healer Strout had supposedly been encouraging Broderick to take care of the plant himself, not realizing it was deadly shrubbery, and then he was strangled by it. First, isn't it odd that Strout didn't recognize the Devil's Snare? After all, according to what Harry was told during "Careers Advice" in Book 5, Healers need an E (for 'Exceeds Expectations') in Herbology to be considered for the post at all - and we were told that Hermione learned about Devil's Snare during class way back in Book 1! Also, the plant survived long enough to get at Bode, which, considering it likes the *dark* and *damp*, is saying that someone had to be protecting the "little killer". Not words you'd want to use while discussing a hospital, are they? People in care of hospitals aren't supposed to die from their Christmas presents.

We get to witness our forgetful little friend, Neville, as he visits his mentally insane parents. As Mrs. Longbottom (nice hat) is about to work herself up into a lovely, long rant, Neville's mother, Alice, comes shuffling toward him and hands (yup!) him an empty Drooble's Best Blowing Gum wrapper (beginning to come full circle, isn't it?). She then turns away, humming to herself. It might be interesting to note that, while Dudley is specifically stated as humming tunelessly (way, *way* back in the first chapter of Book 5), Alice isn't. Does that imply that her song has a tune? And if so, what does that say about her sanity?

Now, remember my lovely little anagram from above: 'Gold Bribe Below St Mungo's'? Think you can piece it all together by yourselves? I'll help anyway…

Alice, who is staying in the Janus Thickey ward, may not be quite as insane as everyone – including her only son – believes her to be. The gum wrappers she's been giving Neville all these years could really be a clever message-in-a-bottle, if you will. If Neville would only check those wrappers out and work out any clues (Hermione could help) – we might see a recovery in the future for Alice and Frank Longbottom. Lucius Malfoy, using his rather large stash of cash, may have been bribing a Healer at St Mungo's (or the hospital as a whole) to keep the Longbottoms in their incapacitated state – a cowardly attempt to save his own skin from Azkaban; the Longbottoms would most likely have known Lucius was and is a Death Eater, and there's still the nagging possibility that more than just the three Lestranges and Crouch were involved in the torture of the high-ranking Aurors. Someone (a Healer?) has been giving them bubble gum – which could be a means to prevent the remedial potions and charms from taking effect. (Notice – Broderick and Gilderoy, who had both been there a far shorter time, had been making remarkable steps toward recovery, while the Longbottoms seem far less near release.)

You also have to wonder, if the Longbottoms had information on the whereabouts of Vold- *You-Know-Who*, what else did they know? Is it possible they also found out how to defeat the Dark Lord? Don't rule it out just yet; that's my personal conviction.

Now that we have seen JKR's website (www.jkrowling.com) with the wrappers all over the place, you can't tell me that those wrappers are there just for wallpaper. Is there something going on at St Mungo's? Alas, only time will tell as we sit, anxiously awaiting the arrival of Book 6. Until then, my friends, I, like you, will be pondering the many questions here raised. Farewell and fair fortunes be yours.

ADDITIONAL SLEUTHING NOTES

✳ If the anagram comes from JKR, then it needs to work in all languages/translations – just like it did for Tom Marvolo Riddle in Book 2 – so has anyone yet tried to work this out for the other languages?

✳ Could "remedial potions" include a potion in the gum that is *keeping* the Longbottoms "insane"? Or…what if, instead of being *less* effective, "remedial" potions are being used to *augment* in the same way that "remedial lessons" augment? Could they be administering any potions to *augment* Gilderoy?

✳ We already know that music was a clue in Book 1. So, could Alice's humming have a clue of some kind hidden in her tune?

✳ There are "bubble" running bits (repeated words and themes) all through Book 5: the lighting in the hospital, Tonks' bubblegum-pink hair, Snape's pink soap bubbles, etc., and you can't miss the wrappers all over JKR's site – so are those really all there *just* because JKR now likes to chew gum?

---

1 Guralnik, David B. , <u>Webster's New World Dictionary of the American Language</u>, Second College Edition, the World Publishing Company, (Montevideo, Mexico, Rio de Janeiro, Buenos Aires and Havana, 1970), pg. 1201.
2 Scamander, Newt, <u>Fantastic Beasts & Where to Find Them</u>, Obscurus Books, (New York, 2001), pg. 27.

Neville's Gran and the Feathered Crowns of Egypt

JEANNE PERRY KIMSEY ✳ CoS, "SILVER INK POT"
USA (*US Edition*), AGE 44

Inspiration for this Discussion

From the very first time I read about the vulture hat of Neville's Gran in Book 3, I have been fascinated by it. What on earth could it mean? Then one night I was fooling around with anagrams and discovered that "vulture hat" was an anagram for "value truth," and it amazed me so much I started researching hats and headdresses. There are so many online discussions of Neville's grandmother in which people are convinced that she is a wicked crone and a Death Eater. From my research, I believe the opposite.

 NEWT

Neville Longbottom's grandmother makes the strangest of fashion statements: a hat decorated with an imposing stuffed vulture. This would, to our civilized eyes, seem to be a hideous and frightening creature to have on one's head, but Neville's Gran seems to wear it proudly. We know that Neville is certainly a bit afraid of his sharply critical grandmother, but should he be? Is she just good and cranky, or evil—a Death Eater perhaps? Or is she merely modeling fashions for the next Death Day Ball?

In the wizarding world, to be a Death Eater is to join the ranks of the most evil and foul wizards who serve Lord Voldemort. Since a vulture is one of nature's scavengers—a literal "death feeder"—then one can easily come to the conclusion that Mrs. Longbottom is perhaps not on the side of goodness. She certainly seems to scare the daylights out of her grandson. Neville talks about her a lot in the first two books, but the first time she actually appears is in Book 3. Harry sees Neville being "told off" by his Gran for losing his book list.{Ch4, p55} The only person more strict with forgetful-Neville is Professor Snape, who is an ex-Death Eater, himself. In the same book, we find out that Neville's boggart, the thing he is most afraid of, looks like Snape. Neville's Riddikulus spell, used to banish his fear, creates a Snape dressed in Gran's vulture hat, green dress, fox fur, and large red handbag. {Ch7, p137}

Should we conclude that JK Rowling is drawing a connection between the harsh Potions Master and Neville's Gran? Is the vulture hat a symbol of how much they want to kill Neville? Not. (Except maybe figuratively speaking when Neville is acting particularly dense.) In fact, the truth is that they are probably both trying to keep Neville alive.

So, you are probably wondering: "What is it about that vulture hat?" Vultures have been associated throughout history with death and funerals, so it is a natural association. In ancient religions such as Zoroastianism and Hinduism, vultures were sometimes encouraged to prey on the dead, and special "towers of silence" were built for this purpose.[1] Other cultures, though they buried their dead, still sensed a mysterious power in the great vultures, which could magically appear from high in the sky so soon after a death occurred. Nowhere was the vulture held in higher esteem than in Ancient Egypt.[2]

In the tombs of Egyptian kings, vultures are often pictured leading a procession of other creatures, gods, and people through the stages of the afterlife. A walking vulture eventually became the symbol of a sound in the Egyptian hieroglyphic alphabet. Surprisingly, this sound – "mw" became part of the word "mwt," which meant *mother*.[3] The ability of a baby to make an "m" sound and mean *mother* is probably universal, but why in the world did the Egyptians connect that sweet sound to a vulture perched by a dead carcass?

The answer is that, to the people of Egypt who worshipped the sun, a high-flying vulture that soared in the sky was close to heaven. The wide wingspan of these large birds was seen as "protective," like a mother's arms surrounding and holding her children. Vultures are usually seen circling in family groups, so they were venerated as symbols of love and affection. The most important vulture to the Egyptians was the Griffon Vulture or "Gyps Fulvus." In that species, males and females look just alike, so the Egyptians believed that they were all female and all mothers. Since a vulture will forcefully protect its young, the Griffon Vulture became a symbol of the goddesses who watch over mothers and children.[4] The main mother goddess of Ancient Egypt was called "Mwt," or "Mut," meaning *vulture*. She was worshipped in the city of Thebes. Sometimes she wears the vulture crown, and other times she is depicted with wings. She was also a goddess of the moon and had a "crescent-shaped" lake near her temple. Each year, a statue of Mut was placed in a boat and sailed around the lake to ensure fertility. Sometimes Mut appears with three heads—one is a vulture, one is a human, and one is a lion—another Gryffindor House symbol. Mut's official title was "Mut, the Great Lady of Isheru, the Lady of Heaven, the Queen of the Gods."[5]

The second great vulture goddess was called "Nekhebet," a protector of Upper Egypt and guardian of mothers and children. She often appears sitting beside "Wadjet, the cobra goddess" of Lower Egypt. She is depicted in many forms: a woman with a vulture crown, a woman with a vulture head, a full cobra with a white crown, and a vulture with a white crown.[6] Her "talons" often hold the "shen" or symbol of eternity, which is reminiscent of Gran's handbag that she holds with her "shriveled, claw-like hand."{Book 5, Ch23, p513}.

Nekhebet was seen as Pharoah's special protector, often shown hovering over his head. The famous golden funerary mask of Tutankhamun (King Tut) is crowned with both the Cobra "Wadjet" and the vulture "Nekhebet." This meant that Tut, the boy king, was protected in both the north and south of Egypt.[7]

Nekhebet is also linked to combat and the fierceness of war. She exists to protect the Pharoah from his enemies. Often a fiery sun disk symbolizes the king, with the cobra and vulture on either side. This symbol is known as the "Eye of Ra."[8] We know that Nekhebet is a sort of combo-goddess, part vulture and part snake. We must look again at the symbolism of Neville's most hated professor, Snape, dressed in Gran's clothing. For JK Rowling to show us the "Head of Slytherin" with a vulture crown on his head is quite enlightening! The fact that the vision was of "boggart" Snape, and not his real self, would be secondary. The vulture and cobra together are "protectors" of mothers and children, so perhaps there is more to Snape than meets the eye. The Egyptian motifs in that scene are clear. The second boggart (Parvati's) is a "blood-stained bandaged mummy."{B3, Ch7, p137}

Each mother goddess, like Neville's grandmother, wears a feathery "crown" with the body and head of a Griffon vulture. The name "griffon" or "griffin" is meaningful, of course, because Neville is a member of Gryffindor House, associated with courage. Interestingly, the derivation of "griffon" or "griffin" is from a Hebrew word which means "cherub".[9]

Are there clues besides the vulture hat that link Neville's Gran to the royal mother goddesses? In Book 5, when Harry and his friends run into Neville and his Gran at St Mungo's hospital, Gran seems to show many qualities of a royal background. She speaks "graciously" to them, "proferring her hand regally."{Ch23, {p513} She is not described as being "critical" of Neville, but she is "sternly appraising" of him and calls him a "good boy". {p513} Obviously, she loves her only grandson and only chides him for not telling his friends the sad story of his parents, who were "tortured into insanity by You-Know-Who's followers." {p514}

If you think about it, Frank and Alice Longbottom's insanity almost completely rules out a Death Eater connection for Neville's Gran. We have Neville's assurance that his Gran supports Dumbledore, and doesn't believe what she reads in the *Daily Prophet* about Harry and Dumbledore being insane. {Ch11, p219}

Another clue, perhaps, is that the words "Vulture Hat" are an anagram for "Value Truth." That seems pretty clear to me! In the world of Harry Potter, things and people are often not what they seem. Neville's Gran, with her alarming appearance, is often critical and harsh, but she is helpful, too. Perhaps her main failure is her tendency to constantly compare Neville with his father, Frank, which lowers Neville's self-esteem. As the story goes on in future books and leads through the war with Voldemort, Neville will have to find his own way to fight and survive. Will his Gran realize that he has powers she might have overlooked? Whatever happens, Neville's Gran will undoubtedly be there, right behind him, hovering, as all great mother-goddesses do.

------------------------------ ADDITIONAL SLEUTHING NOTES ------------------------------

✳ Wizards so often associate color with their Hogwarts Houses, and we see here that there is some snake-related symbolism with vultures – so should we be concerned that Gran likes green dresses? On the other hand, is this a hint that there is regal Egyptian blood (think Half-Blood Prince) in the family?

✳ Is the vulture link to Snape a hint that he could be a vulture Animagus, or is that image just one of JKR's clues to identify a Death Eater? Can we be sure that this "clue" isn't being used on Gran as well?

✳ Neville is already showing confidence in Book 5 – will he be less fearful of Gran in the future?

[1] Houston, David. <u>Condors and Vultures</u>. Voyageur Press. Stillwater: 2001. p51.
[2] Ibid, p51
[3] "Mut". http://www.crystalinks.com/mut/html, p1.
[4] Ibid, p2.
[5] Ibid, p3, 4.
[6] "Nekhebet." http://www.crystalinks.com/mut.html, p3, 4.
[7] Ibid, p2.
[8] Ibid, p3.
[9] Morris, William, editor. "Griffin." <u>The American Heritage Dictionary</u>. Houghton Mifflin. Boston: 1976.

"MAGICAL WHAT'S-MY-NAME" BY GILDEROY LOCKHART (AN AUTOGRAPHED AUTOBIOGRAPHY)

CECI ✳ NEW CLUES FORUM
ARGENTINA (*UK Edition*), AGE 30

Inspiration for this Discussion

When we first meet Gilderoy Lockhart in The Chamber of Secrets, *we see him as a funny charac-ter incapable of holding his wand straight and an absolute coward, who only cares about being famous. However, when we see him again in Book 5, we are teased with more information. I found some of that information odd, so I went back to research him. I came up with several very suspi-cious coincidences that made me dig a little deeper, which reinforced, once again, that the first impression is not always the correct one.*

HANDFUL

We are aware that all that glitters is not gold. Gilderoy Lockhart is no exception.

Before meeting him in Book 2, we learn that he is a wizard who has written several books, and is very charming. The only people who actually admire him, or should I say fancy him, are his female fans (yes, even Mrs. Weasley and Hermione!). We finally meet him in person at Flourish and Blotts. On that occasion, Lockhart notices Harry—even as he's squished in the middle of a crowd, signing autographs (one of his favorite hobbies). Coincidentally, that occurs, of course, at the same time that Lucius Malfoy "handed" Tom Riddle's diary to Ginny and when Arthur and Lucius had their fight. Lockhart was happy.

When classes start at Hogwarts, we wonder what this year will have in store for Harry, Ron, and Hermione. When they are about to have their first lesson, they see Professor Sprout in the company of none other than Lockhart who had been "helping" with the care of the Whomping Willow. {Ch6, p70 *UK*} Another coincidence? In their discourse, he states, "*I just happen to have met several of these exotic plants on my travels . . .*" {Ch8, p100} Any Devil's Snare, Mandrake or Mimbulus Mimbletonia? Is he just bragging as usual, or does he truly have an intimate association with some exotic shrubbery?

During his Defense Against the Dark Arts Class, Lockhart portrays himself as a humanitarian, claim-ing his priorities are ridding the world of evil and creating harmony between all magical and non-magi-cal peoples. Is he sincere? How about when he proclaims his credentials as "*Gilderoy Lockhart, Order of Merlin, Third Class, Honorary Member of the Dark Force Defense League*"? {Ch13, p170} If you think about it, a "Dark Force Defense League" isn't the same as a Defense *Against* the Dark Arts League. It actually sounds as if it could be a league that defends or supports the use of the Dark Arts. There is also the tiny issue that he did try to use a Memory Charm on a couple of twelve-year-old kids. Maybe we should won-der if he, or that group, is supporting the use of Dark Arts.

It is in one of his own classes that we are first led to believe Lockhart is an inept wizard. He couldn't even handle pixies. Lockhart tries a spell, without any effect, and the pixies succeed in leaving him wand-less. The coward then "*dived under his…desk.*" Eventually, he rushes out of the room, closes the door behind him, and leaves the trio to capture and lock up the pixies. {Ch6, p78-80} The second-year students have no trouble doing that.

When Harry hears the Basilisk voice for the first time, he is in Lockhart's office, which is also close to the location of the first victim.{Ch9, p107} Lockhart offers to make the Mandrake Restorative Draught himself. Then, Harry, Ron, and Hermione also see him at Hagrid's hut along with a half-plucked rooster. This is one of the best parts, and I think we all overlooked it. Lockhart just happened to be around the Whomping Willow, the Chamber entrance, Mandrakes, the rooster, and especially when Lucius slipped Ginny the diary.

In Book 2, everyone seems concerned about the safety of the students. Even Lockhart *"seemed [to have] been up most of the night, patrolling the fourth floor."* {Ch16, p213} Gilderoy patrolled the fourth floor? Can we believe that he has the students' safety in mind? Isn't there an entrance to a hidden passage on the fourth floor? How long has the secret corridor been caved in? The twins used it until that winter. If it wasn't caved in at the time, I wonder where it leads and if Lockhart knew about it?

Lockhart doesn't exactly come across as a humanitarian when he willingly tries to *"Obliviate!"* two innocent kids and willingly leaves Ginny to die in the Chamber. He says he can't help Ginny, since he doesn't know the chamber's location. He does seem to know one thing—he brags that his specialty is Memory Charms. {p320} The trouble is, he can be nasty, sly and dangerous with them. Well, if there is something we can't accuse him of, it's being humble. *"Lockhart stopped abruptly in the middle of counting the number of murders he had prevented."* {Ch9, p108}

There is a scene that really bothers me. After Ron forces Lockhart through the entrance to the chamber, he keeps Lockhart under control by pointing his wand at him. Lockhart then gets to his feet and dives at Ron, knocking him to the ground. {Ch16, p224} For someone who is inept and cowardly, he sure is fast and coordinated (beats out two star Quidditch players!).

However, Gilderoy does show signs of bravery. In the Dueling Club, Harry is surprised to see Lockhart smiling. He feels that if the look Snape is giving Gilderoy was meant for him he'd have been *"running as fast as he could in the opposite direction."* {Ch11, p142} For someone who is so cowardly, Lockhart doesn't show the slightest fear. Oddly, I would have expected Lockhart to faint or find an excuse to avoid it, but he just stands his ground and does nothing at all. Is he that brave or that stupid?

When Lockhart thinks it better to teach the students how to defend themselves by learning how to block spells, he says, *"Let's have a volunteer pair—Longbottom and Finch-Fletchley"* {p143} ...Neville, yes, that's right—Neville Longbottom, the boy who can't stay on a broomstick, and is usually considered useless and even dangerous (especially to himself). The first person he thinks about is Neville, and now Lockhart is in the same ward with Neville's parents. Yet another coincidence. Now I can't help but wonder about Finch-Fletchley's background. His mother is at first unhappy about sending him to Hogwarts before she decides that maybe it would be good for their family to have a "fully trained wizard." {Ch6, p73} (*Fully* trained? Hmmm...) It is interesting how he ends up as the next Basilisk victim...

Hermione always has great ideas—like when she wanted to make a (quick and simple) Polyjuice draught to find out who the Slytherin heir could be. Aside from being a very dangerous feat, the recipe for that potion is, of course, in the restricted section of the Hogwarts library. She need a teacher's signature to access it, and who else, but Lockhart? *"It would help me understand what you say in Gadding with Ghouls about **slow-acting venoms**."* {Ch10, p123} Slow-acting venoms and Basilisks—where have we seen them before?

We are told that Gilderoy is a patient in the "Janus Thickey Ward"—the ward for "long term residents." So, how long do you need to stay to be considered a long-term resident? The name of the ward is highly suspicious. Janus Thickey was assumed, by his wife and kids, to be dead, only to be found alive with another woman.{FB p27} Janus is the Roman god of archways (like the veil one), doors (like the Department of

Mysteries and the locked room) and passages (like the ones we see in each book). Janus is usually represented with two faces looking in the opposite direction. Is someone in the ward double-faced? Someone thick, maybe? Do we know anyone thick? Looking at Lockhart from Ron's point of view may be revealing: "'*No teacher's going to fall for that,' said Ron. 'They'd have to be really **thick**.'* (Of course, Lockhart did!) {Ch9, p121}

It is so difficult to determine if there is anything Lockhart can do (besides Memory Charms). We do know that he has a huge fan base and corresponds with them personally. When the boys are punished due to their spectacular arrival by flying car, Harry winds up in Lockhart's office, helping him write letters to his fans. (What do we know about Gladys Gudgeon and Veronica Smethley?) This is the first character in the book whose quill is particularly well described. His quill is followed by Rita's quill, which had the specialty of twisting the truth, and Umbridge's quill which helps the user remember the messages he/she writes. Now, in Book 5, we are reminded that Gilderoy has a "special" quill, too: "*A rather battered peacock-feather quill from his pocket.*" {Ch23, p450} Why does JKR bring up Lockhart's quill around the same time that we are worried about Umbridge's?

The Healer in St Mungo's tells us that Lockhart isn't dangerous, but that could be Rule 4. First, she says that the door is always locked, and Lockhart "*must have slipped out while [she] was bringing in the Christmas presents…*"{p451}. She also says he likes to wander around. So this is clearly not the first time he does it. How can he wander around so much with the door "always" locked? I wonder where he went to and when…

We get a sneak peek of the other ward patients. One of them is the Unspeakable Bode from the Department of Mysteries. Bode isn't speaking any recognizable language, but he does seem to have a lovely plant. Didn't Lockhart say he had familiarity with exotic plants? We also have a veil-like curtain that is concealing two patients, so they and their visitors have more privacy. Last but not least, we see Lockhart's wall, "*covered with pictures of himself.*"{p451} We know that the Lockharts in the pictures can at least move, speak, and smile. We also know he gives a lot of autographed photos to his fans. I wonder who has some of them (certainly Gladys and Veronica)? Can those pictures communicate with him? It is very interesting to think of all the information he could gather that way. It makes me think of Bill Weasley's remark about Dumbledore only caring about staying on the Chocolate Frog cards.

The Healers stop talking about Bode when the curtains are pulled back, revealing Alice and Frank Longbottom and their visitors, Neville and Gran. Well, the world seems to be tiny. Funny how Lockhart's "retirement" takes him to the same ward as the Longbottoms and Bode. After Harry tells Ron and Hermione what he knows about Neville's parents, Hermione asks, "'*Bellatrix Lestrange did that?' There was a long silence, broken by Lockhart's angry voice.*" {p455} Why was Lockhart so angry?

I definitely think that Lockhart is not the incompetent, invalid wizard that we are being led to believe. What do you think? And, I don't believe we've seen the last of his award-winning smile.

ADDITIONAL SLEUTHING NOTES

✳ We know that Gilderoy is an expert in memory charms – what are the chances he is also an expert in *removing* memory charms?

✳ If Mr **Lock**hart keeps finding himself outside of locked wards, then could there be a possibility that he is also good at one other kind of spell – unlocking spells?

✳ Is Lockhart as incompetent as he appears? The wizards he impersonated had fought werewolves, banshees, and vampires (some of the most dangerous creatures in the wizarding world), so he would have had to outsmart some really powerful and clever wizards to place memory charms on them – was he really that clever or does he have yet another talent? Just how "charming" is his smile? Could he have any Legilimens skills?

ALASTOR MOODY: FRIEND OR FOE?

ERIN KNUTSON ✳ NC, "MOMTHATSAFAN"
USA (*US Edition*), AGE 31

Inspiration for this Discussion

I was attached to Alastor Moody from the moment he transfigured Draco Malfoy into a ferret. I admired how he treated Harry's Defense Against the Dark Arts class as adults, but with a gentle guiding hand. It solidified my belief he was a good guy. Yes, I was shocked and dismayed that this Moody turned out to be an imposter! From that point on, I vowed to watch Moody's every action to look for signs of a repeat capture. The legacy of an Auror was there before Harry's eyes, if he would only take advantage of it and use it to better prepare himself for the onslaught of attacks to come from Voldemort and his minions. Since the original Moody character was an imposter, we lost out getting to know the real one. But is this yet the real one? I have explored the contradictions we keep seeing with this character, and the questions we have about his true nature. As Tom Riddle's diary said, "Let me show you!"

 HANDFUL

Alastor Moody has intrigued and confused me with his diverse character traits since his introduction in Book 4. There are many facets to the character we call "Mad-Eye Moody." What we know comes from Barty Crouch Junior's (aka Imposter Moody) portrayal of him and our brief encounters with the "real" Moody. The detailed description of Imposter Moody's entrance into the Great Hall in Book 4, reminds us of similar scenes from Book 5. Can our knowledge of Imposter Moody be a true characterization of Alastor Moody, or does this deception veil who and what Moody really is?

Our introduction to the character of Alastor Moody happens at the Weasleys' home. Unfortunately, we never get to actually meet him. Mr. Diggory is calling on Arthur to help Moody out of a tight spot. *"But if the Improper Use of Magic lot get their hands on Mad-Eye, he's had it—think of his record—we've got to get him off on a minor charge..."* It seems that Moody thought someone was trying to abduct him and set his trash bins on attack mode.{Book 4, Ch11, p160 *US*} We learn in this passage that Moody was a well-known and respected Auror in the era of Lord Voldemort, and Arthur is the only one who can get Mad-Eye off the hook. Many in the wizard community now think he is paranoid and jumpy around anyone, whether a Dark Wizard or not. Diggory thinks Mad-Eye *"started jinxing everything he could reach through the window."*{p160} What happened in Moody's past that makes him paranoid and skittish? Was it anxiety from his days as an Auror or the fact that so many good witches and wizards lost their lives to the followers of Voldemort? Why would the Improper Use of Magic office be so quick to punish Moody? What other "criminal" uses of magic have there been during his days as an Auror?

We don't see much of Mad-Eye in Book 5. I think JKR purposely avoids showing us too much of Moody and his background. However, there are some interesting questions surrounding him:

Where did Moody spend his recovery after being in his trunk? Was it at the questionable St Mungo's Hospital?

Is Moody really as paranoid as everyone made him out to be in Book 4?

Why was Moody so ineffective during the battle with the Death Eaters at the Department of Mysteries?

Moody does not appear to be *overly* paranoid based on what we have witnessed. His initial contact with Harry during Book 5 shows some paranoia when he questions Harry's authenticity and tries to fly the group ragged before reaching number twelve Grimmauld Place. But then there are several examples that contradict this paranoid nature.

Moody lets Dumbledore's handwritten message (though burnt), float into the wind. Given all the methods of repairs and recreation that magic has, wouldn't it be easy for a witch or wizard to reconstruct the destroyed message with even a portion of parchment, should they find it? Why would someone so paranoid make such an amateur mistake as this?

When the kids arrive at Platform 9¾, Moody is missing, but he later arrives with the luggage. Since Harry's arrival is so important and worthy of yet another guard, why doesn't Moody accompany the group to the station instead of taking the trunks? Shouldn't the most experienced Auror in the group accompany Harry and not the luggage? Was something placed in the luggage that we don't know about? He says he is going to tell Dumbledore about Podmore's absence (again), but did he really report to Dumbledore, or to someone else we don't know about? {B5, C10, p180}

During the return trip to Hogwarts after Christmas break, Moody is again suspiciously missing from the guard. {Ch34, p522-524} Moody is insistent on a winding route during Harry's first trip to number twelve. Why is he missing from the guard on the Knight Bus? He should be one of the wizards guarding Harry during his journey to Hogsmeade. Why is the guard significantly smaller during this trip to Hogwarts? Shouldn't there be more Order members guarding Harry than just Lupin and Tonks? Could Moody's absence be attributed to his blunder at St Mungo's? Is Moody's character as deceptive as Imposter Moody, or are we simply seeing an aging Auror making too many mistakes?

The battle at the Department of Mysteries also brings about questions regarding Moody. How is it that a powerful Auror is down and out of the fray before the battle even begins? Moody is past his prime, but you would think that he would still have some of his reflexes from the days of Lord Voldemort's reign. Instead, we see him bleeding and his magical eye rolling across the floor. {B5, Ch35, p802} When Imposter Moody was unveiled in Book 4, his eye was also rolling across the floor.{Ch35, p682} Why do we keep seeing his eye rolling on floors? In the hospital wing at Hogwarts, Moody's eye isn't in its socket—it's next to him on the table.{Ch36, p700} We also see a single eye in the shop on Knockturn Alley.{B2, Ch4, p49} Is there a reason for this repetition? What is JKR trying to tell us about Moody? Does it mean we are not *seeing* the true Moody during these ordeals?

It seems throughout the two novels in which Moody is involved, the only time we are reasonably certain we have the "real" Moody is back when he sics the dust bins loose on Barty and Wormtail. Therefore, we don't even know for sure if the real Moody is the same person we see in Book 5. What is Alastor Moody really like? We know what everyone remembers about the famous Auror Moody, but how true to his actual character is this perception? We never actually see Moody fight a Death Eater. The only spell we have seen him cast is the Disillusionment Charm {B5, Ch3, p54}. We know he can fly, has a seven-tiered trunk, a picture of the original Order members, a wooden leg, an electric-blue magical eye, a chunk missing from his nose, drinks only from his own hip flask and that he had two invisibility cloaks. We can speculate on his actions, but there is so little concrete canon to support our ideas. Only JKR knows whether the Moody we see will be a good guy or bad guy in the end.

——————————————— ADDITIONAL SLEUTHING NOTES ———————————————

* JKR has told us in interviews that we would see the real Moody, but have we seen him yet? If so, is he now so decrepit that he will be a liability?

* Moody performed the Disillusionment Charm without spoken words {B5, Ch3, p54} – is that normal, or is that an example of his power?

* Why are there so many allusions throughout Book 5 to trunks, noses, rubbish bins, legs with chunks taken out of them, and one-eyes? Would JKR be trying to trick us by making Moody an imposter *again* or is she hinting at another imposter in our midst? Or, could it all be pointing to something very important about eyes (including Harry's)?

JUDGE FUDGE

ERIN KNUTSON ✳ NC, "MOMTHATSAFAN"
USA (*US Edition*), AGE 31

Inspiration for this Discussion

This discussion along with "Barty Crouch Jr: A Good Son Gone Bad" was originally part of a larger paper submitted by this author. We, at WWP, felt it was significant enough to stand alone as an extremely fascinating discussion.

HANDFUL

CORNELIUS OSWALD FUDGE: BUMBLING MINISTER, GOBLIN CRUSHER, OR DEATH EATER?

Fudge plays the concerned Minister of Magic for the first three novels in the septology. In Book 4, Fudge begins to lose his jovial disposition. Once so dependent on Dumbledore and Dumbledore's advice, Fudge has turned on him, and now has the *Daily Prophet* questioning each action Dumbledore makes, whether as Headmaster of Hogwarts or as a member of the Wizard Governing Body. At the beginning of Book 5, we are told that Dumbledore has been removed as Chief Warlock of the Wizengamot. This is due to pressure from Fudge, augmented by Fudge's skewed portrayal of Dumbledore and Harry. Fudge modifies the account of what happened at the end of the Triwizard Tournament to make Harry and Dumbledore look like lunatics, unable to tell fantasy from reality. We know now for certain, from JK Rowling's website {www.jkrowling.com}, that Fudge is going to be kicked out of the Ministry. I'm sure this tendency to misrepresent the "facts" is what has lead to Fudge's downfall for Book 6.

I find it interesting that Fudge is portrayed as an individual with many biases and prejudices. We are first exposed to Fudge's prejudicial nature at the end of Book 4 when Dumbledore says, *"I think it possible that it is you who are prejudiced, Cornelius."* {Ch29, p580 US} Dumbledore reminds us of Fudge's bigotry after the Dementor administers its kiss upon Crouch Jr., *"You are blinded...by the love of the office you hold, Cornelius! You place too much importance, and always have done, on the so-called purity of blood!"* {Ch36, p709}

Intentionally or not, Fudge controls the *Daily Profit* and uses it to assist Lord Voldemort and his followers. Fudge's blatant lies allow the Death Eaters more time to organize their members. Fudge's trial of Harry allows him to skew the events that happened and to make more Ministry officials turn a blind eye to the real situation at hand. Therefore, even if not a Death Eater, Fudge is assisting Lucius Malfoy and his cronies. Fudge keeps Malfoy closely informed of events at both the Ministry and at Hogwarts, while his appointment of Dolores Umbridge as Defense Against the Dark Arts professor and subsequently Headmistress of the school is clearly in Lucius' best interest.

It would seem to be impossible to align oneself with all these people and not have some understanding of their true intentions. This kind of behavior comes from many years of practice and did not suddenly occur overnight. As we know, Malfoy has made no secret about his desire to have Dumbledore removed from Hogwarts. Malfoy also has made it clear that he lacks compassion for other magical creatures and those wizards and witches who do not come from a pure-blood background. It would seem to be impossible to have constant contact with Lucius Malfoy and not know these facts about his personality and "interests". To accept donations and help from Lucius is to accept his beliefs and ideals. I believe Fudge knowingly buys into Malfoy's plans and assists him with devious schemes, and I cannot believe that Fudge is so naïve that he cannot catch on to the evil intentions of Lucius and his plans. This close friendship of Fudge and Malfoy lends more credence to Fudge either being a Death Eater, or completely endorsing their pure-blood mania.

Fudge and Dolores Umbridge maintain a close association due to their Ministry positions. This constant contact allows Umbridge to see Fudge's personal view on how to handle Harry's annoying situation. Umbridge instructs the Dementors to pursue Harry in his aunt's neighborhood. It is common knowledge how badly the Dementors affected Harry at the Hogwarts Quidditch match while they were hunting for the escaped convict, Sirius Black.{B3, Ch9, p178} At that time, the Dementors even purposely try to administer their soul-sucking kiss on Harry when they supposedly had no such orders. According to Dumbledore, the Dementors act only on orders from high-ranking Ministry Officials. {B5, Ch8, p146} If the orders were given at the upper level, it would make sense that they had either come from Fudge or his undersecretary. Umbridge admits, "*He never knew I ordered the Dementors after Potter last summer, but he was delighted to be given the chance to expel him, all the same…*" {Ch32, p747} Therefore, logically Fudge must have been in control of the Dementors at Hogwarts, in Book 4, when they try to "kiss" Harry. Is this yet another deception on Fudge's part?

There is also the issue of the large number of Dementors being called into both Hogsmeade and Hogwarts. It is a definite possibility that Fudge knew what was going on with Pettigrew and that Sirius did not murder Peter. Fudge is (conveniently) one of the first people to get there after the street blows up. "*I was Junior Minister in the Department of Magical Catastrophes at the time, and I was one of the first on the scene after Black murdered all those people.*" {B3, Ch10, p208} It is possible that Fudge could have modified memories so that Black was implicated in Peter's murder. Since Fudge has control of the Dementors for Sirius' escape, it seems he would still be the man in charge of the Dementors when the ten Death Eaters escaped Azkaban. Fudge tells the *Daily Prophet* in an interview, "*We are, however doing all we can to round up the criminals and beg the magical community to remain alert and cautious.*" {B5, Ch25, p545} He still seems to be in charge, as implied by his role of spokesperson to the *Daily Prophet*, so, he should have at least as many Dementors searching for the escaped Death Eaters. Instead, the Dementors are absent and the Death Eaters are allowed to reunite with their master, Lord Voldemort.

What happens to Fudge when they kick him out of office? His loyalties are questionable, he lacks responsibility, and has an uncaring attitude towards the community in general. Will he be tried in his own court? Or will he quietly "disappear" so that he can't give testimony to what he knows about Lucius and any spies in the Ministry? Could he join or re-join the Death Eaters? There is enough supporting evidence to allow us to place him in the column of potential Death Eaters not named by Lord Voldemort in Book 4.

My verdict is, this definitely qualifies him for a complimentary mask and cloak (wink). How do other HP Sleuths judge him?

——————————— Additional Sleuthing Notes ———————————

* ✳ Was Fudge ever really in control of the Dementors? How did Dolores "order" them?
* ✳ Some would immediately point out that Sirius said that the world is not split into good guys and Death Eaters, and yet, could Fudge have carried out all those heinous acts for Lucius Malfoy for that long and not been sucked into their ranks? If not, do you judge him differently – just because he doesn't bear the Mark?
* ✳ In speculating on his loyalties and future, it may be useful to know – is it Fudge's prejudice or love of money that drives him most?

Is Something Going on at St Mungo's?

Helen Poole ✳ CoS, "Virtuousdream"
England (UK Edition), Age 17

Inspiration for this Discussion

When I first heard about the call for articles and looked at the categories, I was immediately drawn to this topic—not only because I believe it is quite an important place within the world of Harry Potter, but also because I became deeply paranoid that something was going on at St Mungo's when reading the books. This was especially noticeable in Book 5. It wasn't until I began researching the idea of a potential evil influence that I began to notice there was also *another* side to it. A key theme within JK Rowling's books is that there's always the good to counteract the evil, and vice-versa. It was through this theme that my theory developed into the discussion below—using selected evidence from the books, and good old dictionary definitions, to research the hints given to us by JK Rowling regarding character names. It is even more interesting just to see how Harry Potter theories from other fans could support my essay, making this truly exciting to write.

 HANDFUL

JK Rowling (Jo) informs us that there are top medical experts in their field who work at St Mungo's Hospital for Magical Maladies and Injuries, so the wizarding hospital must have an excellent reputation. The reader would assume that St Mungo's, only briefly mentioned in Book 4, is quite normal . On the other hand, a more cynical reader may perceive all is not right when viewed in context—correlating where the institution is mentioned and by *whom*. However, further suspicions are only speculative…until Book 5. The fifth book invites a more questioning perspective on the hospital's intentions. Plot events surrounding the hospital make a sharp-minded Harry Potter fan develop a nagging suspicion that there is *something going on at St Mungo's.* Is St Mungo's supporting Lord Voldemort?

At the same time, evidence suggests that, in the spirit of Mungo Bonham (the founder of St Mungo's)[1] Dumbledore is working within the hospital to counteract the evil within. This theory, although developed in Book 5, is first suggested in Book 4. I will present both sides.

Voldemort's Influence

Throughout Book 4, evil characters are associated with St Mungo's; the first mention of the hospital is Fudge informing Arthur Weasley of Lucius Malfoy's 'generous donation' to St Mungo's. {Ch8, p92 UK} Additionally, malicious newspaper articles report St Mungo's experts' degrading opinions on Harry's scar troubles. They show a less-than-supportive, condescending attitude towards Harry, and call his pains a 'plea for attention.' Rita Skeeter, aided by the oh-so-sweet-and-caring Draco Malfoy, is (not unexpectedly) responsible for these spiteful newspaper articles.

Book 5 just adds fire to this developing theory by revealing substantially more evidence. For instance, Draco Malfoy subtly mocks Neville, 'informing' Harry of the '*special ward for people whose brains have been addled by magic.*{Ch17, p321} How is he so well informed about what is occurring at the hospital? Again, in the same section, Malfoy airs his 'important' opinion, *'my father says it's a matter of time before the Ministry has [Harry] carted off to St Mungo's.'* Do Lucius Malfoy and the Ministry have control over who is committed to St Mungo's? Of course, the statement by Draco could be just part of Malfoy's bluffing, yet there is an obvious relationship between the Ministry and St Mungo's. The Ministry of Magic collects donations for St Mungo's—*'ALL PROCEEDS FROM THE FOUNTAIN OF MAGICAL BRETHREN WILL BE GIVEN TO ST MUNGO'S.'*{Ch7, p118} Lord Voldemort's Death Eaters have 'connections' at the Ministry (Macnair's department, Lucius's 'friendship' with Fudge), raising suspicions that they could be manipulating St Mungo's through this relationship and this so-called 'money' is being used with questionable intentions.

Within the hospital itself, there have been several incidents that, on the surface, appear to support a more negative view. Isn't it highly coincidental that the apparent lack of imperturbable charms on doors is a casual, everyday occurrence—especially in a place where the welfare and comfort of patients is number one? What about patient confidentiality? (Unless there is no such thing in the wizarding world.) Eavesdropping is made easy, whether you are Fred and George Weasley, or someone equally as sneaky.

Of course, as mentioned in Book 5, the doors on the 'closed ward' are 'usually kept locked'{Ch23, p451} That could possibly be interpreted as a way to prevent perfectly sane patients from escaping, effectively imprisoning them. Is this the case with Neville's parents? Are the gum wrappers a means of communication to try to alert someone to their predicament? Adding to this, the murder of the Unspeakable, Bode, heightens suspicion—as the *Daily Prophet*, itself, questions how a Devil's Snare managed to get in unspotted…unless it was *deliberately* unnoticed? The Healer, Strout, also increases suspicions by being *'unavailable for comment,'* and although she is suspended, the promised *'full inquiry'* never appears to have happened. {Ch13, p254,255}   It is the Healer, herself, who stated 'we've seen a real improvement in Mr Bode.' Inevitably, Bode's death under these circumstances causes suspicion about the hospital. All the above evidence makes perceptive Harry Potter fans develop an immediate distrust towards St Mungo's, and wonder how much Lord Voldemort is behind every tiny 'innocent' incident. Well, isn't he a lot lately?!

DUMBLEDORE'S INFLUENCE

And yet, there is more than one way to interpret the evidence. For instance, although the Ministry of Magic solicits donations for St Mungo's, the relationship can, of course, be strictly business. Likewise, locked doors can be innocent and caring when used for the protection of mentally unstable patients. And, this lack of security would benefit good spies too!

I feel it is likely the hospital, itself, is not responsible for the bad incidents – it may have only been a few individuals. To support this, there is some interesting background information and dictionary definitions associated with St Mungo's and its founder, Mungo Bonham.[1] St Mungo was a 6th century English monk known for good deeds. The 'Bon' in Bonham is defined as *Good; valid as security for something*. This name suggests that that founder was good and would, therefore, (if a form of himself had somehow survived), aim to achieve good, not evil. One of the definitions of 'ham' is *the thigh of the hind leg of certain animals, especially a hog*. Could there be a relationship to Hogsmeade or the Hogs Head Inn?

Dumbledore has an excellent ability to detect the 'action' in the wizarding world. Arthur's 'accident' developments within the hospital are monitored through the *'portrait of Dilys Derwent who was a former Headmistress of Hogwarts.'*{Ch29, p655} This portrait communication, utilizing the old headmasters and headmistresses, allows Dumbledore to acquire knowledge of events in St Mungo's, significantly aiding him in his actions within the hospital. Could anyone else have a similar yet *sinister* network in place there?

Further evidence of this theory is hinted at through death warnings. Before Book 5 was released, this death was hyped up to be not only a tear-jerker, but also 'significant.' Could the significance be related to something going on at St Mungo's? Time-turners have been previously used to aid the good side. Could someone be using the time-turner to travel back and try to warn people of the events around Sirius's death? A possible death clue was found by some extremely sharp readers in the chapters of events at St Mungo's. The arrangement of the ward signs using the first word of each signpost spells out 'creature dangerous Dai Serious'.{Ch22, p487} This sounds just like 'Kreacher dangerous, die Sirius.' This is quite an uncanny warning and provides growing speculation that there may be something beneficial going on in St Mungo's. When regarding Jo's writing style, the coincidences are just too great.

Muggles are allowed treatment at St Mungo's—possibly suggesting Dumbledore's influence—as Lord Voldemort's side would never allow this.

JK ROWLING'S INFLUENCE

Despite these evident hints, Jo knows every reader will be on the alert for deeply entwined clues. Could these simply be red herrings that are just waiting to be analysed to death on Internet forums and chat rooms—to throw us off of craftier, more significant clues? St Mungo's is a vital service, curing injuries and saving lives (we'll see plenty more of that in the upcoming war, unless a magical miracle occurs). It also provides a very useful place to hear about events happening in the wizarding world, (both good and evil) and would serve as a suspicion-free meeting point to pass on information.

In conclusion, this speculative theory could lead to some key plot developments in Books 6 and 7 if it is true. Manipulation of St Mungo's can lead to disastrous consequences, but if manipulated by the good side, some really positive things could happen if Dumbledore has any influence. Only time, and Books 6 and 7, will tell...

──────────── ADDITIONAL SLEUTHING NOTES ────────────

✳ Why couldn't they cure Arthur? Why was the venom so unknown – what kind of snake was it? Who was treating Arthur and couldn't cure him? Who finally did cure Arthur, and How? Can we trust all the Healers?

✳ Why were there apparently so many people in there with 'illegal' injuries? Were they doing experimental charms – similar to Luna's mum and even Voldemort's own spells?

✳ We know the Ministry is collecting donations for St Mungo's, but can we be sure where the donated money goes? Did Harry's donation end up in Fudge's pocket?

✳ How did the kids get into the other wards so easily? How did Lockhart get out?

✳ The Devil's Snare and the calendar may have been sent by two different people, but if not, why did Bode's killer also send him a calendar of Fancy Hippogriffs? Would Newt Scamander's mother {FB, pvi} be able to shed any light on this? Could it have any relation to all the experimental beasts we've been encountering lately?

The Ministry
of Magic:

Employees Only

A SHORT INSIGHT INTO THE SHORT-SIGHTED PROBLEMS OF THE MINISTRY OF MAGIC

HELEN S. SHAW ✳ NEW CLUES FORUM
USA (*UK Edition*), AGE 15

Inspiration for this Discussion

When I first heard of the fan book idea, I was ecstatic. Here was my chance to be published in a book, and to write an essay about something I really enjoy. It was fun to do (even though I still managed to go over my deadline dates). I want to say, thank you, whoever you are, for buying this! I can only hope that I made this essay worth your while. Happy sleuthing!

 HANDFUL

The problems in the Ministry of Magic run deep. Anyone who has read the *Harry Potter* books can see that. However, subtle clues throughout the text of the books show that the corruption in the Ministry is probably more deeply entrenched than anyone imagined. There would seem to be no one cause for these problems, but if we look carefully into the books, and think things through diligently, we may be able to find out what is wrong with the Ministry and how the magical world may go about fixing its problems.

We are told right in the beginning of the series that the wizarding population is dissatisfied with the Ministry of Magic's performance. On the boat ride from the rocky cove in JK Rowling's *The Philosopher's Stone* {Book 1, Ch5 p51 *UK*}, Hagrid mentions that the Ministry of Magic is "messin'" things up as usual'. That tells us the Ministry of Magic's problems have been bad enough to be noticeable for *at least* five years. However, when I was rereading Book 5, I spotted another small, hidden clue. In Chapter 6 {p108}, Sirius mentions that his grandfather was awarded an Order of Merlin, First Class, for "Services to the Ministry", which Sirius says means that he "donated a load of money." That sounds suspiciously like a bribe, and only a corrupt government would sink so low as to take bribes. Taking into account that this is Sirius' grandfather, that means that we are going back three generations – this Order of Merlin title could have been awarded anywhere from 80 to 120 years ago – depending on how old Mr. Black Senior was when the award was given. Obviously, the Ministry has been on a downhill trend for quite a long time.

Something else about the awarded Order of Merlin struck me as being odd in relation to the Ministry. Doesn't it seem a little weird that Sirius' grandfather got an Order of Merlin, First Class, when Fudge was reluctant to give Snape the same for the capture of the most dangerous prisoner of all time (or so he thought)? And yet, at the end of Book 3, Fudge tells Snape that he will get an Order of Merlin, Second Class, or just *maybe* First Class. Strange. Apparently, at the Ministry, the importance of awards changes with the circumstances (that is, helped along with some galleons).

The same inconsistency seems to happen with Ministry punishments – especially to Harry. In his second year, Harry got an official warning for the Hover Charm in his house that wasn't his doing. Then, in his third year, he didn't get punished at all for blowing up his aunt. In his fourth year, he was falsely accused of conjuring the Dark Mark, so why is it that in his fifth year, the Ministry of Magic tried to expel him from Hogwarts for *saving* his and Dudley's lives? Then, of course, we can't forget the whole I-Must-Not-Tell-Lies episode with Umbridge and her horrible black "quill of pain". True, circumstances change, but I don't think that even in the most drastic situations, a good government would let punishments vary like that. It seems as if Fudge lets his personal worries and hopes interfere with his business life.

The key part of any major organization that determines whether it will succeed or fail is the people running it. One day I was sitting, relaxing, and thinking about Harry Potter (I do that a lot), when Curious Thought No. 1 struck me. How many major characters that work in the Ministry do we actually *like?* The names Arthur Weasley, Kingsley Shacklebolt, Nymphadora Tonks, and Alastor "Mad-Eye" Moody come to mind, among others. Then, however, "Curious Thought" No. 2 struck me. I thought about these four names, and it occurred to me that everyone who we know *and like* that works in the Ministry *is also in the Order.* I can think of plenty of other people working in the Ministry, but most fans would like to strangle them. Just some examples are: Barty Crouch Sr. (who turned his back on his own house-elf and son), Dolores Umbridge (set Dementors against Harry, tortured students, and makes us want to punch her), Percy Weasley (deserted his family against all evidence that Voldemort had returned), Ludo Bagman (cheated, lied, stole, and bribed), McNair (works for Voldemort and was going to execute Buckbeak), and of course, the Big Cheese, the Head Honcho, Cornelius Fudge (I'm not even going to go into what's wrong with this guy).

Fudge is a major reason that the Ministry is so "Fudged" up. His entire campaign is founded on the wrong ideals. Besides his financial motivations, he wants everyone to revere him and to be blissfully happy, even though deep down, he knows Voldemort *has* returned. His position as Minister of Magic is more important to him than telling the world the truth and securing the future of the wizarding world. He loves his position so much that he dared to use the *Daily Prophet* for his personal good and to make Harry and Dumbledore look like fools. Now that the truth has been revealed, I'm sure that Fudge, along with Percy Weasley, is smacking himself in the head.

JK Rowling told us on the World Book Day chat that by the end of Book 6 there would be a new Minister for Magic. The big question is—who? There was a possible clue in Book 5 as to who might be the lucky guy. Ron jokes, in Chapter 29, "Careers Advice", that Gryffindor had about equal chance of winning the house cup that Mr. Weasley had of becoming Minister. Funnily enough, they *did* win the house cup that year. So, how does "Arthur Weasley, Minister of Magic" sound? Well, that theory was just a dungbomb. JK Rowling, on her website said the next Minister of Magic would *not* be Arthur.

Now, frazzled HP fans are wracking their brains thinking of anybody else who could fill those shoes. My personal desire would be to see Lupin in that job—but I don't think the magical world is quite ready to accept a part-human Minister. One name comes to mind, though. Earlier in this essay, I wrote that we don't like anyone in the Ministry who isn't in the Order—however there is an exception to that. Amelia Bones is a competent person to be the next minister—she is unbiased, strong-willed, and doesn't let other peoples' opinions influence her judgment. She is also well liked by virtually everybody— that is to say, we haven't been introduced to any characters that don't like her. So, Amelia Bones is a good choice. However, I wouldn't put it past Jo to introduce us to a whole new character. Right now we are in the dark – we can only wait and try to be patient until book 6 comes out.

After what happened at the end of Book 5, the Ministry is sure to undergo some major changes in the near future. I'm quite sure that the *Daily Prophet* will be singing a different tune about Dumbledore and Harry, and that Cornelius Fudge will have a lot of hexes thrown at his house. I shudder to think of all the Howlers and Bubotuber pus that Fudge will have to endure. Well, he deserves it.

ADDITIONAL SLEUTHING NOTES

* Why was it that the Ministry tried to expel Harry—not the school board? Does that mean the school board is already completely controlled by the corrupt members of the Ministry?

* How far does the influence of the Malfoys' money extend?

* Why did JKR answer the FAQ – as to whether Arthur was going to be the new Minister for Magic – with *"Alas, no,"*? {www.jkrowling.co.uk} Does that sound optimistic?

✳ FUDGE & MACHIAVELLI ✳

CALEB GREINKE ✳ COS,
USA (*US Edition*), AGE 14

Inspiration for this Discussion

I was nine years old when I first discovered *Harry Potter and the Sorcerer's Stone* in 1999. From the very first chapter (I admit, I wasn't immediately drawn in on the first page) I was completely enraptured with the notion that there could be a world within our own world where people were able to practice genuine magic freely and that there actually were fantastic creatures such as goblins and gnomes. I was able to escape into a different world where I could observe the life of Harry Potter. I've had a big interest in politics for a few years, and as I read the series, I started to draw links between Cornelius Fudge and political doctrine that was written hundreds of years ago, and doctrines created in the last century. I had read bits and pieces of Niccolo Machiavelli's *The Prince*[1] and came to the conclusion that an analysis should be done paralleling Fudge's and Machiavelli's philosophies. I reread *The Prince* and started jotting down the key points Machiavelli makes and diagramming connections between Fudge and the book. Then I mapped out how my piece would flow and started completing my discussion.

12

Over the years, the name "Machiavelli" has become synonymous with evil and treachery. But should "Machiavellian" be interchangeable with "Fudge-ian"? In 1513, the Italian political philosopher, Niccolo Machiavelli, wrote one of the first political "how-to" books, *The Prince*. In it, Machiavelli delineates how a good prince, or any leader, should govern his principality. The main theme throughout *The Prince* is that a good leader ought to keep his power no matter what the cost or what he has to do. Certainly this theme can be applied to Cornelius Fudge's politics. We will examine Machiavelli's philosophy and writings, Fudge's actions as well as his presumptive philosophy in JK Rowling's Harry Potter series. How does Fudge run the Ministry of Magic? What is Fudge truly thinking when Harry Potter defies him? These answers and more can be found within Niccolo Machiavelli's *The Prince*.

We see the Minister of Magic, Cornelius Fudge, introduced to the Harry Potter canon, in the Book 2. He debuts in the middle of the Muggle-born attacks, where an unknown person or monster is petrifying Muggle-born students. At this point in the novel, the culprit is still unknown. Folding under the pressure from the citizens, Fudge condemns Hagrid (an innocent suspect) to a temporary stay at Azkaban prison under the guise of safety for the students. In reality, Fudge only acts because he has "*got to be seen doing something,*" {Ch 14} lest his favorability amongst the people goes down. Machiavelli writes in *The Prince*, Chapter 17, that: "*...A prince must not worry about the reproach of cruelty when it is a matter of keeping his subjects united and **loyal**.*"

Furthermore, Lucius Malfoy notifies Dumbledore that the school governors have voted to relieve him of his position as Headmaster. At this time, Fudge could have stepped in and stopped the order, or at the very least, more aggressively criticized it, but he chose not to. Machiavelli writes in Chapter 9,

"…*One cannot honestly satisfy the nobles without harming others…*"

While Dumbledore was not physically hurt by being forced into leaving, the order did hurt the overall condition of Hogwarts, and could have caused more Muggle-born deaths. True to what Machiavelli wrote, Fudge decided to harm the well-being of Hogwarts just to satisfy the school governors. Fudge's actions in Book 2 are just a taste of what is to come.

It is in the conclusion of Book 4 that Fudge begins denying the return of Voldemort despite all of the evidence presented. It is also at this same time that Fudge shows how much he was willing to back the articles written by Rita Skeeter by launching his campaign of discrediting Harry through allegations of mental instability.

It is when we were able to read Book 5 that we obtained our most meaningful insight. In this installment of the series, Fudge finally and openly exhibits his philosophy.

Machiavelli states that a wise leader should consider all the harmful things he must do and do them all at once. Fudge does them in close succession to each other. First, Fudge starts feeding the *Daily Prophet* newspaper bogus information. That is part of a campaign of misinformation in which Fudge portrays the magical society as being completely safe and free from all possible harm. Second, he strips Dumbledore of his titles of Chief Warlock of the Wizengamot and Supreme Mugwump of the International Confederation of Wizards. Next, Fudge attempts to expel, silence, and discredit Harry in the Wizengamot trial. And ultimately, he appoints the deceitful Senior Undersecretary to the Minister, Dolores Umbridge, as the new Defense Against the Dark Arts professor.

With the allegations made by Harry that Voldemort has returned, it is clear that the Ministry of Magic uses propaganda to influence the *Daily Prophet* into what becomes, in essence, a puppet of the government. The *Daily Prophet* gives voice to Fudge without any concern for verifying what he is telling them, which ultimately discredits the newspaper. In fact, the problem becomes so bad that Harry is forced to give his story about Voldemort's return to *The Quibbler*.

It's not mere shock and disbelief that keep Fudge from notifying the magical community of Voldemort's return—it's the political implications that would come with such a warning. Machiavelli writes in chapter 18, "*It is necessary* [a leader] *have a mind ready to turn itself according to the way the … changeability of affairs require him.*"

Fudge does exactly that: new laws, new trial procedures, removing those who dare to speak out. His philosophy appears to be that censorship is fine when what's being censored could harm his favorability rating amongst the people or his re-election chances. What he probably fears the most is that his reputation will be tarnished. But Fudge's censorship of Voldemort's return goes even deeper and, yet again, can be related to the philosophy of Machiavelli. Machiavelli reasons in Chapter 19, "*It is to your advantage to follow* [the common people's] *inclinations in order to satisfy them.*"

It's clear that Fudge went to great lengths to satisfy and not to scare the people, even if the people's safety was in jeopardy.

The second thing Fudge carries out is the removal of Dumbledore, by which Dumbledore has his title of Supreme Mugwump and Chief Warlock stripped of him. While it is unclear whether or not Fudge was directly responsible for the removal of the titles, it is certain Fudge would have stopped the action if he had wanted to. In the course of Book 5, it is clear that Fudge consistently viewed Dumbledore as a major threat, and looked for any possible way to have him sacked as Headmaster or at the very least, discredited.

The third thing Fudge does is to paint the picture that Harry is a mentally unstable teenager who only wants fame and notoriety. Fudge viewed Harry as a greater threat to his position as Minister of Magic than Voldemort. He also saw Harry as the tool by which Dumbledore could become the new Minister of Magic. Other than Dumbledore, Harry was the single most dangerous voice who was trying to spread the word of Voldemort's return. What better way to discredit your opposition than to make your opposition appear to be a combination of insane, disturbed, and pompous? Machiavelli writes in Chapter 18, that, *"...Princes who have done great deeds are those who have ...known how to manipulate the minds of men by shrewdness..."*

Fudge does seem to have become a master at manipulation of the public when it comes to matters of the Dark Lord's return. Although Fudge was not aware that it had been Umbridge who had ordered the two Dementors to Little Whinging, he barely allowed Harry to tell his story and immediately discounted it as nonsense–despite all the evidence and testimony presented by Harry, Dumbledore, and Arabella Figg.

The final stroke of his series of actions was the appointment of Umbridge as the new Defense Against the Dark Arts professor. Some would look at the appointment as just a simple post appointment gone awry as the school year progressed. But the real reason for the appointment was for Fudge to have an insider at Hogwarts. Percy Weasley states in a *Daily Prophet* article that Umbridge is partially there to provide the Minister with on-site feedback of the situation at Hogwarts. This role of Umbridge, to provide feedback, is done under a guise, that being the *improvement of education*. With this, Umbridge is now able to find out what's happening at the school and perhaps discover what Dumbledore's plans are. Along with the capability to spy on Fudge's enemies, another reason given for the appointment is presumably to undermine the efforts of Dumbledore to ready Hogwarts for Voldemort's return. Fudge ensured that the students would not be taught any defense techniques of substance and restricts what professors are allowed to teach. This is planned as the first stage of what will become a purge of those undesirable staff members who are loyal to Dumbledore once Umbridge becomes High Inquisitor.

One would think that propagandizing the magical community through control of its newspaper, discrediting both a former hero of the people and a highly respected wizard as well as stationing an insider at Hogwarts would be enough for Fudge to achieve his goals. Apparently not. Machiavelli writes in Chapter 18, *"...He should not stray from the good, but he should know how to enter into evil when necessity commands."*

As the story progresses, Fudge passes a series of "Educational Decrees" which give Umbridge, as the High Inquisitor, supreme power over even that of Dumbledore. With a loyal subject like Umbridge, Fudge is also able to ensure that he will have a permanent presence within Hogwarts, or as Wizengamot elder, Griselda Marchbanks, put it, *"an outpost for Cornelius Fudge's office."*{B5, Ch15}

Upon the realization that Dumbledore and Harry would not be letting go of their assertion that Voldemort had truly returned, Fudge began to fear there was more behind the claims. He began to fear that others, most notably, Dumbledore, were plotting against him. Machiavelli writes in Chapter 19, *"When external affairs do not change,* [a leader] *has to fear that they may conspire secretly..."*

Overtaken by the fear that Dumbledore and his followers are plotting a coup of the Ministry, Fudge seeks any excuse for which Dumbledore can be either exiled or sent to Azkaban, and anything for which Harry can be expelled. His lust to eradicate his opponents climaxes in chapter 27. In this chapter, "the Ministry of Magic are Morons Group" (better known as, "Dumbledore's Army") is betrayed by Marietta Edgecombe, and Dumbledore deceitfully explains to Fudge, just to save Harry from expulsion, that the DA was formed as an army, which would be used to dislodge Fudge from power. Because Fudge did not know that Dumbledore was lying, this actually added fuel to Fudge's fire to purge supporters of Dumbledore.

All of these examples combine to provide a deeper understanding of Fudge's dealings and his similarities to Machiavelli. We've discussed no less than seven links between Fudge and Machiavelli, and I'm sure that upon an even deeper assessment of the texts, one could find more. Hopefully, the reader will come away from this with a better understanding of Fudge's motivations behind the way he conducts his operations as Minister of Magic, and why he does the things he does — all this through a Machiavellian lens and an observer's point of view.

─────────────── ADDITIONAL SLEUTHING NOTES ───────────────

* Did the *Quibbler* political cartoon of Fudge holding a sack of gold and choking a goblin have a basis in reality?

* Do wizards have any ethics policies? Is the Wizengamot supposed to handle that function? Is it covered in their Charter of Rights? Are there any ethical members left?

* Will Dumbledore be able to weed out any of the insurgents?

[1]Machiavelli, *The Prince*, Peter Bondanella and Mark Musa Translation, Oxford University Press, 1979.

THE TYRANNY OF THE DEATH EATERS AND THE SPREAD OF CORRUPTION

A.L. CARPENTER ✳ NC, "RIDGEBACK" (RB)
USA (*US Edition*), AGE 33

Inspiration for this Discussion

The most prevalent reason for my obsession with Harry Potter has been JK Rowling's plotline of a rebellious boy fighting tyranny. She has added her own smart details and insight to a common literary vehicle and has made an important issue available to all age levels.

 12

"... There is this issue ... about the bad side really advocating genocide to exterminate what they see as ... half-blood people…"

—JK Rowling
video interview on Warner Bros. DVD release
of the film *Harry Potter and the Chamber of Secrets*

In Book 2, of the Harry Potter septology, readers have their first experience with the slippery underbelly of the modern wizarding world, when introduced to the offensive slur "Mudblood". {Ch7 US} We watch one of the most prominent themes of the Potter series unfold as Ron Weasley battles a mouthful of slugs. We begin to see the scars on the tapestry of the wizarding world where so many innocents have been wiped out by a magical version of genocide.

It began with a wizard boy...an "orphan" whose mother was a witch and whose father was a Muggle. The distraught orphan, an intelligent and talented (if a bit deranged) student at Hogwarts, began to displace his anger toward the Muggle world that his father represented. The boy, Tom Marvolo Riddle, transformed himself into Lord Voldemort, the Dark Lord, and began to seek supporters for a new platform that would purify the wizard race and bring it back to a perceived glory. The platform included a strategy to wipe out all wizards who were either Muggle-born or half-blood (like Riddle himself), and bring Lord Voldemort to absolute power as the political patriarch of the wizarding world—with his Death Eater forces flying below him.

Little is known about the Death Eaters. We have been informed that except in very rare cases they do not allow Muggle-born members .{www.jkrowling.com - News} We can assume many of them are as wealthy as the Malfoys and the Blacks, or at least from families of high social status, like the Crouches. We are only told of the Death Eaters' technical prowess in the Dark Arts...the tortuous Unforgivable Curses...and about the malevolence and hatred that lurk in their hearts. While we are allowed to know the background details of the clandestine resistance (The Order of the Phoenix), the Death Eaters remain cloaked in mystery.

It is improbable that one could create an absolutist society without becoming a victim of the very society one idealized. Perhaps this is why so little is known about the Death Eaters, who remain shrouded, even in the pivotal graveyard scene of Book 4, when the only witness is meant to die.{Ch32} Despite the verbal roll call given by their leader, the Dark Lord, they remain hidden (even from the other members of their twisted regime). They are anonymous soldiers...a wizarding Schutzstaffel (SS)...in a virulent war.

Within wizarding society there is but one way to distinguish the Death Eaters. In a superb retaliatory move, JK Rowling places the Dark Mark, a tattoo of sorts, on the arms of the militia instead of upon their innocent victims. The Dark Mark strongly parallels the swastika that the Nazi Party wore on armbands and flew on flags. With the shout of "Morsmordre", the same Dark Mark appears in the sky as a sparkling green flag that bears an unmistakable symbol of treachery.

Although many Death Eaters appear to live as normal wizarding citizens, we have been allowed a few glimpses into the abyss of their society. Knockturn Alley is an avenue of Dark Arts, the Black Family mansion is a museum of dangerous artifacts and Draco Malfoy's bragging remarks give much away. During the Quidditch World Cup, little "security risk" Draco insinuates that the Death Eaters have ways of "spotting Mudbloods". Although it is difficult to tell whether Draco's threats are real or imagined, this sort of "measuring of the Mudbloods" recalls the frightening tactics of racial stereotyping performed by Hitler's regime in World War II. The profiling is echoed further by the very definition of a non-pureblood wizard, according to JK Rowling's website: even if a magical child is born from two wizarding parents that child is not considered pureblood if just one grandparent was a Muggle. The Death Eaters' decree is "Toujours Pur" and their aim is to encapsulate the government and the wizarding community within a rigid system of beliefs that excludes Muggle relations and ordains an authoritarian dictator.

JK Rowling touches on the subject of genocide in a much broader sense than simply relating it to early 20th century Europe. She pulls at the most haunting human emotions about prejudice—pointing a "incriminating finger" at all discriminatory atrocities. She even adds a satirical edge with the magical creatures' fight for equality and respect. While we all acknowledge S.P.E.W. (Society for the Promotion of Elfish Welfare)— the "Elf Liberation Front"—as annoying, it does give us pause: should all living beings of equal intelligence and magical abilities be considered equal despite the "species divide"? Well, apparently the centaurs think not, as they are portrayed as highly intelligent and have decided to "manage their own affairs" {FB pxiii}.

Despite Rowling's broader sense of humanitarianism, she has structured the plotline so that it warns of a totalitarian regime. She has placed careful hints throughout her books for us to pick up like so many glimmering stones, and by the fifth book, the warning signs are stacked high...Enter Cornelius Oswald Fudge (whose last name implies anything but dessert). His middle name is apparently snatched from Sir Oswald Mosley, the famed leader of the British Union of Fascists and brother-in-law to the rebellious feminist-socialist author Jessica Mitford for whom Rowling's daughter is named. Then, there is the underplayed fact mentioned on a Chocolate Frog Card in Book 1, Chapter 6, that Albus Dumbledore, leader of the resistance, defeated a Dark Wizard named Grindelwald in 1945. There is also a school in an unknown area of the North Sea where the Dark Arts are openly practiced and it is rumored to exclude non-pureblood wizards. The name of the school is "Durmstrang", a play on the German "Sturm und Drang" movement that was popular with Hitler. "Sturm" and "Drang" literally translate to "storm" and "desire", respectively. (Wagner and Van Goethe were the movement's most prominent members.) Another glimmer is the name Fabian Prewett, which may be a nod to the British socialist movement "Fabianism".

When we are introduced to Harry's fifth year at Hogwarts, we are faced with the most arresting transformations of the wizarding government in the series. Harry's confrontation with rogue Dementors leads to a seemingly superficial trial before a malformed Wizengamot which has recently ousted some of its most prominent and liberal members, including Albus Dumbledore. The trial seems to be looped to frame Harry with a crime they deny was self-defense. After the trial, Harry happens upon Lucius Malfoy, one of the most prominent Death Eaters, doing business with the twittering Minister of Magic, Cornelius Fudge. The two men are old "friends"—as long as the galleons keep flowing. We are suddenly reminded of the influence Malfoy had over the demise of the hippogriff, Buckbeak, in Book 3.

It is at Grimmauld Place where we meet the resistance – a classless league of wizards who have made a pact to fight evil at all costs. The Order of the Phoenix seems to rival the German resistance, The White

Rose[1], (whose members were found guilty of treason and executed) in dedication, and the Czech Charter 77 (an unofficial alliance of activists who were forced to communicate in a clandestine manner via music, poetry, and the arts) in inventiveness.[2] Of the members, Sirius Black is the most deeply symbolic of Rowling's theme of "choice". Black abandoned a life of privilege and luxury to follow his heart. It is with Sirius Black that we learn the pain (through his imprisonment and death) of fighting for what is right. This resistance is echoed in miniature later on, when Harry and his friends create "Dumbledore's Army" at Hogwarts.

Despite the resistance, the chains keep tightening. Harry quickly learns that the government is controlling the press, and "freedom of speech" has been replaced with a strict doctrine of propaganda. According to the media version of the news, Voldemort has not returned and Harry Potter is insane, egotistical, and attention-crazed. The government's control of the media ensures a façade of strength for the Ministry, while keeping average citizens in the dark. The school curriculum has been "adjusted" (drastically changed) to reflect the interests of the regime. The owl post at school and everywhere is being heavily monitored. Innocent people start to disappear or die, while Death Eaters gain a firmer grip on the increasingly demented and spineless Fudge, who seems much more worried about losing his job than about upholding wizarding rights. The toad-like Senior Undersecretary of the Minister has become the "Hogwarts High Inquisitor" and is imposing more and more paralyzing decrees, banning everything that may undermine her rule. The High Inquisitor, (a nod to another tyrannical reign in Spain/Portugal), finally employs a youth crew to spy upon their peers, turning in any student who defies the creed; this echoes the Nazi Youth, as well as George Orwell's *1984*.

The Death Eaters begin to coil around the ministry, enveloping the feeble, power-and-glory-hungry Fudge with their doctrine. As the Order of the Phoenix begins the fight, average wizarding citizens ignore the truth. The truth has not affected them, so they do nothing. Amidst the downpour of letters Harry receives from an interview in a tabloid, shouts of denial and confusion blurt out from parchments as the wizarding community decides whether to close their eyes in response to the impending deaths of Muggles and "Mudbloods".

It is a chilling time in the series because it is all too real. Rowling has never set out to "teach" us, but once more, in her natural and sincere way, she points toward the millions of atrocities that are ignored each day. The wizarding world is sitting on the fence and JK Rowling leaves them, as well as her readers, waiting to tip...

Choice is Rowling's biggest theme, and now it has come down to the choice of following the leader, or doing what is right ... even if one may die for it.

Rowling has created a scenario that ensures balance. Two wizards who have such similar backgrounds and bloodlines are pitted against one another—to prove that it is not nature, or lineage, or heritage that makes us who we are... but what we decide within ourselves and within our hearts.

ADDITIONAL SLEUTHING NOTES

* How far will the war overlap into the Muggle world (we already have Muggles at St Mungos)? The centaurs want to remain neutral (uninvolved), but is that realistic?
* JKR describes her experience on her website while visiting the Holocaust Museum {www.jkrowling.com – FAQs} – is this a foreshadowing of what her wizarding world may become?

[1] White Rose: "A Lesson in Dissent". Hornberger, Jacob G., http://www.jewishvirtuallibrary.org/jsource/Holocaust/rose.html
[2] Czech Charter 77: Kohout, Milan. Interview with A.L. Carpenter. "Schizine". 1994.

✳ THE MYSTERIOUS MAD-EYE MOODY ✳

ERIK SMULDERS ✳ NC, "MAD-MADEYE"
THE NETHERLANDS (*UK Edition*), AGE 15

Inspiration for this Discussion

Who is Alastor "Mad-Eye" Moody and what do we know about him? As far as the books go, we usually see Mad-Eye as Harry does: highly experienced, slightly creepy, paranoid, and exceptionally capable in his job as Auror. He's an intriguing character, definitely not without surprises as HP fans discovered in the last chapters of Book 4. Luckily, no more fake-Moodys have surfaced (as far as we readers know) but there's still plenty of mystery about ol' Mad-Eye.

 HANDFUL

In this essay I will try to discuss the various mysterious topics of Mad-Eye and some speculative ideas. I will break it down into a few points:

> *Career* (Moody's career as Auror. What did he do exactly?)
>
> *Experiences* (What has turned Moody so paranoid? Are other Aurors like him?)
>
> *Skill* (How good was he in his time and is he getting 'rusty'?)
>
> *Eye* (What's up with that thing? What is it? How does it work?)
>
> *Truth* (Could we have another fake-Moody on our hands?)
>
> *Conclusion*

All right, HP Sleuth or not, it's time for us to delve deeper into the wizarding world's most paranoid Dark wizard catcher (…and always remember to keep your wands out of your back pockets!).

CAREER

Based on what we know of Mad-Eye, he seems to be quite experienced as an Auror. From his Dark detectors to his scars, I think we can safely assume the man has seen some action. This, of course, is not that surprising – considering his career was probably around the days of Lord Voldemort's ascension to power during the First War. I always assumed that Mad-Eye was about 60 years old during the events that transpired in Book 4. After doing a bit of math, it's probable that the First War lasted from around 11 years and Book 4 took place about 14 years after that, which would mean that Alastor was in his thirties when all hell started breaking loose in the wizarding world, and he probably started his career around that time. This would mean that he ended up in the worst possible time to be an Auror—with Voldemort and Death Eaters aplenty. So it looks like Mad-Eye immediately got a trial by fire, and considering that he actually made it through the war, he must've had good potential in the first place. Mad-Eye is also considered one of the best Aurors the Ministry of Magic ever had. To quote some Weasleys:

> *"Your father thinks very highly of Mad-Eye Moody," said Mrs Weasley sternly.* {B4, Ch11 *UK*}
> *"He was an Auror - one of the best … a Dark-wizard-catcher," [Charlie] added…*
> *"Half the cells in Azkaban are full because of him."* {Ch11}

And not just the Weasleys, even Sirius praises him in B4:

> *"Moody was the best Auror the Ministry ever had."* {Ch11}

All in all, despite having a difficult career battling the servants of Voldemort, it seems that Moody was one of the top Aurors.

EXPERIENCES

Mad-Eye's most obvious personal trait (for anyone who possibly didn't notice) is his paranoia. The first time I read about him, I naturally assumed that other Aurors were like him, taking their jobs extremely seriously. But after Harry's and Mr. Weasley's trip to the Auror headquarters in Book 5, it looks like fearing possible assassination, as he does, isn't much of a requisite for a career as an Auror.

> *"They … emerged in a cluttered open area divided into cubicles, which was buzzing with talk and laughter. … A lopsided sign on the nearest cubicle read:* **Auror Headquarters**.*"* {B5, Ch 7}

There are, of course, two other Aurors we now know of who definitely take things more relaxed than Mad-Eye: Nymphadora Tonks and Kingsley Shacklebolt. But then why is Alastor so paranoid that he checks food, made within Order of the Phoenix Headquarters, for poison? I believe his experiences in the First War are the cause of that. What do we know of the First War? We know that it was pretty rough. Aurors were probably dying while doing their job and assassination by Death Eaters was also possible. (Look what happened to the Longbottoms.) Mad-Eye must've seen friends killed by Voldemort's servants. All those scars he bears indicate that he's seen some action, too, so it's actually quite logical for Mad-Eye to be "so" paranoid. However, in the almost 15 years since Voldemort disappeared, the Aurors seem to have relaxed.

SKILL

From everything that has been said already about him in this discussion, Mad-Eye seems to be one of the best Aurors ever. I was quite surprised, therefore, to see him go down so soon in the battle in the Department of Mysteries, in Book 5. Weren't you? Not to mention the fact that he was captured and impersonated by Barty Crouch Jr. It's remarkable how Impostor Moody taught his students how to fight the Imperius curse, and yet the "best Auror the Ministry ever had" wasn't able to throw it off himself when he was taken as Crouch Jr.'s prisoner. Even his way of getting Harry into twelve Grimmauld Place (he burned Dumbledore's note with the address, but he left ashes which could be found and restored by Voldemort supporters) is taken into consideration by some sleuths as speculation that it could be another fake Moody. Is it that Alastor simply isn't as sharp as he used to be? I personally go with the latter. Remember, Moody has retired, and he's a bit handicapped with all those scars and injuries (just look at his leg…that's gotta be a drag in a fight with a dozen Death Eaters!. It seems very likely that, amazing though he most certainly was during the First War, Moody's not the invincible Auror he used to be.

EYE

One of the most mysterious things about Mad-Eye is alluded to in his nickname: the Eye. That big, vivid, electric-blue eye that seems to take a look at everything. The most obvious question is, of course: "What exactly is it?" Considering what it can do—being able to look through basically every solid substance, plus invisibility cloaks, and spin around in every direction, which is indeed handy—it seems to be pretty rare. What I wonder most about the thing is whether it actually has a mind of its own or whether Mad-Eye controls every action of it himself. We know that the eye looks at everything continuously, at the most absurd angles and moreover, it's often described that the eye moves so fast it makes Harry queasy. {Ch3} I don't know what HP Sleuths think about that, but I don't think anyone would move his/her eye *that* much, even *if* they're paranoid. Therefore, I'm inclined to believe that Alastor's magical eye is a bit of both: it checks on its own whatever it's interested in, but Mad-Eye can move it anyway he wants, whenever he wants.

Another interesting bit about the eye is exactly when/where did Moody get it? We know that Mad-Eye didn't always have the eye (during Karkaroff's trial in the Pensieve, he's still got two normal ones), so he must've lost one of his own later than that. But we don't have any more data on that particular mystery. Now for the next question: "Where did he get it?" Might it be a Dark Object? There is one other place Harry's seen an eye: Knockturn Alley. {Book 2, Ch 4} Possible connection anyone...?

TRUTH

After the horrible events in Book 4, we know that no one can be trusted in the wizarding world. Crouch Jr. demonstrated how simple it is to impersonate someone without anyone (even Dumbledore) noticing and, as mentioned, some have speculated that Mad-Eye may be impersonated again. When the Weasleys, Tonks, Harry, and Moody visit Mr. Weasley, after he was attacked by Nagini, why does Mad-Eye talk openly about the fact that Voldemort could be possessing Harry (Dumbledore instructed everyone not to) when his eye can see directly through the ward door, noticing Harry and the Weasley kids eavesdropping on him?

Regardless, I don't think Mad-Eye's being impersonated again. First of all, it would be weird for Jo to repeat exactly the same thing. Second, I think that in the case of the Grimmauld Place entry scene, Moody knew for sure that nothing of that note remained, except scattered ashes. Third, I think Moody did indeed see that Harry and the Weasleys were eavesdropping on him with Extendable Ears, and deliberately exposed Harry's possession so Harry became aware of the fact. From Chapter 14 in Book 4, if Imposter Moody was true to the real Moody's personality (Dumbledore sure thought so) we know that it doesn't matter to Mad-Eye how bad or worrying some news can be, if only you can use that knowledge to be prepared. I think this is exactly what Moody was trying to achieve here. That way, Harry *knew* Voldemort could be possessing him and could be trying to deceive Harry by showing him those dreams.

CONCLUSION

I think that all the points that I've discussed about Mad-Eye Moody give us some idea as to what we can expect from him in the future. There's still a lot to discover about him (especially about that eye) but we do know a lot about him already. We know that he's not invincible, nor is his paranoia unfounded. His scars, physical and mental, give us a slight impression of just how brutal it was in the First War, and if we are to believe Professor Trelawny's prediction, the second one will be even more horrible. I think it is clear that Mad-Eye will continue to fight against Voldy and his scum to the very last breath. I'm not sure he'll be an amazing help in battle (sigh) but I think that he'll be a mentor to Harry, nurturing his ambition to be an Auror. Moody can teach Harry a great deal: what it's truly like fighting the Dark Arts and just how difficult and dangerous his job is.

Well, I hope I've cleared up some things about Alastor's character in this essay and that you've enjoyed yourself reading my ideas about Moody as much as I've done typing them. Keep on sleuthing and keep your eyes peeled! Constant Vigilance!

ADDITIONAL SLEUTHING NOTES

✳ Did Mad-Eye lose one eye or give it up willingly like Odin in Norse mythology?

✳ If a Death Eater can never quit his job, can an Auror ever retire?

Objects of Mystery and Things That Go Bump in the Night

THE ROOM OF REQUIREMENT
(AKA THE COME AND GO ROOM)

CHRISTINA "FLAMELSAPPRENTICE" CONLEY ✳ NEW CLUES FORUM
USA (*US Edition*), AGE 23

Inspiration for this Discussion

I think it goes without saying that we all wish we had a Room of Requirement at our personal disposal. I mean, who wouldn't want to have a room that on a whim created the user's every wish and demand? I know I'd like to have a personal study fitted with a 60-inch plasma TV, a nice, cushy couch, and all the cheese and iced tea I can consume waiting for me every evening I come home from a long day. But the truth is…if we all had our own Room of Requirement, would it work the same way? Let's examine the way the room technically functions as well as related story-line events and clues in the book.

 HANDFUL

CONTENTS OF THE ROOM OF REQUIREMENT

As I'm sure many avid readers noticed, the Room of Requirement (RoR for short) seems to contain a lot of, shall we say… familiar items. No, it's not a hex to make you see double. The truth is that we *have* seen these items before! My personal opinion is that the room seems to "pull" objects from the existing contents of Hogwarts.

The most obvious manifestation of this is the cracked Foe-Glass, which hangs on the back wall of the RoR. Harry is almost certain that this is the same mirror that previously hung in Imposter Moody's office. {B5, Ch18, p390 US}

Other objects in the room you probably noticed: the pillows used for stunning, not completely unlike those found in Professor Flitwick's class for practicing stunning spells. {B4, Ch29, p574} All the trinkets and instruments in the bookcase (Sneakoscopes and Secrecy Sensors) have me thinking of Dumbledore's vast collection of strange gadgets. {B5, Ch22 p467}

Other objects you may not have noticed: all the books in the bookcase—possibly from one of the professors' offices or classrooms (we've seen too many book references to know whose), and the whistle Harry asks for to get the class to pay attention—any fan of Quidditch should know this one! (hint: Madam Hooch wears a whistle around her neck at all times for game play). {B1, Ch11, p185} Think this is just another coincidence? Then you're off your broom!

But wait…if the room is pulling objects from the castle, wouldn't this mean that the mirror would still have to be in the castle? Hmmm…maybe we should revise our reasoning a little. Perhaps the room contains objects that had been in the castle at one time or another. You may say that's skirting the issue. But you can see JKR clearly wants the reader to *notice* these objects.

So, how does the RoR *work*? The room somehow simulates the environment and stocks the supplies which best meet the requirements of the "seeker". In Book 5, the room seems specifically to be Harry's RoR—that is, he is apparently the one who willed it into existence, so it came into being from the needs he personally envisioned. But it also seems to go beyond that, since no matter who returns first to the RoR, the conditions are the same as that person left them. Curious, very curious.

Could the room somehow save the image of itself, so when it is called upon again, it is reproduced in the exact condition it was left the previous time? Maybe the room always appears in the identical condition (starting point) each time it is called into existence by the same person/people for the same purpose. Then again, if it is supposed to appear to Harry with the same arrangement, then how can it be altered? And how does it come up for someone else?

Another point of interest is the certain type of ambiance created for the room. The torch-lit walls are reminiscent of the dungeon corridor in the Ministry of Magic. Did Harry think these up or did the RoR pick them? In other words: yes, battling against your enemies or the Death Eaters would be scary (like the corridor) and Harry might want to recreate that kind of atmosphere (consciously or subconsciously). Of course, the DA (Dumbledore's Army) will also be fighting against evil and corruption, hence the Ministry of Magic reference. But, you have to ask yourself was it the RoR's idea or Harry's, and why JKR (as Harry) envisions the room this way—and, therefore, what is she trying to hint about or convey to the reader?

Harry's Subconscious and the RoR

But what's really interesting is when we examine the *psychology* of the room. Technically, the room presents whatever the wishers desire. So, based on what we know about the RoR, how is it that when Harry enters it at for Christmas, it's decorated with things he didn't desire? The room was strewn with golden baubles that displayed his likeness. {Ch21, p452} Harry (after suppressing a gag-reflex) assumes Dobby is the culprit and proceeds to take the decorations down. Can we be sure it was Dobby's doing? This seems to be a contradiction. How could Dobby enter Harry's room without Harry and the room be identical except for his new changes? If the room always keeps itself in the same arrangement, then how could Dobby do this? Is Dobby this powerful to be able to alter the "programming" of Harry's own RoR? We have seen the atypical powers of the house-elf before. Dobby can "Apparate" in and out of the castle and cast powerful spells without the use of a wand. It is also clear that Dobby worships Harry for having freed him from slavery and would be likely to string images of Harry's face from every wall, were it not for some sort of castle etiquette standard.

So, who strung the golden baubles? Did Dobby do it?

Perhaps there is an alternate solution. What if Dobby is not responsible? Once again, we must remember we are reading this story from character perspective. Every scene and event is portrayed through Harry's eyes. He feels very underappreciated and stressed at this time in the story. Ron and Hermione are spending more time carrying out their prefect duties, Umbridge is trying to get Hagrid fired, and, of course, with the O.W.L.s rapidly approaching, there is more and more homework to be done. It's quite possible that (bear with me here) Harry *willed* those decorations to appear *himself*. Sure, he was embarrassed, and took them down, but you know a part of him was flattered and happy to be appreciated…even if it was just a momentary selfish pleasure.

It's also no coincidence that Harry got the ornaments down just in the nick of time before Luna enters. If we consider there are no (or are rarely) coincidences in *Harry Potter*, how very interesting that Luna arrives just as Harry finishes with the ornaments. It's great evidentiary support that Harry may have feelings for Luna that we have not yet seen directly expressed in the books. Or have we? As Luna and Harry exchange words, Luna points out that they happen to be standing under a mass of mistletoe. Bet you just thought that was funny, not a form of foreshadowing. My question is, was the mistletoe left over decorations from Dobby *or* did Harry or Luna subconsciously/consciously wish it to appear? Is Harry the only one who is able to call things at will to the room (see whistle example) or can any of the members? Our only concrete evidence is that Harry can call objects spontaneously to the room, but that's not to say that Luna didn't have a hand in this one. Harry does feel that Luna can understand him unlike any of his other friends. Well, suffice it to say, we'll just have to keep our rotating electric blue eye on this one.

The RoR is certainly funny and interesting, but it's also an insight into someone's mind. Just as the Mirror of Erised plays mind games with the viewer (the mirror displays what the character desires most, and *only* what they desire most) the RoR functions much in the same way. I think we have only begun to see the vast uses for this room. Here's to hoping it reappears (hehe) in books 6 and 7—and if I'm lucky, maybe it'll even be filled with cheese and iced tea. ☺

✳ ADDITIONAL SLEUTHING NOTES ✳

✴ Who invented the RoR? Can the occupant do a "stop program", "save program", or "load program" like the *Star Trek* holodeck? Does the Room exist without a person requesting it? Are there requests the Room will not grant?

✴ Does the entrance to the Room remain visible to all once it is "willed" into existence, or is it only visible to those who know to look for it? Once Harry entered, did the rest of the DA have to also make a "request" to see it? Is the magic at all similar to the entrance to the Leaky Cauldron? Knowing that "*We needed evidence and the room provided*"{Ch p544 UK}, how can the Room be found and used by one's enemies

✴ How could the Room produce cleaning supplies that Filch needed and which he used outside the room (and they functioned) and were presumably used up? Does this mean that the objects were not just temporarily conjured?

✴ Did you notice...

  ☆ On JKR's website—her "RoR" there (the Room behind the locked door) pulls objects from other "rooms"?

  ☆ Her site RoR only *duplicates* items that are found elsewhere. What if the RoR in her books does the same?

THE CLUE MEN SEE IS THE LAKE!

ALISHA HAJOSY ✳ NC, "AUNT REMUS"
USA (*US Edition*), AGE 43

Inspiration for this Discussion

Like so many of my fellow HP Sleuths, I am obsessed with the cyclical nature of Harry's story. I have lain awake many a night, trying to connect all of the hints and clues. The idea for this article emerged when I began wondering why is it that all first years must arrive at Hogwarts via the lake.

Before long, I was spending hours looking through every JKR book I owned, trying to figure out what it all meant. Thinking about the word, "Occlumency", on which many sleuths have used their "Philological Stone" to read, "o cclu men cy", or, "a clue men see", it all fell into place. Could the same be done with Legilimency?

Realizing the importance of the numerous mirror images in the septology, we might consider a "mirror image" of "Occlumency". In a mirror, the image is reversed. Since "Occlumency" is the process of keeping others out of one's brain, and "Legilimency" is the process of getting in; "Legilimency" is the reverse of "Occlumency", and thus, the mirror image. If we break the word down in the same fashion as before, the result is very intriguing. "Le gili men cy" becomes "le gilly men see". The mention of "gilly" instantly brings to mind the egg and the rescue mission in the second task of the Triwizard tournament of Book 4. Harry's success in the second task is due not only to the fact that he learns the secret of the golden egg, but also the fact that Dobby steals gilly weed *and gives it to Harry so that he may breathe and see underwater. These abilities make it possible for him to complete the task. Using "le", the French definite article for the, fits in, since one of the participating schools, Beauxbatons, is a French school. I believe the egg could be a clue hiding in plain sight, and is "screeching" that the lake will play a large role in upcoming books.*

 HANDFUL

JK Rowling, clue master extraordinaire, hides her clues in plain sight. However, like a camouflaged Easter egg, she makes sure they are not easy to spot. Her ability to repeat words and themes, use running bits, and literary references, without giving away the whole story, underlines her talent.

Before Harry begins his journey at Platform 9¾, we are already given clues about major upcoming events involving the lake and underground environs. Rubeus Hagrid, Keeper of Keys and Grounds at Hogwarts, takes Harry to Diagon Alley to buy his school supplies. Accompanying Griphook (the goblin who escorts them to the vaults), "*they plunged even deeper, passing an underground lake...*"{p74} And further on, "*the air became colder and colder... They went rattling over an underground ravine...*"{p75} The key question is: does the lake at Hogwarts connect to any river (above or below ground)?

The grounds of Hogwarts are protected by many charms and spells, according to several sources {B5, Ch23, p500}. The lake is on the grounds, of course. And yet, if we think about it logically and examine the lake closely, we might be able to see a dangerous breach of safety that involves the lake. The very nature of a lake is that it goes beneath the surface, reaching underground. Are the areas *under* Hogwarts protected by the charms and spells?

It seemed strange to me that while all other students were taken to the castle via carriages (or flying **Anglias**), the first-years arrived by boat, no matter how terrible the weather. And why did a gamekeeper have the duty to escort them on this trip? Was it due to the nature of the creatures in the lake? Did it serve as a sort of secret introduction to the giant squid? (The squid is quite friendly with the students, as evidenced by the scene in Book 5 where students are swimming with the squid.{Ch38, p850})

Back when Harry and the other first-years were ferried across the lake for the first time, they found the trip "*carried them through a curtain of ivy that hid a wide opening in the cliff face. . .along a dark tunnel . . .underneath the castle, until they reached a kind of underground harbor. Then they clambered up a passageway in the rock. . .coming out at last . . . right in the shadow of the castle.*" Strangely enough, it is at this moment that Trevor, Neville's constantly disappearing toad, is found.

Thinking about the squid caused me to also contemplate where the squid went during the second task of the Triwizard Tournament. For the Triwizard Tournament, we have three schools competing (that pesky number three keeps turning up), of which the Durmstrang students arrived by water – specifically, the lake. "*Some disturbance was taking place deep in the center—great bubbles were forming on the surface. . .the ship emerged entirely. . .and began to slide toward the bank*" {B4, Ch15, p245}.

The arrival of the ship from the middle of the lake suggests that it has traveled along some route to reach that final destination. Obviously, that route comes out under the lake's surface. JKR describes the edge of the lake as the "bank". Shouldn't that be "shore"? I have always been under the impression that the edge of a river was called a "bank". Hmmmmm…interesting…Gringotts Bank (underground lakes)…bank of the lake….

The idea that Durmstrang's headmaster teaches the Dark Arts is disturbing, and he has just entered Hogwarts' grounds in a very unconventional way. The fact that a former Death Eater (Karkaroff), and his students have an underground route to Hogwarts is definitely frightening.

Harry's trip to the prefect bathroom in Book 4 reveals more interesting references. As Myrtle says, "*I sometimes go down [to the lake] . . . don't have any choice, if someone flushes my toilet when I'm not expecting it.*" {p464} Have we been given as many hints as there are faucets in the prefects' tub? Are we to understand that there are numerous routes that lead to the lake? The most telling thing is that when the toilet is flushed, Myrtle ends up in the lake (and she clearly returns). So, obviously, not only is the toilet a way to get out of Hogwarts, it is also a way to get in.

As Harry frantically searches for a way to complete the second task in Book 4, JKR seems to wink at us from within the passages. Harry is able to gain information he never imagined by *immersing* himself into the Pensieve. Should Harry look into the lake for the danger he knows is coming?

Keeping the thought of the lake in mind, if we look at Book 5, the references begin almost immediately. When Harry encounters the Dementors, his feelings are again described as those of a person drowning.{B3, Ch7, p136} However, instead of the imminent death of Ron and Hermione by drowning, Harry is facing his own death at the hands of the Dementors. Similar to his experience in the lake, Harry "*fought for breath*" until he was able to produce the Patronus that chased the Dementors away.{B5, Ch1, p18}

So, we come to Chapter 24 of Book 5. Interestingly enough, in Book 4, the lake task in the Triwizard Tournament occurred on the 24th, and here we have a chapter entitled "Occlumency" ("a clue men see"). This chapter is full of subtle similarities to the second task of the tournament – including the egg. For instance, Harry can no longer look forward to Quidditch, due to the fact that he is banned from playing by Umbridge. If you will remember, the contest for the Quidditch Cup was cancelled so that the Triwizard Tournament could take place. Also, just before Harry is told of Dumbledore's instructions to teach him Occlumency, we see Harry playing chess with Ron, "egging" on his castle to defeat a pawn of Ron's. {Ch24, p517} So, Occlumency is supposed to help him defend himself from someone getting in. Is this another clue that the lake is susceptible to someone getting in?

Funny, but on her website {www.jkrowling.com}, JKR joked that we should keep an eye out for "Squidward". Is the giant squid the "ward" that keeps the lake safe? What would happen if it were injured or killed? And why do the merpeople have drawings of their people chasing the giant squid with spears? {B4, Ch26, p497}

Now, let me try to bring all of this together in a simpler form. I believe that the lake at Hogwarts is dangerously accessible. If the lakes and rivers are connected—and it makes sense that they could very well be—then both Hogwarts and Gringotts are vulnerable. Note that the centaurs and *merpeople* are the only two species that opted to not be classified as "Beings" by the wizarding world. Additionally, goblins are not listed in *Fantastic Beasts and Where to Find Them*, so are probably Beings – however, they were absent from the classification meeting, therefore, we can't be sure. {FB, pxii}. So, the merpeople do not participate in wizard affairs, and goblins are, essentially, wild cards in the upcoming conflict. Having their own governments exclusive of the wizarding world makes it imperative that diplomatic efforts be made to gain the favor of these creatures. We already know that goblins and centaurs have abilities that wizards do not. It is only practical to believe the same of the merpeople.

While Bill and Charlie are in a good position to help with the goblins and dragons, only Dumbledore, as far as we know, has a relationship with the merpeople. If he has, like so many times before {Book 4, Ch 26, p505}, placed unfounded trust in the inherent good of a people, Hogwarts may very well be in big trouble. Could the merpeople be unwittingly manipulated by Voldemort and his followers to allow access into the lake, thus into Hogwarts? We already know that a wanted murderer found his way into the castle, and the Basilisk also found its way from below through the pipes and plumbing. These are huge hints that something or someone even more horrible may be making their way from the depths below. Let's just hope someone discovers it in time!

Harry begins his journey to Hogwarts on the lake, and I believe his journey will end there. I believe that the battle for good in the wizarding world will be fought there, and that everything and everyone that have gone on before are in preparation for that final confrontation.

Until then, keep your noses in the air for those stinky smells, your ears to the floor for those squishy sounds, and your eyes in the mirror so you know what's behind you!

ADDITIONAL SLEUTHING NOTES

✳ If merpeople are as fearful of magic as Harry believed {B4, Ch26}, are they easy prey for Dark wizards?

✳ Does plant-lover Neville have any special skills or relationships concerning water plants?

✳ Why exactly would the merpeople (who seem like pretty nice guys) be chasing the giant (who seems pretty nice) squid? {B4, Ch26}

✳ Those water clues are awesome, but did JKR mean "le gilly" or "legi" – meaning *read* in Latin? Extra clues and or rewards in role-playing and video games are called "Easter Eggs", and we know that JKR knows about those, so could those egg references be pointing to clues?

✳ Who rescued Dennis when he fell out of the boat in Chapter 12 of Book 4? The squid could have done the deed, but what about the merpeople?

✳ Mirrors and Time ✳

Dana Bielicki-Maffei ✳ NC, "DBMaff"
USA (*US Edition*), Age 33

Inspiration for this Discussion

My fascination with mirrors began when I was a small child; my dad used to tell me the story of *Snow White* at bedtime and the parts of the story that interested me the most were the parts where the wicked stepmother held consultation with her mirror. It was curious to me since my own mirrors didn't behave in the same way — they only showed me a reflection of myself and my surroundings and offered no advice or insight despite innumerable attempts on my part to open up a dialogue with the "spirit" I swore was in there somewhere.

As I got older, despite spending hours and hours in front of mirrors primping and hair-spraying, I fell out of touch with my mirror suspicions until I went away to college and began studying history. In providing me with a new way of looking at the past through the interpretation of events, people, and culture, I began to realize that what we see when reflecting on the past is not necessarily reality. Hmmm... well, if that is the case, then how about what we see when we look in a mirror? Aren't mirrors and historical studies the same things—devices meant to capture and reflect moments in time? Realities from the viewer's perspective.

And then there is the time element—time is also relative and while it is based on nature, our monitoring of time and need to harness and control it is wholly man-made.

The inspiration for this essay began with these early thoughts, but ultimately bubbled up when Sirius presented Harry with one of his two-way mirrors. That drew all of my thoughts about mirrors, time, and representation to the surface. This discussion is the beginning of my attempt to bring these three elements together in a meaningful way.

🦉 12

The mirror is one of a handful of commonplace objects that has inspired more than a few superstitions. In times of old, young women were warned that if they stared too long at the reflection cast from a mirror, eventually the Devil would appear. Breaking a mirror is thought to carry with it bad luck, and in some cultures, mirrors in the home are covered when a person dies. Given these kinds of customs and beliefs, it is easy to understand why mirrors also appear so frequently throughout literature as both literal and symbolic devices. Mirrors, for example, serve as key story elements in famous works like *Snow White*, *The Lord of the Rings*, *The Canterbury Tales (The Squire's Tale)*, *Macbeth*, and the works of Lewis Carroll. This tradition has been carried on throughout the five published Harry Potter books, wherein JK Rowling incorporates/utilizes a variety of mirrors with different appearances and uses.

Mirrors encountered thus far are:

1) mirrors that we know interact with the viewer – Foe-Glass, the mirror in Harry's room at the Leaky Cauldron, the mirror at the Weasley home in The Burrow, and the Mirror of Erised; and the hand-held mirrors Sirius Black shares with Harry and

2) mirrors that haven't yet shown interactive capability – the mirrors that hang in Dolores Umbridge's office, Moaning Myrtle's bathroom, and Voldemort's lair.

One common trait shared by all of the interactive mirrors is the ability to communicate information to the person looking into them. But there is something unique about the hand-held mirrors that Sirius Black shares with Harry in Book 5 that makes them very special – a connection with the concepts of time and space. They seem to have a brand of magic assigned to them, which allows both time and space to be manipulated or transcended.

Sirius' mirrors are clearly communications devices, as Sirius explains to Harry. But we have yet to find out if these mirrors can also bridge time and space. Could they "reunite" Harry and Sirius, who, at the close of the book, exist in different dimensions? We are unsure what lies on the other side of the veil though which Sirius was pushed. However, as it was a "door" that defies the physics of our world, we can safely argue that the final destination is not of the same time-space dimension that Harry occupies. If (and I acknowledge these are big "ifs") Sirius had his mirror with him at the time he passed through the veil, and if Harry's mirror has not shattered though his "careless packing" of it, then it is possible that we may see these mirrors used to help Harry and Sirius bridge the gap of time and space that separate the two realms in which each exists. Yet the actual implications of the crack cannot be ignored. In the case of non-magical mirrors, cracks distort and corrupt the reflected image so we need to be suspicious about whatever is represented in Harry's mirror should it be functional at a future point in the story.

It is also possible that Rowling is using mirrors as gateways for entry into other dimensions. JK Rowling's mirrors, magical and non-magical alike, do one thing in common – they "reflect" a state of existence in the present for whatever image is displayed to the viewer. In reflecting, mirrors encapsulate alternate versions of reality—a reversed vision of the present reality that exists in its own two-dimensional space. Therefore, mirrors create a new and distinct instance of time and space. Now, what if Rowling has taken up this idea, thrown in a touch of Lewis Carroll and as with the looking glass created for Alice, gifted some of her mirrors with the ability to transport the viewer into that new dimension…or though time and space to a different location?

We already know that a dual "reality" exists in Harry's world as demonstrated through the existence of number twelve Grimmauld Place, St Mungo's Hospital, and Diagon Alley. A physical location with the size and complexity of Diagon Alley cannot simply be hidden from view. Rather, it must, on some level, exist in a parallel dimension in tandem with Muggle London. If we accept the plausibility of multiple dimensions coexisting within a given space, Rowling has left us some very interesting clues that point to mirrors serving as portals connecting these dimensions. Consider the way the mirror functioned in Lewis Carroll's Through the Looking Glass allowing Alice to follow her kitten into a parallel world. Compelling evidence in support of this parrallel are the kitten plates that hang in Dolores Umbridge's office – right near (what else) a mirror. In Chapter 1 of Through the Looking Glass, the reader finds Alice playing with a little black kitten that "refuses" to fold its arms properly, prompting Alice's threat to put it through the mirror into Looking-Glass House. Alice explains to the kitten that in this other dimension everything is just the same as in the drawing room they occupy in the current time and space, only backwards. The glass changes to a silvery mist, and Alice jumps through and into the new dimension to find things quite different – most critically, that spaces normally invisible in the normal house, exist in plain sight in the looking glass world. By juxtaposing the kitten plates with the mirror Rowling could be making a literary allusion to the Carroll story and clueing us into a possible alternative use for the mirror in Dolores's office. Further, Harry's non-reaction to the presence of the mirror and his seeming fixation with the kitten plates is characteristic of the method Rowling uses to direct the reader toward something important that a character may disregard.

While mirrors in Rowling's world may be able to provide access to new spaces, I do not believe, at this point, that they *alter* time. Rather, they connect different states of reality existing simultaneously within the present time. Mirrors, as already stated, reflect the present. So if mirrors do provide entry to an alternate dimension of space, I believe time in that space would run parallel with time in all her other dimensions. As further evidence of this, we have seen magical objects that are specifically dedicated to time manipulation, like the time-turner. Snape has told us that in magic, time and space matter. {B5, Ch24} Yet time and space, while integrally connected, remain unique entities. Therefore, it is not too far off base to imagine that the manipulation of each requires the use of distinct objects with a dedicated brand of magic.

If this is the case, and mirrors do function as gateways to alternative parallel realties, new possibilities begin to emerge. For example, combine the concept of mirrors as entryways to parallel dimensions with the concept of the Floo Network and possible answers to some of the hottest septology questions begin to take shape. Where did Dumbledore go after he vanished from his office in Book 5, and how is the Headmaster able to move about Hogwarts, seemingly at will? Perhaps he is using conveniently positioned mirrors (similar to the one that covers the caved-in passage, the one in Moaning Myrtle's bathroom, or the one in Umbridge's office) to navigate the halls of the school. Could he even use them to transport himself to a different location altogether (like the Ministry of Magic) in order to help some of his students do battle with Voldemort's Death Eaters?

In the end, only Rowling can answer these questions and explain the magic behind objects like mirrors. So, we readers have to wait for her to unfold the secrets behind her creations. Who knows, maybe mirrors are simply mirrors…but, given Rowling's track record, I personally plan to make sure that I gaze a bit harder and longer at the mirrors that come up in the final chapters of Harry's story.

ADDITIONAL SLEUTHING NOTES

✳ Since they have identical descriptions, are Voldemort's mirror from Chapter 26 in Book 5, and the mirror in Moaning Myrtle's bathroom from Chapter 9 in Book 2, somehow linked like Sirius' mirrors? Would that be scary? How about the mirror concealing the secret passage on the Marauder's Map? How about the cracked Foe Glass? Does it matter that Imposter Moody's Foe Glass in Book 4 wasn't described (at that time) as being cracked? {Ch20, Ch35}

✳ In the Muggle world, bars will use a two-way mirror, so is the mirror in the Three Broomsticks just a mirror? Also in the real world, a smashed mirror still works the same but the range is limited, so how does smashing a magical mirror alter its magical qualities…or does it? Could it still work but the magic be weaker/smaller?

✳ There is always a mirror or picture in Harry's room , no matter where he is staying – could those be for monitoring? What about the mirror in his room at the Dursleys? In Chapter 3 of Book 5, when Tonks went to his mirror, could she have been sending a signal to anyone?

✴ "THE VEIL OF MYSTERY" ✴

A.L. CARPENTER ✴ NC, "RIDGEBACK" (RB)
USA (*US Edition*), AGE 33

Inspiration for this Discussion

It was Sirius Black who got me totally hooked on Harry Potter. Although I had been reading the books all along, it was not until the third novel that Rowling got my full attention. Even in that character's frequent absence, he remains one of the most intriguing parts of the septology. It is only fitting that his death and the object that caused it would become just as intriguing. Here I make a connection from Rowling's veil to a very small part of literary history—the Greek philosophers myths and tragedies.

🦉 12

We know from Nearly Headless Nick in Chapter 38 of Book 5, that the Department of Mysteries is a place where "learned wizards" study various enigmas – including death. It is also very fitting that the emblem of death that stands within the Rowling's Department of Mysteries is that of an ancient veil. Just as Harry's veil is shrouded in mystery, there is no simple explanation for "the veil" of history.

The concept of the veil has preceded the written word as a symbol of mystery and fate. Even the great classical writers such as Aeschylus, Euripides and Sophocles care not to define the relationship between the gossamer device and the fate of humankind. It is understood…and yet it is not understood. The veil is used to imply mystery as much as it is used to imply the departure of life.

The gently-swaying curtain that hangs upon its cragged and ancient herms is an allegory for the known and unknown. It is the doorway to our fates. Nietzsche has masked us with the "Apollinian Veil" to help explain to us that everything in our lives is appearance. According to him, to lift that veil would reveal the full truth of suffering and would cause us to fall into a circling abyss of madness[1].

Harry Potter, like us, is fascinated and drawn in by the veil's soft beckoning and windswept mutterings. He cannot help approaching it any more than he could help digging into his subconscious to listen to his parents' voices in Book 3, when faced by Dementors. {Ch9} In a chilling moment of foreshadowing when Harry first encounters the veil in Book 5, he calls out Sirius' name as he walks around the dais and nearly touches the cloth.{Ch34, p773} It is logical for Hermione to pull Harry away. This object that seems both obvious and perplexing scares her. Her words are cautious at first, then desperate and pleading, and finally demanding as the urgency of the situation becomes more acute. Harry appears to be lured in by the mystery and fails to grasp the danger, due to the veil's mesmerizing beauty and intrigue. Harry seems compelled to touch the shroud.

We are reminded of his near-death experiences in the preceding books and the habit he has of teasing death (like in the graveyard battle scenes of Book 4 or his solo confrontation with Quirrell, when he was just eleven years old). Is his subconscious pulling him toward the archway? Luna, as usual, offers a detached recognition of the veil and merely mentions that she hears voices, too. Neville and Ginny are entranced—unable to move, think or react. Only Ron and Hermione apparently escape the spell.

During the battle in the Department of Mysteries, Harry feels something hit the back of his legs as he backs away from the Death Eaters. It is the stone dais. He climbs it. The Death Eaters stop. They hang motionlessly, like a pack of wolves...panting...waiting. When they speak, their voices are barking rally cries of mockery. Harry lingers on the dais, threatening them. It is unclear what he is prepared to do to prevent the Death Eaters from getting the prophecy. The veil stands like a gaping mouth, a perilous precipice, amid the warriors with their flashing jinxes in the battle scene.

That orifice is reminiscent of a cave...once more recalling images from the ancients—such as Plato's allegory in "The Republic", in which chained prisoners in a cave only know shadows to be the whole of reality. When released, the prisoners become enlightened to the truth that humans are not just shadows, but three-dimensional beings[2]. The cave is a metaphor for Sirius Black's life of imprisonment and enlightenment. It reveals itself full-force in Book 4, when Sirius, as Snuffles, is forced to live in a cave near Hogsmeade. The mystique of the veil and the icon of the cave seem very similar—offering the forbidden, cloaking the unknown. This is but one clue to Sirius Black's demise that we are allowed to gather upon Rowling's path...and if we have not, we beat ourselves upon the head with her heavy tomes afterward. There were other jabbing hints: in Book 5, the *"harsh bark of laughter"*{Ch1, p15}, juxtaposed with a graveyard and the *"darkness that pressed on Harry's eyes"*{p16}, There is also Sirius' cryptic claim that, *"A deadly struggle for my soul would have broken the monotony nicely."* {Ch5 p82}

Sirius's final moment—the gracefully arching fall into the veil—echoes the painting, "Fall of Day" by William Rimmer (made famous by Led Zeppelin's "Swan Song"). The Order of the Phoenix stops, and time seems to freeze as Sirius vanishes beyond the veil, as if he has fallen into a black hole.

Lupin immediately understands the tragedy and grips Harry tightly so he will not follow. Dumbledore stands still, watching...immobile. It is later in his office at Hogwarts that Dumbledore offers his thoughts on Sirius's demise. His reaction is a turning point in the septology: while we consider him to be a sage, he perceives himself as ordinary, weighing his mistakes and acknowledging regret and human error. He takes partial blame for Sirius's demise, wondering how he could have kept such a free spirit behind locked doors. (Not even Azkaban could keep Black prisoner, after all.)

It is the "remotely occupied" Luna whose final words in Book 5 return us to the question of the veil: what is behind it, and whether those lost can return. *"They were just lurking out of sight...you heard them,"* Luna says, affirming everyone's suspicions. {Ch38, p863}

So, is it possible in Rowling's world to go into the underworld and return? The legend of Samhain offers a thin window of time with which to rescue those who slip into the beyond... Samhain, the Celtic New Year[3], is popularly celebrated as "Halloween". It is the night the dead congregate (corresponding nicely with the "Deathday Party" in Chapter 8 of Book 2) and the one night of the year when the veil between the world of the living and the world of the dead lifts, thus allowing us to see our dead, to gain knowledge from them, or even lure them back. The classics embrace similar legends: Odysseus, Orpheus, Aeneas and Alcestis all return from the underworld. Homer's Odysseus[4] and Virgil's Aeneas[5] traveled there to gain knowledge on their journeys—Odysseus to get home, and Aeneas to start a new life, but both after the Trojan War. Alcestis, in Euripides' play named in her honor, willingly dies to save her husband Atmetus' life. Her dedication and bravery are rewarded when Heracles goes to the underworld and retrieves her[6]. Orpheus was not so lucky. Orpheus was blessed with the gift to play the most beautiful music known—beautiful enough to move stone and lull demons. Soon after his short marriage to the beautiful nymph Eurydice, his bride was bitten by a vicious water snake. Orpheus traveled to the underworld to retrieve her and persuaded Hades and Persephone to allow him to recover Eurydice with the music from his lyre. Unfortunately, Orpheus broke the pact with the gods and looked behind him to catch a glimpse of his beautiful wife—which was forbidden—and she was forced to return to Hades while Orpheus returned to Earth alone[7]. Eurydice's hurt foot is eerily reminiscent of Ginny's hurt foot during the battle in the Department of Mysteries in Book 5.

Rowling teases us when Harry almost adds pomegranate juice to a potion- evoking Persephone's sad predicament. (Persephone was kidnapped by Hades. He was persuaded to return her only upon Zeus' command, but tricked Peresphone into eating pomegranate seeds, thus binding her to the underworld during the winter months.) JKR keeps us wondering about the asphodel in the "Draught of Living Death" and about that strange scene where Harry is lying flat on his back in a flowerbed. While the adventures and tragedies of the Greeks do offer pathways to the underworld and back, it seems impossible that the spirits contained by this veil would be within reach. Luna of Ravenclaw, however, has no worries.

The sinuous fibers of the black cloth represent our subsistence… just as the moirae spin life, Homer's Penelope (whose very name means "weaver") continued to symbolically weave and re-weave Odysseus' lifeline. In the *Odyssey* Penelope becomes a symbol of the triple goddess, to which the fates are also linked. Despite 20 years of waiting for Odysseus' return, she remains desirable to the men competing for Odysseus' throne, and thus represents the "maiden". Her age, wisdom, and power represent the "crone". Her relationship to Telemachus, as a mother, and to Odysseus, as a wife, represents the "mother" aspect. The critical scene in Odysseus' home in Ithaca at the beginning of the poem shows Penelope weaving and re-weaving a veil for her father-in-law. The cloth she weaves is to be his burial shroud—yet another symbol of her role as "fate". The triple aspect of Penelope as "fate, also known as the moirae, the norn, and the Weird Sisters, is a re-occurring symbol of the fabric of time being woven by the past, present, and future[8]. This is reflected in Rowling's work, yet again, by Mrs. Black's portrait in Grimmauld Place shrieking from behind her velvet curtain. {Ch4, p78}

One is reminded, too, of the fury Tisiphone[9], who guarded the pillared entrance to wretched Tartarus with her blood-soaked veil. It is Heracles in The Trachiniae by Sophocles that bemoans his fate as he lifts a "veil" to expose rotting flesh. Sophocles used the veil again and again as an anakalypsis—a nuptial gesture to death- while Homer used the veil, cloak and loom as a continuous metaphor for fate. The veil icons have flourished through global myth, religion and literature and are clearly understood beyond the cusp of one culture.

What is the veil, though? It is both familiar and abstract and Rowling does not offer us one thread of textual explanation about what she has in store…or does she? Even if Rowling had written the piece transparently we could count on her for a twist. If we understood the veil, it would not be sitting upon its ancient dais, held by a crumbling, pointed arch in the Department of Mysteries. To borrow from Sophocles' Oedipus at Colonus, "Tis ill to tear aside the veil of mysteries[10]."

────────── ADDITIONAL SLEUTHING NOTES ──────────

✳ Are the alluring voices Harry hears behind the veil that of people, or a magical deception similar to yet another Classical Greek reference – that of Odysseus' lethal Sirens – who lured sailors to their death upon the rocks that surround their island?

✳ Is Harry's veil the wizarding world equivalent of the prisoners inside Plato's cave? Are wizards' perceptions of reality just a "shadow" of our real world, or is it us Muggles who are the ones inside the cave and the magical world the reality?

✳ Is JKR's veil similar in structure to the Greek veil where mortals have been known to enter and exit the underworld, or is it like Isis's veil of mysteries where mortals are forbidden from possessing the knowledge resting in the netherworld?

1 Nietzsche, "Apollinian Veil": Nietzsche, Friedrich. *The Philosophy of Nietzsche*, 1927. The Modern Library.

2 Plato's "Allegory of a Cave": Plato *"The Republic": Great Dialogues of Plato.* translated by W.H.D. Rouse. New American Library. 1956.

3 Samhain. *"Samhain"*. McCormack, Mike. National History Page from National Ancient Order of Hibernians.
http://www.aoh.com/history/archive/samhain.htm.
-Akasha. *"Samhain".* http://www.wicca.com/celtic/akasha/samhainlore.htm
Fox, Selena. *"Celebrating the Seasons".* Selena Fox. Circle Sanctuary, http://www.circlesanctuary.org/pholidays/Samhain.html

4 Homer, translated by T.E. Lawrence. *The Odyssey* 2004

5 Virgil, translated by Robert Fitzgerald. *The Aeneid*. Vintage Books. 1981

6 Euripides, translated by Philip Vellacott. *Alcestis.* Penguin Books. 1975

7 Martin, Richard P. *Myths of the Ancient Greeks.* New American Library. 1975

8 Grimal, Pierre. *The Dictionary of Classical Mythology.* Blackwell Publishing. 1986
Thomas Bullfinch. *Bullfinch Mythology.* http://www.bullfinch.org

9 -Greek Mythology Link: http://www.homepage.mac.com/cparada/GML/Underworld.html
 -Ovid. *Metamorphoses.* Oxford University Press. London: 1989.

10 Sophocles, translated by F. Storr. *Oedipus at Colonus.* William Heinemann Ltd. London: 1912.

THROUGH THE VEIL (...AND BACK AGAIN?)

K.E. BLEDSOE ✷ NC, "ARTEMIS MOONBOW"
USA (*US Edition*), AGE 42

Inspiration for this Discussion

What led me to write this article was the same feeling of utter denial that so many Harry Potter fans had when reading of Sirus' demise the very first time: that feeling of, No, I didn't just see that — did I? No, he didn't really...did he? Come on, it's the old arrow-under-the-arm trick — right? Then comes anger, and a strong desire to throw the book down on the floor in disgust. How dare any author treat a character so callously? Finally, after the initial shock wears off, comes a need to understand. Then come the re-readings, the spotting of clues, the piecing together of theories to explain the "why" of Sirius' fall – and the incentive to look for any sign of hope that we might see our favorite Animagus again. This is my trail of clues...

HANDFUL

Will he…

or won't he…

…return from the veil, that is?

That has been a burning question among HP Sleuths ever since we got our hands on Book 5 and watched in horror as Sirius Black fell through the veil in the Department of Mysteries. Some say, "He's dead. Get over it." Others say, "But wait… the clues! The clues!" Indeed, a close reading of Book 5 reveals many clues suggesting his return, though few can guess how or in what form.

What *do* we know about death in the world of Harry Potter? Ms. Rowling stated in a WBUR Radio interview (Oct 1999) that those who are "properly dead" don't come back. Cedric Diggory's death confirmed this. There was no reviving him once he was killed by the Killing Curse ("*Avada Kedavra!*"). Some of the dead become ghosts, but this seems to be a choice they make at the point of death, as Nearly Headless Nick stated in Book 5. Nick, himself, hasn't been "beyond the veil," and has chosen to remain on Earth in ghostly form. In Book 5, we also see a number of symbolic representations of the same "rule"— showing that while the "container" can be repaired, the "contents" can't be restored. For example, Harry spills a bowl containing essence of murtlap, breaking the bowl. With a wave of his wand he repairs the bowl, but the contents remain spilled.{Ch15, p328} Broken jars of preserved nasties in Snape's dungeon are also repairable, but once again, the contents can't be restored. In the Department of Mysteries, Harry deliberately upsets a shelf full of prophecy orbs. The broken orbs release their contents, and the prophecies are lost.

So it seems that once the body ("container") is broken, the soul ("contents") is forever lost. Thus, if Sirius is "really, most sincerely dead," as the Munchkins sang in *The Wizard of Oz*,[1] then there is no chance that he can return from the dead.

But *is* he…dead?

IS SIRIUS PROPERLY DEAD?

This question really divides into two questions: 1. Was Sirius dead when he fell into the veil? And 2. Did falling into the veil kill him?

To answer the first question, let's take a look at what we know about curses to determine whether the curse that hit Sirius killed him, and then observe what actually happened to Sirius.

THE FATEFUL CURSE

In the battle in the Department of Mysteries, Bellatrix aims a curse at Sirius that is described as a red jet of light. It misses, and Sirius taunts Bellatrix, but she hits him with a second jet that sends him on his fateful tumble. The color of that jet is unstated. Sirius is hit by only one spell (the nature of which we don't know for certain) and Sirius is still relatively young and strong.

Was it the Killing Curse? Unlikely. Every time that particular curse has been used before, its appearance and effects have been described in detail. We know the curse is visible as green light. We also know that it kills instantaneously. Had Harry witnessed Sirius getting hit with the killing curse, would he have tried to go after him? Would he have denied his death? Harry knows firsthand the effects of the curse. Had he seen a jet of green light, had he heard the fateful words pronounced, he would have known Sirius was dead.

OTHER CURSES

What about other curses? Can they kill? We've learned a lot about curses and their effects in Book 5—enough to conclude that the curse that hit Sirius was not enough to kill him. Consider these descriptions, all from Book 5:

1. The attack on Professor McGonagall {Ch31, p721}—the professor is hit *square in the chest* with *four* Stunning Spells all at once, and red jets of light characterize the spells. Madam Pomfrey later says that it's a wonder the attack didn't kill her at her age. So, four Stunning spells at once didn't kill her, though she's injured enough to have to go to St Mungo's and comes back leaning on a walking stick.

2. Hermione is hit by a flame-like purple bolt of light *in the chest*. {Ch35, p792} We don't know what the curse is, but it's a bad one. She ends up in the hospital ward. *But it's still not enough to kill her.*

3. Ginny is hit in the face with a bolt of red light. {p798} She, too, survives.

So, the only curse we've seen that kills with one blow is the Killing Curse. Others can do a great deal of damage, from which a person might die later if left untreated, but they don't kill instantaneously.

SIRIUS' REACTION

Here is where we get real evidence regarding Sirius' state at the moment he fell. He is hit *square in the chest*, just as Professor McGonagall and Hermione were. His eyes widen in shock, rather like Hermione's reaction to the purple flame thing. As he falls backwards, his expression *changes*, first to a look of surprise, then an expression of fear. Sirius *cannot* already be dead as he falls (like Cedric was) or his expression could not change.

DID THE VEIL KILL HIM?

Is the veil a killing machine? The appearance of the veil reveals little. It looks for all the world like a stone archway removed from some ruin, with a black veil draped over the opening. The arrangement of the room, though, is eerie in the extreme, with its rows and rows of benches like an amphitheater. What could possibly be going on in there that would require an audience? Is it similar to a medical operating theater? Or a courtroom? Or an execution chamber?

The only other clue, apart from how it swallowed a man alive, was the sound of voices from beyond the veil, itself. Both Harry and Luna are drawn by the voices as they enter the chamber. In fact, Harry sees the veil move slightly, "*as though someone just touched it*". {Ch34, p773} The first thing he does is call for Sirius, already connecting Sirius with the veil. Ginny and Neville are also transfixed. Why those four? Three of them can see Thestrals, but since Ginny cannot, there must be some other connection between the four. Luna is confident that the voices she heard behind the veil were those of the dead—but then, Ginny noted that Luna only believed things for which there is no evidence. Which character do we believe?

The behavior of the Death Eaters upon entering the veil chamber is interesting. They chase Harry into the veil chamber, but they stop pursuing when he reaches the veil itself. {Ch35, p799} Are they *afraid* he'll step into it? But then it's what the Death Eaters do *not* do that is most interesting. If someone can be killed by falling into the veil, why didn't the Death Eaters try to push or otherwise force others in? Do they know what the veil is? If they do, perhaps it means that the veil isn't some kind of killing machine, or else they would have tried to use it. And if that is the case, *then it's possible that Sirius wasn't killed*.

On the other hand, Lupin tells Harry that Sirius is gone, and Dumbledore tells the Ministry officials that the Death Eaters are tied up and waiting in the "Death Chamber". {Ch36, p817} Which "chamber" is that? He doesn't *specify* the chamber with the veil, though considering the appearance of the room and the fact that much of the fighting took place there, it seems the likely candidate.

Did Sirius die? The clues surrounding Sirius' demise (such as they are), remain ambiguous. If the veil kills, how? If it doesn't, what does it do? Clues in the Department of Mysteries relate to time, which could point to the veil being a portal through time. Notice also that Sirius appears to take "*an age to fall*" in Harry's view. Granted, that could simply be the drama of the situation. But...an *age* to fall? Did he fall into the world of the dead, as many HP Sleuths assume, or did he, in fact, literally fall back through an age, into time?

We've also seen, indirectly, the actions of the vanishing cabinet at Hogwarts, into which Fred and George stuffed Montague. He turned up days later in an upstairs toilet. We don't know exactly how a vanishing cabinet works, but Sirius certainly "vanished" through the veil. One of the great mysteries regarding wizarding magic is where things go when they are vanished. If Montague can be vanished and end up in another place days later, what about other vanished items—or people? {B5, Ch28, p627}

Can Sirius Return?

Faithful fans of Sirius Black all hope, of course, that he'll make a return, hale and hearty once again. But is it possible? "Returning" clues abound in Book 5, but whose return they foretell is difficult to say.

The bell jar was one of the most obvious clues, with its hummingbird that hatches, ages, and de-ages back to the egg. Interesting that it doesn't really die—it "de-ages." And when the unnamed Death Eater gets his head stuck in the jar, his head changes to a baby's head, back to adult, then back to baby again, at which point the luckless Death Eater pulls away with a creepy and surreal result. Since the bell jar can be penetrated, it clearly isn't just there to house and protect the pretty little hummingbird display. The whole instrument is meant to be used. For what and by whom?

The same room holds a cabinet full of small hourglass-like instruments that Harry surmises are time turners. When the cabinet is upset, the glass panes repeatedly shatter, repair, and then break again. {Ch35, p790} This defies the rule established earlier: that things once broken lose their contents forever.

The time turners are restored to wholeness, but only through tampering with time.

Shortly afterwards, when Voldemort attacks Harry, Fawkes actually *swallows* Voldemort's Killing Curse, dies, and from the ashes is reborn. {Ch36, p815} This gives a whole new meaning to the term "Death Eater," and embodies an obvious death-rebirth clue.

In regards to Harry's wish to talk to Sirius, Ginny says that, *"anything's possible, if you've got enough nerve."* {Ch29, p655} *Anything*, Ginny? Is that a clue? She also says she learned that from Fred and George. And speaking of Fred and George, we've had lots of clues that our favorite twin troublemakers are highly-skilled wizards who have been dabbling with time travel (consider, for example, their lunatic bet at the Quidditch World Cup). Is their dramatic "breakout" scene in Book 5 a foreshadowing? Will they help Sirius "pull a Weasley"?

Then there is a statement by Cornelius Fudge that made true-blue Sirius fans leap from their chairs on a second reading of the book. On page 614 {Ch37}, he says, *"Or is there the usual simple explanation involving a reversal of time, a dead man coming back to life, and a couple of invisible Dementors?"* Fudge was undoubtedly talking about the final events of either Book 3 (with Pettigrew's return) or Book 4 (with Voldemort's return), but my goodness— "a dead man coming back to life." If this isn't a huge, finger-pointing clue, then Ms. Rowling isn't playing fair.

The most endearing and uplifting clue, however, has to be Luna's statement to Harry on page 863 {Ch38}, when Harry sees Luna putting up a notice that a lot of her things are missing, asking people to bring them back. She says this happens a lot, though we've not seen her specific notice before, only a vague reference to lost-and-found notices. Luna isn't worried about getting her stuff back. Notice what she says:

"They'll come back, they always do in the end." {Ch38, p864}

Without knowing what the veil does to a person who falls into it, it's difficult to say whether one can survive in body. But if Luna's statement is as prophetic as many hope it is, and with multiple possibilities of mirrors, portraits, and the like lurking about, then it's quite possible that we haven't seen the last of Sirius Black.

ADDITIONAL SLEUTHING NOTES

* ✳ Did the Mimbulus Mimbletonia Stinksap that hit Harry, Neville, and Ginny back in Chapter 10 have anything to do with their being most sensitive to the veil?

* ✳ During the battle in the Department of Mysteries, what happened to Ginny, Ron, and Luna? If Ginny can be correlated to Eurydice and Ron had a close encounter with Pluto, would that mean they could have been following in the footsteps of Orpheus?

* ✳ Even Dumbledore joked to Fudge about a man returning from the dead, so is it out of the question?

* ✳ Dumbledore is convinced that Sirius is dead, *"'Am I to understand,' said Phineas Nigellus slowly from Harry's left, 'that my great-great-grandson — the last of the Blacks — is dead?' 'Yes, Phineas,' said Dumbledore",* {Ch37, p826} but does he know what the veil is? Can we be sure that he is right? What does Luna say about such things? {Ch38, p862} And what did JKR mean when she said that, *"The sun was rising properly now"*? {Ch37, p826}

THE CHAMBER OF THOTH

S.P. SIPAL ✳ NEW CLUES FORUM
USA (*US Edition*), AGE 38

Inspiration for this Discussion

While researching my first essay on "Geomancy: The Alchemy Gems in Harry Potter", I came across several references to the secret documents and Chamber of Thoth, which bore a striking resemblance to themes and images within the Harry Potter series. So, of course, I had to investigate further.

 NEWT

The Chamber of Secrets held a very important secret, right? A secret that caused dissension between Slytherin and the other houses. A secret that was used as a destructive tool by Tom Riddle, resulting in the death of a young girl (Moaning Myrtle) in the past and the petrification of several more in Book 2. However, I am convinced that JKR is not yet done with this story—and that the Chamber of Secrets may contain another, much greater secret, still to be revealed. After all, the Chamber of "Secrets" is not singular, but plural…

To reveal this possible new secret, I need to first discuss a strangely coincidental ancient Egyptian legend. The secret Book of Thoth and the Emerald Tablet—the Egyptian "Holy Grail."

THOTH AND AN ANCIENT EGYPTIAN LEGEND

Ancient Egypt is well known for its worship of the serpent, especially in the cult of Thoth. The temples of that cult were supported with serpent-entwined pillars, and Thoth, himself, was represented as carrying a caduceus—a staff entwined with serpents reaching toward the head of a winged solar orb. According to Claudius Aelian, a second-third century Roman naturalist, basilisks were kept in Egyptian temples, and whoever they happened to bite were divinely favored[1] (Harry?). Thoth, who many believe to have been a legendary king later deified, was associated with wisdom, learning and magic. While he is credited with inventing astronomy, geometry, medicine and music, he is best known for inventing writing, and was called "the scribe of the gods" and "the lord of books."[2] Legend also describes him as the author of the famous *Book of the Dead*,[3] which was a guidebook of spells to help the deceased pass through the dangers of the underworld and attain eternal life. He was often portrayed with an ibis head (a heron-like bird with a crescent beak) or as a baboon (monkey-like).

Thoth was the most learned of all the gods and recorded the sum of universal knowledge in countless books and the most important Emerald Tablet. All of which were later hidden in a golden box that was buried in a tomb, or a secret chamber, an inner sanctuary of a temple, or, according to another version, in the twin pillars at Heliopolis and Thebes.[4] The Emerald Tablet, which has been quoted from and known to exist for over 2,000 years, was a succinct outline of this universal knowledge and highly revered throughout the centuries. Even Alexander the Great is reputed to have viewed the Emerald Tablet and studied the Thothian documents, then erected the famed library at Alexandria to house them.

Since antiquity, the Emerald Tablet has served as the cornerstone for alchemy (indeed it is very old magic). Of the various translations of the Emerald Tablet that have come down throughout the century, two are notable to Harry Potter fans: one by Dr. John Everard in 1650, and one in the late nineteenth century by H.P. Blavatsky, the author of *Isis Unveiled*.[5] (Interesting title, eh? See side-bar at the end of this article). *Coincidentally,* there are an Everard and a Vablatsky in HP—Everard is one of the old headmaster portraits who goes to check on Mr. Weasley when he is bitten by the snake {B5, Ch 22, p469}. Cassandra Vablatsky is the author of Harry's third-year divination book, *Unfogging the Future* {B3, Ch4, p53}. Clues to an Emerald Tablet link?

The Emerald Tablet is considered to contain all the knowledge needed to create the Philosopher's Stone of legend, which, in its true sense, is the transformation of the seeker's soul. Its message is interpreted in seven steps, each of which advances the inner-personal transformation of the human-lead into the philosopher's stone, or enlightenment. Perhaps each of those levels corresponds to a year of Harry's growth at Hogwarts. Through his writings, Thoth *"succeeded in understanding the mysteries of the heavens [and] revealed them by inscribing them in sacred books which he then hid here on earth, intending that they should be searched for by future generations but found only by the fully worthy."*[6]

One intriguing legend, as recorded on a papyrus over 2,000 years old, details an even more ancient version of the entwined quests of two sons of pharaohs—both with magical powers but living several generations apart—in their search to find the Book of Thoth.[7] Setna, the son of Ramses the Great and also a renowned scribe, heard of the magic Book of Thoth and went to look for it in the tomb of another prince, Naneferkaptah, buried in Memphis, just south of Cairo. Entering Naneferkaptah's burial chamber, Setna discovers Naneferkaptah's wife and son's ka (their personified souls) guarding the body of Naneferkaptah (and the book), even though they, themselves, were buried hundreds of miles away at Coptos.

Ahura, Naneferkaptah's wife, recounts to Setna of her husband's quest to find the Book of Thoth—how he had forsaken everything until he located it, ignoring all those, including herself, who begged him to leave it be. The book was buried at the bottom of the Nile, hidden within a series of seven nested, locked boxes (each one increasing in alchemical value from iron to gold), and guarded by all types of dangerous creatures – the last and most deadly being a deathless, invincible serpent. Each time Naneferkaptah killed the snake, the snake reappeared in a different, more deadly form. The only way Naneferkaptah was able to finally defeat the serpent was to slice it in two and put sand on both ends so its halves could not reunite. He read the book, made a copy of it, and soaked the copy in beer until the script came off, and then literally drank the words down. Unfortunately, Thoth became enraged at his chamber being violated and his book stolen. Naneferkaptah's son died, then later his wife, and finally he himself, with the book bound to his body and buried with him.

When Ahura finishes her tale, she informs Setna that he has no claim to the book which her family gave their lives for. Setna responds by threatening to steal it. Naneferkaptah's *ka* challenges Setna to a board game of chance, winner to take the book, but as Setna starts losing, he uses an amulet to overcome Naneferkaptah. Setna escapes with the book. Naneferkaptah causes curses to fall upon Setna until he repents and returns the book to Naneferkaptah's tomb. As compensation, Setna must bring the bodies of Naneferkaptah's wife and son from their burial place in Coptos and reunite their family in death so their souls can rest peacefully. Setna does this and thus proves himself worthy.

Note how in Ahura's story, the guardian serpent returned in a changed form each time it was killed—very Voldemort-like. We have seen how, after each encounter with Harry, Voldemort changes form—in Godric's Hollow, he becomes vapor-Voldy; at the end of Book 1, he goes from a parasite on Quirrell's body back to Vapor-Mort; at the end of Book 2, from a viewed memory to spilled ink; Book 4—from a disgusting fetus to a corporeal body; and finally Book 5, from a body of his own to inhabiting Harry's body (if only briefly...we hope). I wonder if sand will work on old Voldy? Also, notice in the Setna legend how the "ghosts" can still affect the present events and how the board game is reminiscent of the game of chess in Book 1.

Not only was the Book of Thoth a legend to the ancient Egyptians, but it later became well known in various disguises (with slightly different locations and protections) to the Greeks. The Greeks knew Thoth as Hermes, then in an amalgamation of Hermes and Thoth as Hermes Trismegistus (Hermes the Thrice-Greatest). Much later, medieval alchemists revered the knowledge contained in the Emerald Tablet and considered Thoth to be the father of alchemy, under whatever name they chose to call him.

Though details from the legend of the Book of Thoth differ between the various sources, they usually hold certain key elements in common:

1) great, secret, magical knowledge for those worthy of it in future generations to discover, hand-written by Thoth himself (who many legends ascribe as an ancient king before being deified).

2) knowledge hidden from the unworthy, usually in a golden box, but almost always underneath—under a river, inside a tomb, within a pyramid or in a pillar in an inner chamber of a temple. A contemporary theory is that it's hidden under the Great Sphinx![8]

3) a box protected by a lethal creature, usually a serpent.

RESEMBLANCE TO JKR'S CHAMBER OF SECRETS

A secret chamber underground (even under a large body of water)...in a place resembling a temple...with a large, ancient monkeyish statue...caduceus-styled pillars...guarded by a fearsome, invincible snake (and a snake-like villain who changes form with each "death") – are all elements of the various Book of Thoth legends. All of these objects can also be found in the Chamber of Secrets. Coincidental? I believe JKR modeled the Chamber of Secrets after the secret chamber of Thoth, and if that is indeed so, Harry has not yet discovered the chamber's second and greater secret. But I believe he will.

Each serpent-entwined pillar that lines JKR's chamber bears a striking resemblance to the caduceus, the staff (wand) of Thoth/Hermes. According to legend, upon encountering two serpents trying to devour each other, Hermes threw his wand between them. The serpents entwined about it, reaching toward the top—that of a winged orb (sometimes a bird, symbolic of the bennu/phoenix)—as they strived toward a higher consciousness, the flight of the spirit, the eternal life of the phoenix. The caduceus thus reconciles basic opposing forces, good and evil—in alchemy, solar and lunar, or male and female. The union of the two snakes results in the birth of the Philosopher's Stone—"represented as a golden ball with wings at the top of the caduceus."[9] It signified unity, harmony, and enlightenment. As many have already speculated, the Golden Snitch seems to be the head of the caduceus, and as such, a symbol of the Philosopher's Stone. This could mean that what Harry needs most (knowledge and transformation of self) may well lie within this Chamber of Secrets.

That statue Tom Riddle addresses as Salazar Slytherin could very well be the embodiment of Thoth, whom Slytherin may have descended from or worshiped, or JKR could be conveying a metaphor for Thoth. The statue was "ancient and monkeyish" {B3, Ch15, p307}, just as Thoth is described. At the temple of Thoth in Hermopolis (Egyptian Khmunu), four colossal statues of baboons stood guard.

I do not believe Slytherin built this elaborate chamber, which in description bears all the marks of an ancient temple, only to house a snake. Salazar may not have been as bad as we've been led to believe. It is possible that he was a master alchemist and used this chamber to conduct his secret experiments, expand his esoteric knowledge, and ultimately hide his own book of knowledge, just as Thoth did. Perhaps Slytherin created his own Emerald Tablet, a record of his alchemical experiments and knowledge, a record of his own quest for immortality. Think of it—that book could actually be hidden—if not within one of the pillars, then buried under the feet of the great statue...right where Ginny lay—facedown—when Harry discovered her.

We have seen that books are an extremely important theme running through the *Harry Potter* series. For instance, we have our book-loving Hermione, the book that revealed Flamel in Book 1, Tom Riddle's Diary of Book 2, the biting *Monster Book of Monsters* in B3, the book given to Neville that revealed the gillyweed in B4, and the very intriguing *Nature's Nobility: A Wizarding Geneology* of B5. What might that last one reveal—a clue to the Half-Blood Prince, perhaps? Indeed, books have been used to reveal a major plot element in each of the five HP books thus far released. Could these books be pointing to an even greater, secret book yet to be uncovered? (And don't you think Hermione would be able to sniff out a book even twelve stories underground in a secret chamber? She would be critical to locating any book.)

Another curiosity, in Book 2, ch. 9, p. 145, Ron says that the Chamber of Secrets "rings a sort of bell," and it "might've been Bill" who mentioned it. *Might've been Bill? Bill...his* brother who was a curse breaker in Egypt (Book 3, ch. 1, p. 8). Hmm—maybe Bill's been searching for Thoth's secret chamber as well. I believe we'll see Bill's expertise from his past experience as a crucial plot element in the next couple of books.

DIVINING THE CHAMBER AND THE BOOK

What would the hidden book reveal? The Thoth book of secrets, besides transforming the reader into a powerful magician, enabled the reader to know the language of animals (a Parseltongue parallel?), gain knowledge of the universe and be granted immortality. Ultimately, the Book of Thoth served as the vehicle for discovering the mission, or destiny, of one's own soul.

Isis, Egypt's lunar and mother goddess, is strongly aligned with Thoth as a winged goddess, a magician and a healer. She wears her own symbol of mystery and esotericism: the veil of Isis. Quite interestingly, Isis is viewed as the star, Sirius. An inscription in her temple at Sais reads: "*I am that which is, which hath been, and which shall be; and no man has ever lifted the veil that hides my Divinity from mortal eyes.*"[13] To lift the veil of Isis is to pierce the heart of a great mystery. The veil of Isis is not only the veil of death, but also the veil of ultimate life.

I believe the Chamber of Secrets and the Veil Room in the Department of Mysteries, are both linked in theme and plot in the *Harry Potter* series, drawing upon the mysteries of Thoth and Isis. Both rooms are secret underground chambers, both hiding (in my opinion with CoS) deep secrets of human learning and mysteries. And both seem to be connected to the question of life and immortality. If I am correct, the Chamber of Secrets could ultimately reveal one side of this question, and the veil another. Hermione, through her books, could be the guide to unlocking the deeper secret of the Chamber of Secrets, while Luna, a modern Isis, would help to lift the veil in the Department of Mysteries for Harry. I see it as no coincidence that it is Luna Lovegood who seems to most understand the nature of the veil in the Department of Mysteries.

As to what lies behind the veil, I don't think it will be merely a lot of dead people, but rather a peaceful knowledge of what makes up the mysteries of life and, more importantly, how to live it fully.

Tom Riddle may have gotten his start in the Dark Arts here in JKR's secret chamber, conducting his first alchemical experiments to make himself immortal. JKR has alluded to our need to question why Voldemort did not die when the Avada Kedavra curse rebounded.[10] As a practitioner of alchemy, he could have studied the Slytherin Tablet, if it exists, and be far enough along the alchemical path of transformation that he has some protection from death, but not yet attained true and complete immortality. Thus his eyes glow red—red being the last stage of development before the final gold of the Philosopher's Stone.[11] Tom is the opposite of Harry. He seeks immortality to live forever—he wants the Philosopher's Stone—to use it. Harry seeks knowledge and transformation of self—along with his hero's desire to save all those around him. Thus by looking for the Stone for its true essence, he will find it. Dumbledore's lesson from the first book may very well play out in the last.

It's hard to imagine Riddle leaving behind such a valuable book if he did indeed find it. Maybe he did not find it. Maybe he found it and couldn't open it. Or maybe he found it, and used it, but left it behind believing, as he was the last of the line of Slytherin, no one but himself would be able to access it. But by marking Harry, he gave that power to another—the power to open the Chamber of Secrets, find the book and, perhaps, thus vanquish him by use of that book.

Could such a book contain a clue, a link, to the mysterious and awesome power behind the locked door at the Department of Mysteries? Though I definitely believe love is part of the alchemical equation of transformation, I do not believe it is the only one. There is a seventeenth century riddle (riddle, get it?) of what is most necessary to obtain the Philosopher's Stone.[12] The answer is essentially primary matter, but primary matter in this riddle is interpreted both as love…and imagination. JKR said in an interview at Royal Albert Hall in June 2003 when questioned as to whether she believes in magic: "I believe in some kinds—the magic of imagination and the magic of love." In the world created by JKR, imagination should not be discounted lightly. It is a powerful tool of creation, and redemption.

One last note on Thoth should be mentioned. Thoth is the god who equipped Isis with words of power to bring her dead husband, Osiris, and later dead son, Horus, back to life. As a potential parallel, Harry could suffer a death experience at the hands of Voldemort, and the chamber's secret unlock a key to his resurrection as well.

My speculation is that Harry will return to the Chamber of Secrets and, with Hermione's and/or Ginny's help, discover a book of secrets that will enable him to complete his own transformation of character—the unifying of the entwined serpents (caduceus) within himself (or between himself and Voldemort). This secret, this book, if it exists, could also show a different and better side to old Slytherin, and thus, lead to the unifying of the four Hogwarts' houses, reconciling Slytherin and Gryffindor especially—all ultimately enabling the defeat of Voldemort. Ironically, Riddle's hero, old Slytherin himself, may guard the most important clue to the defeat of Voldemort. Harry, the worthy seeker, may find the Holy Grail of ancient Egypt, Slytherin's own Emerald Tablet.

─────────────── ADDITIONAL SLEUTHING NOTES ───────────────

✳ Are the nesting boxes from the legend of Setna also a Mad-Eye Moody reference? Does his trunk with the seven compartments conjure an analogy?

✳ If there are any secrets hidden underground, could there be any clues hiding at "the Burrow"? Could this be one of the Egyptian treasures Bill has been working on?

✳ How does the information about books correlate with all those ink and quill running bits (themes and references) in Book 5? Also, didn't Harry just get himself another diary? Is that a good sign?

✳ Could an Osiris coming back from the dead be considered a possible parallel for "Sirius will return"?

✳ Could the caduceus symbolize Dumbledore's entwined snakes from Chapter 22 of Book 5— the "essence divided"? If so, could that mean Harry and Voldemort could somehow peacefully coexist? Could that be what all the Hermes/Mercury references in the septology mean?

✳ One current theory regarding where the Book of Thoth is hidden is under the Great Sphinx – could that stone beast relate to the excerpt shown to us from book six on JKR's website, where we see a description of a lionesque character? Could that also be Gryffindor or the Half-blood Prince?

1 http://www.sacred-texts.com/etc/oph/oph07.htm

2 Doty, William G., ed., *World Mythology*, Barnes & Noble Inc., (London, 2002), p. 17.

3 Budge, E.A. Wallis, *The Book of the Dead*, translation of the Papyrus of Ani in the British Museum, (London, 1895), p. 3.

4 The pillars are well documented throughout history. Known as the Pillars of Hermes, they were later brought together and moved to a third temple. Herodotus described them thus: "'One pillar was of pure gold,' he wrote, 'and the other was as of emerald, which glowed at night with great brilliancy.' In *Iamblichus: On the Mysteries,* Thomas Taylor quotes an ancient author who says the Pillars of Hermes dated to before the Great Flood and were found in caverns not far from Thebes. The mysterious pillars are also described by Achilles Tatius, Dio Chrysostom, Laertius, and other Roman and Greek historians." Hauck, Dennis William, "A Hyper-History of the Emerald Tablet", http://www.alchemylab.com/hyper_history.htm.

5 Blavatsky, H.P., *Isis Unveiled*, J.W. Bouton Press, (New York, 1877).

6 Garth Fowden, *The Egyptian Hermes*, Cambridge University Press, (Cambridge, 1987), p. 33.

7 Translated from an ancient scroll of papyrus (which was housed in the Giza Museum), by the eminent Egyptologist W.M. Flinder Petrie: Petrie, W.M. Flinder, *Egyptian Tales*, second series, Methuen & Co., (London, 1913), pp.87-141.

8 See Hancock, Graham and Robert Bauval, *The Message of the Sphinx*, Three Rivers Press, (New York, 1996).

9 Hauck, Dennis William, Sorcerer's Stone: A Beginner's Guide to Alchemy, Citadel Press, Kensington Publishing Corp., (New York, New York, 2004), p. 247.

10 JK Rowling at the Edinburgh Book Festival, August 15, 2004.

11 Hauck, Dennis William, *Sorcerer's Stone: A Beginner's Guide to Alchemy,* Citadel Press, Kensington Publishing Corp., (New York, New York, 2004), p. 106.

12 Hauck, Dennis William, *Sorcerer's Stone: A Beginner's Guide to Alchemy,* Citadel Press, Kensington Publishing Corp., (New York, New York, 2004), p. 39.

13 http://www.themystica.org/mythical-folk/articles/isis.html

Symbolism:
Reading the Runes

✳ TYING TOGETHER ALL THE MAGICAL KNOTS ✳

JEANNE PERRY KIMSEY ✳ CoS, "SILVER INK POT"
USA (*US Edition*), AGE 44

Inspiration for this Discussion

Each time I read The Order of the Phoenix, *I am struck by the number of times the word "knot" is used to describe different groups of people. Why would that word be important? Until recently, I had no idea that throughout history, knots have been seen as magical. Also, in some online discussions, people are now associating Theodore Nott, a Slytherin boy, with Malfoy's gang. This is because Voldemort specifically named "Nott" as one of the Death Eaters in the Circle at his birthing party in Book 4, and a "Nott" was then captured at the end of Book 5, along with the parents of Draco Malfoy and Vincent Crabbe in the Ministry of Magic. At the end of Book 5, Theodore Nott was hanging out with Draco Malfoy, Crabbe and Goyle. I wanted to figure out for myself if "Nott" was related to the word "knot," and what it might mean for the future. Could this Slytherin unite against Voldemort with Harry? Recent comments by JK Rowling herself certainly helped me along!*
{www.jkrowling.com *Extra Stuff*}

 12

In Book 5, the word "knot" is used over and over to describe different groups of people, and to draw attention to various characters. Like knots holding together a tapestry, these references seem to lead us to conclusions about unity and strength. The "stringy" Slytherin boy, Theodore Nott, also appears in this book. Could his name be meaningful as a pun? Has JK Rowling given us any clues in the text and elsewhere about his importance?

Twice, the word "knot" is used to describe members of the Order of the Phoenix, a group dedicated to fighting the Lord Voldemort. When a group arrives at Harry Potter's home on Privet Drive, Harry and Professor Lupin lead the "little knot of wizards" through the house. {Ch3, p49 *US*} Then, when Harry arrives at Order Headquarters, number twelve, Grimmauld Place, he sees Professor Snape at the "very center" of a "dark knot of people."{Ch4, p76}

The symbolism is obvious: the Order is "bound" together to defeat Voldemort. Their fates are "tied" to each other, and to Harry.

There are other groupings described by the word "knot." Fred and George Weasley and their friend, Lee Jordan, perform experiments in the middle of "*a knot of innocent-looking first years.*"{Ch13, p252} Harry must push himself through a "*knot of tall Slytherins,*" when Professor Trelawney is attacked by Professor Umbridge. {Ch26, p594} Harry is even knotted up on the inside! He feels a "*miserable knot in his chest*" when he thinks he is about to be expelled from Hogwarts for fighting off a Dementor attack. {Ch2, p33} I think this is indicative of how much Harry thinks of Hogwarts as "home"—where his heart is. Later, when he leads his friends to the Department of Mysteries to rescue Sirius Black, he feels a "*knot in his stomach,*" probably a knot of fear and guilt, that he may have led them all to their deaths "*for no reason at all.*"{Ch35, p782}

One other interesting group of note: the newly-introduced Metamorphmagus character, Nymphadora Tonks, and her parents Andromeda and Ted, have an unusual last name. {Ch 3, p49} Surprisingly, or "not" surprisingly, "Tonks" is an anagram for *Knots*.

What could all these knots have to do with the magical world? Is the use of the word a clue? I think any word used over and over in the Harry Potter books becomes a sort of incantation, so let's look a little deeper.

Binding spells, or spells based upon knots and tying are considered very ancient magic. The Hebrew word for "enchanter" is *hober haber* or someone *who ties magic knots*.[1] Many Egyptian hieroglyphics represent ropes or cords tied in knots, including the "ankh" symbol which means *life*.[2] Important gods are pictured carrying the ankh, which looks like a cross with a loop strap for a top. The goddess Isis has a different magical knot called a "tyet," which is definitely a symbol of magical protection.[3]

Amazingly, the Greek word for "knot" also means *spell* or *charm*.[4] The Latin word, "fascia," means, *bandage* and is the root word for *fascino* or *bewitch*, and "Fascinum" is the Latin word for *witchcraft*.[5]

Throughout history, knots were used for magical spells of binding or release. Witches in the British Isles used to sell knotted cords to sailors—and the belief was that once a sailor was out to sea and needed the wind, untying a knot would release it![6]

The "Hercules" or "Square Knot" is often seen portrayed in Greek and Roman art. The clothing of gods and goddesses is often seen joined by this sort of knot.[7] One symbol of the Greek god Mercury is a "caduceus." A caduceus has two intertwined snakes twisted and knotted around a wand of power.[8] Remember, in Book 5, after a huge serpent attacks Mr. Weasley, Dumbledore's "silver instrument" shows two smoky snakes twisting into something like a caduceus, which he says are "in essence divided."{Ch22, p470} They are "joined" or "knotted," but still separate entities. This is crucial to understand because, at the end of the book, Voldemort once again possesses Harry, and is repelled by Harry's "choice" to die and rejoin his beloved godfather, Sirius Black. {Ch36, p816} The power of love that "ties" Harry to Sirius, "unties" the link with Voldemort.

Interwoven patterns are the hallmark of Celtic design. The Celts decorated everything from headstones to jewelry to illuminated manuscripts with a pattern of intricate knotwork. Animals, plants, humans, saints, gods, and demons flow together, showing the way all life is connected.[9] Book 5 has the same type of structure—different strands and knots are woven together to form the tapestry of the story.

The Celts, who worshipped the "triple" goddess, believed a three-loop knot called a "trefoil" was sacred.[10] A shape similar to the trefoil can be seen even today on some British pottery made in the County of Staffordshire. This three-loop shape, sort of a "rope pretzel," first appeared on a Saxon stone cross around 805 A.D., and is now known as the "Stafford Knot."[11] A macabre story from the area says the knot is a hangman's knot used to execute three criminals at the same time, but that is just legend.[12] The same knot is found on patterns of the British Order of Garter and the Order of Saint Patrick.[13] Will this have some significance for The Order of the Phoenix?

KNITTING

If we are talking about "knotting," then maybe we should also talk about "knitting." Most needlework is based on knots, and magical knitting has widespread appeal in the wizarding world. We see Hermione trying to free the house-elves by knitting countless little hats. {B5, Ch21, p451} Mrs. Weasley seeks to protect her children and Harry with her yearly hand-knitted Christmas sweaters. {Ch23 p502} Some characters are also associated with lace—Mrs. Figg with her "crochet-covered" furniture {B4, Ch7, p80} and Madame Trelawney, with her lacy shawls. {B5, Ch12, p236} Do these items protect them? Susan Bones, a friend of

Harry's, may have a connection to lacemaking. "Bone Lace" is made using little weights of wood or bone to keep tension on the threads as they are plaited together.[14] Susan appears in the Book 5 with her hair in a "*long plait down her back.*"{Ch16, p338}

Lace doilies, which are delicate knots, are often reminiscent of spider webs, and this has an ancient tradition. In Greek mythology, Arachne was a mortal woman who had great skill at weaving and embroidery, but claimed her weaving skills were better than those of the goddess of wisdom (and war) and weaving, Minerva.[15] (Of course, at Hogwarts we have Minerva McGonagall, who often wears the woven tartan plaids of Scotland. {Book 5, Ch 21, p462}) In the myth, Arachne challenges Minerva to a web-spinning contest, using wool thread on a loom. Their web "canvases" become interwoven with scenes of gods and people in a tapestry-like design. In the end, Arachne's arrogance angers Minerva, who turns the woman into a spider.[16]

UNITED KNOTS

The Staffordshire Country motto is "*The Knot Unites.*"[17] A similar motto, this time in Latin form, has been adopted by the city of Stoke-on-Trent, home of Wedgewood and Spode china. On the English coat-of-arms for that city are the Latin words "*Vis Unita Fortior,*" a very "Rowlingesque" phrase that means, *United Strength is Stronger.*[18]

It sounds like something Dumbledore might say, doesn't it?

The ideas in these mottos are almost identical to the meaning of the "Sorting Hat's New Song" from Book 5 {Ch11, p204-206}. The venerable hat gives a warning for the students to unite against "external, deadly foes" or "crumble from within."

THEODORE NOTT

At this point, let's take a look at a boy named Theodore Nott, and see if we can discover his place in our tapestry.

Nott is briefly mentioned in Book 1 while being sorted into Slytherin. {Ch7, p121} Yet, he is not a "regular" in Malfoy's circle of friends, and isn't seen talking to them until Book 5. Hermione has to identify the boy to Harry. {Ch26, p583} Though Nott is not mentioned by name, he is widely believed to be the "stringy" Slytherin boy in Hagrid's class who can also see thestrals and watches them eating with "*a look of great distaste on his face.*"{Ch21, p445} What Harry knows is that Nott's father is a Death Eater and follower of Lord Voldemort, because he saw the elderly wizard bowing to the Dark Lord at the graveyard in Book 4. {Ch33, p651}

Nott's name sounds like "knot". Is this intentional? We know that JK Rowling likes puns and wordplays, such as "Grimmauld Place" sounding like "Grim Old Place." So why can't Nott be another "knot"?

The name may also have mythological importance. The Norse goddess of the night is called "Niht" or "Nott". She drives a chariot drawn by a magical horse with a "frosty mane."[19] There is another person in Book 5 who is associated with both flying horses and goddesses of the night, and that is Luna Lovegood.

Luna appears at one point in the story with her hair "*in a knot on top of her head.*" {Ch13, p261} "Luna" is the Roman name for the goddess of the moon, also known as Artemis, Diana or Selene. She drives a silver chariot pulled by horses across the night sky.[20]

See how all these different threads are being woven together? "Nott" and "Luna" are basically names for the same goddess!

Recently, JK Rowling wrote an intriguing page about Nott and Malfoy on her official website. Among other details, she writes that Nott was raised by a single parent, who is an elderly Death Eater, and that Malfoy considers Nott to be his "equal" based on his being a "pure-blood" wizard. However, she does not say what Nott thinks of Malfoy in return. He has definitely lost his mother, which perhaps explains why he can see the Thestrals. Rowling writes that Nott is *"a clever loner who does not feel the need to join gangs, including Malfoy's."*

Clearly, the fact that the author has a lot to say about Nott means that she may have future plans for this boy. Can we guess what might happen to him? One clue is that Nott is a parallel to Professor Snape. In Book 5, Harry looks into "Snape's Worst Memory" and sees a boy who appears *"stringy...like a plant kept in the dark."* {Ch28 p641} Compare that description to Nott, who is not only "stringy" {Ch21, p445}, but "weedy." {Ch26, p383} Though Theodore Nott has been raised by a Death Eater father, he can still become a force for good like Sirius Black did against the tradition of his Slytherin family. Perhaps he will be the Slytherin who is "not" bad. It is hard to imagine Harry accepting the son of a Death Eater into his group!

Near the end of Book 5, when Harry and his friends tangle with the Death Eaters at the Department of Mysteries. The elder Nott (who presumably was the "stooped" Death Eater Harry saw at the graveyard in Book 4) is injured. Lucius Malfoy is heard shouting, *"Leave Nott,* **leave him, I say,** *the Dark Lord will not care for Nott's injuries..."* {Ch35, p788} The lack of compassion shown by Malfoy Senior is not surprising. In the same place and time, Neville Longbottom, a mere boy and not a powerful wizard, manages to carry the wounded Hermione Granger on his back and never considers leaving her behind! {p794} Neville chooses to be "connected" to his friends. Indeed, the rare unity of the children helps them fight against adults with greater powers, and survive.

As Book 5 ends, the Death Eaters are imprisoned, but we do not know the extent of the elder Nott's injuries. It may be that he lies near death. We do know that Theodore Nott is not seen again with Malfoy, Crabbe, and Goyle. The Malfoy gang tries to attack Harry on the train, but Nott is not involved. {Ch38, p864}

What will become of Theodore Nott? Does he know that the other Death Eaters at the Department of Mysteries left his father behind in pain? Will this make it difficult for him to be friends with Malfoy? If Nott's father is unable to care for him, who will become his guardian?

Will Nott somehow "bind" the Houses of Hogwarts together? Or will the "ties" that connect the Order of the Phoenix become unraveled? As the scenes of this book flow and twist into the tapestry of Book 6, will Slytherin and Gryffindor learn to unite for the common good and become stronger? If the Sorting Hat's warning is heeded and all four houses tie together, the noose could tighten around the Dark Lord and lead to his defeat.

<hr>

✳ ADDITIONAL SLEUTHING NOTES ✳

* Harry's magical penknife, given to him by Sirius, was supposed to be able to "undo any knot"{B4, Ch23}. Does this sound like a reference to the "Gordian" knot – a highly complex puzzle knot that was "solved" by Alexander the Great – who just *cut* it apart? (he cheated) Also, wasn't Harry's penknife destroyed by a door to a certain room in Book 5?

* Harry's heart is what saves him from possession by Voldemort – are the knots Harry feels in his chest somehow related to love knots?

* In the French translation of Book 1, one of Mrs. Figg's cats is called "Mignonette", which seems to relate best to the Kneazle-like translation *ground pepper*, however, the primary meaning of the word is a *lace doily*—should we add that to our knot-like references?

* Does the Celtic knot (which has no beginning or end) reinforce the ongoing themes in Harry Potter of rebirth and all the cyclical clues?

* It was a knot that was (literally) a "key" to Book 3 – the entrance to the secret passage under the Whomping Willow was accessed by touching the "knot" – are all these knots story line or septology clues?

1 Day, Cyrus Lawrence. *Quipus and Witches Knots: The Role of the Knot in Primitive and Ancient Cultures.* University of Kansas Press. Lawrence, Kansas: 1967, p51

2 Ibid, p52.

3 Ibid, p52.

4 Ibid, p52.

5 Ibid, p52.

6 Ibid, p44

7 Ibid, p54

8 Ibid, p54

9 O'Brien, Deborah. *Celtic Decorative Art: A Living Tradition.* The O'Brien Press. Dublin: 2000. p8

10 Ibid, p. 24

11 Bullfinch, Thomas. *The Age of Fable or Stories of Gods and Heroes.* The Heritage Press. New York: 1958. p70.

12 "The Stafford Knot" http://www.staffsmarq.freeserve.co.uk/projects/staffknot.htm p1

13 Ibid, p1

14 Bath, Virginia Churchill. *Lace.* Henry Regnery Company. Chicago: 1974. pgs. 146, 153, 190-196

15 Bullfinch, p70

16 Bullfinch, p70

17 "Meaning of the Staffordshire Knot". http://www.thepotteries.org/markguide/knot_meaning.htm, p1

18 Ibid, p2

19 "Niht/Nott". http://www.ealdriht.org.niht.html, p1

20 "Diana or Luna". http://www.wordsources.info/luna.html, p2

✳ PINK STINKS ✳

JULIE MAFFEI ✳ NEW CLUES FORUM
USA (*US Edition*), AGE 13

Inspiration for this Discussion

While reading the Harry Potter series, I noticed an abundance of pink things, and began to think about what it could mean. I especially noticed that pink was significant in describing the characters of Pansy Parkinson and Dolores Umbridge, as well as various interesting objects. It made me wonder if there is something significant about the color.

HANDFUL

I believe that the color pink is used frequently by JKR as a symbol. Some examples of this that I want to explore are: Tonks' bubble gum pink hair; Dolores Umbridge's pink "Alice band" and pink sweaters; the pink dress robes that Parvati Patel and Pansy Parkinson wear to the Yule Ball; Dudley, Lockhart's robes, the Fat Lady's dress; and Hagrid's umbrella. The color pink is used to identify many things in JKR's world.

Let's start with Hagrid's famous pink umbrella. {B1, Ch3 US} We know that it is an object through which he can perform magic, despite having been prohibited from doing so. It is obvious the umbrella is concealing the pieces of his snapped wand—somehow Mr. Ollivander appears to have suspected that. {Ch5}

The next example is Dolores Umbridge's pink "Alice band" and pink sweaters. {B5, Ch11} Since pink is typically associated with young girls, I have a feeling that Dolores wears her pink sweater and pink "Alice band" to make herself appear nice and innocent, while hiding her true nastiness. We know that she is an evil toad (think black quill and sacking of Dumbledore). Therefore, the pink sweaters and hair band are intended to trick people and students into thinking she is someone who can be trusted. Basically, she makes herself look innocent on the outside, while she is just plain rotten on the inside.

Both Parvati Patel and Pansy Parkinson wear pink dress robes to the Yule Ball {B4, Ch23}, but would they mean different things? Parvati's best friend is Lavender Brown and the two of them giggle and "squeal" when they are together. {B3, Ch6,7 / B4, Ch13} In this case, pink may be an indication of their girlish qualities. However, we really don't know that much about Parvati.

Pansy wears pale pink, but instead of it symbolizing her girlish nature, she (like Umbridge) uses pink to make people think she's really nice. In reality, she is very nasty to people. For example, Pansy calls Neville names, compares Hermione's looks to an animal, and it is strongly implied that Pansy might be responsible for Hermione's Bubotuber pus hate mail. {B4, Ch28} Pansy tries to use pink to give the image of being sweet and caring, when in truth, she is just like all of the other Slytherins we loathe. Pink doesn't help her at all.

Ever since Book 1, Dudley has been referred to as pink, round, and fat or chubby. {B1, Ch2} Just those words make a picture of a porky, pink pig. In fact, in Book 1, Hagrid grows a pig's tail on Dudley. And that color, pink, may also hint at a "sissy" behavior. We know from Book 1 that Dudley is scared of wizards and that he cowers from them. {Ch4} Later in Book 5, we see Dudley panic and pass out when the Dementors enter the alley and attack him and Harry. {Ch1} Over and over, we see that Dudley, with his pig-like nature, is a bully who may constantly pick on Harry, but his bullying nature seems to conceal a coward who goes to pieces at the first sign of real danger.

Tonks' bubble-gum hair is another pink thing. {B5, Ch3} She is one of the youngest Aurors ever. Not surprisingly, of the many choices of hair color, JK Rowling picks pink—a feminine color usually associated with young girls. Pink could be a sign of how young and inexperienced Tonks is as an Auror. However, most pink things appear to be hiding a secret natures or identities. There seems to be a definite pattern here! Therefore, the pink hair could also relate to her abilities as a Metamorphmagus and how she can conceal her identity by changing her appearance at will. Could the pink also symbolize a hidden secret about Tonks that we have yet to learn? Needless to say, I am going to keep an eye on this one.

Of course, there is Lockhart and his favorite pink robes. In fact, everything Lockhart likes seems to relate to the color pink. He even says his favorite color is lilac. {B2, Ch6}. It's not a stretch to say that Lockhart is cloaked in deception.

Another important pink object is the dress on The Fat Lady in the portrait. The Fat Lady guards the concealed entry to the Gryffindor dormitory—her portrait hangs over the actual door. {B1, Ch6} Her dress is yet another example of pink symbolizing something that is hidden from plain view.

Each of these is a perfect example of the symbolic use of pink to hide something. So, in summary, I think JK Rowling uses pink as a symbol for femininity, cowardice, inexperience, and most importantly, a *concealed* object, secret or hidden trait. Have you been watching those pink things?

ADDITIONAL SLEUTHING NOTES

* Can the fact that the Weasleys all turn pink when they are hiding something be at all relevant?
* What would the pink soap bubbles that come out of Snape's mouth be concealing? Would it be something in his words, or are they to make us think bubble gum (wrappers)?
* Based on this "pink stinks" theory, knowing what we have read in Book 5, should we be surprised Petunia would wear a pink cocktail dress?

HOGWARTS HOUSES

SONIA MARKOVIC ✶ NC, "SILVER"
USA (*US Edition*), AGE 17

Inspiration for this Discussion

I remember reading Harry Potter for the first time when I was in seventh grade. Since she is so intuitive, my mother bought me a copy of Book 1 as a graduation present. After that, there was no stopping me! I collected all the other Harry Potter novels as they came out and have diligently reread them many, many times. There is something special in the world of Harry Potter that is not found in other literature. Harry is not the perfect boy and his life has been far from good (or even fair). He never gets to meet his parents, is tortured by his aunt, uncle and cousin, and lastly, has to deal with death, firsthand. He does not have the typical fantasy story life, where I would wish I could slip into his shoes and become him. In fact, at times I even feel sorry for him. However, this non-perfect character is what attracts me to Harry because there is no perfect person in real life. JK Rowling is able to create a "willing suspension of disbelief" worthy of Samuel Taylor Coleridge ("Rhyme of the Ancient Mariner"), and the sorting gives us special insight into the school that is the foundation of Harry's world.

 HANDFUL

Over a thousand years ago, the four greatest witches and wizards of the time began Hogwarts School of Witchcraft and Wizardry. These four founders were Godric Gryffindor, Salazar Slytherin, Rowena Ravenclaw and Helga Hufflepuff. They lived in harmony, each teaching those students that he or she liked best.

Hufflepuff and Ravenclaw were the best of friends, as were Gryffindor and Slytherin. But soon their disagreements about which students ought to be included in the school became a point of contention, causing the Houses and their founders to turn on each other. Divided, each house wanted to be the one that would rule Hogwarts.{B5, Ch11} The fighting finally stopped when Slytherin left, but since then, the Houses have never been united as they were supposed to be. In Book 5, the Sorting Hat warns Hogwarts students to heed the signs of danger, and that the sorting, in itself, might bring the end that it fears. This "end" is probably the end of Hogwarts.

Hogwarts, of course, has a great heritage, and it would be a devastating blow if the school fell. To survive what is coming, Hogwarts will be strongest if the houses are united and working together. However, through the system of sorting, each student becomes attached to his or her own house instead of to Hogwarts, as a whole. This leads to stiff competition that evolves into animosity between the different houses. Near the end of Book 5, Hermione comments that the problem with Quidditch is that it creates rifts between the Houses, rather than uniting them.{Ch26} It causes the students to look for a way to taunt their Hogwarts companions, such as Zacharias Smith, rather than working together. One of the first things Harry learns about the wizarding world is that Slytherin turns out bad witches and wizards, and that Hufflepuff is full of "duffers" (clumsy or useless people). {B1, Ch5} Three of the houses feel pressure to be the best, while Hufflepuff just feels left out. {B4, Ch18} How did it get to this? What do we know about the houses that might tell us if there is hope?

Each of the Houses has its own Head of House and animal mascot that provides the best insight as to the personalities of the people within that house. Those personalities help define the problems and the hope for a strong Hogwarts.

Gryffindor has a reputation of being courageous, strong and heroic, like their Head of House, Minerva McGonagall, who alone faced four wizards.{Ch31} Their mascot, the lion, goes along with this idea, since lions are brave and valiant (they're also a symbol for the United Kingdom). A griffin is a mythical creature with the head of an eagle and the body of a lion. Gryffindors also have griffin-like qualities. They are fierce when threatened but also chivalrous. Members of Gryffindor House are known to do many great deeds and are very outgoing. Interestingly, their bravery is augmented by humor—consider the antics of the Weasley twins and Lee Jordan. Since the lion is considered the "king" of all animals, is there an overtone that Gryffindor may rule over the other houses?

Slytherin's Head of House is Professor Snape, and their mascot is a serpent. This was because Salazar Slytherin was a Parselmouth (had the ability to speak to snakes) and could even control a Basilisk, considered the "King of Serpents". As we now know, he really did build a Chamber of Secrets to hold a Basilisk for his heir to control. Snakes are considered slippery, sly and treacherous, and so it follows the witches and wizards in Slytherin are slippery, sly and cunning; they are "sly there in". Also, the snake is a "slithering" creature. Slytherins are always involved in everything and they create havoc whenever they can. The Slytherin reputation is well known, and though they are disliked, they are also generally left alone (perhaps out of self-preservation)!

The **Ravenclaw** Head of House is Professor Flitwick and the mascot is the eagle, a highly intelligent bird that hunts its prey, just as the Ravenclaws hunt for knowledge. Ravenclaw House is most known for its intelligence and wit. The very name "Ravenclaw" also describes the students in that house. A raven's claw is notoriously sharp and pointed and is used for finding food. The Ravenclaws are "sharp of mind."

The Head of **Hufflepuff** is Professor Sprout, the Herbology teacher, and the House's animal is the badger, which is slow and steady, quiet but diligent. Similarly, the people of Hufflepuff House are gentle, but hard workers. The badger lives in the ground, and is a nocturnal, burrowing animal, part of the weasel family. Although they are Gryffindors, could this connect the Weasleys to Hufflepuff in some way? Now, the name Hufflepuff has several meanings. *Huff* means, "to be annoyed" and *puff* can mean: "to blow short blasts" (Huff and Puff), "extravagant praise", or "a jam pastry". *Huff le puff* could then be interpreted to mean "an annoyed jam pastry", but I am *fairly* certain that JK Rowling did not intend this definition. ☺

Rarely is any great honor bestowed upon Hufflepuff; that is why Cedric Diggory was so important to the House—because he gave Hufflepuff the fame they never had. It is also why Cedric was so incredibly noble when he offered Harry the cup at the end of the Tri-Wizard Tournament; he was willing to deny Hufflepuff House the kind of glory it had not had for hundreds of years—on principle.

After Cedric's death in Book 4, Dumbledore states that unless the people who are against Voldemort stand united, there will be no hope for any of them. He goes on to say that the only way to fight against Voldemort's "powers of discord" is to show a strong "bond of friendship and trust".{B4, Ch37} Of course, there are certain students (such as Malfoy, Crabbe, and Goyle), whose parents support Voldemort; therefore so do they. There is no chance that the Houses will unite if one segment of the students is not willing to believe in choices and reject Voldemort's doctrines—the major issue over which they are fighting. In Book 5, Nearly Headless Nick says that in times of peril, the Sorting Hat gives out warnings and they are always the same: *"Stand together, be strong from within"*. {Ch11} It counsels that all the Houses need to stand united, overcoming the feelings of animosity and competitiveness between them. However, in the

"Sorting Hat's New Song" chapter of Book 5, Seamus says that his mother wanted to pull him out of Hogwarts simply because fellow student Harry Potter believed in Voldemort's return. This created discord *within* Gryffindor House (never mind the other Houses), and plays right into the hands of Voldemort.

With the coming of the Second War in Book 6, the Houses need to begin to stand as they did a thousand years ago, when they were created and all the founders were still friends. Otherwise, Voldemort will easily conquer Hogwarts. Dumbledore once said about Hogwarts in Book 4 that *"we are only as strong as we are united and weak as we are divided."* {B5, Ch37} At this point, it seems Hogwarts needs a miracle for it to unite, since that would necessitate Draco Malfoy joining Dumbledore's side. However, the Sorting Hat in Book 5 says that Godric Gryffindor and Salazar Slytherin were "best friends" {Ch11}, so maybe there is still hope for Draco and Harry. Hogwarts' motto, "Draco Dormiens Nunquam Titillandos" (never tickle a sleeping dragon)[1] provides confidence. Maybe Hogwarts is simply a sleeping dragon and when provoked by Voldemort, it will become strong and united, and ready to fight.

ADDITIONAL SLEUTHING NOTES

* How is it that this fragmentation mind-set was never purged from the spirit of Hogwarts? Were the original founders truly different parts of a whole, or were they compromising their ideals? Was it simpler to blame Slytherin for all of it?

* Why has Hufflepuff become more visible lately (e.g. Susan Bones)? Are they the nurturing "healers" who will be the champions for unity?

* What are the chances that Hogwarts will unite? Was Umbridge's "Inquisitorial Squad" any indication of what could happen? Will there be unity or in-fighting within each House? Will Luna become a literal outcast from Ravenclaw (think about her "stolen" belongings)?

---

[1] JKR appearance at Royal Albert Hall, June, 2003

GEOMANCY AND ALCHEMY GEMS IN HARRY POTTER

S.P. SIPAL ✳ NEW CLUES FORUM
USA (*US Edition*), AGE 38

Inspiration for this Discussion

I'm a writer as well as a Harry Potter fan. While researching my current fantasy project, I came across Earth Divination, Earth Magic: A Practical Guide to Geomancy, *by John Michael Greer. As I skimmed through the book, I noticed divination characters named* Fortuna Major, Caput Draconis, Albus *and* Rubeus. *Of course, being a Harry Potter fanatic, these caught my attention, and I had to read more...*

 NEWT

INTRODUCTION

Geomancy, a system of divination documented by Cornelius Agrippa, was highly popular in the Middle Ages. Geomancy is based on the principle that Earth's energies could be contacted, honed and intuitively understood, by a geomancer so they could answer questions about the future. Though many methods of probability and chance were used to "draw the earth energies," the most common was for the geomancer to cut a series of lines or dots in soil or sand. These dots were then formed into "characters", using a set system of interpretation (based on binary numbers), with a total of sixteen character possibilities.

Caput Draconis and *Fortuna Major* are two of these geomantic characters. "Caput Draconis" (Head of the Dragon) is the first password into Gryffindor tower that Harry learns in Book 1. {Ch 7} In geomancy, Caput Draconis is defined as: "A doorway leading in. Favorable for beginnings and gain."[1] It signifies the beginning of something new and positive—highly appropriate for the beginning of Harry's new life. Similarly, in Book 3, "Fortuna Major" (Greater Fortune) is used as the Gryffindor password. Fortuna Major, when relating to relationships, means an important and intimate relationship that will profoundly affect one's life is about to come one's way. That's right on the mark for Book 3 when Harry meets Sirius.

Albus and *Rubeus* are two other geomantic characters with a special relationship. Albus (white) represents peace, wisdom and purity, while Rubeus (red) indicates passion, power and violence. The sixteen geomantic characters are divided into eight pairs of opposites. Albus and Rubeus are one set of opposing figures.

By JKR's accurate use of the geomantic passwords, it's clear to me that she is definitely aware of geomancy and, thus, of the implications behind the choice of names for Dumbledore and Hagrid—their role in the septology probably carries geomantic hints as well.

This discussion will analyze how Dumbledore and Hagrid reflect their geomantic characteristics, how they relate to each other, and their interaction with Harry. I will also focus briefly on a few related symbols from alchemy that refer back not only to Dumbledore and Hagrid, but bring in Sirius Black and Severus Snape as well. Finally, I'll provide an overview on how these geomantic and alchemic clues could play out in the final two books. Throughout this discussion, when using the terms Rubeus and Albus, I am referring to the geomantic characters. When referring to JKR's characters, I shall use Hagrid and Dumbledore.

ALBUS AND RUBEUS

To explore where the geomantic clues lead, we need to delve a bit more into the characters Albus and Rubeus. First, let's look at a chart, which highlights the major geomantic differences between the two figures:

	ALBUS (WHITE)	RUBEUS (RED)
Planet/Element	Mercury/Earth	Mars/Fire
Sign/Element	Gemini/Air	Scorpio/Water
Character	"Peace-loving, honest, pure and charitable."	"Hot, passionate and fond of strong language. Tends to stir up trouble."[2]
Description	"Illumination, wisdom…Spiritual growth and harmony. Patience, thoughtfulness and the ability to balance all areas of life."[3]	"Rubeus is a figure of passion and involvement in life, balancing the abstract detachment of Albus."[4] Rugged and emotional.

Note: This chart bases the planet, element and sign attributions according to Cornelius Agrippa—who as *coincidence* would have it, Ron mentions three times {*Book 1, Ch 6, p102 US*} on the Hogwarts Express in his desire to collect Agrippa's Chocolate Frog card. Agrippa, an alchemist of the 16th century, was both feared and revered in his day as a sorcerer. He was most famous for his book *Occult Philosophy*, of which "Of Geomancy" was a part.

Albus is considered a positive figure, while Rubeus is negative. This means if Albus appears in your geomantic chart in regard to a question, the outcome you seek is usually favorable, whereas if Rubeus appears, except in certain situations (love, war, and agriculture), your answer is unfavorable.

HAGRID

I believe the geomantic description of Rubeus fits Hagrid quite well. Hagrid does possess a combatant nature, which he expresses at various times—starting from his first encounter with Dudley Dursley (think pig tail) to his self-defense against Umbridge's minions during the Astronomy O.W.L.s altercation in Book 5.

As Sirius says in Book 5 {p302}, *"the world isn't split into good people and Death Eaters."* Good and bad reside in each of us. Which aspect wins out depends on the choices that we make. Hagrid also has a dark side. He comes from half-giant blood, and according to Hagrid in Book 4, maternal instincts were not in his giant mother's nature. Ron agrees, *"they're just vicious, giants…it's in their nature, they're like trolls…they just like killing."*{p430} Ron states this as a matter of fact that "everyone" knows. But we're not sure whether we believe Ron's statements. Hermione seems to make a bit of progress with Grawp after all, and we see Hagrid as one of the most compassionate characters in the Harry Potter world—he apparently makes the right choices.

Still, Hagrid does have a violent side, including a temper that spins out of control on more than one occasion. We also know he has a passion for large, dangerous and lethal creatures; indeed in Book 2 Ron and Harry almost get killed due to his edict to "follow the spiders." Rubeus' zodiac sign is Scorpio (a scorpion), often described as intense and powerful. In Book 4, ironically, Hagrid breeds a creature (a skrewt) with a hard shell body and a stinger in its tail—very similar to the scorpion.

Hagrid's low education level though, leads us to believe that he's not a pivotal character. He's easy to gloss over when compared to wizards of a caliber such as Dumbledore, Snape, Voldemort and Malfoy Sr.'s. But I think this is a false perception. Just as Malfoy does not recognize Hagrid's worth, I think the reader is led to misjudge it as well.

If asked to give the names of the most powerful adult witches and wizards in the Second War, whom would you choose? Certainly Dumbledore and Voldemort, and probably Snape and Malfoy and possibly McGonagall, Molly or Arthur Weasley, and Bellatrix. You might even mention Umbridge and Fudge. That's ten. But would you list Hagrid anywhere in your top ten?

Could Hagrid be important in a magically powerful sense? In doing battle? Of course, he plays an important role in the story, but with his lack of magical education, it's more "behind the scenes"—allying the giants and playing the older brother/friend to Harry and Hermione. Surely he's not a five-star general in the all-out war. Or, are we being lulled into a false security where Hagrid is concerned? A person can fail without being evil. A good heart does not always win the day. I could see Hagrid's temper leading him into an unwise choice. True to Rubeus, Hagrid's passion dominates his reason.

As many Harry Potter fans believe, (and as the geomantic clues highlight), Hagrid, keeper of keys and grounds at Hogwarts, may also be the keeper of a major septology secret.

DUMBLEDORE

Albus, while being a positive geomantic symbol, is also a rather weak one. Surely no one would ever associate weakness with Dumbledore! He's the most powerful wizard of his day and the only one Voldemort ever feared. The defeater of Grindelwald. And maybe JKR did not intend the "weak" attribute of Albus to apply to her Dumbledore. But no one is perfect, as fifteen-year-old Harry comes to realize at the end of Book 5. Harry is not the only one who makes a mistake.

Dumbledore's greatest strength is also his weakness—he sees the good in people and easily trusts them. Each book gives us an example of Dumbledore not accurately perceiving another wizard's true nature – Quirrell in Book 1, Lockhart in Book 2, Pettigrew in Book 3, pseudo-Mad-Eye (Imposter Mad-Eye) in Book 4, and Harry's maturity in Book 5. (However, I have to give the caveat that the reader doesn't know the whole story yet about Dumbledore's perceptions of these individuals). Imposter-Mad-Eye says about Dumbledore, "*he's a trusting man… Believes in second chances*" {Book 4, p472}. You'd think Barty Crouch Jr. would be one to know this, but just whose perception is skewed?

So, Dumbledore may or may not trust too easily. He says at the beginning of Book 1 {p14}, "*I would trust Hagrid with my life.*" Let's hope it does not come to that or that Dumbledore's judgment is proven fatal. After all, Rubeus is the geomantic character for violence (the antithesis of Albus Dumbledore).

MY ANALYSIS AND WHAT THIS MEANS FOR HARRY

I suspect Hagrid has a bit of a darker and more powerfully magical side than he is given credit for; simultaneously, I think it's entirely possible that Dumbledore is not quite the God-like all-knowing wizard as he's portrayed. When it comes to deciphering others' characters, I believe he tends to see their potential, rather than the reality. In the end, it is my belief that these two characters are just as upfront as they appear to be.

What I believe JKR has done with the geomantic opposites of Albus and Rubeus is to show two sides of the same coin. Even though Dumbledore and Hagrid are diametrically opposed, they're on the same team. One will fight side by side with the other, yet their personalities are complementary. This dichotomy suits their relationship with Harry perfectly. Each offers a fatherly example to Harry in his own way. Harry can garner their different strengths and go to each for their own brand of support and understanding. As always, diversity contributes to growth. In this case, it contributes to Harry's growth.

What do I think will happen in the last two books of the septology based on this geomantic interpretation? What it leads me to think is that before the end of the series, Dumbledore and Hagrid will possibly come into direct conflict. More than likely, over Harry and with his best interests at heart. My own theory is that is entirely possible Hagrid will figure into a death threat against Dumbledore—hopefully by saving his life.

Just a sidebar of interest: the zodiac sign associated with Albus is Gemini. Gemini is, of course, the twin. Could Albus and Aberforth be twins? And if so, how would that relate to the septology?

THE ALCHEMY LINK

It is, however, possible that JKR's geomantic clues regarding Rubeus and Albus are leading the reader in another direction. While she includes a few geomantic symbols and metaphors in her work, (as described above), the *Harry Potter* series is far richer in *alchemical* symbolism. Geomancy flourishes alongside alchemy and, indeed, shares a similar interpretation of symbols and an understanding of the laws of nature and our place in the cosmos. Many alchemists practiced geomancy, including Agrippa and Paracelsus.

A key factor to emphasize here is most alchemists, and definitely Agrippa and Paracelsus, were versed in alchemy—not only in the transformation of lead into gold, but the transformation of a base character into a spiritual enlightenment...their individual selves.

According to the table shown earlier on Albus and Rubeus, Albus (white) represents Mercury (and thus the element mercury), while Rubeus (red) represents Mars (and thus the element sulfur).

Mercury and Sulfur

Mercury and sulfur are the two essential elements in alchemy used in the production of the Philosopher's Stone. "In alchemy, red, standing for sulfur, forms a duality with white."[5] Mercury, being the symbol for white, is also known as quicksilver—an accurate description of Dumbledore. Maybe that is why he seems to seep through the very cracks of Hogwarts and be everywhere at once. Also, in his office, various silver instruments surround him, and don't forget his silver-colored hair and beard,

Sulfur also is known as brimstone, and could easily be linked to Hagrid's volatile personality and temper because it's a fiery, passionate element.

Salt

In his work with alchemy, Paracelsus added a third primal element—salt. According to Paracelsus, mercury represents the spirit (or intellect), sulfur the soul, and salt the body. Salt, at times, is symbolized by black because of its relationship with the earth. In JKR's world, I think this earthy, physical element is embodied in the character of Sirius Black. According to Dennis Hauck in *Sorcerer's Stone*, "*Salt is actual-*

ly the key to alchemy, the beginning and end of the Great Work". It is the imperfect matter at the beginning of the experiment that has to be destroyed and dissolved to release its essences, which are reconstituted into the more perfect form at the end of the experiment."[6] The process of alchemical transformation is divided into three stages, characterized by black, white, and red. *"According to alchemy, the end result of the Black Phase is that the 'soul departs from the body.'"*[7] Sirius had to die for the completion of Harry's transformation. If we continue with an alchemical transformation, I think there is an excellent chance we shall see a more "purified" version of Sirius in what is to come.

There is a famous alchemical plate in the work of Salomon Trismosin (Splendor Solis, 1535) the reputed mentor of Paracelsus. It depicts three birds in an alembic (alchemist glass still): one red, one black and one white. The bird represents the "Three Essentials":

white=mercury=spirit/intellect

red=sulfur=soul

black=salt=body.[8]

Vitriol

Another primary substance worth mentioning here is vitriol, the most important liquid in alchemy. Distilled from an oily green material, vitriol is a highly corrosive acid.[9] In the words of Paracelsus in *The Aurora of the Philosophers*, vitriol contains *"viscous imperfections...take care above all that the matter [purified vitriol] shall not be exposed to the sun, for this turns its greenness pale."*

Vitriol is sometimes referred to as the Green Lion or the Green Dragon. Green alchemically means possessing life, but not fully mature. The fully mature stone is red. The Lion, and Dragon are both symbols of power, intense and deadly. The Green Lion is sometimes seen as a symbol of corrosive rage and fury. Snape anyone? Vitriol's corrosiveness is a necessary component for the alchemical process of making gold out of lead. Most writers agree that a character does not grow and develop without significant conflict being applied to his life. Snape definitely provides significant conflict for Harry to develop.

Thus, we have a metaphorically abbreviated recipe for creating the Philosopher's Stone. A bust of Paracelsus doesn't have to fall on you to see a link between Paracelsus' symbols as metaphors for the character transformation of JKR's little orphan.

A BIT OF DIVINATION

The final link circles from the beginning of the series: the Philosopher's Stone. In the view I propose, Dumbledore (mercury), Hagrid (sulfur), Sirius (salt) and Snape (vitriol) come together as the primary agents acting to create the alchemical transformation of base metal into gold. And that base metal is...Harry Potter.

Harry is not only the Seeker after the Golden Snitch on the Quidditch field, but the alchemist seeking gold within his own soul. No alchemical transformation can be complete without altering the body, mind and soul. Through Harry's mental studies at school, his physical prowess in Quidditch and his inner development (assisted by his friends), his transformation will be complete.

If we accept geomancy and alchemy as our models, *Harry will be the living embodiment of the Philosopher's Stone by the end of the septology!* What Harry doesn't seek to possess for personal gain in the first book will be earned by his noble character at the end of the series.

--------- ADDITIONAL SLEUTHING NOTES ---------

✳ The Hungarian translation of the name "Rita Skeeter" is Rita Vitrol – would they be associating her with acidic Vitriol (think acid-green quill)? {B4,Ch20}

✳ In addition to being a Potions Master, could Snape be skilled in alchemy?

✳ Could Sirius Black return from behind the veil transformed as Sirius White (think "Gandalf the Grey" in The Lord of the Rings) or will Albus Dumbledore undergo a transformation or rebirth?

✳ What other advances in alchemy were made by Dumbledore and Flamel? Do the goblins know alchemy? If they are so focused on gold, how much value would they put on the Philosopher's Stone? Would they help Voldemort get a Stone...would they help Dumbledore if he had another one...do they even need one? What does Bill know about alchemy?

[1] Greer, John Michael, *Earth Divination, Earth Magic,* Llewellyn Publications, (St. Paul, Minnesota), p. 7.

[2] Ibid., p. 44.

[3] SerenaPowers.com, http://www.serenapowers.com/geomancy2.html.

[4] Greer, John Michael, *Earth Divination, Earth Magic,* Llewellyn Publications, (St. Paul, Minnesota), p. 44.

[5] Biedermann, Hans, *Dictionary of Symbolism: Cultural Icons and the Meanings Behind Them,* Meridian, Penguin Books USA Inc., (New York, New York), p. 282.

[6] Hauck, Dennis William, *Sorcerer's Stone: A Beginner's Guide to Alchemy,* Citadel Press, Kensington Publishing Corp., (New York, New York), p. 59.

[7] Ibid., p. 103.

[8] Alchemy was never static. It was practiced over hundreds, thousands, of years throughout various parts of the world. Thus the colors and symbols could be used in more than one manner.

[9] Vitriol is a broad name for sulfuric acid and some other sulfates.

Time...
and Time Again

TIME OF THE DRUIDS AND THE LEGENDS OF OUR TIME

THOMAS JAYROE ✶ NC, "PIKA"
USA (*US Edition*), AGE 24

Inspiration for this Discussion

Months had been spent on the New Clues MuggleNet discussion board sending countless theories and ideas off into cyberspace and waiting for my fellow fans to evaluate and accept or ravage what I had written. I would post ideas on the message boards, but nothing seemed to stir up the crowd. I didn't know what to do, until on a whim, I decided research Stonehenge. From reading Book 5, I noticed that the Malfoy residence is located fairly close to Stonehenge, and realized I had a little research to do...

🦉 12

"Mr Lucius Malfoy…speaking from his Wiltshire mansion" {B5, Ch15}

Avebury, one of the great ancient astronomical monuments, just happens to be in Wiltshire. How might that relate to Harry Potter?

Book 5 seems to contain several hidden subplots. JKR has told us she left clues throughout the book to help us figure out what is going to happen next, and that with careful sleuthing we could figure them out. Armed with use of running bits (repeated words) and knowledge of the wizarding world, I present my research findings.

I convinced myself long ago that the circle, wheel, round and "TT" running bits were related to time. Stone was another running bit that had not yet been placed, so I figured it was possible they could all relate to each other. Besides, thanks to TV documentaries, I was sure that the Druids had something to do with Stonehenge, so I might as well look into that, too.

After researching Stonehenge and the Druids, I learned that no one is certain who built Stonehenge or for what it was used. It originally was speculated that the Druids built it as a temple to worship the sun, moon, summer and winter solstice, or a combination of the four[I]. Some legends even gave credence that Stonehenge was built by Merlin with his magic (can you believe anyone would suggest that?).[II] However, based on scientific carbon dating, Stonehenge seems to have been built quite a long time before the Druids were even known to have existed.[III] I thought my trail was going to get "Avada Kedavra'ed" right there, but the mention of Merlin drove me to dig deeper. Besides, if it wasn't going to work out, I thought it was still very coincidental that Book 5 had a new character named after a moon goddess (Luna) and briefly mentioned the place that may have been used to worship the moon. If people thought the Druids built Stonehenge or that Merlin constructed it, did that make Merlin a Druid? To answer this question, I had to find out who and what the Druids were.

Essentially, the Druids were the religious group of Celtic culture. They were a nature-loving tribal religion divided into three groups: Bards, Ovates and Druids. A Bard's job in society was to supervise, regulate and lead. Bards wore blue robes, which symbolized justice and truth. They were the storytellers and historians of the tribe. Ovates wore green robes that symbolized new life, and were the inventors and observers. They were responsible for understanding the mysteries of death and rebirth, divining the future, and speaking with the dead. The highest group in the religion was the Druids, who taught science and religion and wore white robes that symbolized light, purity and knowledge. It could take up to twenty years of study to become a Bard, Ovate or Druid in Celtic society, which was why they were so revered. It was their close understanding of science and nature that made people believe the Druids were performing magic, rather than using knowledge. Druids were also believed to have invented rune writing and to have believed in reincarnation. [IV]

I did a double take immediately after I finished reading about the Bards. I thought there was something important about the blue robe, but it took some rereading of Harry Potter to figure it out.

> *"Dumbledore was striding serenely across the room wearing long midnight-blue robes and a perfectly calm expression."* {B5, Ch8, p139}

Well, it wasn't exactly a home run as far as evidence goes, but it was a start. I also remembered that Cornelius Fudge had been described as having a lime-green bowler hat and a bottle-green suit, similar to the color of an Ovate.{B3, Ch3, p43} Even though it wasn't a robe and the evidence was incomplete, I found it interesting, nonetheless. Still, I needed a bigger link; something that could help put the pieces together.

I found it in the form of a Druid symbol—the Sun wheel.

A common symbol in ancient Druidry was the Sun wheel, or wheel of Taranis, the Celtic sun God.

The wheel is identical to other solar wheels and represents the solar calendar. The Solar cross and Celtic cross motifs derive from this symbol."[V]

A Sun wheel? The Druids had a sacred wheel that represented the solar calendar? Not only did this relate to the wheel-like running bits but it also gave a very plausible use for Stonehenge. First, I came across a Lunar calendar and then a solar calendar—there really might be something to this, I thought. I then delved into the information on Taranis, although it was quite limited, and found that he was the Celtic god of thunder (very similar to the Roman god Jupiter), and was associated with forces of change.[VI] God of thunder, lightning bolt scar…it was a stretch, but one I was willing to make. Things were starting to look very interesting, but I still needed more sleuth time. What also struck me, in my research, was that the Druids were believed to have used runes as a form of writing and divination.[VII] Hermoine mentioned her rune classes several times throughout Book 5, and dropped a bombshell in Chapter 31.

> *"'I mis-translated ehwaz,' said Hermione furiously. 'It means partnership, not defense; I mixed it up with eihwaz.'"* {Ch31, p715}

Once again, I had looked into this clue early on. I was so certain that Harry's scar was the eihwaz rune (kind of looks like a lightning bolt if you flip it and rotate and lengthen it…ok, not really convincing), and that it was from the protection given to him from Lily before she died. My focus was solely placed on this one rune and I never bothered to look at any other runes, which was a big mistake. I had missed an important rune that was two runes away from eihwaz—Sowilo, which means "sun" and is the shape of a lightning bolt.[VIII] This sealed it for me—sun, sun wheels, runes, Druids, Stonehenge—it's all there. All signs pointed to JKR using Celtic mythology in her writing. Great, fantastic, super…but now what?

Something was still nagging me. I wondered if reincarnation would come into play, since it's another important Celtic theme. Sigh…more digging.

While researching Druids and reincarnation, I was happy to verify that Merlin was believed to have been a Druid.[IX] At first I thought it was a little funny. Linking Merlin to the Druids was part of what had put me on this quest in the first place and now, after all the information I had discovered, I had dropped that part of my investigation. Yep, good old Merlin was a Druid and he helped out his buddy King Arthur. Nothing new there. Merlin, King Arthur and Guinevere—all mates. Yep, yep, yep, I don't see any clues here. Just because Merlin was a Druid and he was friends with Arthur and Guinevere and Percival and there was a magic sword and…ohhh boy. This "ancient" story was starting to look a little familiar:

* ✳ *"Arthur Weasley, you made sure there was a loophole when you wrote that law!"* {B2, Ch3, p39}
* ✳ *"Ginny (full name Ginevra, not Virginia), is the first girl to be born into the Weasley clan for several generation"* {JK Rowling, Edinburgh Book Festival, 2004}
* ✳ *"Witness for the defense, Albus Percival Wulfric Brian Dumble-dore…"* {B5, Ch8, p139}
* ✳ *"Dumbledore … picked up the blood-stained silver sword…'only a true Gryffindor could have pulled that out of the hat…'"* {B2, Ch18, p334}

Only a "true Gryffindor" could have extracted that sword, much like how only the true king could have pulled Excalibur from the stone. I was starting to see a pattern. Druids, sun wheels, Stonehenge, runes, King Arthur, Merlin, Excalibur, Stone—what else could I pull from these stories? I decided to dig further into the legends of King Arthur and in doing so, found the quest for the Holy Grail to be the most interesting. I have put together some highlights to help you:

> The quest for the Holy Grail began with some of Arthur's knights having a vision of the Holy Grail while sitting at the round table. It had been lost for centuries and had been prophesized that only the Knight who could sit in the Siege Perilous (a chair that had deadly consequences for anyone who sat in it) could find it. Upon seeing the vision, one of King Arthur's knights, Galahad, sat in the Siege Perilous and decided to hunt for the grail with Percival and Bors. It took many years of hard work, but the three eventually found the castle where the grail was hidden. However, only Galahad could enter, as he was the purest of heart (It was said that his heart was so pure he had the strength of ten men and contained every good quality a knight could ever want). When Galahad laid his eyes upon the grail, all of its mysteries were revealed to him and at that moment Galahad wished to be in heaven as his life was complete. He then died.[X]

Now, I had seen an object similar to a grail before (check the title of Book 4 if you can't figure it out), but it was the "pure of heart bit" that had a familiar ring to it.

According to Dumbledore, *"In the end, it mattered not that you could not close your mind. It was your heart that saved you."* {p884}

> The tale of the quest for the Holy Grail is said to be a modified version of an old Celtic legend. In that legend, King Arthur and his Knights travel to the underworld to fetch the Cauldron of Annwfn (a Celtic god) who was said to have been a source of endless replenishment and renewal much like the grail. The quest proves to be too dangerous and many of Arthur's knights die. The story also takes parts from the legend of the cauldron of Bran the Blessed, which could restore to life the body of any dead warrior placed within it.[XI]

So the trail had finally come to death, which at the moment I didn't consider to be a good thing. I still needed to get to the bottom of this reincarnation business. Earlier, during my search for stone circles and reincarnation, I came across a symbol in eastern mysticism of a snake/dragon/worm eating its own tail forming a circle, called an ourobouros worm. This symbol seems to have been around for ages and is said to represent death and rebirth. As the worm eats its own tail it is simultaneously devouring and regrowing itself creating a never-ending cycle. How nice would it be to find a link as clear as this with the Druids? (I could have, had I looked more at Stonehenge in the beginning). The Druids, or whoever built Stonehenge, didn't only build one site. They built many sites all over England, with the most famous being Stonehenge. It was this notoriety that overshadowed one of Stonehenge's little brothers—Avebury.

> Avebury is about 28 acres and is partially overlapped by the village. It consists of a few smaller circles within a giant circle and two stone trails leading off to the left and right. Returning home from hunting one winter's evening in 1648, John Aubrey passed through the village of Avebury, and recognized the stones around him as an ancient Druid temple. Later, William Stukeley visited the site and agreed with Aubrey's theory and published his book Abury, a Temple of the British Druids. According to Stukeley, the trails that run through the circles stretched all the way from the Sanctuary on Overton Hill, to the Beckhampton Long Barrow.[XII]

He interpreted the trails as a great stone serpent passing through the circles, symbolizing the snake's rebirth. Bingo, we have a winner… and a theme…death and rebirth.

It makes sense that this is what JKR could be hinting at, but was there more? Could there be other clues that I had missed? Knowing what I was looking for this time made this an easier task. I just needed to extend my search beyond the Druids and into the Greek and Roman references contained in Book 5.

Many, if not all, of the Roman gods are modifications of the older Greek gods. Generally, the only difference is that they are usually known by a different name. For example, the Roman god of love is Venus, while the Greek god is called Aphrodite. Both have the same stories and legends. The Roman god of war, Mars, and the Greek god, Ares, are similar as well, making the names and legends interchangeable. Knowing that I was looking for a link to death and rebirth, I started searching for the Roman god of the underworld, Hades aka Pluto.

> *"anyway, one of them grabbed Ginny's foot, I used the Reductor Curse and blew up Pluto in his face, but…"* {Ch38, p796}

So Luna blew up Pluto? She did it at the Department of Mysteries, where we seem to have a veil to the underworld? Very coincidental, isn't it? It was time to dig up info on Hades.

> In Greek mythology, the god of the underworld "Hades" (the "unseen") was a son of the Titans, Cronus, and Rhea. He had three older sisters, Hestia, Demeter, and Hera, as well as two younger brothers, Poseidon and Zeus: together they constituted half of the Olympian gods.[XIII]

God of the underworld, check. I knew that. He also had a helmet that made the wearer invisible, while Zeus had a spear that could throw lightning bolts.[XIV] Was this another coincidence? An invisibility helmet?

> *"Firs' we presented him with a nice battle helmet—goblin-made an' indestructible, yeh know…"* {Ch20, p429}

> *"Fred swept the hat on to his head, beaming…then both hat and head vanished."* {Ch24, p540}

Not exactly the same thing, but I was willing to compromise again. Links to Hades were beginning to form, but to what cause? I needed more evidence.

It seems, while guarding the Underworld, Hades got a little lonely and abducted a daughter of Zeus, Persephone, as his bride. Zeus wasn't happy about that and demanded Hades set her free. Hades had to comply, but before he did, he tricked Persephone into eating a few pomegranate seeds (if you eat something while in Hades, you're stuck there). So, a deal was made that Persephone had to stay with Hades in the Underworld for half of the year. I wonder if Hades ever met Professor Snape?

> *"'Salamander blood, Harry!' Hermione moaned... 'not pomegranate juice!'"* {Ch17, p363}

As the king of the underworld, Hades had control of all souls within, and was not known to let many go. He did, however take pity on one man, Orpheus. Orpheus was one of the greatest poets and musicians in Greek mythology and was married to Eurydice the nymph. Orpheus' love for Eurydice was so deep that they were said to be inseparable. Shortly after their marriage, Eurydice was bitten on the foot by a snake and died. Orpheus was so overcome with grief that he decided to follow her to the Underworld and try to convince Hades to release her.[XV] To enter the underworld, Orpheus had to contend with Cerberus, Hades three-headed, watch-dog guardian. Using his musical gifts, Orpheus lulled the giant creature to sleep, allowing him to gain access to the lord of the underworld to plead his case.[XVI]

Once again this *tail* has a familiar ring to it. Not only have we seen a giant three-headed guard dog that gets lulled to sleep by music, {B1, Ch16, p275} but we were also recently introduced to a music box that puts almost anyone to sleep.

> *"There was a musical box that emitted a ... tinkling tune ... and they all found themselves becoming curiously weak and sleepy..."* {B5, Ch6, p116}

While we don't know what happened to this box (Fred and George, or Ginny herself, may have taken it), it serves as a reminder of our friend Fluffy. If this box did somehow escape Molly's "cleaning" we may very well see it again. Back to Orpheus...

At first, Hades refused Orpheus' request, but upon hearing his sad song, the lord of the underworld agreed to set Eurydice free on one condition: Orpheus had to trust that Eurydice was behind him and not look back at her until they reached the surface. But, like so many Greek stories, this ended in tragedy. Just before reaching the surface, Orpheus' curiosity got the best of him and he couldn't resist checking to see if Eurydice was behind him. As soon as he looked back, Eurydice faded back to the underworld and Orpheus never saw her again.[XVII]

Fresh off of Sirius' death, this story really tugged at the heartstrings. Was this it? Was this what was going to happen? All the connections to the underworld, the hints of death and rebirth, Avebury and King Arthur...what significance can all this have for Harry? Near the end of Book 5, Harry feels as if he is *"stretched across two universes."* {p866} Could one of them be the underworld? Is he going to try and get Sirius back?

Based on these many parallels, I believe that Harry and crew could go to the underworld to try to get Sirius back, but much like Orpheus, they would fail. If so, Sirius could make the CHOICE to stay, most likely by sacrificing himself somehow as a final act of love for Harry, much like Lily did.

Until the next book, JK Rowling will have us running in circles.

─────────────── ADDITIONAL SLEUTHING NOTES ───────────────

✳ Is there a link between the poem "Sir Galahad", by Tennyson, and the phoenixes in Harry Potter? ("*My strength is as the strength of ten, Because my heart is pure.*")

✳ In addition to making us think of the Stonehenge monuments, could the double-Ts in Book 5 (TT) represent time or the Greek letter pi?

✳ The Avery and Stonehenge circles seem to relate to all the other imagery that JK Rowling had included in Book 5. Don't they make you think of turning bicycle wheels, the Department of Mysteries spinning room of doors, fiery crosses in a circle, crisscrossing rays of light in a circular Owlery, clocks, a sliced pie (think Fudge here), or the Odin sun wheel? If you can see that, do you also see that on JK Rowling's site that there is a spinning top with spokes?

✳ Didn't Luna blow up Pluto in Book 5? How does that relate to time (Cronus) and the underworld? Did everything that happened in Book 5 happen in front of us, or could some events have been time-shifted?

I http://campus.northpark.edu/history/WebChron/World/Stonehenge.CP.html
II http://www.fortunecity.com/roswell/blavatsky/123/stonebuilt.html
III http://www.aboutstonehenge.info/modules.php?name=Education&file=who-built-stonehenge
IV http://www.geocities.com/~huathe/druids.html
V http://altreligion.about.com/library/glossary/symbols/bldefsdruidry.htm
VI http://draeconin.com/database/gods2.htm#t
VII http://altreligion.about.com/library/weekly/aa022203a.htm
VIII http://www.tarahill.com/runes/aett_2.html
IX http://www.encyclopedia.com/html/m/merlin.asp
X http://www.kingarthursknights.com/knights/
XI http://www.britannia.com/history/arthur/grail.html
XII http://witcombe.sbc.edu/earthmysteries/EMAvebury.html

VOLDEMORT, THE OUROBOROS WORM, AND THE LEGEND OF KRONOS

MARIA ROSARIO ✴ CoS, "AURI DeMEER"
SPAIN (*UK Edition*), AGE ADULT

Inspiration for this Discussion

It's fun to make theories about what is going to happen in the rest of the series. We know that 99.9% of those theories are wrong, mainly because none of us is JKR and there are just millions of possibilities she can devise.

It's great to analyse facts as they are and the information provided... But, what about unexplained facts? Why not add a bit of imagination to the logic of the books? That's when a theory is born. To make a theory is always risky; that's the nature of theories. One single word from JKR in an interview can demolish the best of theories. And of course, none of the theories will be alive after Book 7... Why bother, then? There's only one answer to that question: Because it's FUN! :-)

 NEWT

AN INTRODUCTION TO TIME TRAVEL

Since Time Travel is not possible in the "real world", it's an abstract and even difficult idea to grasp. Other Fantasy/Science Fiction authors have used the concept, and each writer has adapted it to their specific plot needs. They explain the rules of the concept, how it works, and its possible consequences. Every author may have a different vision of it, more or less complex or paradoxical. For example, in Asimov the people who travel to the past may change the course of events and thus lead to a different present. Some writers of popular science, like John Gribbin, view the events as having parallel time lines...

Time Travel is possible in the Harry Potter universe, and JKR introduced us to *her* concept and *her* rules in Book 3, when Harry and Hermione use it to help Sirius Black. The rules in her version are fairly straightforward compared to those of some authors; we'll explain them here briefly as a memory refresher...

CHRONOLOGY OF THE EVENTS INVOLVING TIME TRAVEL IN BOOK 3

Thursday, beginning of June of Harry's 3rd year at Hogwarts, the following events take place between 21 hours and midnight...

1. The Officials of the Department of Magic arrive at Hagrid's cabin to execute Buckbeak. Harry, Ron and Hermione don't actually see what happened, but believe McNair kills him.
2. Shrieking Shack scene; Peter escapes; the Dementors show up.
3. Harry and Hermione are in the hospital. Dumbledore suggests that they time travel to save Sirius. They give three turns to the Time Turner (three hours).
4. Harry saves Buckbeak and in the last moment, realizes he has to be the one casting the Patronus spell.
5. Harry and Hermione use Buckbeak to rescue Sirius and return to the Hospital wing to continue normally with their lives.

Harry's life at the end of Book 3 - No Loop

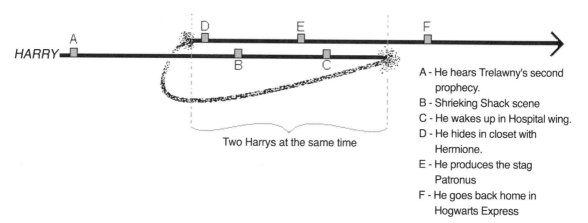

A - He hears Trelawny's second prophecy.
B - Shrieking Shack scene
C - He wakes up in Hospital wing.
D - He hides in closet with Hermione.
E - He produces the stag Patronus
F - He goes back home in Hogwarts Express

RULES FOR TIME TRAVELLING IN HARRY POTTER

After reading Book 3, these are the basic rules to understand Time Travel as conceived by JKR:

1. What has really happened at one moment in time, has happened and cannot be changed. Time travel cannot be used to change something that has already happened.

*That is, Harry and Hermione do **not** travel in time in order to save Buckbeak. Buckbeak never died, although Harry thought he did.*

2. Time travelling **is not a continuous circle**: once the character re-lives the time (traveled backwards), he continues his normal life, next to the temporary line of the other characters.

This means that each person lives the experiences on their temporary line a single time. That is, when Harry and Hermione return to the Hospital in point 5, they follow life in a normal way from then on. They are not sent back to the past nor return for the second time to point 3.

3. When time travelling, nothing can be done that affects the very time travel decision.

*That is, when Harry (in point 4) sees how Lupin is going to turn into a wolf, he **cannot do anything to avoid it**. He cannot go to Lupin and say to him, "take your wolfsbane potion, Lupin; take it, and everything will happen as planned: we will take Wormtail to the court and Sirius' name will be cleared". No. If he did so, Harry and Hermione would have changed history and never would have ended up with the situation that they needed to use the Time Turner (in point 3) and then Harry would never have had the opportunity to tell Lupin, "take your wolfsbane potion". In other words, it would create a paradox.*

4. To avoid that type of paradox, the free will of the characters is artificially constrained. That is, in a normal situation, nothing would prevent Harry from warning Lupin or taking his invisibility cloak. However...

    "How can you stand this?" he asked Hermione fiercely. "Just standing here and watching it happen?" He hesitated. "I'm going to grab the cloak!"

    "Harry, no!" {B2, Ch21}

Hermione is the voice of the author at this moment. JKR *disguises* the free will constraint by creating a **"magical law"** that says *the one that travels in the time must never be seen*. Then Hermione explains that *law* to Harry, so that he doesn't go fetch his cloak. In other words, *"Nobody is supposed to change time"* is the *disguised* way to explain the rule without meddling with *free will* and other things more difficult to understand.

THEORIES & TIME TRAVEL IN BOOKS 6 AND 7

The concept of Time Travel has been so neatly introduced in the HP series that it would be a *waste* not to use it afterwards. :-) In other words, why would JKR bother to make Harry and Hermione travel in time, when she had millions of other interesting and original ways of saving Sirius? Why introduce it and explain all the rules? Why come back to it in Book 5 showing again the *Time Turners* and the *Time Room*, to remind us of the existence of *Time Travel*?

That's why we believe that Time Travel will appear later in the series. :-)

OUROBOROS: THE SERPENT BITING ITS TAIL

The Ouroboros Worm (serpent biting its tail) was well-known in Ancient Egypt and Greece. It represents the cyclic nature of the Universe: the Creation that emerges from Destruction and the Life that emerges from Death. Therefore, it is also a symbol of Immortality. Now, when you look at a serpent symbolizing endlessness, what does it remind you of? Right! Voldemort in his quest for Inmortality! This is when I thought Voldemort could be somehow involved in Time Travel, Voldemort could be the *serpent biting its tail...*

THE ASTROLOGICAL PERSONALITY OF VOLDEMORT

> *"I was saying that Saturn was surely in a position of power in the heavens at the moment of your birth... You were born in midwinter?"*
>
> *"No,"* said Harry, *"I was born in July."* {B2, Ch13}

This may appear, on the surface, to be nothing more than Professor Trelawney's own lack of "sight", however, because we know that Voldemort and Harry are linked through the scar, it is very likely that Trelawney was mistaking Tom Riddle's birth, for Harry's. She can be a genius sometimes...☺

According to standard astrology, Saturn is the ruling planet for the sign of Capricorn (December-midwinter).[1] Another Harry Potter fan, Sam Avila, recently shared her ideas comparing Voldemort to the representation of the astrological Saturn, and the Roman god of the same name. The similarities between the two personalities help give credence to my Ouroboros theory.

REPRESENTING SATURN

The astrological sign of Saturn is often known as "The Devil". Saturn is represented as an old man, bearing a scythe in one hand and an hourglass in the other. These symbols are found in many representations of Death (or the Grim Reaper) and are undoubtedly linked to Saturn...[2]

Isn't this a wonderful representation of Voldemort? JKR describes Voldemort as having skeletal features (not to mention the black cloak :-)) On one hand, he's Death & Evil (the scythe), on the other hand he's linked to Time, and to an HOURGLASS no less. When an hourglass ends its time it's turned around and begins timing again.

THE OUROBOROS THEORY

One of the questions that arises in the Harry Potter series is: How did Tom Riddle, while he was Hogwarts, know that the Chamber of Secrets existed. My theory postulates that, *as Slytherin*, he left a piece of "coded advice" for his future self.

JKR stated, in an interview, that there was a *deliberate* typo in Book 3 that declared Tom Riddle to be Slytherin's *ancestor*.{Scholastic.com, October 2000}. If Tom Riddle was the last remaining heir of Slytherin, wouldn't that imply that Slytherin would be Riddle's ancestor, and not the other way around? According to my theory, Voldemort *is* Slytherin because he was sent back in time.

THE EMERALD TABLET

The Emerald Tablet is one of the main historical books on magic that focuses on Alchemy and the making of the Philosopher's Stone. JKR has explicitly used Alchemy throughout Book 1, and she could very well use it again through yet another method — by means of the book that concerns the making of the stone.

In this Emerald Book, there is a verse, called *The Riddle of the Stone* that reads:

> ***"Visita Interiora Terra. Rectificando Invenies Occultum Lapidem."***

The English translation is, "visit the bowels of the Earth. By rectifying, you shall find the hidden stone"[3] In other words, it could be directly applied to JK Rowling's works: *visit the Chamber of Secrets. By changing history (making things right), you shall find immortality.* It is interesting to note that the Latin "code" is called the *Riddle* of the Stone, and Voldemort was born "Tom *Riddle*", and we all know what he is seeking.

VOLDEMORT AS SATURN (KRONOS)?

I previously stated that Voldemort has an uncanny resemblance to the Roman god Saturn, or Kronos in Greek mythology. Kronos is considered the God of Time. This would fit the description of Voldemort and the Ouroboros theory, because in a sense, he is the God of Time in the cyclical nature of his life. In an ironic way, Voldemort would, in fact, achieve immortality by re-living his life over and over again (like the phoenix, who is reborn from his ashes.) Starting to sound familiar?

According to Greek mythology, Kronos tried to kill his children because *he was foretold that he'd be overthrown by one of them.*[4] In the Harry Potter series, Voldemort killed a lot of people because he was aware of the Prophecy that stated a child would vanquish him. In fact, he was trying to change the future (or is it the past?). Like Voldemort, Kronos slayed his own father, and was tricked by the mother of Jupiter to protect him. Lily certainly tricked Voldemort when she used an "ancient magic" to protect her son. {B5, Ch37} Jupiter, the only child to escape through the help of his mother, vanquished Kronos through the help of his *3 sisters and 2 brothers.* (Hermione, Luna, Ginny; Ron and Neville, anyone?)

THE FINAL FIGHT

Back to the Ouroboros theory, I think in the final "battle" or fight against Voldemort, Harry still won't want to be a murderer and will perform a spell to put him out of circulation so that he can get a trial later. Remember, we already know that Harry would not let Lupin and Sirius kill Peter Pettigrew, and instead opted for a trial for his crimes. {B3, Ch19} I believe Harry could end up using a non-violent spell, such as "Obliviate", which will wipe out his memory.

My theory suggests that Voldemort will either be sent "through the veil" (Remember, it took Sirius an age to fall through the veil—perhaps Voldemort will fall into the "Middle Ages"). Or, Voldemort, in his confused stupor following the battle, could stumble into the Time Room with all the time-turners, and get sent back in time to the Middle Ages, when Hogwarts was first founded.

In the myth of Kronos, Kronos is sentenced to the Tarturus prison, located in the deepest level of the mythological underworld. According to the Ouroboros theory, Voldemort is sent either "through the veil" or enters the Time Room, both of which are located in the deepest levels of the Ministry of Magic.

VOLDEMORT: FOUNDER OF HOGWARTS?

Kronos ends up banished to an area in Italy called Latium, where he changes his name to Saturn. In my theory, Voldemort (who doesn't remember who he is) changes his name in the Middle Ages to Salazar Slytherin. (Perhaps the name was even given to him because he could converse with snakes).

Why the Middle Ages? We know from canon that Hogwarts was founded during that time, but it was also during the time that Quidditch was invented. I bring this up, because if we follow the theory that Voldemort entered the time room, it is possible that the vehicle through which Voldemort time traveled, was studying this moment in history. There are other facts that help support this theory. We know from *Quidditch Through the Ages* that Gertie Keddle lived in a marsh during the 11th century (around the time Hogwarts was founded). The Sorting Hat also tells us in Book 4 that Slytherin came from fen (that is, a marshy area). Gertie kept a diary (maybe she got the idea from Slytherin/Voldemort/Tom Riddle), and her last name "Keddle" is Scandinavian for "cauldron". If all this is so, it wouldn't be the first time that Tom Riddle starts a new life with the help of a cauldron.

In Latium, Kronos/Saturn demonstrated his leadership abilities and became an important person who taught the ancient Romans how to farm land. Salazar Slytherin, as we know, was an important wizard who founded Hogwarts and taught young wizards and witches how to develop their magical abilities.

My theory suggests that this is when he would have left some sort of clue or instructions, like the Emerald Tablet, for his future self, to find. I believe that following Slytherin's argument with Godric, he built the Chamber of Secrets, hid the book in Hogwarts Library for his future self, and went off to spread his pureblood ideology, and most likely found Durmstrang (where they study the Dark Arts).

THE SERPENT BITES HIS TAIL

Trewlaney's prophecy states that *"for neither can live while the other survives..."*{B5, Ch37} If Voldemort were to be sent back into the past, he no longer lives in the present: he's already dead - he would have died in the Middle Ages. So, Voldemort is dead (in the present) and Harry wouldn't have had to murder him. I think to bring up Time Travel in this way at the end of the series would be a perfect way to tie up all loose ends and bring the story to a full, complete circle. ;-)

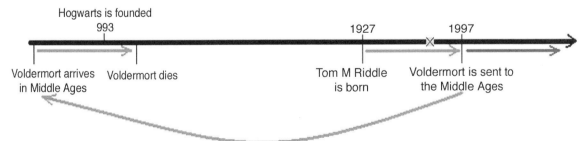

(I consider Voldemort goes back in time in 1997 because the Prophecy was *at the end of row 97...* It would be neat if that fit. ;-))

Saturn (the planet) has a cycle of 30 years. Let me explain...

Saturn takes 30 of our Earth years to complete a turn around the Sun. According to standard Astrology, these *cycles* can be interpreted in a person's life as phases. E.g., Youth, Maturity, Wisdom ("*the last phase, if reached, seems usually to mark the transition either to the next world or else back to a second childhood!*"[5]).

Tom Riddle's relationship with Slytherin ALSO moves in cycles of 30 years. Briefly:

1. Tom Riddle enters Hogwarts. That's his first ever contact with Slytherin. Sorting Hat, etc. (Phase: Youth to Maturity.)

2. Around 30 years later, Tom Riddle comes back to England as Voldemort, once his transformation has been completed. (Phase: Maturity to Wisdom.)

3. 30 years after that, at the end of this year, according to Ouroboros, Tom Riddle is sent back to the Middle Ages, where he finally becomes the very Slytherin himself. (Phase: Wisdom to "next world" or "second childhood"/chance.)

CONCLUSION

Well this is the theory for now. It could go on for ages... :-) As you can see it includes many elements (not only time travel), and although it of course won't end up happening it's FUN to imagine how loose ends are tied under its logic. And of course, this theory is not incompatible with other theories based on Time Travel... For example, what would happen if, when Voldemort escapes and is sent to the past, another person bravely tries to go after him, to catch him? What if that person is Ron? What if he also gets sent back into the past, but about 136 years instead...? (Check Dumbledore's age ;-) ...)

I hope you've enjoyed reading the Ouroboros Theory as much as I enjoyed coming up with it, and you find it useful to create your own theories. Now that I think about it, you can make a very nice theory about Arabella Figg that, among other things, explains why the Quibbler thought Fudge was drowning Goblins. Seriously. :-)

I must thank: my boyfriend for helping me put my thoughts about this Theory in order, Sam Avila for coming up with the connection Voldemort/Capricorn, the people who read the theory and gave me feedback, and all the people who posted in the original CoSForum thread who made the right questions to help develop the idea, or even helped me explain it when it was difficult...

I love ya'll. ;-)

———————————— ADDITIONAL SLEUTHING NOTES ————————————

✳ Are the references to 12s, calendars, planets, etc., that keep appearing throughout the series pointing us to Astrology?

✳ If the instructions for making the Philosopher's Stone are in the Emerald Tablet, and we know Nicolas Flamel made a Philosopher's Stone, does that mean Flamel got a look at the Emerald Tablet? Did Dumbledore (his partner) see it?

✳ If Trelawney has divination powers (seems that she has some), and is sensing Voldemort through Harry when mistaking his birthday, was she also constantly seeing Harry's "death" because she sensed the "mostly-dead" Voldemort through him? When doing palmistry, she also said that Harry had one of the shortest lifelines she had ever seen – would that have also related to Harry's link to the barely-alive Voldemort?

✳ One of the first epic fantasy novels was ER Eddison's *The Worm Ouroboros,* which took place on a planet called Mercury. Considering the cyclical time references throughout the series, could the Mercury-related imagery (Hermes, Caduceus, invisibility hats) also be hints about the Worm Ouroboros? On page ix of Fantastic Beasts, JKR mentions "Mr Augustus Worme of Obscurus Books". Could this be a subtle hint at the Worm Ouroboros book by Eddison?

ii From: http://www.astrologycom.com/saturn.html
   Other Astrology links visited:

      Saturn (conquer the world, discipline, *time restrictions*, teacher - Slytherin...)

      http://www.astrology.com/aboutastrology/interpreting/planets/saturn.html

      Capricorn (ambitious & determined; success, fame, prestige and money - VERY Slytherin...)

      http://www.astrology.com/allaboutyou/sunsigns/capricorn.html

1 The Sun is life, Saturn is death: http://weboteric.com/astrology_planets/saturn.php

2 http://www.alchemylab.com/phoenician_tablet.htm

4 Who's Who in Classical Mythology, Michael Grant & John Hazel, Oxford University Press, 1993.

5 Saturn 30 years cycles: http://www.astrologycom.com/saturn.html

THE PROBLEM WITH TIME-TRAVEL

RICHARD H. JONES ✳ NEW CLUES FORUM
USA (*US Edition*), AGE 43

Inspiration for this Discussion

When I first read Book 3, I didn't understand Time-Turning at all. But I couldn't just let it go. So, I had to reread the passages until I got it. I finally thought I understood Time-Turning after setting up a graph with four different colors to indicate the flow of time, Harry and Hermione passing through the time, time-travel itself, and the important events of the evening. But then looking at the important events, I noticed a problem: "Wait a second, how did Harry get past the Dementors in order to time-travel later?" So I started rereading again, and I noticed from what Hermione said, that in the Potterverse, the past was not fixed and that we could change history, and this led to some disquieting thoughts about how time-travel might be used in telling a story. And I also noticed that Dumbledore seemed to know that time-travel was going on even before Harry and Hermione did. All of this touched off a whole chain of musings.

 12

JKR used time-travel in Book 3 to good effect, and she might use it again. (When asked in a fan interview if Harry would time-travel again, JKR answered, "Not telling!"{AOL chat, October, 2000}) Time travel is key to a lot of speculative fan theories —Ron is Dumbledore; Hermione is McGonagall; time-travel is how Dumbledore knows all he knows; Harry goes back to Godric's Hollow in time to save himself (as a baby). But making it part of the solution to the end of the series may lead to problems. Here's why.

1. HOW TIME-TRAVEL WORKS IN BOOK 3

In Chapter 21 of Book 3, at 11:55 p.m., Dumbledore encourages Harry and Hermione, who are in the hospital ward, to use a Time-Turner to go back in time and save *"more than one innocent life tonight"*. {B3, Ch21} The simplest explanation of the time-traveling events in Book 3 is this: Harry and Hermione skip back through time from 11:55 p.m. to 8:55 p.m. in the blink of an eye and pass through that three-hour period a second time. Time, itself, only happens once—time is not actually "turned" (only the travelers experience the difference). Harry and Hermione jump off while time keeps flowing forward as it always does; it does not repeat itself or stop or go backward – again, only the travelers move about time, while time continues on its path for everyone else. And Harry and Hermione do not magically create duplicates of themselves that somehow pop into and out of existence, but instead, are transported to a different position on the timeline.

The Harry and Hermione who are in the infirmary after 11:55 p.m. become the time-travelers and are sent by the Time-Turner back in time to nearly the same location they were at 8:55 p.m. — via the magic of the Time-Turner. The same Harry and Hermione are now in that same three-hour period a second time to participate in events and save Buckbeak and Sirius. That is, the same Harry and Hermione who traveled up to 11:55 p.m. are now traveling back to 8:55 p.m. to relive the time until 11:55 p.m.; they retain all their memories from their first pass through the period.

Thus, during those three hours there are *two sets of Harry and Hermione*, but they are the same people in two places at once, as Dumbledore joked. Only one set exists going into the evening – the Harry and Hermione who have yet to travel (pre-time-traveling Harry and Hermione). And at the end of the evening, only one set exists any more to come out (the same Harry and Hermione who have now finished time-traveling). Let's call the Harry and Hermione who are attacked by the Dementors Harry1 and Hermione1. The Harry and Hermione who traveled back in time become Harry2 and Hermione2 during the 3 hours that both sets exist.

Pre-time-traveling Harry did not see time-traveling Harry at around 11 p.m. across the lake "before" he time-traveled: both Harrys were present at the same time because Harry had traveled back in time. Yet Harry and Hermione aged six hours during the period of time traveling because they passed through the three-hour period twice. (That's why Hermione was so tired all year!)

To summarize: Harry1 enters the evening, survives the Dementors, and gets to 11:55 p.m. when he then time-travels and becomes Harry2 who participates in the same events from 8:55 to 11:55 a second time. He saves himself (Harry1) at about 11 p.m.

Harry and Hermione do not "change history" that evening from what was written earlier in the book because the actions of time-traveling Harry and Hermione were already visiting our world from the moment the clock reached the time that they were to arrive back (so, were *always part of the events*). They simply participate in the same events twice and see them from two perspectives. That is, the events did come out differently than if they hadn't time-traveled, but both sets of Harry and Hermione were simultaneously participating in the events. Buckbeak was not killed before Harry and Hermione time-traveled and then somehow resurrected by time-traveling Harry and Hermione—rather, time-traveling Harry and Hermione were there all along when Buckbeak was about to be executed and they prevented the execution from happening. That's the only time you can *prevent* something *before* it happens. Pre-time-traveling Harry and Hermione simply misinterpreted the axe's thud and Hagrid's howls. {Ch17, p331, 332}

2. THE PARADOX OF SAVING YOURSELF

Paradox: *"a seemingly absurd or contradictory statement…"*

All time-travel potentially involves one basic danger: you could travel back through time and accidentally kill yourself (or an ancestor). And this leads to a paradox: if you kill your former self, you will not be around later to time-travel or accidentally kill yourself! For example, if time-traveling Harry (Harry2) dropped his wand and could not produce a Patronus— there would be no Harry2 to save Harry1 because Harry1 would have been killed or have had the Dementor's Kiss administered and so would never have reached 11:55 p.m. In short, if Harry had not time-traveled, he wouldn't be around to time-travel!

That paradox leads to a problem in Book 3: how did Harry live through the Dementors' attack *in the first place*? How did Harry1 get past the Dementors so that he could be around to time-travel and become Harry2…who then saves Harry1 from the Dementors? (I want to say, "how did he get past them *the first time*?" but that is not right, since there was only one event that occurred only once – witnessed by two Harrys.) We cannot simply say that Harry2 saved Harry1 and they both were there at 11 p.m. at the same time; that is true, but for a complete answer we need to know how Harry1 could become Harry2. That is, Harry1 had to survive the Dementor's Kiss *before* the time-traveling occurred in order to be able to time-travel at 11:55 p.m. and become Harry2, who could then be there at 11:00 PM to save Harry1 . . . thereby enabling Harry1 to get to 11:55 p.m. for the time-traveling to occur! Whew! How did he save himself *before* the time-travel occurred in order to be able to time-travel and save himself? As Galadriel Waters asks, "Well, how did he get to the future so he could come back and save himself?"[1] And we can't even argue that someone else (for example, Dumbledore or Snape) saved Harry "the first time" because Harry1 was saved by the Patronus and only one Patronus was generated that evening and that was by Harry2.

It is one thing to go back in time and influence events that don't affect your own survival (for instance, saving Buckbeak), but it is another thing altogether when time-travel is *required* to save your own earlier self. You might as well make Harry into his own father. There is a hole in the process here and no theory of time-travel gets around it. Hence, a paradox.

3. PARADOX, CHUCK BERRY AND THE PATRONUS

Let's assume Harry1 *somehow* got to 11:55 p.m. so that Harry2 could be there at 11 p.m. to save himself. However, there is yet another problem: how can Harry2 produce his Patronus? Harry1 couldn't produce one that evening, but he sees the Patronus that Harry2 makes (mistakenly thinking that James produced it), and so Harry2, who is "older" and knows more than Harry1 about what is going on, can later remember that he can produce it. Harry later says to Hermione: "I knew I could do it this time . . . because I'd already done it…does that make sense?" {Ch 21, p412.} Well, no, it doesn't. Neither Harry1 nor Harry2 had done it before that evening. Future Harry2 does recall what earlier Harry1 had "previously" seen, but the Patronus still was only produced once. The two Harrys just see the same event from different perspectives. But since the Patronus was produced only once, it's not clear why Harry2 should now think that he had produced it before based on what Harry1 saw.

That last paradox is the "Chuck Berry" paradox from the movie "Back to the Future". There, the Michael J. Fox character learns Chuck Berry's guitar licks off Berry's records but then teaches Berry those very same licks over the telephone—so, Fox learns the licks from Berry, who learns them from Fox, who learned from Berry, and so on. In effect, the earlier Chuck Berry learns his own licks from the future Chuck Berry. So there is no point in this loop for Chuck to actually *create* the licks! And the same problem applies here: Harry2 can make a Patronus because Harry1 saw him already do it because Harry2 did it because Harry1 saw him do it, and so on, and so on. At no point in the loop can Harry2 gain the confidence to produce the Patronus on the basis that he saw himself already produce it "before" during the evening.

4. THE FATAL FLAW: CHANGING HISTORY

And there is a bigger and more important problem: it is clear from Book 3 that under JKR's magical laws, we *can* change history. Hermione tells Harry that McGonagall told her that *"loads of [time-traveling wizards] ended up killing their past or future selves by mistake."* {Ch21, p399} That is definitely changing history: the "earlier" wizards have been eliminated from history by time-travel events.

Some people will argue that we can't change history through time-travel because of the basic paradox concerning accidentally killing yourself. In fact, frequently a cardinal rule of time-travel in sci-fi is that time-travelers cannot change events that would affect their ability to time-travel. But JKR is the only physicist in the Potterverse, and what she says goes. If she says that time-travelers can change history—for example, by killing their former selves—then time-travelers can change history, and that's that. JKR sets the rules, and that has to be our starting point for thinking about time-travel.

Also, notice that in Book 3, time-traveling Harry2 wanted to run out of the forest when he and Hermione2 were hiding there to get the Invisibility Cloak {p405} and find Wormtail. {p408} Hermione2 had to grab and stop him. She only expressed concern about being seen, but the fact remains that Harry would have changed the history that got them to that point if he had done what he wanted to do. If Harry2 had stopped Wormtail or had just gotten the Invisibility Cloak, all the events of that evening from that point on would have changed. No "laws of nature" or "magical forces" or "laws against time paradoxes" kept Harry from changing history—only Hermione's fast reflexes.

In addition, consider Dumbledore's comment about being careful because time-travel's consequences are complicated and unpredictable. {Ch22, p426} Why would he say that if the past were "fixed" and unchangeable? If our actions during time-travel were somehow fixed and predetermined, his comment wouldn't be needed; and if our actions aren't fixed, then we can intentionally or even just accidentally change the course of events.

The events would have come out differently if Harry and Hermione hadn't time-traveled. Without time-travel, Buckbeak would have been executed. But we can alter the past. So if Buckbeak had died, there is nothing to prevent Harry and Hermione from simply going back earlier and just stealing him, thus saving him. That would change the history we know and would create a new "time-line" in which Buckbeak is alive. But we would never be aware of the changes because we would now be in the new time-line. (Think of the changing time-lines in *Back to the Future, Part 2*.) Thus, we couldn't detect the changes resulting from time-travel. Knowing what has occurred does not determine past events once and for all, but it does determine what events have occurred in *our* time-line. Notice that Dumbledore's reactions in Hagrid's hut {Ch21, p401, 402} do indicate that he knew what was really going on with Buckbeak and so he was aware that Harry and Hermione had time-traveled and were outside. And he seems to have known that the time-traveling succeeded when he was in the infirmary at 11:55 p.m. (see Additional Author Notes)

5. THE MYSTERY OF TIME-LINES

The whole idea of a new "time-line" (a new course of events replacing another course of events) raises some weird questions. Think about changing the past. If Voldemort were to go back now and kill off baby Harry, does Harry Potter just disappear from reality? Or do different time-lines simultaneously exist, one with a Harry Potter existing in it and one with none? Do different realities branch off with every time-travel incident? Does each branch off the main timeline now "exist" in some sense? Is there a whole collection of time-lines of past events existing right now and we are aware of only one? Are any of the branches "more real" than any other? Does Harry pop out of existence or continue to exist in another time-line we are unaware of? And think of the confusing complications for time-lines if two different people, one at Hogwarts and one in London, use a time-turner at the same time.

But in any case, all we can say is that no one has gone back in time to kill Voldemort or to save James or Lily in our time-line. If anyone has gone back in time, they have already done so. No one can go back now and kill Voldemort or save James and Lily because those events have passed and no one did go back to change them—once someone is dead, they're dead.

But that is only *in our time-line*: we are free to go back and kill Voldemort or to save Sirius or to change any other event that has occurred in our time-line, thereby creating a *different* time-line. (So too, earlier in the book once Hermione missed one of her classes {Ch15, p295}, she could not time-travel and take it over again without creating a new time-line.) Of course, if someone does go back and kill Voldemort, *we* would never know about it because we would then be in a different time-line —we would only know about the one in which Harry lives with his parents and never heard of Voldemort because there would be no Voldemort in that time-line.

6. CREATING NEW TIME-LINES

Notice that when Harry and Hermione time-traveled they did not arrive back in exactly the same spot in the Great Hall that pre-time-traveling Harry and Hermione had been in at 8:55 p.m. They "landed" only nearby—otherwise, they would be occupying the same spaces as pre-time-traveling Harry and Hermione. (So too, during the school year the boys notice that Hermione was right behind them at the top of the stairs and then suddenly at the bottom of the stairs after she time travels {Ch7, p129}.)

Harry2 and Hermione2 would have had some unnoticed small effects just by being where they landed, (such as moving a mop in the closet or stepping on something in the forest). But these small effects may have great consequences. (Think of Homer Simpson going back to the age of dinosaurs and stepping on a bug and saying, "That couldn't change anything" only to affect the entire course of evolution.) This is why time-travel's consequences are complicated and unpredictable, as Dumbledore says.{Ch22, p426} Thus, one of the most important wizarding laws is against time-travel {Ch 21, p399}.

But small effects as much as big ones (for instance, saving Sirius) create new time-lines—the size of the effect is logically irrelevant. Thus, just by their presence in the time-period a second time, time-traveling Harry and Hermione must have created a new time-line.

So the mere act of time-travel alters history, and any act of time-travel creates a new time-line. Thus, the distinction between "time-travel to participate in events" and "time-travel to alter past history" does not really hold. There is no difference between going back to save Buckbeak or James and Lily. But we would not know that Harry and Hermione's presence created a new time-line because we would now be in a new time-line with all the changes. What we think occurred is only what occurred in our current time-line.

7. THE ABILITY TO CHANGE HISTORY PRESENTS A PROBLEM

But here's the rub for story-telling: if history can be changed by time-travel, then anything goes. Why doesn't someone just go back and kill off Tom Riddle before he gets to Hogwarts or prevent his parents from meeting? It may create a new time-line in which Harry would live happily with his parents. Or why doesn't Voldemort just go back before Harry was born and kill James as a baby before all this got started? And he can do in Neville while he's at it just in case. (Granted, you would need an industrial strength time-machine to go back years, not the little one Hermione had, but perhaps the thing in the Department of Mysteries is one?) And if at first you don't succeed, you can always go back as many times as you need. (Dr. Who had a rule against that.)

Thus, if we can change history, there is a danger of an unsatisfying ending. The story doesn't have to be restricted to what came before. There does not have to be any continuity or plot development or logic or common sense. You can just use time-travel to get any outcome you want or to fill in holes in the plot—there are no constraints. An author can just pull something out of the blue that changes the whole history of the story in a major way. We couldn't make any predictions based on earlier clues—a whole different time-line could be created. Based on the story so far, it will be disappointing if what "really happened" is that Harry traveled back in time and saved his parents and lived happily ever after.

Still, JKR tied time-travel tightly into the plot in a clever way in Book 3. And if she uses it again, it will be interesting and fun to see what she comes up with.

ADDITIONAL AUTHOR NOTES

TIME-TRAVEL AND FREE WILL

Notice that when Dumbledore first walked into the infirmary at around 11:55 p.m. and saw Harry and Hermione, he must have realized that they had in fact already succeeded in their time-traveling mission. If they had not succeeded, they would have had the Dementor's Kiss applied and would not be in their current condition in the infirmary. So, he knew they must have accepted their time-traveling mission and accomplished their task before he even asked them!

This leads to strange questions about "free will". Is Dumbledore's foreknowledge compatible with Harry and Hermione's free will? Dumbledore already knew they must have done it—so did they really have any free will in the matter? Or did they somehow exercise free will before Dumbledore arrived at the infirmary? Was it now just a matter of fate that they must time-travel? Was it "destiny" and "what was meant to happen"? Could they now refuse to time-travel when he suggests it? It was also, by definition, impossible that Harry2 *not* produce the Patronus because Harry1 saw it—so did Harry and Hermione really have any choice but to use the time-turner? Or does Dumbledore's knowledge of what must have happened and Harry1 seeing the Patronus simply irrelevant to the question of free will?

DOES THE PAST STILL EXIST?

Here's another interesting philosophical issue. Harry and Hermione go back three hours and so 8:55 p.m. somehow still exists at 11:55 p.m. when they leave. The earlier period hasn't gone away. If we can go back to earlier events, does this mean the past events really are not gone at all, but somehow still exist? Are past events constantly occurring? Is the past always there? Is the past still real—a "place" we can go to anytime? How about the future? If time-travel works, our present moment isn't the only time that is real, and our living through this particular moment doesn't make anything real. We like to think the future has not been created yet, but if the present does not "make" time (since the past continues to exist), why can't the future also exist? That we (or any other particular beings) haven't gotten there is irrelevant—our presence doesn't make time real. The present is just our little moment on the already existing continuum of time. Must not the future also be there since no point on the continuum of time is any different from any other? Do our actions choose our time-line among an infinite number of time-lines that now exist? Can we just as easily travel to the future?

ADDITIONAL SLEUTHING NOTES

* If, according to McGonagall, loads of wizards ended up killing themselves, how would she know they killed themselves if they no longer exist?

---

[1] Oxford/American Dictionary and Thesaurus, 2003

[2] Waters, Galadriel. Ultimate Unofficial Guide to the Mysteries of Harry Potter. Wizarding World Press. Niles, IL: 2002. p214

✦ Time Travelling and Turning ✦

Troels Forchammer
Denmark (*UK Edition*), Age 38

Inspiration for this Discussion

The idea of travelling in time is far from new, but has been around for a long time. We are enticed by the possibility of correcting the wrongs and mistakes of the past—whether our own or someone else's.

Using the physicist's criteria, we define time travelling as what occurs when the duration of the journey is different when perceived inside a travelling vehicle and externally (what I will call "subjective" time[I] and "objective" time[II]). The possibility of travelling in time is actually mathematically permissible: special and general relativity states that travelling into the future is completely unproblematic. [7] However, time travelling becomes far more interesting when considering journeys into the past, like that of Harry and Hermione in Book 3.

This essay is based on my writings found at the Hogwarts Library web site [10][11], but rewritten for this purpose. References to further reading are denoted in the text with a number in square brackets.

 NEWT

1 Time Travelling in Potterverse—According to Physics

The possibility of travelling in time is not just for fantasy and fiction writers. It has come up in physics as a consequence of Einstein's general theory of relativity, [1][3][4][7] and while time travelling to the future is today an accepted (though not experimentally tried) aspect of physics, the same is not true for journeys to the past. A number of scenarios have been proposed as to how this can be done using various aspects of general relativity. [1][2][3][4][7][9]

Physicists agree that the current theoretical understanding predicts time travelling as a real possibility, but beyond that, the waters part. [2][13] Some, such as Igor Novikov, believe that the experimental time machine is "just around the corner" (some fifty years, perhaps); while others, such as Stephen Hawking, believe that there is some kind of natural law that prevents time travelling. Yet others, such as Holger Bech Nielsen, are taking a "wait and see" position, claiming that time machines, if they are possible at all, will be something for the far future.

The object of this section is not to describe the physics of time travelling in detail or the long and extremely complex debates about time travelling, time itself and other related topics, but rather to give a brief overview of the more prominent of the contending theories on how a physicist would cope with the paradoxes which are inherent in using "time-turners" and other possible time-travelling methods.

1.1 Metaphysics

A proper discussion of time travelling should begin with an overview of the philosophical and metaphysical questions that relate to this: questions such as time and causation. I will touch very briefly on these subjects; presenting a few of the questions that philosophers face when discussing these questions.

1.1.1 TIME

To understand what time travelling is we ought first to ask ourselves, "What is time?"

That debate is at least as much philosophical and metaphysical as it is physical [7] and I have no intention of attempting a thorough introduction to that ongoing, highly volatile debate. Suffice to say, there are three main ideas, which are, roughly speaking, distinguished by their perception of the past and the future.

* ✳ Eternalism [6][8] postulates that both the past, the present, and the future exists.[III, IV]
* ✳ Possibilism [6] holds that the future doesn't exist yet.[V]
* ✳ Presentism [6][8] claims that only the present exists.[VI] [See pg. 2-physics]

Each of these ideas faces a number of problems—from logic and common usage to other areas of philosophy such as determinism and causation.

Both physicists and philosophers concur that of all possible scenarios, forward time travel is the least problematic and, in particular, it gives no problems with the usual forward understanding of causation.

1.1.2 CAUSATION

Causation: the process of events and/or objects being the *cause* of an *effect.*

Normally, we think of the cause as necessarily preceding (in time) the effect. For example, (a cause) Neville forgets to add an ingredient to his potion; (the effect) his cauldron melts down. Our current perception is that the cause would have to come before the effect. But might this common understanding be wrong? That, at least, is a question that philosophers are seriously considering. [5][3]

The discussions surrounding causation would be far beyond the scope of this essay, and it will have to be enough to note that such questions are not exclusively the domain of metaphysics; physics theorists also seriously consider the possibility of allowing "backwards causation" in quantum physics. [3] And in most (if not all) physical systems, the two directions in time are symmetrical, which means that nothing in quantum theory suggests that the past is more important in terms of causation than the future. [5]

One possible ramification of this is that the eternalist view on time doesn't necessarily limit our free will. We would, in this model, be affected not only by our past, but also by our future, and we, ourselves, would likewise affect both past and future. Sounds a lot like the themes in Harry Potter, doesn't it?

1.2 PHYSICS

Definitions

Moving on to the real purpose of this first section—how *physicists* suggest that we may treat the possibility of time travelling. For that purpose I first need to define a number of terms:

Grandfather paradox[9][7]

> This term refers to the classical set of paradoxes exemplified by the idea of going back in time to kill one's own grandfather before he can beget one's own parent. In other words, this class of paradoxes creates a logically impossible situation.

Causal paradox[7]

> In this essay this refers to the creation of an effect without a cause. If I go back in time to hand myself this article before I even start on it, who then actually wrote this article? In other words, we have an effect (this article) without any cause (someone writing it). This is a sub-class of what, in some literature, is described as "causal loops"[VII]

Circular Causation[7]

Circular causation is not necessarily a paradox as such, event A can cause event B, which then might go on to cause event A. This is possible without loss of consistency if the information related from B to A is gathered in the normal way. The event in Book 3, when Harry realises that he can cast the Patronus Charm because he's already done it is a good example of this. This is another subclass of causal loops,[VII] but is one that allows a consistent history, and as such might be possible.

First order time travelling

Time travelling of the first order is, basically, time travelling without limitations. Specifically, it means that you can go to places in space-time where you can affect your present. In the following, I will use it to refer specifically to journeys of that kind.

Second order time travelling

Time travelling of the second order is a subset of first order time travelling. Second order time travelling specifically excludes travels within your event horizon. This means that you can freely go back 200 years, if you like, but you must then end up 200 light years or more from your starting point.

Time machine

Unless I specifically state otherwise, I will use this to refer to any device that can be used to perform first order time travelling.

Now we proceed to the discussion of how we can deal with the possibility of paradoxes. [1][4][7][9] In general, physicists are none too sure how to handle the possibility of time travelling. The following is a walk-through of some of the most prominent suggestions and theories on how to handle this possibility.

TIME THEORIES

1.2.1 The Immutable Past

This is in many ways the simplest possible explanation that allows time travelling. According to this hypothesis, there is only one timeline for all eternity. It is not possible to change the past in any way because what has happened stays happened. Named after Russian physicist Igor Novikov [3][9], this idea is often referred to as "Novikov's Globally Self-consistent Loops in Time" or "the Hypothesis of Consistent History".

The logic behind this is that if I go back to yesterday, I will experience the same "yesterday" that I lived through yesterday. The actions I perform after going back were *already* performed and incorporated when I first experienced that day.

One variation of this theme is inspired by quantum physics.[VIII] According to this theory, the future is still in some unknown state: containing a superposition of all possible futures. As the future, from moment to moment, becomes the present, the state is observed, and the "wave function" collapses. In other words, the true state becomes known as it is observed, and at that moment all the other possible outcomes (the "indetermination") cease to exist. Once the state is known it cannot be altered, and we get the same immutability of the past as described above. This is obviously linked to the probablistic view on time.

This does not really affect my ability to assert my free will in the past time that I arrive in, but as the effects of my free choices are already observed, there is a limit to which *results* I can achieve. It does, however, require that the universe (or whatever) conspires to force me to act in accordance with the observed past.

This strange conspiracy of nature is the most powerful objection to this theory. On the other hand, no one protests when the laws of physics prevent us from being able to walk on walls. The strength of this theory is that it allows for time travelling of the first order, while resolving any possible paradox in a neat way.

1.2.2 THE ALTERNATIVE TIME

The Alternative Time theory suggests that whenever the past is changed, a new world "branches off" from the original. In this new world the changes will take effect, while in the original, nothing will have changed. [3][4][6][7][8][9]

It is not clear exactly when a new time branches off. If the original history can include the possibility of the time travellers arriving, but not changing anything, then it would be possible to travel in time without creating a new world. On the other hand, it would seem more natural that the original history did not include time travellers, and that a new time is inevitably created whenever someone travels back in time.

For the time traveller, this idea can be very uncomfortable. Once he has changed the past he will be in the new world without any way to get back to his origin. Therefore, when the time traveller leaves on his time journey, he will disappear from the original timeline, never to return. In the new timeline, there possibly will be two instances of him (unless one of him has died).

This theory is obviously related to the *many-worlds theory* [IX]—the idea that at every moment in time, an infinite number of possible futures branches out: one for each possible combination of outcomes of every single choice in that instant. While the two ideas are related and easily can be combined, neither of them requires the other to be true.

The advantage to this theory lies in allowing changes to the past (while punishing the traveller severely) in a way that avoids paradoxes. The main problem with this explanation is the creation of a whole new universe every time the time line branches: where is the energy for that going to come from? It is, however, being seriously considered in modern physics:

> *"… the idea of parallel universes and alternative histories as a solution to the time travel paradoxes is also now being taken seriously by some (admittedly, not many) researchers, including David Deutsch, in Oxford. Their research deals with both time, and relative dimensions in space. You could make a nice acronym for that – TARDIS, perhaps?"*
>
> —John Gribbin [3]

1.2.3 NO TIME MACHINES

Professor Hawking has suggested another approach: that, *at most*, second order time travel is possible (and perhaps not even that). Hawking proposes that some kind of "Chronology Protection Law" causes wormholes to collapse before they can become time machines. As Hawking put it in a public lecture, "*This picture would explain why we haven't been over run by tourists from the future.*"

The main advantage of this theory is that it disallows any paradoxes without the complex theories of causation necessary for the immutable past. The disadvantage is that it is not possible to express this theory in the mathematical language of physics, which means that it is not testable: a bad thing for a physical theory.

1.2.4 NO TIME TRAVEL

"The theory of boring physics"

It is inevitable that someone would suggest the boring explanation: that time travelling is impossible [6]: wormholes (assuming they could exist) become unstable before we can use them for time travelling or something else prevents them from becoming time machines. There is nothing much to say about this; the theories and equations that predict time travelling are not yet testable, and may of course be wrong.

The greatest disadvantages of this theory are that it *is* boring, and it requires some hitherto undiscovered restrictions on the theories of physics.

2. Time-Turning and Potterverse

In the context of Potterverse we know that time travelling of the first order *is* possible, so that we immediately get to dismiss the more 'boring' theories ;-)

On the other hand, we have to include a paradox potential: that of the changeable past. This will obviously create the possibility of temporal contradictions of all kinds, but authors have been known to ignore that before. The idea of actually changing the past has been used often in fictional works and can be played out in several ways: the author can ignore the possibility of paradoxes and just write in changes to the past (though these might, of course, be seen as paradoxical in themselves), or can even choose to include specific paradoxes for literary effect.

To discuss how time works in Potterverse, let's look at what actually happened in the last chapters of Book 3.

The important thing to remember when discussing these events is that irrespective of how time works in general in Potterverse, only one timeline is involved. Events happen only once—even if Harry and Hermione get to experience them twice.

The timeline for these events is analysed in detail both in [10], where the focus is on the parallelism of the events and in [12] where Hollydaze focuses on the sequentiality in external time. Both accounts, however, are based on the observation that the two descriptions of this period are consistent with each other. The older Harry and Hermione don't do anything in Chapter 21 that is inconsistent with the preceding chapters—specifically when Harry, Hermione and Ron hear "*the sounds drifting from Hagrid's garden,*" "*the unmistakable swish and thud of an axe,*" and a little later, "*a wild howling*". All of this is completely consistent with the events as described later, when we learn that the swish and the thud was when Macnair "*seemed to have swung it into the fence in anger*" and the howling is referred to being precisely the same, explaining that "***this time** they could hear Hagrid's words through his sobs.*"

One comment that has given rise to much confusion is Harry's explanation to Hermione "*I knew I could do it this time because I'd already done it…*"{Ch 21} Harry goes on to ask "*does that make sense?*" and, yes Harry, that makes perfect sense.

It is an example of "circular causation", and to understand it we must look at Harry's personal time, which continues uninterrupted first through the experiences of Harry above and then the experiences of Harry†. Following this time-line, Harry first sees the Patronus chase off the Dementors and then sees the person who cast the charm. Later he realises that he, himself, cast it and then realises that he will be able to do it. In the traditional view, this may indeed be a reversion of cause and effect, but as noted earlier this is not necessarily a logical problem; causation is satisfied in Harry's personal time, so it may be possible.

Within Potterverse we know, as stated above, that travelling backwards in time is possible. That much is an irrefutable fact. Furthermore, based on McGonagall's warnings, Hermione tells Harry "*when wizards have meddled with time ... loads of them ended up killing their past or future selves by mistake!*" {Ch21} Whether this is actual fact; a misunderstanding by Hermione; or Professor McGonagall engaged in a bit of hyperbole[X] has been much debated.

Hermione is generally a very trustworthy character, though she *has* been known to be wrong. Rowling addressed part of this in the interview on the *Harry Potter and the Chamber of Secrets* DVD when she said she uses Hermione to tell her readers things because "*Hermione has read it somewhere. So, she's handy.*"

It has been argued that this means that Hermione's statement above does not fulfill the requirements for Hermione being the mouthpiece of Rowling as she is not relating something that she has read somewhere, but rather something she heard from McGonagall, who is *not* included among Rowling's reliable sources. It should, however, be noted that even if true, this doesn't mean that Hermione's statement can be automatically dismissed; at most, it means that it is not at the same level of reliability as something she has read in a well-researched book. It can be argued that we should, by default, trust Hermione: she is reliable and is often used to divulge important information.

Whatever the personal opinion of those arguing the nature of time in Potterverse, most readers agree that nothing actually *changed* in Book 3 between the two descriptions of the same period[XI]. In this respect, the events play themselves out as if they followed the 'immutable time' model from physics.

Using that model, one might say that Harry[†] and Hermione[†] go back in time to ensure that the past happens 'correctly'. This is, however, strictly from the point of view of their subjective timelines. In the terms of the single objective timeline we have Harry, Harry[†], Hermione and Hermione[†] acting as free-willed agents, similar to the explanation of the Immutable Past. (Inviolability of the past does not remove the free choice of the time-travelling wizards – their free choices are already incorporated in the past.)

This is, of course, not the same as saying that this is definitely the way time works in Potterverse. The exact reproduction of the past that we witnessed in Book 3 could be due to random chance, or it could be because Rowling has decided only to describe the final history.

What is it, then, that the time-turner does? Well, it simply takes the person(s) wearing it back to a point in time. It does not create a copy of the person, but he or she is now able to relive the same time again. They are still the same individuals, but although for a short period are in the same general space, they are functioning on different personal time clocks[XII]. Who did all of Hermione's exams? She did herself—by using the time-turner she was able to be at three exams at the same time—but in her *subjective* time, she did them one after the other.

3. Discussion

So, knowing that time travelling really *is* possible in Potterverse, we are left with three possible explanations of Rowling's time laws.

1. Time is truly changeable—changing the past causes the old timeline to cease to exist and be replaced with the new time.

2. Time isn't changeable (as such)—but it is possible to create a new timeline that is different from the original. The original timeline remains unchanged. This is what is described as the Alternative Time, section 1.2.2.

3. Time is unchangeable (as described in my section The Immutable Past)—and Hermione's statement about wizards killing themselves cannot be trusted.

So let me explore the consequences of each of these from a story-telling point of view.

1. Time is truly changeable

If time is truly changeable, we are faced with a subcreation that incorporates the possibility of paradoxes. In addition to this, it is also a very high-powered ability that will obviously unbalance the plot in favour of those who are able to travel in time and we may end up playing the "why didn't they use it there" game forever. In short: allowing a changeable past creates not only the possibility for paradoxes, but it also inevitably creates a number of plot (worm) holes large enough to sail a medium-sized aircraft carrier through (e.g., the USS Nimitz).

2. TIME ISN'T CHANGEABLE (AS SUCH)/ALTERNATE TIME

Adopting the alternative time theory will solve the problem of the paradoxes and it will also allow Hermione and McGonagall to be correct![XIII] Unfortunately it will also open the possibility of the creation of alternative time lines in which the events play out differently. This doesn't necessarily present a major problem as Rowling could just say that she is telling the story of only one of these possible time lines.

If we apply this model to the conclusion of Book 3 (and assume that a new world *did* branch out[XIV]) it would mean that in the original world, Buckbeak was executed, Sirius Black was administered the Dementor's Kiss, and the magical world was left without Harry Potter ("*The one with the power to vanquish the Dark Lord*" {B5, Ch37})—definitely not a desirable situation. The same would apply if Harry were to go back in time and change some event so that Voldemort was defeated in the new history: in the original time the magical world would be left with an undefeated Dark Lord and no Harry Potter to vanquish him. This is not necessarily a literary problem: Rowling could be focusing on one world-history exclusively. It would, however, as I see it, be an ethical problem to leave the original history to the undisputed reign of Voldemort. However, as long as this model is not used for major plot points (such as the defeat of Voldemort), I don't see any problem with it—the model doesn't preclude the kind of scenario we saw in Book 3 from occurring within one single consistent history.

3. TIME IS UNCHANGEABLE

Adopting the model of the immutable past will always best maintain inner consistency, both with respect to avoiding paradoxes and the closure of plot holes. It will, however, also have the effect that it constrains the freedom of the author to utilise time travel for literary effect. Only by keeping the readers ignorant of the 'real' events the first time we read about the doubled period (as Rowling did in Book 3) can she maintain the suspense of the story.[XV] In the case of the *Harry Potter* books there is the added complication of Hermione's statement, which must be assumed to be untrue (wizards killing themselves).

There are other problems inherent in using this time model: first and foremost that the characters, when travelling in time, are forced to 'act' in such a way that they create the past as they experienced it the first time around. Instead of a conspiracy of the universe we get a conspiracy of the author, that limits characters' freedom to act (insofar as literary characters can be free-willed at all). This creates a self-imposed limitation on the author and (perhaps more problematically) it creates a possibility for more perceptive readers to guess the plot.

SUMMARY

Ultimately, the choice between the various models must be a matter of taste, as in most matters of art. There is doubtlessly an element of skill involved, and keeping track of the multitude of possibilities when writing a time travelling story can by no means be an easy task. No matter what model an author elects for subcreation, it will require some skill to do it convincingly. Beyond that level of skill, however, it becomes a matter of literary tastes only; all models can doubtlessly be employed with good results, and while some models will alienate a certain group of readers, it will inevitably attract another group of readers. My personal preference, though unimportant in this context, is to favour the model using an immutable time. This is because I put the inner consistency, the 'believability' of the subcreation beyond all else. I agree completely with Tolkien when he wrote that "*The moment disbelief arises, the spell is broken; the magic, or rather art, has failed.*"[XVI] And also when he later requires "*inner consistency of reality*" as that "*which commands or induces Secondary Belief.*"

4. CONCLUSION

> *"The conclusion of this lecture is that rapid space-travel, or travel back in time, can't be ruled out, according to our present understanding. They would cause great logical problems, so let's hope there's a Chronology Protection Law, to prevent people going back, and killing our parents. But science fiction fans need not lose heart. There's hope in string theory."*
> —Professor Stephen Hawking, *Public Lectures*

With respect to Potterverse, I don't think we have enough evidence to resolve the matter either way, and the debate will no doubt continue. My own preference is clear: the immutable time model. Whether Rowling will see fit to follow my tastes is of course still left to be seen (he said with a self-conscious smile).

On the other hand, it is also clear that the "many worlds", or the *alternative time* theory, provides the best possibility of reconciling Hermione's statement using a time model with a consistent history.

Whatever model Rowling has chosen or will choose for Potterverse, I am hoping that a changeable past is not an important part of resolving the plot: the can of worms in terms of plot holes and loss of inner integrity that she will open in that way would be way too big, in my opinion. Book 5 showed that temporal manipulation can be used in several ways, not just for time travelling, and the exploration of these other usages would be, to me, more interesting than another time travelling plot.

──────── ADDITIONAL SLEUTHING NOTES ────────

✳ The bell jar in the Department of Mysteries had no walls – does that mean a time anomaly was self-contained in free space? Would it be considered a "bubble" of time? How large a bubble can exist, and is it always a closed loop?

✳ Is the Pensieve a kind of time device? Do the memory strands stay static, or do they change with the user's experience?

✳ In the wizarding world, is time a parallel existence similar to the concept of the veil separating parallel universes? Would there be "doorways" between those universes? Could the 12 doors in the rotating room in the Department of Mysteries sync up with entrances to various parallel universes?

For those interested in further study in these matters I provided a few websites to other places that give a far more thorough discussion of these subjects, and which, for the most part, provide further references for the diligent and dedicated student (any Hermiones out there?)

[1] Johnson, Neil, "Shaping the Future" from *BBC - Science & Nature - Space - Time Travel*
http://www.bbc.co.uk/science/space/exploration/timetravel/index.shtml

[2] Hawking, Stephen, Public Lectures, "Space and Time Warps" from *Professor Stephen W. Hawking's web pages*
http://www.hawking.org.uk/lectures/warps.html

[3] Gribbin, John, "Time Travel", *John Gribbin's Home Page*, http://epunix.biols.susx.ac.uk/home/John_Gribbin/Time_Travel.html

[4] Arntzenius, Frank, Maudlin, Tim, "Time Travel and Modern Physics", *The Stanford Encyclopedia of Philosophy* (Spring 2000 Edition), Edward N. Zalta (ed.), http://plato.stanford.edu/archives/spr2000/entries/time-travel-phys/

[5] Hoefer, Carl, "Causal Determinism", *The Stanford Encyclopedia of Philosophy* (Spring 2004 Edition), Edward N. Zalta (ed.),

[5] Hoefer, Carl, "Causal Determinism", *The Stanford Encyclopedia of Philosophy* (Spring 2004 Edition), Edward N. Zalta (ed.), http://plato.stanford.edu/archives/spr2004/entries/determinism-causal/

[6] Markosian, Ned, "Time", *The Stanford Encyclopedia of Philosophy* (Winter 2002 Edition), Edward N. Zalta (ed.), http://plato.stanford.edu/archives/win2002/entries/time/

[7] Hunter, Joel, "Time Travel", *The Internet Encyclopedia of Philosophy* (© 2004), James Fieser, Ph.D. (gen. ed.), http://www.iep.utm.edu/t/timetravel.htm

[8] Dowden, Bradley, "Time", *The Internet Encyclopedia of Philosophy* (© 2004), James Fieser, Ph.D. (gen. ed.), http://www.iep.utm.edu/t/time.htm

[9] Nielsen, Malene Steen, "Tidsrejser", *DR, Videnskab & IT Tema*, http://www.dr.dk/videnskabold/minitema/tid/index.asp (In Danish)

[10] Forchhammer, Troels, "What is this problem with the timeline?", *Hogwarts Library*, http://www.hogwarts-library.net/reference/potterverse_faq_VI.html - time_travel

[11] Forchhammer, Troels, "Time Travelling", *Hogwarts Library*, http://www.hogwarts-library.net/reference/time_travel.html

[12] Hollydaze. "Time Line: The End of PA", *The Harry Potter Lexicon*, http://www.hp-lexicon.org/timelines/timeline_end-of-pa.html

[13] Hanson, Mike, "Re: book 7 finale", alt.fan.harry-potter, http://google.ca/groups?threadm=11d49fef.0311121208.47913227@posting.google.com

[1] That is: time, as it is perceived by a time-traveller. This is the personal time line of the time traveller – her 'world diagram, to put it in relativistic terms.

[2] That is: the universal time dimension of physics. Also called "external time".

[3] Treating the entirety of space-time as one four-dimensional coordinate system where there is no fundamental difference between any of the existing in another time is exactly equivalent to existing in another place. This attitude is prevalent among physicists as it is supported by conclusions from special and general relativity.

[4] The language is restricted to the temporal tenses – extra tenses related to space-time would be of great help. Existence can be seen both in the present sense, as 'existing in this instant (of time)', but also in the broader sense as 'existing somewhere in space-time'. It is in this broader sense that it is debated whether the past and future exists.

[5] And thus the present may lead to a lot of possible futures. Whether, if one travels back in time, the future from which the time traveller originated will then exist is unclear.

[6] This creates some serious problems with respect to general relativity where the traditional concept of simultaneity breaks down, and observers in different inertial systems may perceive two events as either simultaneous or separated in time

[7] Causal Loops. These are in general "a chain of causes that closes back on itself. A causes B, which causes C…which causes X, which causes A, which causes B…and so on ad infinitum". The possibility of causal loops in general is debatable, but I have here chosen to treat two subclasses separately.

[8] In which case the wizards went back in time to an alternative world, or created an alternative world at the latest when they killed their past selves. That would mean that it in the new world, they didn't survive to travel back, but that is no problem as they lived on in the original world to leave from there.

[9] Inspired by another interpretation of quantum physics according to the different possibilities represented by the mathematical representation of the state are manifestations of different possible worlds, or realities 'existing' in parallel with our own universe (there was yet another way to use 'exist' – now referring to something that isn't even true in our own reality).

[10] The reason attributed to McGonagall for wanting to exaggerate to Hermione is that the attempt at changing the past is potentially disastrous because the past is (according to this argument) unchangeable, and thus, since the time traveller is bound to be stopped in her attempt to change the past, there is a great risk that this will involve something of a personally catastrophic nature.

[11] Actually the order in which the procession leaves the Whomping Willow changes slightly between the two descriptions, but this is generally held to be an error, and not indicative of a real change of the past.

[12] It is only fair to note that this is one of the problems discussed in philosophy

[13] In which case the wizards went back in time to an alternative world, or created an alternative world at the latest when they killed their past selves. That would mean that it in the new world, they didn't survive to travel back, but that is no problem as they lived on in the original world to leave from there.

[14] A branching of time most likely happened either at the point where Harry and Hermione arrived in the past (as there is, in this model, no reason why the time travelling Harry† and Hermione† should have been present in the original time line) or at the point where the change is first introduced (saving Buckbeak? Changing the sequence they exited the Whomping Willow?)

[15] It may also require that the readers are unaware, or at least uncertain, about whether this specific model is used or not.

[16] Tolkien, J.R.R. "On Fairy Stories" Tree and Leaf. HarperCollins Publishers (London 2001), p. 37 & 47

Bubble, Bubble, Toil and Trouble: The "Potions Master"

✴ ESSENCE OF SNAPE ✴

VICTORIA JONES ✴ CHAMBER OF SECRETS FORUM
ENGLAND (*UK Edition*), AGE 19

Inspiration for this Discussion

In my opinion, one of the most complex and fascinating characters created at the hand of JK Rowling is the ill-natured Professor Severus Snape. The character of Snape is far deeper and more complicated than most of the other characters in the Harry Potter series. He is bitter, unpleasant, and downright nasty, so why don't all Harry Potter readers hate him?

HANDFUL

In *The Philosopher's Stone* (Book 1), we expect Snape to be the villain of the piece. We're convinced that he tried to kill Harry at the Quidditch match, and many of us would have bet our life savings (just like Harry) that he had let the troll in as a diversion on Halloween. When we get to the end of the book and realise that contrary to what we actually believed, Professor Snape has been going out of his way for a whole year to keep Harry alive, we are surprised to say the least.

How could we have misjudged this man? Why did we assume that because of his venomous appearance and general nastiness he was in league with Lord Voldemort? I know that when I first read Book 1, I passionately hated Snape. I felt he was unnecessarily cruel to Harry and, indeed, the majority of his students (after all, who needs to be called a 'dunderhead' on their very first day at school?). When I finished the book and realised that he really wasn't as bad as I had previously believed, I was still a little unsure about him. After all, what was all that business Dumbledore mentioned about hating James Potter's '*memory in peace*'? {Ch17, p217}

In Book 2, we see several more examples of Snape's nastiness towards Harry and we hate him for his unfairness (yet we quite admire his dislike for Lockhart). Although we're not keen on him, it's still in the back of our minds that he saved Harry's life the previous year and therefore can't really be evil. We also recognize that Professor Dumbledore trusts Snape (true, he trusted Quirrell and look what *he* was up to!). We see that Snape wastes no time this year trying to get Harry expelled and taken off the Quidditch team and we continue to ponder why he hates Harry so passionately—and why he also hated Harry's father.

In Book 3, we get an insightful look into the workings of Professor Snape's mind. We begin to find out more about his hostility towards James and see his reaction when triumph eludes him twice in this book: once when he fails to get Harry expelled for sneaking off to Hogsmeade, and then when Sirius Black escapes (meaning Snape can kiss goodbye to the Order of Merlin once and for all). We can't help but dislike Snape in Book 3 a little bit more than we did in the last one, and applaud his downfalls as triumphs for Harry and the rest. However, I also think that in this book, the whole Snape situation is portrayed less caustically than in the previous books. For example, some of the nastiness is turned toward him this time – the Marauder's Map insults Snape to his face, while Sirius allows the unconscious Snape's head to keep banging on the ceiling as they are returning from the Shrieking Shack. Yet, we see Snape's hatred for Harry intensify, culminating by the end with Snape in a total rage. It becomes apparent that regardless of what went before, Snape is a nasty piece of work with a serious grudge – although, as Dumbledore said, "*some wounds run too deep for the healing.*"{B5, Ch37, p735}

Despite his grudge and his attitude, because Snape is such an enigma, we find ourselves quite intrigued by his behaviour. (After all, he has maintained his aura of unpleasantness for an extremely long while.)

In my opinion, it is in Book 4 that Snape really comes into his own character. We find out that he used to be a Death Eater, but switched sides to join with Dumbledore. With this revelation, all sorts of questions are triggered in our heads such as: why did Snape change sides? And why is Dumbledore so sure that Snape can be trusted? In Book 4, we can appreciate Snape's good side – as we see he risked his life against Voldemort. We are given the opportunity to either dislike or admire him throughout the book. But, whatever we feel towards him, by the end of the novel we are forced to acknowledge his allegiance when it is hinted that he has to go back to Voldemort. We appreciate that this is very risky and he could potentially lose his life. I believe it is at this point in the series that we readers can appreciate this man, who has shown himself to be unpleasant, formidable, and at some points downright scary, as essentially a 'good guy'.

But what about Book 5? In there, our feelings about Snape seem to be a continuation from the last. We are dimly aware that he's not the nicest person in the world, but we also know *that he's up to something* concerning Voldemort, something that apparently entails him risking his own life. Like Harry, we treat Snape with much more curiosity at this stage, and are desperate for more to be revealed. We feel this attraction through the book's progress, but it is when Snape explains disdainfully that Dumbledore has assigned him the task of giving Harry private Occlumency lessons that we are able to start becoming really captivated.

The revelations about Snape's misery, both as a small child and as a teenager, come as a bit of a nasty shock. The less intelligent amongst us (and I include myself in this) had never thought of the possibility that Snape had a life of suffering and misery *before* his involvement with Voldemort. We had simply assumed that some people are just generally a bit horrible, and he was one of those people.

The further revelation that James Potter had made young Severus's life sincerely miserable was also a bit of a shock, and we could finally begin to empathise with the reasons behind Snape's loathing for Harry. Snape fans found themselves able to fully appreciate why Snape's hatred of Sirius, James, and to an extent Remus Lupin, is so intense, and also in some ways share in Snape's dislike of these characters.

When I reached the end of the fifth book, I found my feelings toward Snape to be incredibly mixed. I felt that I had a far greater understanding of his past life and experiences, but at the same time, I couldn't help thinking that, had Snape not terminated Harry's Occlumency lessons, then Sirius Black could have survived. For an hour or two, after reading Book 5 for the first time, I couldn't help resenting my favourite character. Why did Snape have to be so stubborn and petty? Harry had seen one of his worst memories…. So what? He had known how important the Occlumency lessons were. Surely his stupid pride wasn't more important than a man's life? After I'd calmed down (and dried my eyes) I started to think. In that period between Harry being held captive in Umbridge's office, and his arriving at the Ministry for Magic, Snape had done an awful lot of running around. He had worked out Harry's intentions and raised the alarm, telling the Order where Harry and the others had gone, and for what purpose. Had Snape not raised the alarm, it is possible that Harry and his friends would have died at the hands of Voldemort and the Death Eaters – ensuring the ascension to power of Lord Voldemort, and the continued rise of the Dark Order. Surely Snape's actions do more than counterbalance his prior behaviour?

As the release of the sixth book in the septology edges ever closer, we are left with a number of questions to ponder in regard to Snape. Now, after everything we've learned, there still has to be (even for Snape fans) a tiny part of us that, like Ron, questions whether Snape truly is on the 'good side'.

At the end of Book 4, Voldemort tells his supporters about the one who has left him 'forever' and would be killed{Ch33, p565}; if we assume that Crouch Junior was the loyal one and Karkaroff the cowardly one, then logically it would seem Voldemort must be speaking about Snape. However, by the end of the fifth book (a whole year later), Snape is still alive. It strikes me as strange that Voldemort would wait so long without killing Snape. It is this fact that makes me (and I'm sure other readers) seriously ponder what it is that Snape must have told Voldemort on the night of his rebirthing ceremony (if they made contact).

Another possible theory is that Snape is spying on both sides to keep himself alive—after all, self-preservation is a skill greatly associated with Slytherins. However, as Hermione takes delight in telling anybody who will listen, Dumbledore trusts Snape and if there's one thing we can be sure of, it's that Dumbledore is certainly nobody's fool.

Something else that I have pondered with regard to Snape is whether Rowling can allow a character like him to survive the series? It's obvious that there will always be a degree of mutual enmity between Snape and Harry, and from everything that Harry says at the end of Book 5, we know that he has no intention of forgiving Snape for his role in Sirius's death. However, I am confident that a point will eventually come when Harry has to acknowledge Snape has risked his life to ensure the continuing success of the 'good side'.

It seems to me that the only way Harry will ever accept that there is a decent human being encased within Snape's greasy exterior is if the formidable Potions Master dies in an act of grand heroism while saving Harry's or another important character's skin. Only then will Harry be able to respect Snape without 'losing face' or disrespecting the memory of his godfather. As a Snape fan, the death of Snape is not something to which I look forward. However, I think it's the only way Rowling will be able to allow Harry to accept Snape's sacrifices, at least without subjecting her audience to a 'pleasant' Severus Snape.

The thing that puzzles me most of all about Snape is why Harry Potter fans all over the world have such a deep-rooted affection for him. He isn't funny like Ron or full of wisdom like Dumbledore, he doesn't have the 'devil-may-care' attitude of Sirius or Hagrid's penchant for dangerous creatures. Instead, he's ill-natured, sarcastic and sometimes downright cruel, but this doesn't put us off. I think the reason that Snape has so much appeal as a character is because he is a glorious caricature of nastiness. He delivers cutting remarks with ease, takes delight in worrying his students to the point of nervous exhaustion, and sneers and billows his way around Hogwarts. Most readers love a 'bad guy', and whilst Snape's not Voldemort or even Draco Malfoy, he is still in possession of a personality so different to Harry's that we cannot help but find it appealing.

I think another reason that so many people love the character of Snape is because as readers, many of us feel we can relate to him and can compare his experiences to our own. More readers than would like to admit have come from a home where their parents fought. Others have been bullied at school, or made to feel badly because they weren't the same as everyone else. Some people know what it's like to have such a desperate desire to 'fit in' that they've mixed with the wrong crowd at some point, and many of us know how to hold a grudge (for decades if necessary!).

Snape is such a real character because there are elements of him which we share deep down. We see his experiences and associate them with our own. Snape is able to make us laugh with his put-downs and we want to cry when we catch a glimpse of his tortured past. The best thing about Snape is he's so much fun to read about, and as Snape fans, we can be safe in the knowledge that the best is yet to come with him.

─────────────── ADDITIONAL SLEUTHING NOTES ───────────────

✳ Why does Dumbledore trust Snape so much? Could there be a magical bond? Is it similar to either the debt between Harry and Wormtail? If so, what happens when debt is finally repaid? Or is it a protection like the one between Harry and Petunia – that Snape is safe *only* as long as Dumbledore is safe?

✳ If JKR feels the way she does about Snape, is she implying that there is not enough good in him? Is Snape capable of redeeming himself? What would make a bully change?

SNIVELLUS, PROFESSOR, DEATH EATER, AND SPY: THE FOUR FACES OF SNAPE

ANNA-LOUISE GEORGE ✳ NC, "COOKIE"
ENGLAND (*UK Edition*), AGE 17

Inspiration for this Discussion

As a character, Professor Severus Snape has fascinated me throughout the books. Writing this has been quite difficult in that there was so much I wanted to put in. After poring over countless books and websites, I hope I included everything that's most relevant.

12

Snape's personality and life don't appear to be homogenous (integrated), but seem to exist in blocks of separate personalities: Snivellus, Professor Snape, Death Eater and Spy. Professor Snape is one of the key figures in the Harry Potter series. As the books have progressed, we as readers have been given an antagonistic relationship with him; just as we begin to develop a more tangible understanding of him as a character and his significance in the series, another inaccessible attribute of his personality is revealed. He is one of the only constant characters of whom we have an in-depth understanding. But at the same time, he is also one of the most enigmatic.

Throughout the Harry Potter series, Snape has been rather unpredictable. Why is that? He is a very complex character. Indeed, there are four distinct facets to his personality. In what way does all this make Snape significant?

SNIVELLUS

Let's start from the very beginning (a very good place to start). But where do we begin? Do we look at our introduction to the snarky Potions Master in the first book? Or do we go as far back as we feasibly can to the image in Book 5 of the "dark-haired boy" crying in the corner, watching his father shout? I think this reversed Legilimens scene, where we see a stream of memories, is one of the most important in establishing Snape as a key character in the series—not necessarily that the memories he is forced to revisit will reveal any details later on, but the mere fact that we now have this much knowledge about Snape sets him apart from the other characters. We know so little about most of the characters' childhoods and backgrounds, yet Snape has his proverbial guts spilled out unwittingly to Harry and us.

Our biggest insight into the personality of Snivellus comes from witnessing his interaction in the Pensieve with Lily Evans and James in Chapter 28, 'Snape's Worst Memory'. "*You're lucky Evans was here, Snivellus…*"

"I don't need help from filthy little Mudbloods like her!" {B5, Ch28 p571}

Aside from the intriguing anagrams of Severus Snape and Lily Evans' names (Perseus Evans, Aly Snivel), the fact that Snape has yet to ever insult Lily in front of Harry perhaps points to some kind of relationship or emotional attachment. We know that the memory, as part of the plot, serves to disillusion Harry about his father. This could be done without Lily's involvement, plus it is Snape who pushes her away. Since we don't hear Snape talking that way about Lily (his 'Mudblood comment') in the present, it suggests he had a major change in attitude.

Was Snape always the instigator, or was he a victim himself? From what we observe through the *'Protego!'* Charm and later in the Pensieve, Snape didn't have a happy childhood or adolescence. We see him either alone or being abused, which hints at a possible rationale for the seemingly unpleasant man he has become. Yet, it isn't until the end of 'Snape's Worst Memory' that Harry begins to empathize with Snivellus, conceding that he knows *exactly how Snape felt*, when being taunted by Harry's father. We might also want to look at Snape's reaction to Harry's memories of his early childhood, when Harry asks, *'Did you see everything I saw?'* Snape replies *'To whom did the dog belong?'* {Ch 24, p472} Even though Harry bristles at the inquiry, there is nothing offensive or hostile in Snape's comment. In fact, it may be quite a wake-up call to Snape that one of Harry's relatives set their vicious bulldog on him, so at this point in the story, it looks like Snape and Harry could work things out after all. While we recognize their similarities, it appears Snape and Harry don't—or at least if they do, it's only briefly, and quickly forgotten.

The connection between Harry and Snape is made clear in the 'Seen and Unforeseen' Chapter, where Harry is forced to relive the humiliations *'inflicted upon him in primary school'* {Ch26, p520}, while similarly, Snape relives the traumas and humiliations in his childhood. Why Snivellus didn't place these memories in the Pensieve also could be relevant. He, like Harry, may have forgotten that he still possesses these memories—or perhaps so many of his memories are like this that it's only worth putting the worst of them in the Pensieve.

Harry and Snape's interaction here could foreshadow even worse events if they don't come to a mutual understanding. Harry clings onto Snape's injustices (most of the time with good reason) and Snape doesn't seem to be able to look past Harry as James, Version II. These paralleled sets of memories, resulting in two very different people, are highly suggestive of JK Rowling's theme of 'the choices we make'.

THE PROFESSOR

How Snape responds to the delicate precision of potion-making and Occlumency, versus his reaction to Harry viewing his memories, can be a measure of the balance between Snape as a professor and as a grudging man. When Harry recalls the memory of Cedric in the graveyard during his first Occlumency lesson, Snape, *'looked paler than usual, and angrier.'* Snape may be both: angry that Harry is failing to master Occlumency, and upset that, as a Professor, he should have been able to help Cedric.{Ch24, p473} What if Snape couldn't help save him because he was in the Death Eater circle at the time?

In this scene, he appears more aggressive and angry, not the collected Potions Professor we know. He is even hypocritical to his own words as he, too, becomes emotional. This draws a distinction between Harry failing here at Occlumency and failing later, when Snape discovers Harry's dream about Rookwood during another lesson in Chapter 26. In that lesson, he remarks to Harry, *'you are neither special nor important.'* While that is the disdainful Potions Master we all know here, after Harry's angry outburst, Snape remains calm and cold; even after Harry breaks into his memories, Snape is still collected, though shaken and pale. In fact, he gives what must be the slightest hint of a compliment to Harry in Snape language, *'but there is no doubt that it was effective.'* What do all these mixed reactions point us towards? Perhaps Snape is first and foremost a professor whose responsibility it is to look after the students, but he is constantly in conflict with his own emotions.

THE DEATH EATER

In contrast to Snivellus and Professor Snape, we have Snape as the ex-Death Eater and as spy extraornaire. Well, perhaps Snape is no 007 (no women for one thing), but in the present, he works secretly for the Order of the Phoenix as a spy (truly dangerous espionage). These are the two roles we know the least about; yet JK Rowling has dropped some big hints…

In order to speculate about his role as a spy, we need to look at his motivation for being a Death Eater. We can happily use canon to theorise why Snape became a Death Eater. Chapter 28 shows us his Slytherin attitude towards Muggle-borns. We also learn that he was picked on and had, what we believe to be, an abusive father. Plus, he was possibly often alone. All this seems like reasonable motivation for Snape's Death Eater background. He probably had a need to belong to a group, and to have power and control, too. In the most simplistic sense, these would simultaneously provide good enough reasons to try to break away from Voldemort, as the benefits of power and belonging are illusions. We can all surmise being a Death Eater is no fun at all. But this can't be the only reason it didn't work out—it must be deep and personal.

As an ex-Death Eater, Snape is in a good position to play the part once more and, therefore, spy on Voldemort's inner circle. However, there are several questions we need to raise in considering how Snape would go about rejoining Voldemort. It was publicly (at least in front of a whole jury) announced that Snape was a spy. How did Voldemort react to this? He has to know, doesn't he? Did Snape attend the Rebirthing Ceremony for Voldemort? What is Snape's relationship with the other known Death Eaters?

Voldemort's reaction is what could be construed as the most difficult one to understand, as we have several pieces of seemingly contradictory information. Snape was revealed to be a spy, so presumably this information would filter down to Voldemort somehow, and as we know, Voldemort does not forgive or forget. Yet, we also know that Lucius Malfoy, a known Death Eater, is still in contact with Snape. Sirius Black comments that Snape is Malfoy's 'lapdog' {Ch24, p460} and Umbridge later declares: 'Lucius Malfoy always speaks most highly of you!' {Ch32, p657} Would Snape still be so 'tight' with Lucius Malfoy if he were on Voldemort's hit list? Also, in the 'The Death Eaters' chapter in Book 4, Voldemort talks about the three missing Death Eaters—one is a coward, one is faithful, and one who has 'resigned'. Even if Snape were one of the three missing Death Eaters, Voldemort used the phrase, 'One, who I **believe** has left me forever' {B4, Ch33, p565} 'Believe' is an ambiguous word, which means whoever that certain Death Eater was can still revert to the dark side. We are drawn to the conclusion that Voldemort believed Snape was his spy against Dumbledore, making Snape a double-agent—leaving us all a little shaky about where his loyalties lie.

Speaking of loyalties brings us to the Quirrell confrontation in the first book. In Book 1, Voldemort is possessing Quirrell, so shouldn't he know that Snape is working for Dumbledore? Then again, wouldn't Snape sense Voldemort? Could Snape have believed Quirrell wanted the Stone for himself? There's something odd about what happened that year.

So, if we smooth out all the creases, we see it is feasible that Snape could walk right back into that circle… or perhaps he never walked fully out of it.

The Spy

We know Snape works for the Order, but the question is, what does he do? We are given an ambiguous answer to this in Chapter 26. After Harry suggests in a temper that finding out what the Dark Lord is saying to his Death Eaters is Snape's job, Snape replies, 'That is my job.' {Ch26, p521} This confirms our initial suspicions from Book 4, where Dumbledore in the Pensieve scene tells the court that Snape turned spy against Voldemort at a 'great personal risk' and that he is again playing spy. How Snape is spying brings up many questions.

When is Snape available to spy? What methods does he use? (Veritaserum? Pensieve? Polyjuice? Legilimency? Occlumency? Animagus? Metamorphmagus?) Deception runs rampant through the Harry Potter series, and we see many ways to spy and gather information from one's enemy. How many of these ways can we connect directly to Snape? There are certainly some running references to Animagi, especially to bats. '*Not unless he can turn himself into a bat or something,*' said Harry. {B4, Ch29, p491} Also, being hung upside-down like a bat in 'Snape's Worst Memory' from Book 5 might be an obscure clue. These questions touch upon Snape's process of spying, without even beginning to examine the reasons *why*.

Why Snape turned spy is a juicy bit that JK Rowling seems intent on keeping from us until the end. We can map out his life to a degree, but it becomes blurry in the transition from Death Eater to spy. Dumbledore has shared quite a few things with Harry that he considers secret (Neville's parents, for instance), but won't yet give Harry the reason why he knows Snape turned from Voldemort. Nor will Dumbledore reveal why he so vehemently trusts Snape.

The only other character to outwardly trust Snape is Hermione, who remarks in Book 5, '*I think Dumbledore's probably got plenty of evidence, even if he doesn't share it with you, Ron.*' {Ch12, p212} We know that in Book 3 Hermione keeps Lupin's secret. It makes you speculate whether she knows more about Snape then she's letting on…

SNAPE WHO?

And speculating is what we Harry Potter Sleuths do. I expect Snape will be a surprising source of revelations of the past. I also think we can conclude that Snape will play a pivotal role in the future of the series—the question is which personality will eventually dominate?

ADDITIONAL SLEUTHING NOTES

* Why was Snape not present at the rescue in the Department of Mysteries? Was he "lying low" so he wouldn't have to become involved in situations where he would have to declare his loyalty?
* Which parts of Snape's personality are what he wants to be vs. what he can't control?

THE SOCIOLOGY OF SEVERUS SNAPE

KARI RATLIFF ✳ CoS, "DOG STAR"
USA (*US Edition*), AGE 22

Inspiration for this Discussion

The character of Severus Snape has intrigued me ever since I first read the Harry Potter books in late 2001. I went to the first movie just for the sake of seeing what all the hubbub was about—I bought the first three books the next day. I devoured the books in the span of a few days, falling in love with the series immediately. The further I got into it, the more I began to like the ill-tempered Potions Master. It was at that point that I also began to wonder what events in this man's past must have shaped him into the person portrayed on JK Rowling's pages. Enter the field of sociology, my minor at East Tennessee State University and a field that appealed to a lifelong interest of mine — figuring out what makes people tick. As journalism major, I am also passionate about writing, so when you put the two together, posting and analyzing on fan forums is a perfect fit for me. Through discussions about the character in many threads on the Chamber of Secrets Forums, I began to form several theories (all grounded in the field of sociology) about why Severus Snape is the way he is. Upon reading Harry Potter and the Order of the Phoenix, *the tiny glimpses we were given into Snape's childhood and adolescence only served to confirm theories I was already cultivating. I began to feel more and more like I was on the right track. This essay contains rationalizations and analyses of several facets of the cunning but cranky professor and seeks to find scientifically-supported explanations for his often-baffling behavior.*

 12

Professor Snape, resident Potions Master at Hogwarts School of Witchcraft and Wizardry, is one of the most hated, most loved and most perplexing characters in the series. The reasoning behind many fans' hatred for him is easy to understand—Snape hates Harry. Since we're all fans of Harry, it would make sense to hate anyone who dislikes him, right? So then, why don't we all hate Professor Snape? Why do some of us design fan sites dedicated to the "greasy git" and create thread upon thread dedicated to analyzing his character on Harry Potter forums? Why are we creating clubs in his honor, adorning our virtual desktops with Snape wallpaper, skipping straight to the chapters where we know he has the biggest parts …well, you get the picture. Are the people who love—and sometimes sympathize with—Snape really just entirely off their rockers? No, I don't think so, and I'm not just saying that because I'm one of them.

The allure of Severus Snape, for the most part, lies in the aura of mystique that surrounds him—and his mysterious past is the portion of the character to which many of us are drawn. However, we readers are not completely in the dark about Snape's past, thanks to the many clues JK Rowling has given us along the way. But these are still just clues, and the character's past remains largely shrouded in darkness. Instead of having the key to figuring out such a complex character handed to us, we have to look for it, and the field of sociology holds many such keys to explaining Snape's behavior. Of course, trying to explain his erratic (sometimes bordering on violent) behavior is half the fun. By using standard, sociological analysis techniques, we can get a glimpse into the potential motivation for Snape's behavior.

For our first few pieces of the puzzle that is Snape, let's look at his early years. We don't know much about this period in our dear potions master's life, but what we do know could be very significant. The most crucial moments in our psychosocial development occur in the first several years of life. It is during our childhood when we begin to develop a sense of self and start figuring out where we belong in the grand scheme of life. Most of us are raised by loving, nurturing parents who provide a favorable environment for healthy social development. By contrast, when the home environment isn't conducive to normal development, disaster can result. Children form many lasting ideas about themselves (including whether they see themselves as strong, weak, smart, stupid, loved and cared for…or merely tolerated)[1] based on their parents' and others' behavior toward them.

We gain an important glimpse into Snape's childhood in Chapter 26 of Book 5, during one of Harry's Occlumency lessons. When Harry casts his Shield Charm, he sees snippets of Snape's memories, one of which features a *"hook-nosed man shouting at a cowering woman, while a small dark-haired boy cried in a corner."* If we assume for the purpose of this discussion that the "hook-nosed man" is Snape's father, the "cowering woman" his mother, and the "small dark-haired boy" is Severus himself, then it's obvious the Snape household was an abusive one. Documented sociological research suggests children who are the victims of physical or emotional abuse will bear the emotional scars from that experience for their entire lives and find themselves virtually unable to form healthy relationships as adults.[2]

This seems to be directly in line with the Snape we see outwardly portrayed in the books—a loner who doesn't seem to have a friendly or positive relationship with anyone. Instead, he likely drives others away with his overbearing, authoritarian tendencies, which could be seen as a late-blooming overcompensation for having felt weak in contrast to his "strong", authoritarian father (even if this image was derived from putting an undue positive spin on a bad situation). Or it could also be seen as delayed overcompensation for the weakness he felt at being teased during his own school years, as he was by Sirius Black and James Potter. Everything he does seems to be one great, big defense mechanism aimed at keeping others from discovering the "true" Snape under the rough exterior.

But why is Snape so afraid of people discovering whom he really is inside? For the same reason most people put on airs to look tough or authoritative—they feel weak and don't want others to see them as such. One would have to be a fairly sensitive person to need the kind of thick, outer shell Snape has built for himself over the years, and most people who put such effort into never letting their emotions show are largely doing it because they have been burned by doing so in the past. Young Sirius' and James' nickname for Snape—"Snivellus"—suggests that just such a thing may have happened, since "snivel" means to sniffle, whine or complain tearfully. From this nickname alone, it becomes apparent that Snape probably wasn't always so tough. In fact, he may have been exactly the opposite in his school years.

In Chapter 28 of Book 5, (appropriately titled "Snape's Worst Memory") readers see a scene in the Pensieve from Snape's school days—something Snape presumably views as one of the most humiliating moments in his past, and one he wants no one to know about. In that memory, Harry witnesses his father and Sirius teasing and torturing a 15-year-old Snape, while their classmates look on and laugh. Experiences such as this one, piled one on top of the other (as they are, in the real world, they are almost never isolated incidents), cause serious, emotional consequences for their victims, although the bullies never stop to consider that. Victims of bullies bear lifelong, emotional scars in the form of low self-esteem and sense of self-worth, all because someone wanted to have a little "fun". Victims of bullying often suffer from a terminal lack of confidence in social situations, or overcompensate by being nastily totalitarian when they find themselves in positions of authority. And Professor Snape certainly falls in the latter category.

It seems Snape was an outcast throughout most, if not all, of his childhood as well as his years at Hogwarts. In Book 3, we learn that Sirius thoughtlessly risked Snape being killed by werewolf Remus Lupin during their sixth year at Hogwarts, yet Sirius was hardly punished for his transgressions. Events like this fit the general tone of perception most people at Hogwarts seem to have had for the Marauders and Snape. The Marauders were popular Gryffindors, and people looked upon them as if they could do no wrong. But Snape was unpopular, a Slytherin, and had a reputation for being into the Dark Arts. So, who were people more likely to sympathize with—James and his Marauders or Snape?

The more events like this transpire, and the more the bullies' victim sees his attackers go unpunished or even rewarded in some cases, the more he begins to feel resentful and isolated from society. Social acceptance is an integral part of healthy development, and when a person feels rejected by his peers, the emotional effects can be devastating. Even worse, when that person becomes desperate for social acceptance, he may engage in destructive or deviant behaviors to gain any semblance of acceptance to fill that void.[3] This chain of events is one potential reason why Snape joined the Death Eaters, who perfectly fit the bill of a deviant subculture.[4] Additionally, in desperately seeking acceptance and camaraderie, young Snape was vulnerable to Lord Voldemort's alluring propaganda and fell victim to it. When he realized what he had done, he may have wanted out, thus leading him to return, desperate for help, to Albus Dumbledore at Hogwarts. Given Dumbledore's personality, he could very likely have been one of the only people who ever seemed to show an ounce of caring for young Severus Snape.

Another sociological concept that is central to the development of Snape's character is the self-fulfilling prophecy, a daughter concept of famous sociologist Howard Becker's labeling theory.[5] Readers find out early on in Book 1, that Slytherins are people best avoided because *"there's not a witch or a wizard who went bad who wasn't in Slytherin."* Right from the outset, anyone who has the misfortune of having the Sorting Hat call out, "Slytherin!" while atop his head is automatically branded as being a Dark Wizard in training. Any Slytherin is labeled as deviant, regardless of whether or not he has ever engaged in deviant behaviors (such as practicing the Dark Arts). As this label becomes more pervasive, those who are being labeled begin to lose interest in fighting it and may start to participate in the behavior they have been accused of having.

Since people already thought Snape was well versed in the Dark Arts (even though there has been no concrete evidence of this, as of Book 5), perhaps he decided he should just go ahead and do it. What was there to lose? Besides, it could make him seem tough, and maybe then people would leave him alone. Being prematurely labeled as someone involved in the Dark Arts, coupled with desperation for acceptance and belonging, could have been the perfect combination to lead Snape directly into Voldemort's fold. In fact, Sirius' claim in {Book 3, Ch27} that Snape was an expert in Dark Arts when he first came to Hogwarts could also be a product of a concept called retrospective labeling. This portion of labeling theory involves the reinterpretation of a person's past to incorporate the beginnings of deviance committed in the present, regarding that those beginnings were present in the original events.[6]

Snape's life has obviously not been an easy one, and doesn't appear to be getting easier anytime soon. However, it does look as if it will become progressively easier with each new book to understand why some of us find Snape so intriguing. Based on what we know, people aren't born evil, mean or nasty—society makes them that way. And Snape is a perfect example of what happens when events that are detrimental to healthy psychosocial development happen one after the other, leaving that person emotionally disabled for life.

So the next time you find yourself hating the "greasy git", think about what kind of childhood he must have had. Think about how he came to be the person we now know as Severus Snape, resident potions master of Hogwarts School of Witchcraft and Wizardry.

─────── Additional Sleuthing Notes ───────

✳ Why was the Order of Merlin so important to Snape? Is it because of his Slytherin ambition, or could it relate to his insecurities? Does he need external validation of his worth?

✳ Who knew about the Marauders incident?

✳ How does the self-fulfilling prophecy relate to JKR's theme of "choices"? Even though Snape may have been predisposed to turn into a Dark Wizard, wouldn't it ultimately be his choice?

✳ Why do people like Snape (a bully) so much? JK Rowling, is a bit concerned about it, saying, *"This is a very worrying thing"…"Why do you love him? Why do people love Snape? I do not understand this. Again, it's bad boy syndrome, isn't it? It's very depressing."*{*JK Rowling, Edinburgh Book Festival, August, 2004*}

[1] Macionis, John J., Sociology, Prentice Hall, (New Jersey, 1997), p133.
[2] Ibid, p472
[3] Ibid, p213
[4] Sullivan, Thomas J., Introduction to Social Problems, 5th ed., Allyn and Bacon, (Boston, 2000), pg. 7.
[5] Macionis, John J., Sociology, Prentice Hall, (New Jersey, 1997), pg. 210.
[6] Ibid, p211

PROFESSOR SEVERUS SNAPE:
A CASE OF CAULDRON MELTDOWN?

J. LIBBY ✴ NEW CLUES FORUM
USA (*US Edition*), AGE 35

Inspiration for this Discussion

Professor Severus Snape has long fascinated me. He is such a complex and mysterious character. The more information I receive about Snape, the more I want to know. He raises my suspicions— I find myself questioning his motives for practically everything he does. Is he scapegoat, bullying antagonist or master strategist? Is he misunderstood or even a hero?

In the beginning of the series, Snape seems a perfect picture of calm, cool and collected, with a demeanor that is usually as cold as ice. What makes his chilly persona crack, exposing the bubbling depths of his wrath? "A boy like no other…perhaps?" {B4, Ch23, p514}

I am always struck by how unlucky Snape seems to have been ever since Harry made his debut at Hogwarts. Snape and Harry seem to be working toward the same goal but they have quite different methods. How does Harry manage to rob Snape of his glory and recognition time and time again? I find it fascinating to watch Snape's tightly controlled persona unravel in each of the progressive books. So, I want to track the demise of Snape's control and his descent into his inevitable meltdown. I have so many pages of notes on Snape that it's hard to narrow it down. I hope I have not missed too many overt points, and that I have been able to highlight some normally overlooked ones.

12

How is it that Snape's soft-spoken personality can become an overflowing cauldron of contempt in a matter of minutes due to "Famous Harry Potter"? The mere sight of Harry seems to light a flame under him. Harry can push Snape beyond the realm of his calculated control and sometimes, it seems, out of his mind. Harry, alone, is the one who can light Snape's fuse, and then the fireworks really get going.

The image of Professor Snape is that of a thin, "sallow-skinned" wizard with "a curtain of greasy black hair" and a "hooked nose."{B1, Ch7, p126 *US*} He is often described with "billowing" black robes flowing out behind him. Snape is also a sinister man with black, cold, empty eyes, resembling "dark tunnels" which "glinted malevolently" when provoked. {B4, Ch17, p276} Luckily, Snape has the dark personality to match his unique appearance. He has no qualms in calling his students "dunderheads" or "moronic." Snape usually sides with Slytherin when student arguments erupt in or around class. He looks as though *"Christmas had been cancelled"* when he fails to have Harry and Ron expelled.{B2, Ch5, p81} He looms in the background, trying not to laugh as Professors McGonagall and Dumbledore examine Mrs. Norris. When Gilderoy Lockhart suggests asking him for a love potion, Snape looks as if he would poison the first person who would dare ask. Of course, he actually did plan to poison Harry in class in order to test his antidote. {B4, Ch18, p300-1}

Harry seems to pick up on Professor Snape's animosity rather quickly. After his first lesson with Snape *"he knew he'd been wrong. Snape didn't dislike Harry—he **hated** him."*{B1, Ch8, p136} We are all chasing red herrings throughout the first book—eager to condemn Snape as the vicious villain. It is shocking to find him a spy for the Order. One of the hidden clues to Snape's disposition is his display after the Quidditch match he refereed. He doesn't seem to be the "hock-a-loogie" type, with his quiet, intense presence, but there he goes for all to see and spits on the ground after Harry wins the match. {B1, Ch13, p224} Is it a small glimpse of his contempt for "Famous Harry"? I think Snape was only suffering from a case of humble pie and found the taste not to his liking.

At times, Snape seems to confuse Harry with his father, James, which is apparently a common occurrence among people who knew the elder Potter. However, Snape doesn't make a flattering comparison when he tells Harry his father was an arrogant show off. "*Strutting around the place with his friends and admirers…The resemblance between you is uncanny.*" {B3, Ch, p284} He goes on to tell Harry that, like his Quidditch-star father, Harry thinks he is above the rules. (How many times do you think James caught a snitch under Snape's rather large, hooknose? One time too many is my guess!)

Snape seems to have a great concern about rules and the breaking of them. He points out Harry's inability to follow them on many occasions, such as when Snape confronts Harry in Chapter 14 of Book 3 about his "head" being seen in Hogsmeade. Maybe Snape has such an issue with following "the rules" because he was usually the one on whom James broke them!

I see a huge parallel between two events that involve Snape—one with James and the other with Harry. In Book 5, we get a glimpse at Snape's "worst memory", which concludes with James dangling Snape upside down for all his classmates to see (including his gray underpants). In Book 1, Snape has his leg bitten by Fluffy and Harry startles Snape, who is in the teacher's lounge being tended to by Filch, in yet *another* compromising position. "*Snape's face was twisted with fury as he dropped his robes quickly to hide his leg.*"{Ch11, p182} The contorted look of rage on Snape's face is so horrific that Harry has a hard time banishing it from his mind that night so he can sleep. Was that another James flashback for poor Snape? Is that why his reaction seemed a bit over the top?

It may not have been as heroic a gesture as first believed, but James did save Snape's life. Nonetheless, James' death doesn't seem to have softened Snape's hatred of him either: "*You'd have died like your father, too arrogant to believe you might be mistaken about Black.*" {B3, Ch19, p361}

In Book 3, Snape seems to have reached a critical point. One of his least favorite classmates, Marauder Remus Lupin, is appointed as teacher of the Defense Against the Dark Arts, the very position Snape covets. Plus he has "James Jr." to contend with on a daily basis. The kicker is that Sirius, his "arch enemy", is on the loose. I think the stress is just a bit too much for him. To no avail, Snape has been warning Dumbledore that Lupin would be trying to help Sirius. Snape dreams of catching Sirius—that would be his crowning achievement and ultimate payback. But Harry manages to snatch away his visions of glory once again. When he finds out he has been robbed of his "Order of Merlin, First Class", he boils over into a full rage. His normal approach of silky-soft threats is turned into a screaming fit (most unbecoming).

"'*YOU DON'T KNOW POTTER!*' *Snape howled, pointing at Harry and Hermione. His face was twisted; spit was flying from his mouth.*" {B3, Ch22, p419} Unfortunately for Snape he is unable to prove it. It is then that things between him and Harry unravel completely. I think this is the defining moment—when Harry replaces James as Snape's most hated Potter. Snape develops a curious twitch and "*he was constantly flexing his fingers, as though itching to place them around Harry's throat.*"{p429-430} The summer apart did not, as far as I can see, cool any of the animosity. Harry and Snape seem to hate each other more than ever.

Does Snape set such high standards for following rules because he is the Potions Master? Potion making is a highly precise branch of magic. These concoctions must be made in a very specific manner, regardless of how one feels; otherwise, all your efforts are worthless. But when followed precisely, incredible elixirs can be created. Snape seems to find extreme satisfaction in keeping this area, as well as his own emotions, always under control. In contrast, Harry seems to be pulled willy-nilly by his heartstrings, letting his highly charged emotions rule his decision-making. Snape has learned to detach, to a point. Perhaps this is his reason for being a "superb Occlumens."{B5, Ch24, p527} And yet, this superb Occlumens doesn't quite rid *himself* of all emotions, does he? Although he may consider himself unemotional, Snape appears to be drawing from negative energy. Perhaps that is why he uses Dumbledore's Pensive—to draw out the memories that are so highly charged, for he can't seem to focus with them stirring around in his mind.

Based on the information about emotions, I have a theory about how Snape is such an effective Occlumens. It comes from Sirius' description about being able to fool the Dementors to escape Azkaban. His frustration from knowing that he was innocent wasn't a happy thought exactly—so the Dementors could not take it away. Maybe Snape uses his **anger** as a way to keep people out of his mind, or to keep focused on the task at hand.

Snape tells Harry that Lord Voldemort can almost always tell when someone is lying to him. He informs Harry that Legilimency is Lord Voldemort's tool to extract information. We know at several junctures in the series that Harry is convinced Snape can read minds. Snape never really explains how Legilimency is performed, but does say the mind is not read like a book. Clearing one's mind is a safeguard to keep it from being broken into, or at least not handing Lord Voldemort its keys. Snape seems to enjoy enraging Harry before each Occlumency attempt. Is his goal to see if the "Famous Harry Potter" can master another highly skilled branch of magic… or is Snape trying to foil Harry's attempts to overthrow Lord Voldemort so he can *finally* be the one to step in and save the day? Are his motives calculated or emotional? Unfortunately, because Snape is such a good Occlumens, we don't know the answer.

We don't know what Snape's motives are, but he appears to give Harry help when it seems very unlikely. In Book 1, he saves Harry from Quirrell's curse. In Book 3, he "saves" Harry in the Shrieking Shack. It seems irrelevant to point out how wrong his assumptions or motives are for doing this—the fact is, he shows up. In Book 4, Snape is right beside Dumbledore when Harry is saved from the fake Mad-Eye Moody. Finally, in Book 5, Snape is Harry's last hope in saving Sirius. Even though I am sure he doesn't want to, Snape pulls through. He even goes into the Forbidden Forest to look for Harry. All of this is highly suggestive. It could just as easily be pointed out that in all of those instances, Snape could have been trying to ruin Harry's plans. But was he reacting or calculating? What is it about Harry that sets him off?

And yet, Dumbledore trusts Snape. Like Harry, we don't know why Snape is on his second chance or what he did with his first one. But for now—I'll have to take Dumbledore's word for Snape's trustworthiness.

And also for now, I'll have to wonder why Harry keeps driving Snape's cauldron to the boiling point. Will this meltdown spill over into books 6 and 7?

ADDITIONAL SLEUTHING NOTES

* As Harry grows up and becomes stronger, will he begin to take advantage of Snape's emotional instability?
* Occlumency seemed to be causing Harry some head-splitting problems -- could it also be causing some of Snape's problems?

PROFESSOR SNAPE AND THE DEFENSE
AGAINST THE DARK ARTS POSITION

S. SCHWEDER ✳ CoS, "SERPENTINE"
GERMANY (*UK Edition*), ADULT

Inspiration for this Discussion

I have always been puzzled by the fact that even though Snape is a very good dueler and very interested in Defense Against the Dark Arts, Dumbledore refuses to give him the position. Since Dumbledore always has his reasons for doing things, it made me wonder why he continues to hire DADA proffessors that do not last more than one year, and is keeping Snape as the Potions Master instead. I question whether the position too close for comfort, or if Dumbledore has another underlying reason for refusing Snape.

HANDFUL

In each of the Harry Potter books we've been told that Professor Snape wants the Defense Against the Dark Arts (DADA) position. In the first four books we always heard it from third persons—which has caused suspicions, and theories to go along. But in Book 5, we're told at last that it's true, by the Potions Master, himself: Snape does indeed want the Defense Against the Dark Arts position. He has even been applying for it every year since he started teaching at Hogwarts. And Dumbledore has been refusing him year after year. {B5, Ch17, p323}

I find this puzzling. Why does Snape insist on that position when he's so capable as a Potions Master? Both the Mandrake Restorative Draught in Book 2 {Ch9, p110} and the "particularly complex" Wolfsbane Potion in Book 3 {Ch8, p118} were prepared by him, and worked fine. As for his teaching abilities—Snape isn't a nice teacher, granted, but he's effective. In spite of his demeanor in class, his students keep succeeding in the end-of-year exams. Even High Inquisitor Umbridge in Book 5 was impressed with how advanced his Potions class is. {Ch17, p323}

The other question is why does Dumbledore keep refusing him? Just because there's nobody to take over Potions? Dumbledore found—and hired—enough candidates for Defense Against the Dark Arts even if not all of them were capable, and he can't possibly believe Defense Against the Dark Arts to be less important than Potions. None of it adds up, or does it?

To shed more light on these questions, let's take a closer look at Defense Against the Dark Arts on the one hand, and Dark Arts on the other. Both advanced Dark Arts spells and advanced Defense Against Dark Arts spells seem to depend pretty much on the state of mind of the spellcaster.

The basis of advanced Dark Arts magic is presumably a negative state of mind—evil intent. The Unforgivable Curses are obviously powerful Dark spells, and to cast them you have to really "mean them". This is certainly valid for the Cruciatus Curse, as we've been told by Bellatrix Lestrange in Book 5 {Ch36, p715}, and probably for the Imperius and Killing Curses, too. Even Dark creatures or beings are distinguished from other magical creatures by their evil intent, such as Redcaps, Kappas and (at full moon) werewolves.

Advanced Defense Against the Dark Arts magic, on the other hand, seems to be based on a positive state of mind. Book 3 tells us that to defend yourself against boggarts you need a mental image that makes you laugh {Ch7, p101}. The Patronus is a powerful spell against Dementors, but you need a happy thought to cast it. {Ch12, p176} Maybe it's similar for other advanced Defense Against the Dark Arts spells. Even Legilimency and Occlumency from Book 5 would allow the same pattern. They appear to be advanced subjects—obscure skills that apparently aren't on the Hogwarts syllabus, otherwise Harry could have been taught by any NEWT student. Consider that Occlumency, as a "defensive spell," needs a calm and empty mind shielded from emotions. {Ch24, p473} Legilimency, as an "aggressive spell," requires an intrusion into someone else's mind, and could actually be considered a Dark Art. {Ch24, p468} The spells seem to be like two sides of a coin.

Why would Snape want the Defense Against the Dark Arts position so badly? According to Sirius in Book 4, Snape was already very skilled at Dark Arts as a first-year and he became a Death Eater later. {Ch27, p460} But Book 5 tells us that he did work hard for his Defense Against the Dark Arts O.W.L., and he's been after the post since he first started teaching. {Ch28, p564} Yet, Dumbledore keeps denying him the position. Why? Does he distrust Snape, in spite of his words? Does he not find him competent enough? Or, is it because of the emotional state necessary for Defense Against the Dark Arts?

Dumbledore states his trust for Snape throughout the books, despite his past and without giving a concrete reason. And yet, according to JK Rowling in an appearance at the Royal Albert Hall in June 2003, Dumbledore *"feared that [the Defense Against the Dark Arts position] would bring out the worst in him"*. What is that supposed to mean? If he were worried that Snape would use his Dark Arts knowledge against the students, he would surely have kept him from Potions as well. Poisons, anyone? We aren't told of any student actually poisoned though—rather, we hear of several potions accidents prevented in time. In Book 3, when Snape subs for Lupin, he doesn't curse anyone either—he "only" gives subtle hints about Lupin's true nature (which seems to have gone unpunished by Dumbledore). {Ch9, p127} Even after the Pensieve incident in Book 5, when Snape would probably be in the mood for an Unforgivable Curse, all he does is smash a jar at Harry. {Ch28, p572} Obviously, Dumbledore has good reasons to trust Snape, not only about his loyalties but also about the safety of his students.

Competence doesn't really seem to be an issue. Granted, Snape placed Kappas in Mongolia {B3, p129}, while in Newt Scamander's *Fantastic Beasts and Where to Find Them*, they are described as Japanese water demons.{p23} However, Scamander has been wrong before about Acromantulae and Basilisks not existing in Scotland. {p2, 4} Surely, Lockhart can't be called any more capable than Snape. Then there's Umbridge's teaching method of having the students read a book, which demands even less Defense Against the Dark Arts competence than Lockhart's pixies.

Could Dumbledore's reasons, then, lie on the emotional plane? Snape seems to be quite unbalanced in his emotions. We know him as a resentful person who is able to hold grudges for a long time. His vengeful attitude toward Sirius and James is one example, or his transferred resentment to James' son, Harry, is another. His temper seems to vary from unpleasant to highly volatile. Also, he doesn't take kindly to disrespect. When he subs for Lupin, the students question his temporary position—and in his reactions, he comes across even nastier than he usually does in Potions, the field where he enjoys an unquestioned authority.

The dueling scene in Book 2 {Ch11, p142} is a good example of what the problem is, when we see Snape's ill temper in connection to Defense Against the Dark Arts. His Expelliarmus spell is supposed to only disarm Lockhart, but in addition, it slams him violently into the wall. Maybe it is just because Lockhart is no real opponent for him—but Snape seems offended when Lockhart offers to take his place in brewing the

Mandrake Restorative Draught, and upon being introduced as Lockhart's assistant, Snape looked "murderous". {Ch9, p110} It's safe to assume that he didn't have any kind thoughts to spare for his opponent, and that may well have added to the effect of his spell.

Other Defense Against the Dark Arts spells pose a different problem. The Patronus charm, for instance, raises the question of whether Snape would be able to conjure up a memory happy enough to cast it. True, if in Book 5 the idea of Umbridge being sacked is good enough for Harry, the idea of Harry's expulsion could probably do the same for Snape. But in Book 3, Harry finds it hard enough to get there in the first place. {Ch12, p176} It's open for debate to how well Snape gets along with Defense Against the Dark Arts practice as opposed to theory. Still, who knows if he won't surprise us with a happy memory worthy of a Patronus?

Snape's ill temper is obvious, but we know very little about his positive emotions. They haven't been explicitly mentioned so far, but that doesn't mean that they don't exist. The fact alone that he not only left the Death Eaters but even turned spy on them *at great personal risk*" (and is apparently doing the same now) is strong proof that he isn't as bad as he appears. {B5, Ch26, p513, 521}, Snape's words are nasty, but his actions speak a different language, and it's partly because of him that Harry's still alive. Clearly, somewhere under his cold surface, he does care about his students, including rulebreaking Harry and Neville the Potions disaster. Dumbledore knows this. His trust in Snape is unwavering, in spite of Snape's past, and apparently in spite of his behaviour in class. But there might be even more. Snape's words in Book 5 about "*fools who wear their hearts proudly on their sleeves*" being "*easy prey for the Dark Lord*" are very powerful. {Ch24, p473} Could he have been talking about his own experiences, and warning Harry not to repeat his own mistake?

Apart from his anger issues, the first thing to spring to mind is the possibility of a love interest—somebody loved and lost, for instance. Fair enough, for Dumbledore keeps underscoring the importance of love to Harry. However, JK Rowling doesn't seem to support that idea. During the "Connection" interview in October 1999, when asked about a love interest for Snape, JK Rowling said (laughing): "*Who on earth would want Snape in love with them? That's a really horrible idea.*" Right after that she reacted "stunned" to a remark about a redemptive pattern to Snape because of something we will find out in Book 7. The first part might be interpreted as an indication for unrequited love or something alike, but the second part seems to be even more important.

The concept of love can, but doesn't have to, mean a love relationship. It can also mean love in the sense of caring, and in that broader sense much more would seem possible. For instance, could Lily have been the only one who cared for Snape as a friend? Between his unhappy life at Hogwarts and his family, if she was a friend, he seems to have alienated her in the Pensieve scene. As for the present, the concept of love as caring would open up different possibilities for Snape to be redeemed and regain his emotional balance—and if this is true, the solution might be closer than we think. In Book 5, independent of personal sympathies, we see Snape as a recognized member of the Order, and his spying activities seem to be of vital importance. {Ch4, p67, 73} This acceptance into the group, respect and recognition of his work, and the possibility to redeem himself may go a long way to boost his self-esteem and help him balance his emotions.

We have also seen Snape's efforts to protect his students, including Harry, plus he's begun to realize the extent of Harry's powers. He knows about Harry's ability to throw off the Imperius curse, which seems to be a rarity, especially when compared to the Crouches and Moody in Book 4. {Ch28, p471} And it would be a miracle if he hadn't heard of the slain Basilisk and Harry's diverse encounters with Voldemort. Now, in Book 5, he begins to show grudging respect. While in Potions class, his surface attitude to Harry remains unchanged, yet in the one-on-one Occlumency lessons we see him behaving more civilly towards Harry. Not a single point docked, sound advice on the "how" and "why" of the lessons—though still delivered in

Snape's snarky style {Ch27, p458, 468}—and twice we even hear him utter backhanded praise. {Ch30, p472, 522} Besides he has now seen a new side of Harry which must remind him of his own childhood. {Ch33, p521, 564} Finding Harry in his Pensieve must have crushed quite a bit of the budding respect, but the things he has learnt about Harry's abilities and memories are still there. There may be hope yet.

Snape's reasons for changing sides, whatever they are exactly, might be an insight into his actions as well. Again, we know about Snape's tendency towards vindictiveness and long-held grudges, but we also knew his protectiveness for those about whom he cares. Hatred and/or revenge for whatever evil deed done to him or somebody he cared for would be a plausible motivation for Snape to realize his mistake, turn on his former Master and his comrades, and even now, keep pursuing activities against them. It would also account for his persistent pursuit of the Defense Against the Dark Arts position in spite of his Potions skill. For Dumbledore, it would be a solid reason to trust his loyalty, but too Dark an emotion for him to allow Snape to teach DADA. It may be the emotions Snape would draw from in order to teach Defense Against the Dark Arts could easily turn out to be the wrong ones. Similar to the Duelling scene with Lockhart—and an aggressive use of Defense Against the Dark Arts spells would be a disastrous thing for students to learn. It would blur the lines between Defense Against the Dark Arts and Dark Arts.

Dumbledore keeps stressing the importance of love. Could that be the key? Could he be waiting for Snape to tap into the right feelings before he can appoint him to the Defense Against the Dark Arts position? It would tie in with in Lily's sacrifice in Book 1, Dumbledore's own feelings for Harry in Book 5, and the "power the Dark Lord knows not".{Ch12, p216 / Ch37, p739,741} Snape's turning on Voldemort, and his later deeds, have brought him closer to the end of his inner transformation and to redemption, but that's still not enough to get him there—he needs love for that, and as yet, he doesn't have enough of it. So, he's stuck with Potions.

During her appearance at the Royal Albert Hall in June 2003, JK Rowling's words—that Dumbledore refused Snape because he "*feared it would bring out the worst in him*"—didn't seem to imply that the Defense Against the Dark Arts position is actually jinxed. Dumbledore rather seems to have filled the post for only a year each time (for example, with Moody in Book 4), possibly to re-evaluate Snape's suitability on a regular basis. {Ch14, p186} So far, Snape doesn't seem to have met the requirements yet (poor guy…). But chances are that he won't be denied the Defense Against the Dark Arts job forever. Due to his past and his spying activities, he must have valuable inside knowledge about Voldemort, which will come in handy for Harry and the other students. Therefore, in my opinion, we're likely to see him get the job...either in Book 6 or 7.

─────────────── ADDITIONAL SLEUTHING NOTES ───────────────

✷ Dumbledore wants Harry to address Snape as "Professor" – could that support this theory?

✷ When Snape threw Harry out of his office, was that exploding Jar thrown, or did it just explode in place? Was it Snape's version of wandless magic?

✷ Is the key to Legilimency a "focused" mind?

✷ How does the Ministry detect underage magic? Can they detect any magic? Would being associated with the Dark Arts allow for Snape to be detected by Voldemort, or somehow leave himself more open to Voldemort?

✷ Was Snape really "teaching"? Would this be an effective way to teach any complex subject such as violin or downhill skiing? Is Snape just a bad teacher?

✴ THE PUBLIC SNAPE ✴

CINDY ERIC ✴ NEW CLUES FORUM ✴ WWW.DESIGNERPOTIONS.COM
AUSTRALIA (*UK Edition*), AGE 25¾

Inspiration for this Discussion

What a person chooses to wear (or not to wear) can usually tell us a lot about the person – in life, and especially in fiction. JK Rowling's quote that Snape "wasn't about to put on a turban" inspired me to take a closer look at what Professor Snape does wear, and what that may tell us about him, or at least what he would like us all to believe about him…

 HANDFUL

"I know all about Snape, and he wasn't about to put on a turban"

JK Rowling
AOL Chat, October 2000

Snape and a turban? We think not. But this little piece of information that Rowling "let slip" about our Potions Master tells us quite a lot about him.

It tells us that in Rowling's mind, Snape does, in fact, care about what he wears, which means that appearance is important to him (the public Snape). He cares about what people see when they look at him. JK Rowling's comment, therefore, also tells us that Snape probably *chooses* to wear only black—which he does almost all the time (rare exceptions being the Slytherin vs. Gryffindor Quidditch game in Book 3 where he wore green robes, and the late-night wanderings in his infamous long grey nightshirt in Book 4).

Why has the author decided to depict the character in this way? What does the character's choice of clothing tell us about him?

Let's start by looking at black, (which also happens to be my favourite colour). I like black because it is elegant, quiet, mysterious, and strong. It does not scream out "look at me" like red, nor does it promise to be gentle like (shudder) pink. Though, when you pass a person on the street clad completely in black from head to foot, you cannot help but take a second look. In this way, black contradicts itself—it is strong and captivating without even trying to be. Black is *literally* the opposite of white in that the scientific definition is: white contains *all* colours of light, while black is a lack of light or colour.

Of course, the answer could be this simple—perhaps Snape wears black because it is his favourite colour.

Or is it more symbolic than that? (In literature, it usually is.)

Figuratively, according to the Oxford Dictionary of Phrase and Fable, the word "black" "*has traditionally implied foreboding, evil, or melancholy*". Looking at it from this perspective, and coupling it to the rest of Snape's appearance, a slightly different picture is painted. What else do we know about him (physically)? He has black, greasy hair, pale sallow skin, uneven yellowish teeth, and is gaunt. This reminds me very much of a quote from Shakespeare's 'As You Like It': "*Everything about you demonstrating a careless desolation…*"[1] That also fits with the horrid underwear scene in Book 5, so Snape may, in fact, be very depressed.

Now, let's not look at it strictly from one perspective – w*ho else wears black exclusively in the wizarding world?*

1. Death Eaters and Lord Voldemort (it's the uniform)
2. The Weird Sisters (torn fashionably in a number of places)
3. Hogwarts students (it's the uniform).

Could Snape be influenced by one of these fashion statements?

1. Technically, Snape is still a Death Eater—he has the Dark Mark on his arm, and the job of a Death Eater requires a lifetime of service or death, {B4, Ch33} and (last we checked) Snape is still among the living...But I highly doubt that it is as simple as this.

2. The Weird Sisters, who play popular, mournful-sounding tunes with bass guitars, bagpipes, violins, and other instruments that remind me very much of a few Muggle bands. And although it is possible that Severus is a huge Weird Sisters fan, I consider it unlikely that he would choose to wear black constantly simply because of something that trivial.

3. He isn't a student anymore either (just thought I'd state the obvious). Thus, given Snape's nature, it doesn't seem difficult to imagine that he chooses to wear black because he feels most comfortable in them. It is the image of himself that he wants to project to the public; black is a part of his personality and character—both literally, and figuratively.

Then, there's that grey area...

Snape also appears be very fond of grey in his nightshirts – a lighter shade of black; an intermediate between two very strong opposites. My definition alone already implies a certain symbolic meaning:

Something that is not "all" or "nothing", often referred to as "neither black or white", is said to be "grey". The Oxford Dictionary of Phrase and Fable qualifies it further as "*an area of law or morality which does not fall into any predefined category, and which is a matter of uncertainty…*"

Put your hand up now if the above quote reminds you of a certain Potions Master. If your hand is not in the air…detention!

What is Snape really doing? Why would he sleep in grey? Because he likes it? We still don't know.

Snape is the perfect grey – seemingly caught in the middle between Death Eater and Order of the Phoenix member. A man with two "masters", one white, the other black…and a true enigma.

———————————— ADDITIONAL SLEUTHING NOTES ————————————

✱ The students at Hogwarts are required to wear black as a uniform, do the teachers have any dress code as well? What about Lockhart?

✱ Is Snape's grey nightshirt symbolic of his indecisive nature – reflecting a dilemma as to whether he should work for the good side or return to his former Death Eater self?

---

[1] Shakespeare, William. "As You Like It". Act 3, scene 2. Lines 144-145.

SEVERUS SNAPE AND MOLLY WEASLEY: COMMON THREADS

JEANNE PERRY KIMSEY ✳ CoS, "SILVER INK POT"
USA (*US Edition*), AGE 44

Inspiration for this Discussion

I never would have associated Molly Weasley with Severus Snape if it weren't for Book 2. Once I realized that they throw parallel "tirades" toward Ron and Harry in that book, I began to look for more similarities. And I certainly did find them—these two characters seem so similar, they could be related (except in appearance, of course!). And Hermione Granger seems to be just a younger version of both of them. It will be fun to look for these same sorts of comparisons in future books.

 HANDFUL

Severus Snape and Molly Weasley appear to be as different as night and day. Molly is a kind, red-haired mother of seven children. Professor Snape is a dark, coldly sarcastic Potions Master. Molly is fond of Harry Potter, treating him as one of her own children, giving him extra food and extra hugs. Professor Snape, on the other hand, treats Harry with contempt, speaks dismissively to him, humiliates him in class, and never even gives him a pat on the back.

Surprisingly, JK Rowling repeatedly writes similar scenes for both characters in which they exude almost identical emotions, opinions, and even behave alike. Why would these two characters have anything in common? What can we learn from their similarities? Do clues about them appear in the words and actions of Hermione Granger, a student, who often echoes the opinions of both these adults?

Molly and Professor Snape both obviously believe in following "the rules" and obeying those in authority. Their motto seems to be "Break a Rule—Get a Tirade." They are disciplinarians, and not always easy-going. Yet, neither Molly Weasley nor Professor Snape ever resort to any punishment more cruel than extra cleaning or hard work. They shout and fret, but it is mostly bluster.

Just like Snape, Molly is associated with cauldrons, and Snape is the only other character who stirs a cauldron with his wand. Snape and Molly both do a sort of practical magic—not flashy but highly effective.

Did these two characters have a similar upbringing? Were they reared by strict parents? Such resemblances make one wonder if they could be related somehow, despite their obvious physical differences. Of course, the main clues we have are from the things they say in the text, so let's look at that.

Though we come to know the often-vindictive Professor Snape in Book 1, it isn't until Book 2 that we hear enough from Molly to compare the two characters. When Fred, George and Ron "rescue" Harry from the Dursley's house using the flying Ford Anglia, the twins expect to sneak past their mother and go to bed. Instead, she meets them in the front yard, wearing the look of a "saber tooth tiger":

"So…Have you any idea how worried I've been?" says Molly in a deadly whisper." She then gives them an angry tongue-lashing that makes her tall sons "cower." She informs them that many bad things could have happened, including dying, being seen and Mr. Weasley losing his job. Her presence and power in

this scene are overwhelming. {B2, Ch3, p33}

By the time school begins, though, Harry and Ron seem to have totally forgotten her admonishments. When they miss the Hogwarts Express, Ron's first idea is to steal the car again! {Ch5, p69} And Harry follows happily along, until they crash into the Whomping Willow. {p74-75} They try to sneak into the school, but Professor Snape is waiting for them, and like Molly, he already knows what the boys have done. Look at how closely his language and demeanor mirrors Molly's—it's uncanny:

"So," he said softly, "the train isn't good enough...wanted to arrive with a bang, did we boys?" {p78} He then proceeds to read to them from the *Daily Prophet*, making them both feel ashamed by pointing out that they were seen by many Muggles and that Ron's father will probably face questions at work for owning a magical car. {p79} He also threatens to expel them, and seems upset when Dumbledore dismisses the idea. {p81}

Having Snape and Molly begin their tirades with "**So**" is presumably intentional on JKR's part. Both adults point out the danger of being "seen" and the repercussions for Ron's father. The things they say sound almost like echoes of one another.

Snape meets the boys holding the rolled-up newspaper.{p79} This motif is seen again in Book 4, when a worried Molly greets her family after the Dark Mark appears at the Quidditch World Cup. She is clutching a rolled-up copy of the *Daily Prophet*. {B4, Ch10, p145} And the parallel is reinforced again when Molly has the last word about the car during the Howler scene. She sends Ron an exploding letter called a "Howler," in which she echoes Snape's sentiments again: *"I wouldn't have been surprised if they'd expelled you,"* and *"if you put another toe out of line, we'll bring you straight home."*{B2, Ch6, p88} In hindsight, this statement seems to foreshadow Snape's appraisal of Harry in Book 4, when he says Harry has been *"crossing lines ever since he arrived here."* {B4, Ch17, p276}

JKR had to have put these clues in to tell us something we need to know – but what?   One thing is certain: Professor Snape and Molly Weasley both command respect from the children in their care. They also get their attention. After Molly's Howler shrieks its message, *"A ringing silence fell."*{B2, Ch6, p88} That silence is "heard" again in Book 5: *"when Snape closed the dungeon door with an echoing bang, everybody fell silent immediately."* {B5, Ch17, p362}

Molly is just as suspicious as Snape, and can often tell when someone is keeping secrets. She enters rooms almost silently, and comes up behind people with stealth – another trait in common with Snape. After the Weasley twins give Dudley Dursley a "ton-tongue toffee" in Book 4, their father tries to cover it up before Molly finds out. But Mr. Weasley is no match for his wife, who appears behind him suddenly and wants to know what is going on, her *"eyes narrowed with suspicion."* {B4, Ch5, p53} An almost identical phrase is used to describe Snape's eyes during Occlumency lessons, when he thinks Harry is being disrespectful: *"his eyes narrowed malevolently".* {B5, Ch24, p530}

Indeed, one wonders if Molly might be skilled at Legilimency: the ability to tell when someone is lying. {B5, Ch24, p531} She and Snape both seem gifted with this skill. In Book 3, Snape correctly assumes that Harry is sneaking out to the town of Hogsmeade, even though it is forbidden. He forces the boy to turn out his pockets, and finds Zonko products and the Marauder's Map. {B3, Ch14, p285} Molly shares the same uncanny knack for digging out the truth, as seen in the following conversation with her son, from Book 4:

> "George!" said Mrs. Weasley sharply, and they all jumped, . . . "What is in your pocket?"
>
> *"Nothing!"*
>
> *"Don't you lie to me!"* {Ch4, p68}

George is ultimately unable to stop his mother from finding the ton-tongue toffees in his pockets, and she makes them come flying from all over the house. Perhaps Snape and Molly have had so much experience with children, that it just seems as though they are reading minds, but it is often maddening for the children themselves.

There are many other examples. For one, they both come up against Sirius Black, Harry's beloved godfather. It's probably no accident that, at the end of Book 4, the ever-perceptive Dumbledore sends all adults from the room except for Snape and Molly. Together, they witness the return of Sirius Black, and are both obviously shocked and angry. {Ch36, p712} Perhaps Dumbledore knows something of their natures, and realizes they will have a hard time trusting Sirius and dealing with his relationship with Harry. Dumbledore is certainly correct about that!

The fur begins to fly as soon as Harry reaches Grimmauld Place, headquarters of the Order of the Phoenix and Sirius' family home. In the lazy lull after dinner, Sirius suddenly brings up Voldemort's name and causes a "frisson" (chill) to spread through everyone at the table. We are told that Molly's *normally kindly face looked dangerous.* {B5, Ch5, p87} Her final statement in this scene appears rude to many readers, yet it brings home an important point. She says, as her lip curls in Snape-like fashion, "*... it's been rather difficult for you to look after him while you've been locked up in Azkaban, hasn't it?*"{p90}

Bang! That's a shocker coming from Molly and some readers will think that is a low blow. After all, we know that Sirius Black was wrongly imprisoned for killing Harry's parents, and now he is forced to stay in hiding at Grimmauld Place. The only way to understand this almost cruel remark is to remember that she sees Harry as one of her own children, so she naturally wants to keep him out of danger, and Molly just does not trust Sirius Black.

Meanwhile, Severus Snape has his own "kitchen confrontation" with Sirius Black. The very fact that these outbursts are happening away from Hogwarts, in a domestic setting, makes them seem more real—almost like a child-custody battle. From the time Harry enters the room, Sirius lets Snape know that it is his house, Harry is his godson, and no one is going to tell Harry what to do except Sirius himself. Sirius gets angry when Snape just tries telling Harry to sit down! Snape, who hates being shown disrespect as much as Molly Weasley, still tries to control his temper, but gives Sirius the full "lip curl."{Ch24, p518-521}

Of the children, Hermione often echoes the opinions of both Snape and Molly. Hermione sometimes has problems with Sirius Black as well. When she tells Sirius that it is too risky to talk through the fire while Dolores Umbridge resides at the school, he tells her, "*You sound like Molly.*"{B5, Ch14, p301} Sirius also ignores Hermione's pleas to treat Kreacher, the house elf, with respect. {p303} Like Professor Snape and Molly, Hermione feared that the Order will be put in jeopardy if Sirius didn't follow the rules. Ron tells her, "*Sirius is right ...you do sound just like my mother.*"{Ch18, p378} Although she has been known to bend them, Hermione is generally a stickler with the rules above all else, just like Molly and Snape.

Of course, we also know that Hermione is a high achiever who practically lives in the library, and in that respect, she may be a parallel to Snape. Hermione is seen two hours after her O.W.L. exam, "*still clutching the exam paper.*"{Ch31, p712} When Harry later views "Snape's Worst Memory", he sees a fifteen-year-old Snape "*still absorbed in his own examination paper.*"{Ch28, p643}

So can you learn anything about the mysterious Snape by studying Molly and Hermione?

One thing that is plain is Snape's traits are also present in those who care for Harry. These are complex characters who are not exactly what they appear to be at first glance. Though Molly is loving and sweet, she is also a raging disciplinarian, a sarcastic opponent in an argument, and sometimes a hopeless romantic (when it comes to a certain Gilderoy Lockhart). Molly's worst fear is the death of her family—

as seen in Order of the Phoenix when her "boggart" turns into the dead bodies of her husband and children.{B5, Ch9, p175} Will we ever learn Snape's worst fear? With all the similarities, you would expect his boggart to be the loss of a loved one—but who does he love?

So far, we have seen only one side of Snape—the darkly Slytherin side. However, it would not be surprising if appearances are deceiving with this aspect of his character as well. In the Pensieve scene in Book 5, we discover Snape had a rough childhood, that he was bullied by Harry's father, and that Harry's mother stood up for him. As we learn more about Harry's parents we undoubtedly will know more about Professor Snape.

So what do you think? Does Snape have a domestic or romantic side, as Molly does? Does he have a socially conscious side like Hermione? Is his tough demeanor just an act? And why do Snape and Molly sound so much alike? Hermione probably already knows the truth, but JK Rowling just won't let her tell us yet.

ADDITIONAL SLEUTHING NOTES

* Was Mrs. W the studious type, like Hermione and Snape? Were either Severus or Molly prefects?

* JK Rowling said that Molly's maiden name was Prewett (www.jkrowling.com – Extra Stuff), and that Voldemort killed members of her family – is there a parallel for Snape?

* Both Molly and Snape have high-strung personalities – what effect will the stress of war have on them?

✳ SNAPE'S PATRONUS ✳

BRENDAN R. COURTSAL ✳ NC, "THE CROOKSHANK"
USA (*US Edition*), AGE 8

Inspiration for this Discussion

When I was in kindergarten, lots of kids' families were reading Harry Potter to them and I got interested in it. My Mom had already read the books, so I asked her to read them to me. Mom was psyched because she likes them so much and so does my Dad. I loved the first two books, but the Basilisk was a little scary. I thought it was cool how JK Rowling mentioned things at the beginning of the books, like how everybody thought Snape was bad in Book 1, and she tricked you in to thinking that. But really, he was trying to help. I like that, because she finds a way to keep her secrets and then reveals them at the right time. I found Book 3 even scarier than Book 2, but it was also pretty interesting. I am in the middle of reading Book 4 myself. I think it was amazing how Mad-Eye Moody could show the kids the Unforgivable Curses, but I don't think he should have done it.

I like how Harry admired Professor Lupin and how Lupin was so great at teaching. I thought the idea of Harry's Patronus being like his Dad was awesome.

HANDFUL

I overheard my Mom and Dad talking about Snape's Patronus after the chat with JK Rowling on World Book Day. I was thinking about Snape's Patronus and an idea just hit me what his Patronus could be. I discussed this with my Mom, and she posted my idea in the JKR Chat scroll [thread] on the MuggleNet Forum because no one else had mentioned it.

When I was asked to do this discussion, I knew I would have to do some research. I did most of my research in Book 3 because it had a lot of Dementors in it and has Harry's Patronus. I also looked at the parts in Book 5 about Dementors, Patronuses, and Snape's father. According to Professor Lupin in Book 3, a Patronus is an anti-Dementor; it's a guardian that protects you from a Dementor. It's made of a "positive force" and can't be harmed by a Dementor. Each wizard's Patronus has a different form, and it's not the same as another wizard's.{Ch12}

We have only seen three Patronuses in the books: Hermione's otter, Cho's swan, and Harry's stag.{B5, Ch27} Now, Harry's father could turn into a stag (his Animagus form), so I think that it means he's Harry's guardian, because Harry's Patronus, his own protector, is a stag. I don't know enough about Cho and Hermione to know if their Patronuses represent their parents, but it is one possibility. That is my theory.

In Book 5, Harry sees Snape's father in a memory.{Ch26} I think that was Snape's dad—they do both have hooked noses. His father was really mean and so are Dementors. If Snape's Patronus is like his father, his Patronus could be a Dementor.

I think that Snape and Dementors are related in some way because, when JK Rowling uses like words to describe different things, it often means they're connected. I've also noticed that Snape is mean. Kind of like his dad in his memory.{B5, Ch24}. I looked for descriptions of both Dementors and Snape in Book 3 and Book 5. I saw that JK Rowling used these words to describe them both: black, cold, dead-deadly, sweep-sweeping. Also, Snape and the Dementors both wear black.

Why do I think that Snape's Patronus is a Dementor? Because the way JK Rowling describes Snape and Dementors and Snape and his father is very similar. Plus Snape's father is mean like a Dementor.

If Snape met a Dementor and yelled "Expecto Patronum!" and conjured a Dementor Patronus, maybe the Dementor would be so surprised to see another Dementor that it would give Snape time to run away… Or maybe the Dementors would stare at each other wonderingly… Or, this part might be a little silly…a lot silly! Maybe the Dementors would walk arm-in-arm and go off to tea, and Snape would be able to run to safety while the Dementors were having their lovely tea! But I think it would work because they probably wouldn't attack one another because they work together in the books.

These are my ideas! I hope you like them.

──────── ADDITIONAL SLEUTHING NOTES ────────

* Are Dementors good guardians? They did a good enough job at Azkaban, but do they actively "shield," or do they rely on the devastating effect they have on people? How will Voldemort make use of them in the war?

* Molly Weasley has been described as a "saber-toothed tiger"{B2, Ch 3, pg. 32}, which would make a highly effective Patronus. Thinking of how she can strike fear into even Fred and George, would a Patronus of Molly, herself, be effective? Can a Patronus be a human, or is it always a creature?

* What are Dementors and how do they communicate? Are they an extension of Voldemort's psyche? They seem to have a "group mentality"—so do they also have a unified focus about their loyalty to the Dark Lord? Is there any chance that one or more think independently and could break from "the hive"?

Severus Snape and the Cult of Fear

"Inkwolf" ✳ Chamber of Secrets Forum
USA (*US Edition*), Age 39

Inspiration for this Discussion

When I first read *Harry Potter and the Sorcerer's Stone*, amid the hullabaloo of the release of Book 4, my reaction was actually, "Well, that was a pretty average book, considering the fuss… but I really liked Snape." As time went on, the books got better and better…and so did Snape. The Dueling Club scene was the clincher: I was officially a 'Sevage,' one of the savage Severus Snape fans.

While waiting endlessly for Book 5 to be released, I fell to discussing the books online with fellow enthusiasts. Imagine my surprise that most of them felt that Harry was the central figure in the books! I soon found it my sworn duty to defend Snape from indignant Harry fans, and dove into the books, examining his actions more closely. Strange things came to light. Snape performed heroic (or at least worthy) deeds in every book, the hallmark of which were a profound lack of appreciation by anyone else. His most horrible threats were carefully kept idle. His accusations and suspicions of Harry were generally fully justified and understandable. And strangely enough, when arriving at the Shrieking Shack, Harry and Snape ran through the exact same course of action (Snape with a much nastier verbal commentary, of course). So, with every act of a hero to his credit, why was Snape so blasted… nasty? Why the threats, the bullying, the sneering? Why the talent at finding the most offensive way to say anything? Was it all just due to really poor people skills?

Order of the Phoenix was finally released, with its tantalizing glimpses into Snape's past. Many of us had speculated something of the sort, but now the ideas were confirmed. And slowly the reason for Snape's behavior clicked into place.

It's about a lifelong relationship with fear.

Severus Snape, master of terror! His every word is calculated to frighten. Even his appearance is designed to intimidate: the black cloak, the stalking gait, unkempt, angry, bat-like, his skin pale from the darkness of the dungeon.

Snape's primary social skill seems to be his ability to inspire fear in people, and he uses it freely. He makes terrifying threats—mostly idle. In Chapter 7 of Book 3, he threatened to test Neville's incorrect potion on his pet toad, then conveniently vanished to the other side of the room while Hermione fixed it.{p126} In Book 3, he threatened to take Sirius Black directly to the Dementors, but when Black was unconscious and at his mercy, Snape took him to the castle.{Ch21, p387-8} In Book 4, he threatened to use Veritaserum in Harry's pumpkin juice{Ch27, p517}, but when Umbridge actually tried to do it in Book 5, Snape supplied a fake potion.{Ch37, p832}

Snape can sneer any student into silence. His class dreads his displeasure. He is Neville's greatest fear.

And Snape doesn't stop at intimidating students. Quirrel was warned in the darkness of the forest that he did NOT want to be Snape's enemy.{B1, Ch13, p226} Lockhart was frightened into trying to flee the castle by Snape's suggestion that it was time for him to face the monster of the Chamber.{B2, Ch16, p226}

Why does Snape rely so heavily on intimidation? Where did it start? During his Occlumency lesson, Harry saw a vision from Snape's mind of a shouting, hook-nosed man – probably Snape's father.{B5, Ch26, p591} This was Snape's first model of male power, a man who terrorized his cringing wife and crying child. From this example, Snape learned that to express himself as a person of strength and power, he must induce fear. Fear could deter his bullies and tormentors. Fear could crumble opposition. Fear could keep people at a safe distance. It's likely that Snape's school reputation of being an expert in the Dark Arts {B4, Ch27, p531} and perhaps even his joining the Death Eaters, arose from his attempts to make himself as fearsome as possible. Some of his angriest moments in the books arise at Harry's rare discoveries of his vulnerability...the time he was wounded by Fluffy {B1, Ch11, p182}, and Harry's foray into the Pensieve.{B5, Ch 28, p640} In both cases, Snape generated tantrums of terrifying rage, resealing any cracks that might have weakened the aura of terror he uses as both a shield and weapon.

Even extreme bravery is no match at times for Snape's aura of fear. On arriving at Hogwarts, Harry Potter was sorted into Gryffindor, the house that represents the quality of courage. If courage is the rejection of fear, then that makes Harry and Snape true opposites. Harry's greatest fear was fear, itself, according to Lupin.{B3, Ch8, p155} Through hard work, Harry conquered the Dementors and his greatest fear.

But Harry has not yet conquered his fear of Snape!

Though anger is apparent in many confrontations between the two, fear is often the driving emotion. Harry runs in terror from Snape's rage after the Pensieve scene, he hides in fear of Snape catching him out of bed on the stairs{B4, Ch25, p466}, he cringes in horror at the idea of Snape learning his secrets through Veritaserum. Thus far in the series, there isn't a book where Snape does not succeed in making Harry afraid of him. To Harry, Snape represents his own failure of courage.

The Order of the Phoenix can obviously only be strong if it is united. Considering the relationship between Harry and Snape, how can it be? Is there any hope for the two to even co-exist, let alone support one another? The answer may lie in Snape's relationship with Dumbledore.

Why did Snape leave the Death Eaters to risk his life as a spy for Dumbledore? Voldemort is the most feared wizard in the world, and therefore (if fear is equal to power in Snape's eyes), the most powerful. Is it because Voldemort may not be the most powerful after all, as he is said to fear Dumbledore? Possibly. But there is a much more important theme in the books. Snape's relationship with fear goes beyond his inflicting it on others. He lives in fear, himself. From what we have seen of his childhood experiences, he was mocked and tormented by his peers. By the time the humiliating experience that Harry witnessed in the Pensieve occurred, Snape was already angry, solitary, and clearly expecting to be attacked at any moment. Experience had already taught him that people were likely to hurt him if they could.

He hasn't forgotten the lessons of childhood. By frightening people off, he keeps them at a safe emotional distance. When he discovers something wrong at the school, he investigates alone: Snape rarely asks for help. When he is all bloodied from three-headed dog bites, he doesn't go to the school nurse to be magically healed: he turns to Filch, who bandages him Muggle-style. Filch, whose status as a squib probably makes him non-threatening, and whose foul temperament identifies him as a fellow terrorist. Snape is never seen in Hogsmeade with the other staff members, or joining their chats in the hallway. He keeps to himself. He jealously shields his vulnerability. He will not give anyone the chance to hurt him again.

Snape trusts no one.

And yet, in spite of his dark past as a Death Eater, in spite of his harsh words and fearsome manner, in spite of whatever crimes he may have committed… apparently in spite of common sense… Dumbledore trusts Snape. By trusting Snape, Dumbledore is opening his heart to him, and leaving himself vulnerable to betrayal and hurt. By utterly refusing to fear him, Dumbledore is able to get around Snape's defenses and get closer to him than anyone else can. To a man who can trust no one, this gift of trust must seem the ultimate act of courage.

And Snape clearly does not take that trust lightly—it was the first thing he spoke of when Crouch/Moody claimed that Dumbledore had ordered his office searched. {B4, Ch 5, p471} Snape's gratitude for Dumbledore's trust, and his pride in having maintained it, are evident. Why else would he keep Lupin's secret so long? Why else would he so fiercely defend Dumbledore when he is accused of cheating at the Triwizard Tournament? {Ch17, p276} In return for trust, Snape has given Dumbledore loyalty—something Voldemort apparently failed to earn from him.

Harry, like Snape, grew up in an atmosphere that did not promote trust. Harry, too, is disinclined to ask for help, or even to ask questions. And he certainly does not trust Snape! Surely Harry has some reason to feel trust. In Book 1, Snape saved Harry's life during Quidditch, and was watching out for him during the whole book. As for the rescue at the Department of Mysteries, in the fifth book, Snape did his best to protect Harry as well as his own old enemy, Sirius Black. Dumbledore said that one of his "useful spies" had warned him that the Potters were in danger. Snape was a Death Eater who turned spy for Dumbledore.{Ch 30, p590} How many Death Eater spies does Harry think Dumbledore had? When will he make the connection?

Sadly, the very fear-inducing skills that Snape relies on for his own emotional protection seem to have killed any gratitude or acceptance Harry might have felt for him. Harry learned early on to despise bullies, and Snape's cruel words weigh more with him than Snape's well-intended actions. Five years of Snape's intense, unfair, immediate dislike of Harry, five years of Snape's classroom bullying, five years of hearing Snape's threats and taunts.

Many of the characters who do have Harry's trust also loathe Snape. Lupin clearly did not trust Snape enough to risk reviving him in the Shrieking Shack to prove Sirius Black's story to him.{B3, Ch18, p361}. Black, himself, accused Snape of still being a Death Eater and of planning to use the Occlumency lessons to harm Harry.{B5, Ch24, p520} Small wonder Harry went into those lessons with such resistance! Harry certainly has some justification to distrust Snape.

But distrust is only another name for fear.

If the Order is to be united, I feel that Harry is going to have to finally reject that fear and take a major step. Harry must learn to trust the man he despises. Against his fear, against past wrongs, against suspicion, even against common sense, Harry must trust Snape.

It will be an act of courage worthy of a Gryffindor.

ADDITIONAL SLEUTHING NOTES

* Why did Snape keep Lupin's secret for so long? Why did he reveal it? Could it be when he found that Harry did whatever was needed to accomplish his goals, that Snape decided to do the same? Or could it be that Snape was afraid of what people might say about his part in the events at the Shrieking Shack, so he lashed out at the others first – before anyone had a chance to do it to him?

* Did Snape go to Grimmauld Place to inform Harry about his Occlumency lessons – with the specific purpose of announcing it in front of Sirius?

* Snape is quite sensitive to the respect he gets from Dumbledore in spite of his past {B4, Ch25, p472}, so why hasn't he learned from Dumbledore that to gain respect without resorting to fear tactics, he has to show respect to others too?

VOLDEMORT'S PAWNS

ALEXANDER BENESCH ✳ "STIC" CoS
GERMANY (*UK Edition*), AGE: ADULT

Inspiration for this Discussion

As soon as the first Occlumency lesson began in Book 5, my reading speed dropped dramatically. The things I have read and learned in my life about Intelligence services, interrogation techniques, mind-control and psychology made me suspect Snape in a way I had never anticipated. I began to write everything down to sort out my thoughts and evaluate my theories. At an early stage, I posted a few bits on the CoS forum, but the fan book stirred my ambition and I spent hours (that felt like minutes) writing the complete essay with everything in place. I hope I'm able to surprise you and that you enjoy reading it!

🦉 HANDFUL

"*Time and space matter in magic, Potter!*" (Severus Snape) {B5, Ch24 UK}

"*Remember - No distractions.*" (Stic)

The more I read Book 5 with those things in mind, the more I am becoming convinced that Lord Voldemort (LV for short) is the most outstanding strategist of all characters and that Snape is indeed helping him execute his plans.

LV needed three things implemented to successfully lure Harry into the Department of Mysteries:

A) Harry needed a motivation to go there—a false vision of a person in danger, who Harry would try to save under any circumstances.

B) Harry's mind had to be opened further to make it possible to give him the faked vision.

C) Harry somehow had to be told where to go (the Ministry of Magic/DoM) without someone actually telling him and drawing attention to it.

As LV cannot personally reach Harry while the boy is at Hogwarts, the only objective LV could accomplish from a distance was (A) but he needed (B) and (C) taken care of before that. It logically follows that in order to even consider this crazy mother of a plan, LV needed somebody *inside* Hogwarts who could handle objectives (B) and (C).

Now this "somebody" could only have been Severus Snape, who was ordered by Dumbledore to give Harry Occlumency lessons.

OBJECTIVE (C) - THE FIRST OCCLUMENCY LESSON

Consider the possibility that Snape might have received his new mission from Voldemort only moments before he gives the first Occlumency lesson.

Objective (B) was likely to take quite a few lessons to achieve but (C) could already have been taken care of in the first one: when Snape does the Legilimens spell for the first time, he "*had struck before Harry was ready, before he had even begun to summon any form of resistance."* {B5, Ch24, p471} The year before, Harry had been able to resist the Imperius Curse of Impostor Moody at the very first try. Jo reminds us here that Harry has extraordinary powers regarding Defence Against the Dark Arts. See how he handled Snape's Legilimens spell: the Potions Master gets only a couple of short flashes and, sure enough, when he reaches the memory of Harry's love interest Cho Chang, he gets thrown out of Harry's head. Harry even manages to produce a kind of non-verbalised stinging hex!

That accomplishment deserves recognition, yet Snape shows suspiciously very little appreciation for Harry's huge achievement while criticising: "You lost control."{p472} Harry believes it, as he has almost no theoretical knowledge about Occlumency, and has to trust the judgement of his teacher. Harry rightfully complains about getting no instructions from his tutor about defending himself: *"You're not telling me how!"* Snape chooses to ignore the content of Harry's accusation and distracts him: "Manners, Potter!" {p472}

Snape not only doesn't give Harry any information about how to defend himself against the Legilimens spell, he even chooses to increase Harry's anger by taunting him for one of his memories and heightens Harry's fear, *"Now I want you to shut your eyes."* {p472} Remember, this is only Harry's first lesson—he is a 15-year-old male wizard, suffering both adolescent and true life-and-death stress already—something Snape *must* have known. You typically can't teach a human being how to swim by just throwing him into a lake and hoping he'll do it, but do you also tie an extra big stone to that person's leg if you try that method?

At that point, one could still argue that Snape only wants to prepare Harry for the worst, to "teach him the hard way." However, check out Snape's reaction after Harry shakes off his Legilimens spell for the second time: despite Snape's efforts to make it darn near impossible for Harry to defend himself, he gets no more than three short flashes of Harry's memory this time. The last image is one of Harry's most horrifying memories: Cedric Diggory. {p473} Harry sees a memory from last year *as vividly as if he was really at that graveyard, again* and he pulls out: "NOOOOOOO!" {p473} Snape again gets thrown out of Harry's head. That wasn't a NOOOOOO! of defeat, it was a NOOOOO! of regaining control and shaking off that horrible image and the spell along with it!

If Snape had just tried to teach Harry the hard way, he should now have been extremely happy with himself as his strange method of teaching had worked out quite well. But Snape is *unnerved* and says just the opposite of what is actually true: *"You are not trying, you are making no effort. You are allowing me access to memories you fear..."* {p473} **Not trying? No effort??? Not true** – a complete lie. Allowing him access? Yes, about the same amount of access as the "superb" Occlumens Snape allows to Harry. In one of the following lessons when Harry uses the *"Protego!"* Spell, Snape has to shake off his *own* Legilimens spell, and Harry receives a few memories of *Snape's* fears before the Potions Master can break free. {Chapter 26, p521} Compare Harry's ability to Snape's ability in fighting off the same, equally powerful Legilimens spell. There is basically no difference! Harry does as well in his first lesson as a trained Deatheater, yet Snape keeps telling Harry that he is not getting it.

You should be as worried about that as I am. Why was Snape "paler than usual" (as always when he's really scared), and "angrier" {p473}—when he should be perfectly content with the success of his teaching in the first lesson? If, as I believe, Snape was trying to accomplish his mission for LV, his behaviour makes perfect sense: he begins to realize that he might disappoint the Dark Lord and is therefore shaking in his boots.

Now, with the next Legilimens spell, Snape seems to give it all he can. He gets a few flashes of Harry's memories and then reaches the one of the black door, the corridor... and Arthur Weasley leading Harry off to the left, down a flight of stone steps... "*I KNOW! I KNOW!*" Harry recognizes *for the first time ever* that the corridor he had been dreaming about for months is in the MoM / DoM. And..."*It looked as though, this time, Snape had lifted the spell before Harry had even tried to fight back.*" {p474} That last quote is very cleverly constructed. One way to read that is that Snape had deliberately and intentionally lifted the spell all three times when, in reality, he only did so in the *last go*. Then Snape keeps prompting Harry until he remembers "*...and I think Voldemort wants something from ...*"{p475} Slam Dunk[i] At this point, Snape has achieved objective (C). Harry knows where to go.

All of a sudden Snape immediately ends that lesson and says to Harry: "*You are to rid your mind of all emotion every night before sleep; empty it, make it blank and calm.*" {p475} *Excuse me???* That is *all* the help, instruction and training Snape gives Harry to stop him having these dreams/visions at night? Wasn't stopping the dreams supposed to be the most important reason for the Occlumency lessons? Is this how Harry gets trained? This is ridiculous! Snape *must* have known that Harry, with the incredible load of terrible stuff happening to him, could *never ever* empty his mind before sleep without any real help, training, or proper instructions.

If there is one additional thing to make it absolutely sure that Harry won't be able to close his mind before sleep it is this: "*And be warned Potter... I shall know if you have not practised...*"{p475} A threat, obviously. And obviously it works! At the end of the following busy day, Harry remembers that he's supposed to be practising. No big surprise that Harry's mind automatically jumps to the threatening Potions Master and how he loathes him and Umbridge. And no big surprise that a dream about the Dark Corridor follows in which the mysterious door is "ajar" for the first time.

OBJECTIVE (B) - THE PLAN IS ADVANCING

Not more than an hour after the first Occlumency lesson, Harry breaks down in the Gryffindor dormitory because he feels LV is the happiest he had been in 14 years. Why is Jo so specific about the timing?

The next day, people read in the *Daily Prophet* about the Azkaban breakout, and Ronald Weasley concludes: "*There you are Harry. That's why he was happy last night.*" {p481} I am not convinced of your assumption, Ronald. Note the emphasis on "the happiest in 14 years"—what was LV so extremely happy about *14 years ago*? He thought he could kill the only child (who would ever be able to destroy him) as a 1-year-old because he knew which two babies matched the descriptions of his fragment of the prophecy. I don't believe LV would, 14 years later, be happy in a similar amount just because he had released some of his Deatheaters from Azkaban. I say he was that happy because the plan he came up with just a few hours before was greatly advancing. That plan would not only bring him the complete prophecy, but would also finally result in the death of the only one who could ever vanquish him.

One objective had already been accomplished by Severus Snape. One down, two more to go: Snape continued objective (B) of the operation: In the Occlumency lessons he did nothing more than ruthlessly attack Harry's mind over and over again. Harry's brain was aching from the force of Snape's spells and he was convinced that his defence against his dreams "*was getting worse with every lesson*". Harry felt that he was "*turning into a kind of aerial that was tuned in to tiny fluctuations in Voldemort's mood*" {p488} and even more important, "*he was sure he could date this increased sensitivity firmly from his first Occlumency lesson with Snape.*" He dreamt about the corridor leading to the entrance to the DoM almost every night, and he was convinced that Snape's lessons were "*making it worse*". {p489}

Hermione may trust Snape because Dumbledore trusts him—but she and Dumbledore haven't got a clue about what's really going on in those lessons. Unlike us, they don't know what is being said or taught, and more importantly: what is not said and not taught.

OBJECTIVE (B) - THE OCCLUMENCY-LESSON IN CHAPTER 26

Jo reminds us that this second Occlumency lesson takes place "*a couple of weeks after [Harry's] dream of Rookwood*" {Ch 26, p520} I'm sure that since Arthur Weasley's attack, LV has tried very hard not to give Harry access to anything he shouldn't receive. As the memory of the Rookwood-questioning, which Harry had witnessed, was a most sensitive one, I am sure the Dark Lord had dropped the ball with this. That was something Harry should definitely not have seen. When Harry saw Voldemort's eyes and the white face looking back at him in the mirror, he again pulled out because of the raw terror he felt. LV would have again recognised that Harry had been inside his head, although he may not have known *how long* Harry had been in there or how much of this particular memory (or which *other* memories/thoughts) Harry had caught. If it had been too much, LV's wonderful plan could have been out in the open (drat!). That could have been inconvenient.

Before LV could continue with his plan, he may have needed to find out how much of what Harry had accessed. If so, he needed somebody to find that out for him.

Snape. Sure enough, in the Chapter 26 Occlumency lesson:

"'*The last memory,*' said Snape. '*What was it? I mean the one with a man kneeling in the middle of a darkened room.*'" Interestingly, Snape asks Harry "softly" about his dream of the Rookwood-interrogation. {p520} Snape seems to have cast himself in the role of interrogator (since when does he speak softly to Harry?). Harry lies that it was just an ordinary dream he had and gives Snape no further information about it. Snape, of course, knows it's a lie and his voice becomes "low" and "dangerous" when he changes his approach of interrogation. Snape tries to make Harry feel guilty, by asking why he is giving up his evenings to this tedious job. {p520} FYI – making someone who is being interrogated feel guilty for withholding information usually heightens his/her will to confess.

Snape then asks Harry the *other* very important question LV must have been dying to have answered: "*How many other dreams about the Dark Lord have you had?*" {p521} It sure seems as if Snape is trying to determine if Harry had caught anything else besides the questioning of Rookwood. Harry lies, and Snape's lousy interrogation attempt fails once more, since he can't force Harry to divulge his information. Snape becomes so angry that he seems to make a mistake when he says: "*it is not up to you to find out what the Dark Lord is saying to his Death Eaters*". {p521}

Snape has been skimming through Harry's memories and seen a variety of stuff. It really seems as if Snape has been specifically searching for this all along. Notice how he wastes no valuable time by actually teaching Harry to defend himself against the Legilimens spell.

When Snape tries again, our young hero resists better than ever. For the first time, he is still able to see Snape in front of him and he has enough control to actually raise his wand and do a spell: "*Protego!*" {p521} Snape's *own* Legilimens spell backfires onto himself and the professional Occlumens needs about the same time to shake it off as Harry usually does. Shouldn't Snape now be *super-content* with the success of his teaching? But instead, he is highly agitated and angry.

Snape becomes tense, and hits Harry again with the Legilimens spell. That time, it is not only a lot stronger, it also seems to have a completely new effect:

Harry is "hurtling along the corridor towards the Department of Mysteries", "moving so fast he was going to collide with it" and "The door had flown open!"

Harry sees a "black-walled, black-floored circular room lit with blue-flamed candles, and there were more doors all around him". {p523} Harry has never yet dreamt about this. In fact, he has never even seen the place before, so how could Snape have *extracted* it? Snape must have either *given* Harry these images with this last spell or somehow made it possible for the Dark Lord to give them to Harry:

Harry begins to realize that something is not right, but Snape uses his old tactic to distract him and to stop his stream of thought: "*You are not working hard enough!*" {p523} In the next moment, the lesson ends abruptly by the noise of Professor Trelawney getting sacked and the reader is also once more distracted from the really important things by a loud kaboom.[ii]

THE LAST OCCLUMENCY LESSON

In Harry's last Occlumency lesson, Snape doesn't get to do the Legilimens spell at all because Draco interrupts him right at the beginning. Umbridge needs help with removing Montague from a toilet and the Potions master leaves the room.

After Snape finds Harry messing with the Pensieve, he stops giving lessons. How convenient. Objectives (C) and (B) were already accomplished so maybe it was just that Voldemort didn't need Snape to work with Harry any more. Now that Harry (C) knows where to go to find this door, and (B) has his brain prepped for LV to waltz right in, all that is left is for LV to plant a little motivational thought.

OBJECTIVE (A) - THE FINAL OPERATION

To launch the final objective (A) of the plan, LV still needs to know which person Harry would try to rescue at any lengths. Well, luck and Kreacher are on LV's side and he finds out that person is Sirius Black.

But, you ask, didn't Snape try to save Harry's life when he searches the forest for him and Hermione? Here is my interpretation—see what you think:

Snape could have followed Umbridge, Harry, and Hermione into the forest. Then, when all the kids start off to London with the Thestrals, he could have given the other DEs the "green light", the confirmation that Harry has indeed been successfully lured into the trap and has set off for the MoM. According to Dumbledore, Snape checks Headquarters to find "*that Sirius was alive and safe in Grimmauld Place*" {Ch 37, p732}, also a perfect excuse for him to check if Harry has somehow managed to contact his godfather or anybody else from the Order in the meantime.

Snape does wait a while for Harry to return from the Forest with Umbridge (he "grew worried" according to Dumbledore) {p732}, before he finally contacted "certain Order members at once" at Grimmauld Place again. {p732} At once? But he waits, and why does he do *that*? As Snape has no clue about Harry's secret Defence-Against-The-Dark-Arts group, he would logically figure that this bunch of kids will not last five minutes against the Deatheaters. The DE's figure they will quickly take The Prophecy from the youngsters, kill them all, and return to Voldemort in no time. Snape could wait just long enough before raising the alarm so that the Order-members will arrive too late at the DoM—meaning they and Dumbledore will only find the dead kids and probably Ministry people, ready to arrest them. As we know, it is only because Harry and the others have secretly trained in Defence Against the Dark Arts all year that they are able to defend The Prophecy long enough against the Deatheaters for the Order to arrive.

Snape? He will (again) appear as if he has been helpful and loyal to the Order the whole time.

This scenario will bring LV the complete prophecy (*and* the only one who could ever vanquish him) on a silver platter *while assuring his spy, Snape, maintains his place inside the Order!* It was…

The… Perfect… Plan…

…foiled again.

A psychologist I know once told me *"every strength that is overdone becomes a weakness."* Bravery becomes a people-saving thing and trusting people becomes being naïve. LV knows the weaknesses of his enemies and he knows which buttons to push to make them do what he wants. Unfortunately, everyone has a weakness that LV can exploit.

I believe Lord Voldemort created Snape as the man-who-needed-a-second-chance – specifically for Dumbledore.

ADDITIONAL SLEUTHING NOTES

* Was Snape taunting Harry about Marge's dog or did he feel a very *slight*, momentary pang of empathy – that he had to crush with a sarcastic commentary before it was noticeable to Harry (or himself)?

* Why would Snape have opened Harry's mind? If it is true that was his intent, was his purpose to just to let Voldemort in, or was it also to obtain information for himself (Snape), as well?

* We still don't know how one gets out of a Pensieve – does Harry?

* Could Harry have been created for Dumbledore? Sirius was used as bait for Harry and Dumbledore has now admitted his weakness for Harry ("We fools who love…") {B5, Ch37} Is that setting up Harry as a trap for Dumbledore as well?

* Why was Snape not present at the rescue in the Department of Mysteries? Was he "lying low" so he wouldn't have to become involved in situations where he would have to declare his loyalty?

Editor's Note: This discussion was considerably longer than what was asked for in the guidelines, but due to several factors, we were happy to allow the length. As you see, the research, depth, and presentation are exceptional. But most importantly, it offers one of the few perspectives that focuses on the bullying and malicious aspect of Snape's character – which may or may not be redeemed. In fact, at the Edinburgh Book Festival {2004}, JK Rowling made firm statements that she doesn't understand why so many fans are enraptured by Snape, and that it is a "very worrying thing" to her. (Don't know what she'll say if she ever she sees this section on Snape, hehe). Now, that doesn't sound as if she had redemption in mind for Snape, and she definitely categorized Snape in with Draco as a "bad guy" and not the hero (*"I make this hero – Harry, obviously –"*). Having said, that, Snape is clearly fascinating and JKR has been known to trick us with her comments. However, until Snape shows his true colors, causing pain for amusement is a bullying tactic that is not easily excused, and it keeps suspicion focused on Snape. What choice has Snape made? What were his intentions and motivations in Book 5?

---

i Slam Dunk (n.) – English sland; exclamatory phrase referencing a clear shot in Basketball, similar to a goal, or a hole-in-one.
ii Kaboom (n.) – English slang; Loud noise, mimicking an explosion.

Who Is The
Half-Blood Prince?

WHO IS THE HALF-BLOOD PRINCE?
(OR A MAGICAL WORLD OF POSSIBILITIES!)

JK Rowling has announced that the official title of Book 6 is *Harry Potter and the Half-Blood Prince* (HBP). She has challenged sleuths to guess the identity of the Half-Blood Prince, however she has given us just a mere handful of clues to help figure it out:

   1)   The HBP is neither Harry nor Voldemort (nor Tom Riddle).

   2)   *"'The Half-Blood Prince' might be described as a strand of the overall plot…it was not part of the story of the Basilisk and Riddle's diary…" "The link I mentioned between Books 2 and 6 does not, in fact, relate to the 'Half-Blood Prince' (because there is no trace left of the HBP storyline in 'Chamber'.) Rather, it relates to a discovery Harry made in 'Chamber' that foreshadows something that he finds out in 'Prince'."* {www.jkrowling.com F.A.Q.}"

As soon as the title for Book 6 was revealed behind the "locked" door at www.jkrowling.com, the MuggleNet Forums immediately went to work deciphering the clues and the list of suspects. Many sleuths believe the HBP might be a legend from the past that Harry has to discover. This may very well be the case, so the possibilities are not limited to current, living characters, but historical characters as well. However, as the title is "prince," we have limited (if you can call it that) the possibilities to only the males of the species.

In the table below are the possible (though not always usual) suspects that WWP pondered, followed by the forums' perspectives on those possibilities. Under **WWP Ponders** are listed key highlights positively supporting that character as the HBP. Any evidence suggesting that character is ***not*** the prince is listed under **The Forum Debates**.

Just to clarify, the term "half-blood" could mean any kind of non-homogeneous breeding. That would cover marrying outside a race, a social status, an ethnicity, or even a species. Therefore, we cannot know which kind of half-blood JKR has in mind. It is possible that she could mean a human with a parent who comes from a different human-type designation such as race or social status (think Disney's *Aladdin*), it could mean someone who is a cross-species (think Crookshanks), or it could even mean a non-human with a parent who comes from a different type of social designation (think *Aristocats*). So, we can't make any assumption as to whether the "Prince" is human, cross-species (including part-human,), or completely non-human. In fact, since this is a wizarding world even if the Prince is part-human, the royal blood may even flow from a non-human lineage (e.g. lions)! This makes it very difficult to speculate on who could be carrying that royal blood.

We know sleuths will continue their excellent investigative work in ferreting out the clues (stay clear of bouncing ferrets!).

WWP PONDERS		THE FORUM DEBATES
• Could have been a prince • Garners respect	BLOODY BARON	• A baron, even historically, is usually distinguished from a prince
• We don't know anything about their mother, could be a witch	COLIN OR DENNIS CREEVEY	• Both definitely seem to be Muggle-born; no knowledge of magical world
• Could be a "prince among elves" • Could be a half-blooded elf	DOBBY	• It is unlikely the Malfoys would settle for anything less than pureblood house-elves
• Could see him as a prince • Very powerful wizard • Maybe explains why he likes Muggles	ALBUS DUMBLEDORE	• This would probably make Aberforth a prince as well, and the title is not plural • Already plays a large enough role
•Definitely a half-blood	SEAMUS FINNEGAN	•Seems to be just a background character
•He has fire and leadership •Half-man	FIRENZE	• If he is a prince, it is unlikely that he would be cast out by the other centaurs
•Powerful and respected	FILIUS FLITWICK	• Doesn't appear to be anything but a professor
•Wouldn't surprise anyone if he were half-blood •A lion implies a regal persona	GODRIC GRYFFINDOR	•Has been dead for 1,000 years •Harry is not a Half-Blood Prince, so that either eliminates Harry as heir of Godric or Godric as HBP
• For some reason, Grawp is smaller than he should have been	GRAWP	•Grawp seems to be strictly a giant
•The giants are famous for many struggles and switchovers among their leaders •Hagrid is half-blood	RUBEUS HAGRID	•We don't know if Giants have royalty •He already has such a big part •Rita Skeeter probably would have found out when she interviewed Hagrid
•Couldn't you just see him as a prince?	VIKTOR KRUM	•Attends Durmstrang, which seems to admit only purebloods •We've been told we will see him again, but not soon
•He thinks he is very important •His favorite color is lilac—purple is the color of royalty •Maybe the HBP is his new "personality"	GILDEROY LOCKHART	•JKR has presented him as a 1-joke character, not important to the future stories

WWP PONDERS		THE FORUM DEBATES
•We know from JKR that Lupin is a half-blood He could be hiding a royal lineage	REMUS LUPIN	•Umbridge was scared of him
•He has the "prince in rags" and sleeper character attributes	NEVILLE LONGBOTTOM	•He's pure-blood
•Could the title warlock have "princely" implications?	WARLOCK PERKINS	•Is only mentioned in passing •Seems to only be a background characte
•Could be half-blood We don't know for sure	PETER PETTIGREW	•Not quite himself or a key figure in Book 2 •Rats aren't exactly "kingly"
•He's a "king" by name	KINGSLEY SHACKLEBOLT	•Was only introduced in Book 5
•His heir is half-blood	SALAZAR SLYTHERIN	•Would seem pureblood, but don't know that for sure
•A powerful wizard •Maybe rejecting his Muggle side?	SEVERUS SNAPE	•Hard to imagine with his attitude him being a HBP •Unlikely a Death Eater would be half-blood
•JKR said we'd meet a good Slytherin •How about Blaise Zabini or Theodore Nott?	SLYTHERIN STUDENT	•No mention made of his family roots; possibly pureblood being in Slytherin
•Precedent set of an animagus living as his animal counterpart for years undetected, and in that same boys' dorm room no less	TREVOR	•No direct evidence of being a wizard
• For some reason, Grawp is smaller than he should have been	GRAWP	•Grawp seems to be strictly a giant

JK Rowling has already discounted: Harry, Tom Riddle/Voldemort, Mark Evans, and Dudley

Other Possibilities:

Justin Finch-Fletchley, Draco Malfoy, James Potter, The Weasleys, Non-humans, Portraits or Ghosts, Ancient and/or Legendary Characters, etc....

(Note: The Half-Blood Prince doesn't have to be living, or living within Harry's timeframe.)

PONDERING THE IDENTITY OF THE HALF-BLOOD PRINCE...

TROELS OFFERS A THEORY

Who might this be? The only thing we know is that a story line involving this Half-Blood Prince didn't make it into Book 2, but unless the foundations for this story line are still in Book 2, there is nothing we can say about anything. Consequently any intelligent guesses apart from "someone new" must take their outset in Book 2. The main plot of that book revolves around the age-old conflict between Gryffindor and Slytherin; not only the Hogwarts houses, but also the two founders themselves (Godric and Salazar) who are represented by the modern heirs to their conflict: Harry Potter and Tom Riddle (the latter also being the heir to the flesh of the founder he represents, whereas we don't know about the former).

We know that neither Harry nor Tom is the half-blood prince, and consequently I think that it is most likely that the Half-Blood Prince is either Godric Gryffindor or Salazar Slytherin, and that the abandoned story line was to be a part of the back-story. This was possibly something that would form part of the explanation for what either Harry or Tom has become today. Note that both of their modern representatives are, themselves, half-bloods sharing the virtues, values and prejudices of the founder they represent.

ARTEMISMOONBOW OFFERS A THEORY

Right now I think the best candidates are Godric Gryffindor or Salazar Slytherin. Here's my line of reasoning.

The HBP plot was spliced out of Book 2, leaving nothing of the storyline. Yet it's hard to pull a story-line out completely without leaving a clue or two, and JKR says that there's something that Harry discovered in Book 2 that will be important in HBP. So the HBP plot must have some relationship to the events or themes in Book 2, though it's definitely not a continuation of that plot. With that in mind, there are several important motifs in Book 2:

1) The origins of Hogwarts, including the dissension amongst the Founders that led Slytherin to break away, and to build the Chamber.
2) Harry's doubt about his placement in Gryffindor, later followed by Dumbledore's reassurance that Harry is a "true Gryffindor."
3) The importance of Gryffindor's sword and hat.
4) The theme of "history"—everyone was checking "Hogwarts, a History" out of the library, and Hermione asked Professor Binns, the History professor, to tell them about the Chamber. Binns' explanation took us back to the founding of Hogwarts, and the relationships amongst the Founders.

The Book 6 snippet from JKR's official site may be the Half-Blood Prince. The connection between Gryffindor House and lions seems logical, so it's possible that the snippet is a description of Godric Gryffindor, himself, which makes a strong case for the HBP being Godric.

Salazar Slytherin also figured prominently in Book 2. He built the underground Chamber—and to what purpose, other than housing a basilisk, we do not know. I suspect we'll be seeing that Chamber again, and finding out more about Slytherin, which is one reason I suspect that he could be the HBP. Voldemort was Slytherin's last heir, and a half-blood. Slytherin may have valued pure-bloods, but suppose he was a half-blood himself, just as Voldemort is, and hence his traits came out strongest in Voldemort? It would be mortifying for a pure-blood fanatic to learn that his great powers are the result of being a "mongrel", rather than a toujours pur-blood, but that could be part of the connection between young Tom Riddle and

Slytherin (and later, part of the reason that Voldemort chose to go after Harry rather than Neville).

But I rather suspect Gryffindor over Slytherin. I can certainly picture Slytherin mockingly referring to Gryffindor as a "half-blood prince" and Gryffindor himself taking up the title proudly and in defiance to pure-blood pride.

S.P. SIPAL OFFERS A THEORY

Dobby has had my vote since I found out about the Book 6 title. He was a critical character in Book 2, yet we found out little of his background. The only clues I have for Dobby being half-blood, besides his less than servile attitude, are his long fingers and feet, which are just like goblins. I've not seen another house elf described with long fingers, long feet, and a long thin nose. If Dobby were half-goblin it could very well explain his totally un-elfish attitude toward freedom.

What will it take, besides Hermione, to lead the house elves to freedom? A leader among them. Dumbledore has understood that other living beings will have to take part in the war that is to come. Dobby could well be that leader and a crucial ally to Dumbledore.

I think one of the critical things we have to consider in speculating on the HBP is whether this person will bring something important to the table in the war with Voldemort. I don't think JKR's going to name a whole book after someone who's not a critical figure in this war. The goblins hold a powerful position within the community with all that gold. If Dobby could unite house elves and goblins under Dumbledore, he'd bring a lot of power to the table.

MARY AILES "ZOEROSE" OFFERS A THEORY

There is one character in particular that I would like to see be the Half-Blood Prince. In doing so, I must make the case not only that he may indeed be a half-blood wizard, but also that the term "prince" may be applied to him, even in jest—Professor Severus Snape.

We do not know for sure that Snape is a pure-blood. We assume so because as a student he was in Slytherin, later became a Death Eater and follower of Lord Voldemort, and is now in fact the Head of Slytherin House–whose original founder, Salazar Slytherin, believed only pure-bloods were worthy to be students. The term "half-blood" could be juxtaposed or contrasted against the word "prince" and may be more a term of ridicule than accolade. With this in mind, I am reminded of Prince Don Pedro and his illegitimate half-brother, Don John, in Shakespeare's immortal play *Much Ado About Nothing*. Don Pedro is a charming, popular, and much-beloved prince and leader, while Don John is his brooding and bitter half-brother out for revenge. In the small glimpses we have of James and Snape's relationship, it does appear that their disdain for one another seems to be far more than skin deep. In fact, the term "Half-Blood Prince" could actually be an ironic turn of a phrase used as an instrument of ridicule.

In considering who could be the HBP, there is no character in the Harry Potter series that could be more ironic and more vulnerable to ridicule than this man caught between two worlds, Professor Severus Snape.

ALEXA OFFERS A THEORY

Kingsley Shacklebolt strikes me as regal and the name does conjure images of royalty in chains, even if only symbolically. Quirrell claims he received his turban as a gift from an African prince. Also, Lupin is a favorite of both readers and the books' characters and it would be nice to find there is something hidden in his past that will lift him out of his misery and poverty, but he is a sentimental choice.

And now for the wildest HBP theory on the Internet...
(using canon, of course)

<u>INKWOLF OFFERS A THEORY</u>

It's Argus Filch!

Consider that...

* The Half-Blood Prince was the working title of Book 2, until Rowling decided that the prince's story belonged in Book 6. She has said that Book 2 contains vital clues to Book 6 and the future!

* In Book 2, Harry spends time in Filch's office, discovering his secret Squibbiness. Other secrets might also have been planned to be uncovered, originally. (And, yes, you can be a Squib and a Half-blood at the same time. All it requires is for one parent to be a Muggle-born witch or wizard.)

* Harry notices the Quikspell envelope on Filch's desk. It's purple, the color of royalty.

* The VERY FIRST ATTACK of the basilisk in Book 2 is on FILCH'S CAT! Many fans believe that cats act as 'seeing-eye dogs' to squibs, since they can see dangerous magic that a squib can't detect. Was Riddle clearing the way to eliminating the heir to the throne?

* Filch has been identified by Rowling as the ONLY PERSON who stays at Hogwarts year round. Obviously hiding from anti-royalists and paparazzi!

* Rowling has said that SOMEONE will learn magic surprisingly late in life. As there are few non-magical characters in the book, Filch is a prime candidate for a fuller role...

* There is a mythic tradition of kings in exile doing humble chores...though most of them don't gripe about it as much as Argus does.

* Princely attributes...he is tyrannical, he has a neat and tidy streak, and he prefers to torture those who annoy him. And he keeps files on all his enemies for future reference!

Argus Filch is the Half-Blood Prince...all based on irrefutable canon!

HALF BLOOD PRINCE VOTE SUMMARY

A New Character 17	Viktor Krum 3	Mr. Ollivander 1
Rubeus Hagrid 15	A Slytherin student	Nearly Headless Nick 1
Remus Lupin 11	we don't expect 2	Somebody who thought
Seamus Finnegan 8	Kingsley Shacklebolt 2	he was pure blood
Severus Snape 8	Any half-blood 1	but isn't 1
Dean Thomas 7	Blaise Zambini 1	Stan Shunpike 1
Godric Gryffindor 7	Cornelius Fudge 1	The Bloody Baron 1
Neville Longbottom 7	Dobby 1	The Ghost of a
Albus Dumbledore 5	Draco Malfoy 1	Hogwarts student 1
A Legend 3	Dudley Dursley 1	The Giant Squid 1
Argus Filch 3	Euan Abercrombie 1	The next DADA
Colin Creevy 3	Gilderoy Lockhart 1	professor 1
Salazar Slytherin 3	James Potter 1	Theodore Nott 1

Cross-Reference of Page Numbers
UK and US Hardcover & Trade Softcover Editions

OFFICIAL HARRY POTTER PUBLICATIONS:

Harry Potter and the Philosopher's Stone, Bloomsbury Press, 1997.

Harry Potter and the Sorcerer's Stone, by J.K. Rowling, Scholastic, Inc., 1997.

Harry Potter a l'Ecole des Sorciers, by J.K. Rowling, translated from English by Jean-Francois Menard, Gallimard Jeunesse, 1998.

Harry Potter and the Chamber of Secrets, by J.K. Rowling, Scholastic, Inc., 1999.

Harry Potter et la Chambre des Secrets, by J.K. Rowling, translated from English by Jean-Francois Menard, Gallimard Jeunesse, 1999.

Harry Potter and the Prisoner of Azkaban, by J.K. Rowling, Scholastic, Inc., 1999.

Harry Potter et le Prisoner d'Azkaban, by J.K. Rowling, translated from English by Jean-Francois Menard, Gallimard Jeunesse, 1999.

Harry Potter and the Goblet of Fire, by J.K. Rowling, Bloomsbury Press, 2000.

Harry Potter and the Goblet of Fire, by J.K. Rowling, Scholastic, Inc., 2000.

Harry Potter et la Coupe de Feu, by J.K. Rowling, translated from English by

Jean-Francois Menard, Gallimard Jeunesse, 2000.

Harry Potter and the Order of the Phoenix, by JK Rowling, Bloomsbury Press, 2003.

Harry Potter and the Order of the Phoenix, by J.K. Rowling, Scholastic, Inc., 2003.

Fantastic Beasts and Where to Find Them, by Newt Scamander, Obscurus Books

(U.S. Publisher, Scholastic Press, 2001) for Comic Relief U.K.

Quidditch Through the Ages, by Kennilworthy Whisp, Whizz Hard Books

(U.S. Publisher, Scholastic Press, 2001) for Comic Relief U.K.

Conversations with J.K. Rowling, by Lindsey Fraser, Scholastic, Inc., 2000.

Selected Bibliography

OTHER BOOKS:

The Aeneid, by Virgil, translated by Robert Fitzgerald, Vintage Books, a division of Random House, 1981.

The Age of Fable or Stories of Gods and Heroes, by Thomas Bullfinch, The Heritage Press, 1958.

The American Heritage Dictionary, Houghton Mifflin, 1976.

Celtic Decorative Art: A Living Tradition, by Deborah O'Brien, The O'Brien Press, 2000.

The Concise Oxford Dictionary, edited by Judy Pearsall, Oxford University Press, 2001.

Condors and Vultures, by David Houston, Voyageur Press, 2001.

The Dictionary of Classical Mythology, by Pierre Grimal, Blackwell Publishing, 1986.

Dictionary of Symbolism: Cultural Icons and the Meanings Behind Them, by Hans Biederman, Penguin Books USA Inc., 1994.

Earth Divination, Earth Magic, by John Michael Greer, Llewellyn Publications , 2000.

The Egyptian Hermes, by Garth Fowden, Cambridge University Press, 1987.

Egyptian Tales (Second Series), by W.M. Flinder Petrie, Methuen & Co., 1913.

Euripides Alcestis, translated by Philip Vellacott, Penguin Books, 1975.

Freemasonry and Its Ancient Mystic Rites, by C.W. Leadbeater, New York, 1998.

Introduction to Social Problems, 5th ed., by Thomas J. Sullivan, Allyn and Bacon, 2000.

Lace, by Virginia Churchill Bath, Henry Regnery Company, 1974.

The Message of the Sphinx, by Graham Hancock and Robert Bauval, Three Rivers Press, 1996.

Myths of the Ancient Greeks, by Richard P. Martin, New American Library, 2003.

Oedipus at Colonus, by Sophocles, translated by F. Storr, BA, Harvard University Press, 1912.

The Poetics of Portraiture in the Italian Renaissance, by Jody Cranston, Cambridge, 2000.

The Philosophy of Nietzsche, by Friedrich Nietzsche, The Modern Library, 1927.

Photography 1839-1937, by Beaumont Newhall, New York, 1937.

The Prince, by Niccolo Machiavelli, translated by Peter Bondanella and Mark Musa, Oxford University Press, 1979.

Quipus and Witches Knots: The Role of the Knot in Primitive and Ancient Cultures, by Cyrus Lawrence Day, The University of Kansas Press, 1967.

Sociology, by John J. Macionis, Prentice Hall, 1997.

Sorcerer's Stone: A Beginner's Guide to Alchemy, by Dennis William Hauck, Citadel Press, Kensington Publishing Corp., 2004.

Webster's New World Dictionary of The American Language, 2nd Edition, World Publishing Company, 1970.

World Mythology, edited by Willliam G. Doty, Barnes & Noble Inc., 2002.

INTERNET RESOURCES:

Alchemy Lab: http://www.alchemylab.com/hyper_history.htm

AllWords:
http://www.allwords.com/query.php?SearchType=3&Keyword=thick&goquery=Find+it!&Language=ENG

Angelseaxisce Ealdriht Asatru & Heathen Pages: http://www.ealdriht.org/niht

Behind the Name: http://www.behindthename.com

Baby Name Network: http://www.babynamenetwork.com

Crystalinks: http://www.crystalinks.com/egyptgods.html

Crystalinks: http://www.crystalinks.com/mut.html

Crystalinks: http://www.crystalinks.com/romemythology.html

Darren Jardine The Irishkiwi: http://homepages.paradise.net.nz/darrenj2/irish_slang.htm

Deutsche Welle: http://www.dw-world.de

Dictionary.com: http://www.dictionary.com

Edgar's Name Pages: http://www.geocities.com/edgarbook/names/n/nigel.html

The Etruscans: http://www.etruscans1.tripod.com/

The Free Dictionary.com: http://www.thefreedictionary.com/Janus

Grove Art Online: http://www.groveart.com

Jewish Virtual Library: http://www.jewishvirtuallibrary.org/jsource/Holocaust/rose.html

JK Rowling Official Site: http://www.jkrowling.com/textonly/extrastuff_view.cfm?id=5

The Local History of Stoke-on-Trent: http://www.thepotteries.org/markguide/knot_meaning.htm

Mythical Folk: http://www.themystica.org/mythical-folk/articles/isis.html

Mythography: http://www.loggia.com/myth/janus.html

Oxford Reference Online:
http://www.oxfordreference.com/views/ENTRY.html?subview=Main&entry=t23.e42271

Oxford Reference Online:
http://www.oxfordreference.com/views/ENTRY.html?subview=Main&entry=t23.e43729

Serena's Guide to Divination: http://www.serenapowers.com/geomancy2html

Sketches of Blackley and District: http://www.fdjohnson.co.uk/shorthistory.html

Staffordshire Marquetry Group: http://www.staffsmarq.freeserve.co.uk/projects/staffknot.htm

Wikipedia: http:/www./en.wikipedia.org/wiki/Janus

Word Sources: http//www.wordsources.info/luna.html

MOVIES:

Harry Potter and the Sorcerer's Stone, Warner Brothers Pictures, 2001.

Harry Potter and the Chamber of Secrets, Warner Brothers Pictures, 2002.

Harry Potter and the Prisoner of Azkaban, Warner Brothers Pictures, 2004.

So you think you sleuthed all the clues about Harry Potter?

Then you'd better not read these books.

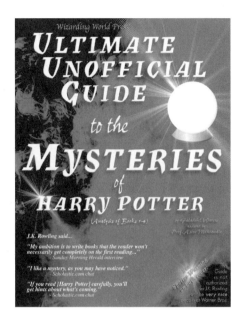

Wizarding World Press'

ULTIMATE UNOFFICIAL GUIDE
TO THE MYSTERIES OF HARRY POTTER

NEW CLUES TO HARRY POTTER: BOOK 5

by Galadriel Waters

The Ultimate Unofficial Guide to the Mysteries of Harry Potter is the original guide which focuses on the basic skills needed to sleuth the Harry Potter books. With over 400 pages, it examines in detail, the wealth of intriguing mysteries that are hidden in the text of the first four books and speculates on what to expect in Book 5 and beyond.

ISBN 0-9723936-1-7 (paperback)

New Clues to Harry Potter: Book 5 allows readers to try out their own detective skills and sleuth out the clues that are hidden in Book 5. It contains over 90 FAQs that help the serious Harry Potter fan understand the books' complex mysteries.

ISBN 0-9723936-2-5 (paperback)